The Ivory Maid

Book 2 of the Transit Star Continuum

K.Britton

Rusty Fish Press

Published by Rusty Fish Press

ISBN (eBook): 978-1-7644942-2-9
ISBN (paperback): 978-1-7644942-3-6

This is a work of fiction. Names, characters, places, and events are either the product of the author's imagination or are used fictitiously. Any resemblance to actual persons, living or dead, or to actual events or locales is entirely coincidental.

This work draws upon global mythic traditions, folklore, and archetypal narratives, reinterpreted within a contemporary fictional context.

This book was created with the assistance of artificial intelligence tools under the direction and editorial control of the author. All creative decisions, intellectual property rights, and derived works remain the exclusive property of the author.

Contents

Prologue - The President

The lights never slept in the Situation Room. They burned over the table like interrogation lamps, reflected off the screens' glass. The screens carried the same nightmare on every channel: Morocco breaking open. Valleys choked with bone. Armoured vehicles blazing like toys. Civilians flooding roads that rescue teams couldn't reach.

When the President entered, no one stood. No one spoke. The only sounds were the low hum of machinery and the distant clatter of bone echoing from the speakers.

He pulled out his chair, sat, and gripped the wood with white-knuckled hands.

"Tell me," he said.

The General, face carved by decades of battlefields, pointed at the main screen.

"Sir. Fez is gone. The dead are moving in formations. Moroccan units have collapsed. They're asking for one thing only: air."

The image shifted. Night vision showed a road lit by muzzle flashes. Skeletons walked into the bullets as if bullets were rain.

Soldiers screamed. Static swallowed their last words. The screen cut to black.

"They don't stop," the General said. "They don't fall like men. Armour doesn't hold. Comms fail the moment they draw near. Sir, we don't have a manual for this."

The Secretary of State leaned forward, eyes rimmed red.

"Rabat is begging for help. Paris dithers. Berlin debates. The UN calls it seismic anomalies. Morocco doesn't have hours—if we wait for consensus—"

"There won't be a Morocco left," the General finished.

Silence clung to the table. The President let it stretch.

He had seen war—floods, fires, men armed or starving. But this was older. The grainy footage looked like prophecy unearthed.

"They rise," he murmured.

No one contradicted him.

He turned to the General. "Options."

"Strike groups, sir. Stealth bombers. Drones. We cut the formations into dust. Buy the living room to breathe."

The Secretary of State cut in. "If we move, we lead. No coalition, no mandate. Every headline will say America bombed Morocco."

The President's jaw hardened. "Better headlines than obituaries."

His eyes tracked the footage—an alley in Casablanca, civilians against barricades, shadows in smoke. Alliances, treaties, elections—all irrelevant if the dead crossed the strait into Europe.

At last, he said, "We answer Rabat. Tonight. With fire."

The General didn't flinch. He nodded, already speaking into a handset. Orders rippled outward like shockwaves.

The Secretary of State lowered her gaze. "It begins, then."

"No," the President said. "It's already begun. We're just late to the field."

Across the ocean, hangars opened. Black wings rolled into the night. Pilots strapped in, hands steadier than breath. Engines woke. In Missouri, Spain, and on carriers, the air thundered. Tankers lifted, drones followed, stealth shapes rose like shadows chasing the moon.

The President stayed seated, watching the live feeds stitch themselves across the walls. Morocco burned in one window. In another, the first American bomber cleared the tarmac and took to the sky.

He thought of the Moroccan Prime Minister's voice an hour ago, thin with exhaustion, begging: *Help us breathe.*

He whispered back into the dark, "You will."

The first flight crossed the Atlantic, eastbound, toward the land where bones marched and the living prayed. And humanity, for the first time in this new war, roared back.

Meanwhile, in Casablanca, Amal had been awake long before the sirens.

The city grew restless—rumours like fire: soldiers vanishing in the hills, shepherds muttering about moving bones, power cuts aligning with whispers of marching feet. Most people laughed at first. Then the phones began to fill with shaky videos no one could explain. By the time the air-raid sirens wailed, no one was laughing.

Amal clutched her son's hand so tightly that the boy whimpered, but she didn't loosen her grip.

They pressed through Avenue Hassan, thousands heading to the port where ships, rumour claimed, would take them to Spain. But the ships never came. The sea was dark and empty, save for the hiss of waves and the glow of burning fuel tanks farther down the coast.

Above them, something cracked like thunder.

At first, she thought it was a storm. Then she saw the lights—ranks of them, steady and cruel, moving with the rhythm of soldiers who did not know fatigue. Shadows swept the boulevard, long and wrong, as if cast by torches instead of the moon.

People screamed, surged, fell.

Amal pushed her boy behind her, heart clawing at her ribs.

A column of figures emerged from the smoke, their armour glinting faint bronze, shields carried high. She wanted to believe it was the army. She prayed it was. But when one stumbled close enough for her to see its face—nothing but a skull grinning beneath a dented helm—her knees buckled.

They marched without sound but for the endless clatter of bone, jawbones clicking like teeth in winter. No orders shouted. No banner raised. Yet the formation pivoted as one, turning its hollow gaze toward the crowd.

Panic broke out on the street.

Mothers dropped bags to lift children. Men shoved, scrambled, and climbed over abandoned cars in the crush. The dead didn't run—they didn't need to. They advanced like a tide that already owned the shore.

Amal dragged her son into a narrow side street, chest heaving. The boy's eyes were wide, fixed on something above. She followed his gaze. On the rooftops, more of them waited. Silent. Watching. Their empty sockets glowed faintly in the smoke. One tilted its head slowly, as if scenting prey.

The boy whimpered again.

Amal pressed his face to her stomach, whispering prayers older than the mosque down the road, prayers her grandmother had whispered in another time of fear.

From far away, beyond the city, came a new sound. A deep, rolling thunder that was not bone.

She looked up through the haze and saw contrails burning faint silver against the night. Dozens. Then hundreds.

Jets.

The sky itself seemed to split as engines screamed overhead. For a heartbeat, the crowd stopped fleeing and lifted their faces. Hope and terror knotted together.

The boy tugged at her sleeve. "Mama," he whispered, "are they here to save us?"

She wanted to say yes. She wanted to believe the fire in the sky belonged to the living. She kissed his hair and held him tight as the ground trembled, not knowing if salvation or ruin had arrived.

Back in Washington, the President saw none of this. Only the contrails on his screen, white lines across black water, carrying America's answer to the dead.

ACT III:
LILITH ON THE MARCH

Chapter 1

The Hop

Ben ran until his lungs burned. Fez's dust clawed his throat raw. Behind him, the city was no longer a city, but a graveyard cracking open—streets buckling under what should never have risen. Even here, he heard them: bone striking stone, shields rattling, a thousand jawbones chattering like winter teeth. The army was awake. Leila was awake. And he, once more, was running.

South-west, the Andes called like a compass in his chest, some pull older than choice. But there was a sea between here and there, and men of flesh could not outrun an army of bone.

He needed wings.

The thought struck like lightning: a plane.

Madness.

He had never flown so much as a kite that held steady. His only time on an aircraft had been as cargo—wedged between passengers on commercial flights, or clinging to the stench of army transports in wars he wanted to forget. But even as the idea surfaced, it took root. South-west demanded more than footsteps; it demanded sky.

He stumbled through an alley, past shuttered stalls and overturned carts, past a woman clutching a child who no longer breathed. The night stank of dust and ozone, of fear made physical. He knew the gendarme would not save him; their rifles cracked and were swallowed by static the moment bone touched barrel. He knew no convoy or bus would drive him past what now marched.

That left the airport.

Men were already fleeing—businessmen in crumpled suits, tourists pale and dragging their luggage, and Moroccan families clutching Qurans and passports.

The terminal had become a hive of shouting, prayer, and gunmetal panic. Ben pushed through them, his shirt clinging with sweat, and Leila's blood dried dark across his chest. Don't look back, she had said. He hadn't. But he still saw her every time he blinked: pale, unbowed, smiling as she turned to face the dead.

The airport fence loomed, barbed wire glittering under floodlights. Soldiers barked orders in Arabic, struggling to control the crowd. Their eyes flicked anxiously toward the city, which now screamed with ancient voices.

Ben kept moving. He angled away from the bottleneck of civilians and sprinted along the chain link fence. He spotted a service gate as a corporal stepped in front of him, raising his rifle.

Ben reacted. He slammed his elbow into the man's throat. The corporal collapsed, choking. Ben snatched the gate key, unlocked the gate, and shoved his way through.

The tarmac opened wide. Heat shimmered off it, though the night was cold. Hangars squatted like sleeping beasts, tails of planes jutting from their mouths. His heart thudded harder: wings. He didn't need a 747. He needed small, fast, stealable.

He ran low, his boots slapping concrete, until he saw it—a battered twin-prop Cessna parked near the far hangar, its white paint stained by desert winds. A ladder leaned against its side, toolbox open. Someone had been working on it.

Perfect.

He clambered up. He slid into the cockpit—and froze. Levers. Gauges. Dials everywhere. His pulse slammed in his ears.

I can't.

Then Leila's eyes flashed in his mind—the gnawing pull in his chest.

You can't, but you must. Keys waited in the ignition. He twisted them. The propeller coughed, spun once, and died. He tried again: cough, shudder, ignition.

Sweat trickled down his back. Footsteps approached. Shouts echoed.

A mechanic burst through the hangar door, wrench raised. "Qu'est-ce que vous—"

Ben didn't let him finish. He slammed the throttle forward. The engine screamed, half-alive, as the plane jerked, wheels rolling. The mechanic leapt aside, cursing. Ben's hands shook on the yoke as he tried to recall every half-forgotten movie, every late-night cockpit documentary. Throttle up. Keep it straight. Don't overthink.

The runway lights rushed toward him, soldiers waving, shouting. Muzzle flashes spat. Bullets pinged the fuselage like thrown stones. Ben ducked instinctively, one hand white-knuckled on the yoke, the other shoving throttle to the limit.

The twin props screamed in protest. The plane gathered speed. Faster. Faster. His teeth rattled. His vision tunnelled. He yanked too soon—the nose lurched, wheels bounced, then slammed back. The fuselage groaned. Another volley of bullets clattered against the tail.

Fly, damn you!

He shoved forward, steadied, then pulled again, smoother this time. The nose lifted. Tyres screamed against asphalt one last second—then silence. The ground dropped away. He was flying.

For a heartbeat, disbelief numbed him. He expected to fall, to stall, to tumble like Icarus. Instead, the Cessna clawed the air, wobbling but aloft, climbing raggedly into the smoke-stained night.

Ben let out a bark of laughter, half hysterical, half triumphant. "I'm airborne!"

The lights of Fez sprawled beneath him, a trembling lattice of orange and white. Beyond, darker still, the mass of skeletal ranks spilled through streets, their shields glinting faintly under moonlight, their phalanxes spreading outward like veins of rot. He saw Leila among them—tiny from this height, but unmistakable in the way the ranks seemed to pivot around her presence. For a mad instant, he thought she turned her face up toward him, as if she knew exactly where he was.

The cockpit rattled, gauges quivering. He forced his attention forward, south-west. His hands moved awkwardly, clumsy on the yoke, but instinct—or something more—kept him level. The propeller roared, the desert spread beneath him like an ocean of stone, and the Andes pulled invisible strings inside his chest. But already, in the back of his mind, a new terror whispered: he had no idea how to land. And if the plane went down—as every sane part of him insisted it should—he knew his cursed gift would see him crawl from the wreckage again. Bones broken, breath ragged, luck twisted like wire. He could not die, but he could still fall forever.

The yoke trembled under his grip, alive in a way no tool or weapon had ever been. Every twitch of his wrist sent the nose wobbling, wings tilting like a drunk staggering between lampposts.

The Cessna was airborne, yes, but it was not steady.

Ben clenched his teeth and tested a gentle pull back. The nose rose too quickly. The engine groaned. The horizon tilted, black swallowing his field of view. He shoved forward in panic—the plane dipped hard, his stomach lurching, the city lights tilting like it meant to spill him out.

"Whoa."

He corrected clumsily, the wings levelling with a shudder. Sweat stung his eyes. Every instinct screamed that this was a mistake, that men didn't simply steal planes and learn as they went. But he was already above the lights of Fez, already beyond choice. South-west. Anywhere but here. He risked glancing at the gauges. The dials jittered like nervous eyes. Airspeed—what was too fast? What was too slow? Altimeter—did that needle mean hundreds or thousands of feet? Fuel—half a tank? A third? He didn't know. Couldn't know. The numbers might as well have been hieroglyphs carved by the Sleeper itself. So he did what he always had—what had kept him alive through fires, wars, wrecks, and Leila's impossible gaze. He guessed.

The yoke nudged left. The plane tilted obediently. He straightened the wings, then nudged right, watching the plane respond. Encouraged, he pulled back to climb. Too sharp—the engine whined. The airspeed needle sank. Suddenly, silence bloomed. The nose lurched skyward, and the propeller froze mid-spin.

The Cessna stalled.

In a single frozen heartbeat, the world stopped—weightless, soundless, a void where breath should be.

Then—the drop. The nose tipped down, and the desert rushed up, black rock and moonlit sand like a tidal wave of stone. Alarms shrieked and loose tools clattered in the cockpit. Ben's chest slammed against the straps. Pull back! His mind screamed. But instinct—a half-remembered lesson from films about stalls—cut through.

He shoved the nose down harder, his heart pounding. Airspeed crept up as the desert loomed like a maw, ready to swallow him. He twisted the ignition key, praying. The engine coughed. Once. Twice. Then caught with a roar. The propeller spun, air flowed, and the Cessna clawed its way back into flight. Ben let out a cry of relief, his voice breaking into a sob. "Ha! You bastard—you thought you had me."

He levelled the yoke, climbed shallow, breath coming in hard gulps.

Trial and error. That was all this would be. He would make mistakes. He would stall. He would bleed fear until there was nothing left to bleed. But he would survive. He always survived.

The night deepened. Stars spread above him, cold and innumerable. Below, Morocco's ridges gave way to emptier desert. Villages flickered like scattered coals. The clatter of bone armies was distant now, but not gone. He swore he could still feel the thrum of their march in his ribcage, the pull of Leila's will dragging at the marrow of his bones.

South-west, always south-west. But the compass on the dash spun uncertainly, and his gut said otherwise. The Andes lie across water. He needed to cross the sea before the Cessna gave up its secrets—or its fuel, and figured the closest land, Cuba, was west. West, then. West to the Atlantic.

He squinted at the gauges again. Fuel was falling—slow, but constant. He had no idea how long half a tank lasted. An hour? Three? Ten? His only certainty was that the sea had to be crossed, and Cuba was his target. From there—south-west again.

He resolved then, aloud, voice hoarse in the small cabin: "West it is. Better to drown with wings than be buried in bone."

To test his path, he banked westward. The nose dipped, wings shuddered, but he steadied it. Lights shifted below—the glow of Casablanca in the distance, a smudge of brightness against the coast. Closer, nearer, the Atlantic waited. The ocean stretched black and endless, swallowing the horizon.

Fear prickled sharply.

Land at least gave you somewhere to crash. Sea gave you nothing. But West was the only way. He tightened his grip, eyes fixed on the stars ahead. Time blurred.

He tilted too far once, wings nearly vertical, the ocean filling the window. Panic clawed, but he corrected, steadying, lungs burning from held breath. Each mistake taught him something.

The Cessna droned on, stubborn and fragile, its stolen pilot stubborn and delicate with it. Together, they pressed west, two survivors in a night that had already claimed too many. The sea below was a black sheet without seam or border, as though the Earth had peeled away and left him suspended above nothing.

The propellers worried the air. Each shiver of turbulence was a giant's hand brushing the wings.

Ben held the yoke tight, eyes burning from hours unblinking.

Stars crowded the windows, sharp and close, and for long stretches it felt as if the plane wasn't moving at all—just pinned between a vault of light and an endless pit of water. The gauges ticked onward. Fuel was bleeding away. He tried not to look at the needle. The hum of the engine lulled him into a half-trance. His shoulders ached, his throat dry as bone dust. Somewhere far below, white crests flickered faintly as moonlit teeth. He imagined what would happen if the Cessna faltered now. The plunge. The cold. The black silence closing in.

He told himself, as he had on the runway, as he had through every escape of his cursed life: Even if it crashes, I'll crawl out again. The words steadied him, though the thought was as much horror as comfort.

Then, a new light. At first, he thought it was a star brighter than the rest, hanging low on the horizon. But it moved. Fast. Eastward. Then another. Then a third. Within minutes, the sky above him was cut with streaks—red beacons, green strobes, steady glows of engines burning hot against the night.

Jets.

Big ones. Their silhouettes slid across the stars, heading east, back toward Africa, back toward the rising terror.

Ben craned his neck, mouth dry. One formation of three, then another higher, then another, until the sky looked like a lane of fireflies sweeping across the dark. He counted a dozen, then lost count. Military. It had to be. Civilian planes would never fly in such numbers, such tight patterns, at this hour. These were fast, purposeful, bristling with unseen weight. Squadrons, whole wings, maybe fleets.

The thought struck hard: the world had seen what he'd seen. The skeleton armies are rising. Leila, smiling among them.

Ben let out a short, bitter laugh. "Good luck with that."

The jets roared overhead, shaking the Cessna like a leaf. His little craft bucked and rattled in their wake. For a heartbeat, he thought they might turn their attention to him—some lone speck off course, unfiled, a smuggler or spy. He ducked instinctively, though he knew it wouldn't matter. One missile and he'd be fire over water. But they didn't see him. Or if they did, they didn't care. The convoys streamed past, wave after wave, all eastward, all toward the rising dead.

Ben sat back, breath ragged, the yoke damp in his hands. The sight of so many war machines lit the night with dread. The gods might have whispered, the ethereals might have stirred, but this—this was humanity's answer. Jets against bones. Bombs against prophecy. It wouldn't be enough. He knew it as sure as breath.

The water below never ended. It seemed the Earth itself had drowned. His eyes blurred, lids heavy. He slapped his cheek, muttered curses, and forced himself awake. Once, he thought he saw a shape on the waves—a white bat-wing spread enormous, gliding silently above the swells. He blinked hard. Only sea. Only dark.

West. Always west until the coast. He prayed for the faintest glimmer of land, the suggestion of lights, anything that wasn't water. His compass wavered. The stars wheeled. But his chest still tugged south-west, faint and insistent, reminding him this flight was only the beginning.

Ben's hands ached, but he did not let go. "Hold together," he muttered. "Just long enough to see land."

The Atlantic was not a body of water. It was a mirror, flat and cruel, reflecting the night so completely that Ben often could not tell where one ended and the other began. The compass needle quivered stubbornly in its little circle, and he clung to it like a drowning man to driftwood. West. Always west. And still—nothing.

Hours had dragged themselves into a blur. His hands were locked around the yoke, stiff as wood. His eyes ached from staring at the endless shimmer below, that maddening consistency of moon reflection rolling without pause. The sea's face hypnotised him. Every wave looked like the last, every ripple another copy of a copy. The sameness drilled into him worse than turbulence.

He had not slept since the fight with Poseidon. Not truly. A few stolen moments of half-consciousness leaning against a bulkhead, maybe, but never real rest. His skull felt packed with gravel. Thoughts wouldn't line up anymore. Images slipped in unbidden—Leila's bloodied smile, Posi slicing blades of water against him, the muffled clatter of skeleton jaws. He blinked them away only to see the sea again, and the sea was worse.

The hours stretched. He pressed on. The compass, the hum, the endless mirror. His eyes watered, his vision swam. He could not tell if he was flying level anymore. He just held on and hoped the Cessna forgave him.

When the moon fell behind a cloud, the sea became worse—an infinite blackness swallowing the windows. He gripped the yoke tighter, terrified that if he let go for even a moment, the plane would roll and plunge unseen into the abyss.

Fatigue gnawed at him. His head nodded again, jerked back up. "Stay awake," he croaked.

His body trembled with the effort. Every second stretched into an hour. Somewhere out there, land waited. He clung to that thought as the only truth left. West. Always west. Until the sea broke. And if it didn't? Then he would fly until the fuel gave out, and the sea would finally have him. But he doubted, even then, that it would hold him for long.

When dawn smeared pale orange over the horizon, he saw them again—contrails stitched eastward, one after another, as if the sky itself had been drafted.

The world was going to war.

The Atlantic had stripped him raw; his eyes no longer trusted what they saw. He expected more ocean—nothing but ocean forever. Then, a smudge on the horizon. It held steady. Dark against the lightening sky. Mountains, not waves.

His chest tightened. Land. Real land. He blinked tears out of his eyes, muttering, "Don't vanish, don't you bloody vanish."

The Azores. He didn't know the name—not yet—but he knew the miracle of seeing Earth after an endless night over water. He had no map, no radio call, no clearance. Just a battered Cessna groaning on empty tanks and a man who had never landed before in his life. The islands rose sharp and green from the sea, volcanic ridges clawing at the clouds. He spotted a strip of flatness glinting in the dawn—an airfield.

Military by the look of it. Runway lights still burned pale in the morning haze.

"Alright," Ben rasped, gripping the yoke. "We're going down, one way or another."

He cut the throttle halfway. The engine dropped to a guttural growl. The plane sagged, nose dipping, fields and coastline rushing closer.

He yanked back too hard—the Cessna lurched upward, nearly stalling. The prop coughed, wheezed. Panic knifed through him. He shoved forward, levelling just enough to catch air again.

Sweat slicked his hands.

The runway grew larger, impossibly fast.

He lined it up by instinct, not skill—wings wobbling, nose drifting. Alarms shrieked. His teeth bared. The wheels hit hard. The plane bounced, skidded, slammed down again with a sound like breaking bones. Metal screamed. The nose wavered, fishtailing across the tarmac. Ben hauled the yoke, boots braced, the world a blur of sparks and concrete.

And then—stillness.

He didn't know it yet, but this was the last moment the sky would let him go without asking for something back.

The Cessna sagged, nose down, engine coughing to death—silence except for his own ragged breathing. Ben sat frozen, hands welded to the controls. He had landed.

God help him, he had landed.

Beyond the glass, soldiers were already running, silhouettes in the dawn, rifles raised. Sirens wailed. He knew what came next: interrogation, custody, questions he couldn't answer.

But for one beat, he let himself laugh—wild, broken, triumphant. "Crossed the bloody ocean… and stuck the landing."

The Andes still pulled south-west in his chest, insistent, unrelenting. But first, he had to survive the Azores.

Chapter 2
The Skip

The cuffs clicked too tightly around his wrists, the steel biting into bone. Ben flexed once, testing, then stilled. The two military policemen flanking him thought they had him contained, another stray pilot in over his head and out of his lane.

They didn't know what he carried—the curse of survival, the gnawing pull south-west, the memory of bone armies spilling into Morocco. They thought they were detaining a man. They were shackling a storm.

They didn't walk him toward a cell. They walked him toward a desk. Paperwork. Questions. Names.

A camera on a tripod tracked his face as it turned. A medic waited with a kit that wasn't for bandages. Ben saw the zip ties on the table—bright plastic, final. The kind used when someone wasn't meant to get their hands back at all.

"Keep walking," the taller MP muttered, his gloved hand pressing between Ben's shoulder blades.

Ahead, floodlights burned across the Azores tarmac, catching the silhouettes of parked aircraft. Fighters, transports, one or two trainers with paint schemes dulled by salt air. Ben's eyes locked on them. Wings. Freedom. Escape.

He kept his pace steady, boots clanging on the steel grates of the hangar threshold. Soldiers glanced over, but none lingered; they had bigger worries with bombers prepping for sorties east.

The war was already spilling outward. The dead were moving, and America was answering with fire.

He had no intention of becoming a footnote in their operation.

The smaller MP shifted closer, rifle angled across his chest. "Eyes forward," he snapped.

Ben exhaled slowly. He counted his breath, counted the steps. Left foot. Right foot. One more shadow. One more heartbeat. He thought of Leila's last words in Fez—Don't look back.

He didn't.

He struck. His shoulder slammed back into the smaller MP, knocking the rifle sideways. At the same time, Ben snapped his bound hands upward, ramming steel cuffs into the taller man's chin. Bone cracked. The taller MP stumbled, dazed, weapon slipping loose. Ben spun, hooked the shorter man's rifle sling with his cuffed arms, and yanked. The man pitched forward, breath blasted out of him, rifle clattering.

Alarms hadn't sounded yet. Shouts hadn't gone up. It was all happening in the blind spot between floodlights.

Ben drove his boot into the dazed man's chest, sending him sprawling, then dropped to seize the fallen rifle. His wrists were still chained, movement clumsy, but adrenaline sharpened every angle.

He jammed the cuff chain into the hinge seam of the hangar door and wrenched. Metal screamed. The cuff chain sheared, leaving one cuff still on his wrist—but his hands were separate.

Free hands. Free air. A chance.

The taller MP groaned, hand reaching for his sidearm. Ben stomped down hard on the man's wrist, kicked the pistol free, and scooped it up.

He didn't shoot. Noise was death.

Instead, he sprinted into the glow of the tarmac. Half the ground crew were already sprinting for hardened shelters—sirens meant drills, and drills meant incoming—not a man running.

Engines growled nearby, turbine whine like predators waking.

Ben darted between parked vehicles, eyes scanning. Too big. Too complex. He needed something flyable, fast enough to cross the Atlantic, but not guarded like a nuke. Then he saw it—gleaming under sodium lights, its nose angled toward the open runway: a Northrop T-38 Talon.

A trainer. Supersonic on paper. Short-legged in reality. With the canopy still half-open, the ladder hanging loose as if some pilot had stepped away for a smoke.

Fate, or something older.

He ran.

Behind him, voices rose—shouts, whistles, the bark of orders in clipped English. Boots thundered. The alarm klaxon split the air, red lights strobing. He was already moving, lungs burning, pistol clutched tight. A spotlight swept wide, grazing his back as he vaulted the last barrier and scrambled up the ladder.

The cockpit smelled of oil, sweat, and ozone. The panel was dark. Dead. Ben's gut dropped—until a ground cart hummed nearby, releasing a cable already hooked to the nose. Whoever had left it ready hadn't expected a thief with nothing to lose. Ben dropped into the seat, fingers trembling but decisive. He shoved the pistol into his waistband, yanked the harness straps across his chest, and found the ignition.

A voice bellowed from below. "Step out of the aircraft! Hands where I can see them!"

Ben ignored it. He twisted the key, pressed switches the way he'd watched pilots do on tarmacs years ago. The jet shuddered. Turbines coughed, then screamed alive.

The ladder rattled as an MP started climbing. Ben slammed the canopy switch. Glass sealed down with a hiss, cutting off the shouts. Bullets pinged against the fuselage, sparks glancing off steel. The MPs weren't waiting for him to comply.

Ben shoved the throttle forward. The jet lurched, wheels biting the tarmac, engines screaming like chained animals released. The ladder tore loose, clattering to the ground as the Talon rolled. Floodlights locked on him. Sirens howled. A jeep roared to block the taxiway. Ben gritted his teeth and pushed harder. The Talon surged forward, wheels screaming, fuselage rattling.

At the last second, he yanked the nosewheel aside, the jet skidding past the Jeep with meters to spare. The guards scattered.

Ben shoved the throttle to its limit. The Talon howled. He wasn't ready. He wasn't trained. But he had wings. And wings were enough. The runway stretched out in a corridor of harsh white light, shimmering in the night haze. Sirens wailed behind him, jeeps giving chase, soldiers firing warning shots that pinged against the tarmac. Ben's pulse thundered in his skull. He jammed the throttle forward. The Talon's twin J85 engines screamed, a howl that vibrated through his bones. The jet bucked against him, raw thrust slamming him into the seat as the airframe gathered speed. Every instinct told him to ease off, that he was moving too fast, that he'd rip the machine apart before he left the ground. But hesitation was death.

The Jeep behind swerved, soldiers leaning out with rifles. A spotlight blazed against the canopy, blinding him for a second. Ben hunched low, teeth gritted, and shoved the stick forward to steady the roll. The nose wobbled, tyres biting the asphalt. The speed dial climbed—eighty knots, ninety, a hundred. He yanked back too early. The nose lurched skyward, the jet wobbling like a drunk on stilts. The stall warning shrieked. His stomach plunged as the engines whined in protest. The Talon dipped hard, slamming back onto the runway in a shower of sparks—the harness bit into his shoulders.

Easy. Smooth. Don't choke it.

He shoved the stick forward, regained speed, let the wheels rattle a few more seconds, then pulled again—gentler, steady. The nose lifted. This time, the wings caught air. The ground peeled away beneath him. A final burst of gunfire stitched the tarmac where he'd been seconds earlier.

He was airborne.

The Talon climbed raggedly, its controls twitching under his untrained hands. He forced himself to focus on the horizon—keep it level, keep it accurate. The gauges swam before his eyes, numbers meaningless, needles jittering like nervous eyes. He clung to the stick, trying not to overcorrect. Every wobble threatened to flip him. The coastline glimmered faintly in the distance, the Atlantic stretching orange and endless beyond. Behind him, base lights shrank, though tracer rounds still clawed the sky.

They weren't about to let a stolen Air Force jet fly off without a fight. A red light flashed on the console. He had no idea what it meant. Oil pressure? Landing gear? Imminent death?

He ignored it. The only thing that mattered was altitude and distance. Put miles between him and the Azores before they scrambled fighters.

The radio crackled. A clipped voice barked through the headset hanging near his ear: "Unidentified pilot—return to runway immediately. Failure to comply will result in force."

Ben grabbed the headset, shoved it on, and said nothing.

Silence was his only answer.

Another voice followed, sharper, commanding: "This is Azores Control. You are flying a United States Air Force aircraft. Return to base now. Last warning."

He yanked the mic away. If they wanted an answer, they could watch his taillights.

The jet rattled through turbulence, the nose pitching. He adjusted, clumsy but stubborn. The deep-blue sheet of ocean loomed ahead, swallowing horizon and sky alike. He exhaled once, slowly. Then a new sound—low, rising, behind him. He craned his neck. A pair of afterburner flares lit the sky like twin suns. F-16s.

They were already in the air, closing fast. Panic clawed him. He'd stolen speed, but not stealth. The Talon wasn't built for dogfights against real fighters. It was a training jet, lighter, simpler. Against an F-16, it was a sparrow in a storm.

"Unidentified jet, this is your final chance. Divert immediately, or we open fire."

Ben laughed—sharp, ragged, half-mad. Fire wouldn't kill him. It never did. But capture would. Capture meant chains, interrogation, and secrets stripped. He couldn't let them hold him.

South-west still pulled at his chest, a compass buried in bone. He couldn't stop. He shoved the throttle to its limit, engines screaming. The Talon leapt forward, cutting low over the waves. Spray burst against the canopy as he dropped altitude.

The F-16s followed, banking hard, sleek predators slicing the night. Missile locks would come any second. He had no countermeasures, no flares. Just instinct, chaos, and the impossible luck that had dragged him through fire, wreck, and war.

The jet trembled under his hands. He whispered through clenched teeth, "Hold together. Just a little further."

Warnings blared. The radio screamed. The F-16s closed. And Ben flew on—hugging the ocean, where only the desperate and the damned dared chase him.

The Atlantic spread beneath him, stretching blue and bottomless, the waves silhouettes save for faint gold crests catching sunlight. The Talon's engines screamed at full throttle, straining against their limits. Ben hunched over the stick, muscles locked, eyes fixed on the thin horizon. Behind him, the afterburner glare of two F-16s carved fire across the sky.

A voice rattled in his headset: "Unidentified Talon, this is Falcon Two. You are ordered to divert and land. Comply now or be destroyed."

Ben tore the headset off and flung it into the empty rear seat. He didn't need their threats poisoning his concentration. The message was clear enough: he was prey, and the hunters had their teeth bared.

The first missile lock warning shrieked through the cockpit. A red light pulsed, steady, insistent.

Ben's pulse matched it beat for beat. He pushed the stick forward, dropping altitude so fast his stomach tried to climb into his throat. The Talon skimmed just above the waves, spray misting against the canopy.

The F-16s followed, disciplined, precise.

Think, damn it. Don't fight them head-on. You can't win. The Talon was lighter, more fragile, but also more twitchy. A trainer wasn't built to hold steady under heavy Gs.

That was his chance.

If he could make the jet dance where they expected straight lines, maybe he could slip their net.

He banked left, hard. The wings shuddered, the fuselage groaning. For a heartbeat, the sea filled every window, dark and merciless. He snapped the stick back, levelling clumsily.

The F-16s swung wide in graceful arcs of light, compared to his jittering zigzags.

The lock warning shrieked again.

He slammed the throttle back, then forward, jerking the Talon into turbulence. The jet bucked like a horse trying to throw him. Sweat streamed down his forehead, stinging his eyes. He gritted his teeth and yanked right.

Something hammered the water beside him—not a missile, a short, controlled burst that turned the surface into exploding spray.

A message without words: It wasn't a miss. It was punctuation.

We can end you whenever we choose.

The F-16s regrouped, their engines howling as they angled for another pass. Ben could almost feel the pilots' disdain, their training screaming at them to finish this quickly.

He didn't give them steady targets. He threw the Talon into another drop, skimming so low that the jet wash kicked up spray, rolling it into walls behind him. His hands cramped around the stick, every correction too sharp, too panicked. The stall warning blared. He eased just enough to keep air flowing over the wings, whispering to the machine like it could hear him.

"Easy. Stay with me."

The gauges were a blur, but one needle stabbed his gut: fuel. Already dropping faster than he wanted to admit. He had no long-range tanks, no backup. This wasn't built for transoceanic flights. He needed luck—and luck, twisted and cruel, had never abandoned him.

The pull in his chest throbbed again, deeper now. South-west. The Andes. Always south-west. Like a compass buried in his ribs. Even with F-16s hunting him, even with the ocean waiting to swallow him whole, the pull never wavered.

Another missile lock. Another shriek.

He jerked the stick right, climbing sharply, then cut throttle mid-rise. The Talon staggered, slowed, nearly stalled.

The F-16s overshot, their sleek bodies flashing past in streaks of light.

Ben slammed the throttle forward again, dropping back to low altitude, the Talon gasping for speed. It worked for now.

The radio crackled again, distant but cold: "Falcon Two to command. Target is evasive. Request permission to fire at will."

He couldn't hear the answer, but he didn't need to. He knew it would come.

A sudden vibration rattled the cockpit. His heart seized—engine failure? No. Just turbulence, or the Talon protesting its abuse.

He grinned through clenched teeth. "Come on, you bastard. Hold."

For a few long minutes, he flew by blind instinct, weaving erratically, forcing the fighters to keep distance.

The morning stretched endlessly, broken only by the glare of the sun and the jagged hum of engines.

Then silence.

No locks. No shrieks. He risked a glance back. Empty sky. No afterburner flares, no shadows. He was alone.

Relief hit—and then the colder thought: fighters didn't just vanish. Fuel was already bleeding.

They could wait him out.

The gauge stabbed again, a needle creeping lower, lower.

He clenched his jaw. He wouldn't reach South-west America. Not directly. Maybe the Caribbean. Somewhere south-west, somewhere he could touch ground before the tanks ran dry.

His vision swam with exhaustion. Every muscle screamed from the fight. The cockpit smelled of sweat and hot metal. He wanted to close his eyes, just for a second. But closing his eyes in this machine meant death. And yet death wouldn't take him.

Maybe that was the true curse: not dying, but living long enough to watch the world collapse around him, to feel the pull of destiny like chains across his chest.

He laughed again, bitter, hollow. "South-west it is. One way or another."

The Talon flew on, fragile and furious, across a sea that had no mercy. Behind him, unseen eyes still watched. Whether gods, ethereal, or men with satellites, it didn't matter. They hadn't caught him yet. And as long as the engines screamed, he wasn't done.

The coastline crept into view at last, a jagged line of mountain against the vast blue sea. Ben's eyes burned from the hours of flying. His shoulders felt carved from stone. The Talon trembled beneath him, every gauge screaming warnings he didn't understand. Fuel hovered just above empty. He had no choice. He had to put the jet down.

The dim line of an airstrip flickered inland, a string of trees to the side. A windsock. A squat building with a single rotating beacon. Not a major base—more like a refuel strip that existed for emergencies and no one else. A narrow ribbon of asphalt offering respite.

He angled toward it, breath shallow, sweat soaking his shirt. His hands shook as he gripped the stick. The Talon dropped altitude too quickly. The stall warning blared. He corrected, jerking the nose upward. The jet bucked, wings wobbling. The runway loomed closer, closer. His speed was wrong—too fast, too hot. But slowing meant stalling, and stalling meant slamming into the earth like a stone.

"Easy," he whispered. "Easy now..."

The wheels kissed asphalt. For a second, he thought he'd made it. Then the nose bounced, slammed down, and the jet skidded sideways. Tyres screamed. The Talon slewed across the tarmac, sparks blazing as metal scraped stone.

Ben yanked the stick, fighting to level it. Useless. The left wing clipped a light tower. Metal shrieked as the wing tore, sending the jet spinning. The canopy rattled, his harness biting into his ribs. The world blurred into fire and shadow. Impact. The fuselage skidded into the grass verge, ploughing deep furrows. One engine tore free in a blossom of sparks. Flames licked the torn wing. The cockpit shuddered to a halt with a violent jolt that nearly snapped Ben's neck—silence, then the crackle of fire.

His ears rang. His vision swam. He tried to move—nothing. Pain radiated through his body, sharp and hot.

For a sick instant, he thought this was it, that death had finally found him. Then breath returned. Shallow, ragged, but real. His chest heaved. His fingers twitched. His cursed gift wasn't done with him yet. The canopy glass had fractured but not shattered. Smoke filled the cockpit, choking him.

He clawed at the release handle, coughing hard enough to vomit. The canopy resisted, jammed from the crash. He slammed it with his elbow, again and again, until the latch gave.

The glass popped, smoke billowed out, and Ben dragged himself through the narrow gap. His legs screamed with every movement, his knee useless, blood soaking his boot. He tumbled onto the grass, rolling once before collapsing flat on his back. Above him, trees wheeled calmly, uncaring.

The wreck burned behind him, flames crawling up twisted metal.

Explosions popped inside the ruined fuselage—hydraulic lines, ammunition, whatever the Talon still carried.

Heat seared his face. He dragged himself further, every inch an agony, until he collapsed against a ditch.

Sirens rose in the distance. Local response, maybe military, maybe civilian. He didn't care which. Capture was still death of a different kind.

He had to move. He clawed at the grass, hauling himself upright. His right leg refused to hold weight, and his vision was spotted with black. But he staggered forward, away from the fire, into the shadows beyond the runway. The pull was still there. South-west. Always south-west. Even broken, even bleeding, he could feel it dragging him onward.

Behind him, the wreck flared brighter, as engines roared closer—trucks or jeeps or worse.

Ben limped into the long grass, teeth clenched, every step an act of defiance. He should have died in the crash. Any man should have. But he wasn't any man. He was the aberration, the one who survived when survival was impossible.

The grass hid him as the sirens closed on the wreck. Ben lived. Barely. And the world would not forget it. He dragged himself further towards a large rock, each breath a knife in his lungs. His right foot dragged wrong, useless, the pain white-hot and nauseating. He crawled into a hollow and collapsed, chest heaving.

He forced himself to look.

His boot was twisted at an angle no boot should twist. Bone hadn't broken the skin, but the joint bulged grotesquely against the leather—a dislocation.

For a moment, black despair threatened to take him. Outrunning fighters, surviving the crash, and now this. But despair was a luxury. Capture would mean cages. He'd seen cages before. He would never go back.

His hands trembled as he unlaced the ruined boot, tugging it free with ragged gasps. The foot beneath was swollen, ugly, already purpling. He braced his back against the rock, gritted his teeth, and wrapped both hands around his shin.

"This'll hurt," he whispered.

He almost laughed. This was the part of survival no one ever put in speeches—the private violence you did to yourself so the world couldn't do worse.

He pulled. The joint yelled. He smothered his scream, a raw animal sound swallowed by pain. For a second, the world dissolved into white fire behind his eyes. Then—crunch—the joint slid home. The agony spiked, then dulled into a deep throb. He lay in the grass, soaked with sweat, shaking uncontrollably.

His breath came in broken gasps. But the foot moved now. Barely, painfully, but enough. He jammed the boot back on, tied it half-fast, and shoved himself upright. His vision blurred, but he staggered forward.

The airstrip stretched quietly beyond the burning wreck. Sirens still swarmed there, engines roaring, voices shouting. But the other end of the field lay quieter, hangars hulking shadows against the sky. That was where the planes would be—smaller craft, maybe a transport, even perhaps another trainer.

He limped toward them, each step a lance of pain, each heartbeat a drum in his ears. The smoke and chaos behind him cloaked his movement. He clung to it, invisible in the shadows. The pull in his chest gnawed harder now. South-west. Always south-west. It didn't care that his body was broken, that his lungs rasped or his bones screamed. It only cared that he kept moving. The hangars loomed—bright, fenced, and watched.

Ben limped toward them anyway, because the pull didn't negotiate. South-west. Always. And somewhere behind him, men with radios were already deciding what he was.

Chapter 3
The Jump

He had a window before the rescue crews would find him. Minutes would do. He stood. The right knee tried to fold, but held. The shoulder had gone tacky with blood where skin had peeled; already the edges tugged together, fresh pain knitting, the curse taking its quiet bites.

He gritted his teeth and waded up through driftwood and scrub, away from the wreck's smoking halo.

The hangars sat over the next rise. He reached a dirt road and climbed, staying off the crown, letting the weeds brush his legs. Wind pushed from the sea, warm and steady; the palms clattered like tin charms. Halfway up, he turned and looked. Multiple rescue vehicles clustered at the end of the runway—smoke billowing, sirens and voices multiplying.

He cut right, crossed a patch of feral cactus, and dropped into a drainage runnel that led him along the perimeter fence. Chain link. Topped with barbed wire, the colour of old blood.

He found a spot where the metal had been bent and rebent by hands that weren't official; a scatter of cigarette filters confirmed it. He shouldered into the gap and slid through, shirt snagging, flesh complaining. Inside the fence, heat rolled off concrete.

Close now: the rectangle of runway, white lines glowing; beyond, hangars with their mouths half open like sleeping beasts ready to wake ugly. A flight of small transports hunkered in the shadows. At the far end, a fuel truck idled, its driver standing, smoking and staring seaward at the fire that used to be a jet. The wreck had bought him time. He moved into it—across a service lane, under a wing, into a spill of dark behind a stack of pallets—just in time—out of the driver's view.

He reached the nearest hangar and slid inside with the door's next breath of wind. Light buzzed in strips along the rafters. Tools on carts, orange chocks, an oil-stained tarp draped over a dead engine like a corpse's sheet.

Three aircraft: a twin with its guts open; a high-wing utility turboprop in pieces; and—under dust—a sleek, long-legged machine, nose pointed toward a door that faced the taxiway. Single engine. Low wing. A tail high enough to look arrogant.

He didn't know models—not really—but he knew shapes. This one had range written into its bones. Slender wings. Fat belly tank. Oxygen ports labelled in a pictogram language he could read only as intent. Someone had flown this across oceans before. He checked the cabin—empty. Cockpit—clean, ready in a way that said someone had meant to take it up before the island exploded.

Keys hung from a red ribbon on a checklist hook. Luck. Or the same force that had hauled him out of fires since he was young enough to mistake miracles for curses. He swallowed and took them.

The seat cupped him like it meant to keep him. He hated that. He hated the way the yoke fit his hands better tonight than it had yesterday, like the world wanted to trick him into feeling at home above the ground.

Don't.

Feet on earth. You live because you come back down.

He ran the checklist with a speed that would have gotten a pilot killed and a thief blessed. Battery. Fuel pump. Mixture. Starter. The engine coughed into a clean whine. The prop blurred, then became nothing—a clear disc that shook the hangar's shadows. Voices. Sirens arrived; the airport snapped fully awake.

Go.

He released the brakes, and the turboprop rolled. It felt eager—too eager. He feathered the throttle, eased it through the half-open door, and nosed onto the taxiway.

"Tower," a voice snapped in his headset—he hadn't realised it lay crooked around his neck—"identify. You do not have clearance."

He pulled the headset off and dropped it to his shoulder. Words were snares. He'd had enough of those.

The runway threshold loomed—white numerals, a rectangle of promise. A Jeep zipped past at the far end and turned, blocking. He pushed the throttle; the turboprop surged and then settled as he eased back. Not yet. The pattern would get you killed. Let them move to the wreck. Let the hole open and step through it.

He coasted along the edge. At midfield, a gap appeared—two trucks, a knot of men, all half-turned toward the ocean. The Jeep at the threshold spun toward the surf.

Now.

Throttle forward. The tail squatted, the nose lightened, the engine's steady whine hardened to a saw's song. He centred on the paint, hands delicate on the yoke as if a rough touch might make the thing buck and throw him.

A figure lunged from the side, waving both arms. Ben kept the roll true; the figure leapt clear, cursing in Portuguese that carried even through the glass.

Speed ran up. Eighty. Ninety. He held the nose low longer than instinct wanted, feeling the wings load, the runway whisper under tyres that didn't want to belong to him anymore.

"Abort! Abort!" the headset shouted at his shoulder.

He didn't.

He eased back. The nose floated. The mains drummed once, twice, then forgot the ground. The island sagged away; Cabo Verde became a mountain in water. Gear up. Throttle back a sliver to stop the worst of the engine's scream. Trim enough that he wasn't strangling the yoke.

Don't overthink. Don't look down.

He looked down.

The fire had thinned, a cruel ember in the side of the runway. The apron littered with rescue vehicles and human ants pointing up.

Out past the island's teeth, the Atlantic spread like an undecided god. South-west tugged him again—deep, bone-level—as if some buried magnet wanted the marrow out of his body.

He set the nose SW, toward the bulge of a continent he couldn't see.

Brazil was a word, a glow he would find; the Andes were the thing that pulled.

He forced his hands to relax by degrees. Tiny corrections. No hard moves. Let the machine work if it wanted to. He wasn't up here to fight it; he was up here because the world wouldn't let him stay down.

"Feet on dirt," he muttered, a superstition said to an empty cockpit.

"Feet on dirt, and this ends."

He levelled at an altitude that felt right. The instruments jittered and settled. The fuel gauges, mercifully, were fat and friendly; someone had left the tanks heavy, maybe for a morning hop to Bolivia, maybe for a medevac leg that would now be late.

Ahead, only the ocean and the thin line where darker blue became a lighter blue. He kept the wings level and flew into it. The sea took him back. It always did. Blue on blue, a skin over depths that didn't care if men crossed it or drowned singing. The turboprop shouldered his burden with a steady animal hum. Thin, eastbound contrails stitched the high sky—military flights still arrowing toward Morocco.

He watched them without envy. Let the living hurl metal at prophecy.

His war was smaller, meaner, and personal.

An hour slipped by. Then two. The engine settled into a rhythm that felt almost like breath. He didn't trust it. He trusted the way the yoke twitched when a gust grabbed the wing root, the way the horizon line wavered by hairs when he over-trimmed, the flicker of a gauge needle that knew more than he did and complained less. Stay level. No heroics. Let the world pass.

Wind shifted—warm, damp; the smell of rain sneaking through the vents. He saw it first as a band of grey, then as a cloud wall. The Intertropical belt was awake—clouds piled on clouds, flashing with silent heat lightning, reflecting off the plane. The turboprop shuddered as he eased left, threading between two curtains of rain and plumes of cloud, the colour of billowing smoke.

"Not today," he told the weather. "I'm already spoken for."

The turbulence punched back anyway—an uppercut that threw his head against the headrest and made the altimeter skip.

He corrected with his fingers more than with his hands. The yoke didn't need orders; it required permission. He gave it, and the wing rolled out of the downdraft like a boxer slipping a hook.

A thin grin cracked his split lip. "Good girl."

He hated himself for saying it. He was making friends with the sky.

The band of storms fell behind him by slow inches. Ahead, the fog eased slowly until the clouds became intermittent puffs in a sea of blue sky. He let his eyes rest on the endless roll of white clouds below him, wondering if the world would reveal itself. The pull in his ribs was constant, like a hand on a leash that never tugged—just insisted. South-west, and then further.

He drank warm water, gagging on the stale tang of plastic. Fatigue crawled along his shoulders; his muscles were getting tired. He shook it off. Sleep was a plummet, waiting to happen.

Sometime later, the world started to darken—not much, just a suggestion of it. As the clouds started to bruise and the Atlantic turned to slate. Far off, gulls wheeled as white flecks.

He almost didn't believe the first line of land. It rose slowly from the sea like a lie—a darker smear where the horizon should be clean. He waited for it to dissolve back into water. It held. The smear became a line, then a contour, then an uneven jaw of coast with green behind it so dense it looked black.

He laughed then, a short, ugly sound. "About bloody time."

No towers. No bright grid of the city. No beacon said land here.

The coast was mangrove and marsh and long skeins of sandbar, the water shot through with coffee-coloured rivers, dragging whole forests toward the sea. He turned south along the shore, hugging the empty. The gauges said he could keep going—maybe far.

He didn't trust "maybe."

He wanted dirt before luck changed tones. A slash appeared in the green. Narrow. Straight by accident more than design.

An old strip, or a new one built by men who didn't want to be found: coral sand tamped to hardness, a single drag mark down the middle where something heavier than a truck had used it recently. No tower. No windsock he could see. Only a leaning shack at one end, dog-legged and sun-bitten, with a tin roof that flashed as the sun set.

He circled once, high enough to make the trees look safe. The strip looked shorter every second he stared at it. *Pick something else*—the sensible part of the skull said.

The rest of him remembered the way the fence had given in Cabo Verde and the way the dead in Fez did not. No second options. Only the one in front of you until it becomes the last.

He set up a long, shallow final, nose a breath down, power steady enough to keep the prop from complaining. The wind was cross and lazy, a sideways push that arrived late. He crabbed to meet it, hating the angle, hating the sight of a runway sliding crooked under his nose.

"Feet on dirt," he told the bones. "Feet on dirt and we walk away."

The last hundred meters happened quickly. The strip jumped up as if the jungle were tossing it at him. He eased power and flared—too much, too soon. The air went syrupy under the wing, and the tail sagged in that hungry way that meant stall was coming. More power. Nose down a hair. The left wheel kissed earth, and the right one refused, a child sulking, and then both decided together to arrive with a bang that rattled his teeth.

The aircraft bounced in a single heave, lifted, and came down harder. He caught a widening swerve with a panicked boot on the rudder.

"Easy—"

Something ahead on the white spine of the strip—a hump of coral or a buried root—didn't hear him.

The nose rolled over it with a crunch that travelled through the cockpit floorboards and into his teeth. The left main snapped. The world yawed left like it meant to throw him into the mangroves. He shoved the opposite rudder and felt nothing. Control went soft, a rope gone slack. The prop chewed sand; the nose dipped; the windshield filled with broken ground.

Instinct screamed Go around.

Hands moved for the throttle. The engine coughed at the abuse, surged, then stuttered. The burst threw him forward into the straps; the stutter robbed the wings of whatever kindness they had left.

Then the slam.

The right gear folded and tore. The nose dug deep, ploughing a furrow that piled coral sand over the cockpit. The prop shattered into knives and splinters. The harness clasp snapped. The windshield cracked, and noise collapsed into a tight, white sound like ripping linen.

He did not black out. He hated that most. He watched it all as if the cockpit were a theatre box where the play came with shrapnel.

The fuselage slewed, lifted at the tail, and came near enough to a cartwheel to count. The canopy frame twisted. The left door gave up. The belly skidded off the coral onto wet grass and then into soft, dark earth that slowed the wreck the way a hand slows a thrown stone.

The harness let go—the plane had decided it was done with him.

He went forward, up and out, through the torn gap where plexiglass had been, through a spray of dirt and steam and bits of aircraft skin that fluttered, torn.

For half a second, he hung in a geometry that didn't make sense. You fall. You break. You heal. Repeat until the gods get bored. Except he didn't fall like a thrown thing. His arms were flung wide because the body does that when it understands what's next, and stupidly, wants more surface to surrender. His chest opened to the air and—there. Not a cradle. A hand.

A pressure. A shape pushing back. It was so small he could have denied it. A millimetre lost to an accident—an extra heartbeat between gravity's footfalls. The ground missed him; it argued. It said not yet in a language as old as breath.

He told himself it was the updraft boiling off the strip, heat lifting the air before the day was ready. He said everything, but the only thing that fit the sensation blooming through his sternum was that the sky knew he was there, and for the first time in his long, stupid war. Something did not want to kill him.

"Don't," he said to the open air, to no one, to himself.

He angled his hands without meaning to. The palms edged, feathers on a bird that had never been taught that word. His body was shaved, a slice from the fall.

The ground shifted from 'incoming' to 'approaching'. Reed tops bent to greet him instead of to spear him.

Then his disagreement with gravity ended. He struck the reeds, not the coral. They folded under him with wet, furious sounds. Mud took his weight poorly. He skipped once, stupidly, and then stopped on his side, half-submerged in sweet-rot water that smelled like a thousand dead things—and then silence, except for the crickets, acting as if nothing had happened.

For a moment, he forgot how to breathe—then remembered, violently. He choked, spat mud, and rolled onto his back. Pain arrived later, angry. Shoulder, ribs, hip, his whole map lit. The curse had run ahead of him, busy and efficient. He tried fingers, toes. All present, functional and outraged.

"Wind," he told himself as he stared up.

The word didn't fit. This had been a refusal.

He shut his eyes. "Feet on dirt," he said, voice rough. "Feet on dirt."

When he finally sat up, the wreck lay thirty meters away, skewed like a fish run aground. Smoke uncoiled lazily from the torn cowling. The strip's shack tilted, window dark—no sirens—no one close enough to care. The jungle watched with the patience of a cathedral.

He should have crawled to the fuselage to search for water, tools, anything. Instead, he stood, because standing put weight in his heels and reminded him that the ground was still a thing. His knees shook once and then found themselves. He faced the strip, then the sky, and reluctantly—he turned his back on both and limped toward the tree line.

He didn't look up again. Not yet. He could still feel the fraction of a second when the air had disagreed with his fall. That was enough to ruin a man who liked the ground. Enough to make him dangerous to himself. He pushed into the green shade.

The jungle was loud in ways the city never was. Not gunfire loud, not sirens or engines. Loud in layers. Cicadas had the top, droning their electric hymn. Under that came a scatter of bird calls, high and mocking. Somewhere lower, frogs repeated the same short syllable like priests too bored to change the sermon.

Ben moved through it half-stumbling, the wet weight of the air squeezing sweat out of him faster than it could dry. Every step felt like a surrender to something old. Vines tugged at his boots, thorns cut his skin. The earth was spongy, black, and smelled of rot.

He breathed hard, ribs protesting, but now complying. He wiped mud from his face, but the gesture only streaked it more. Didn't matter; it was going to get dark soon. He pressed on. No one here cared. At least, no one human tonight, or so he thought.

A mile from the strip—maybe less, maybe more, he had no map—he heard the first voices. Portuguese, barked, clipped.

Men were marking sectors, calling them in on the radios. The jungle swallowed their echoes quickly, but not quickly enough.

He dropped to his belly in the rot and lay still, letting beetles crawl his wrists, willing his lungs to shrink—boots on the trail not twenty feet away. Flashlights darted. The wreck had been noticed after all. A word crackled over their radio—"australiano."

He cursed inwardly. They already knew whose body they expected to find. He didn't move until they moved. When their lights faded into the green, he slid deeper into it, crawling until the mud was up to his chest and the roots above made a lattice strong enough to hide him from anything short of a god.

South-west, his ribs whispered. He almost laughed. I'll get there in pieces if I keep crashing. Maybe that's what you want.

He rose again once the jungle had eaten their footsteps.

The airstrip was behind him, and with it the possibility of another aircraft. That door had closed in smoke. The curse might keep him walking, but it couldn't magic wings out of shredded aluminium. So it would be on foot. On stolen trucks. On boats. Feet on dirt. That had been his promise. No more sky.

He plodded on. The canopy thickened. Light was disappearing. Thorns raked him; sweat dripped into eyes he dared not wipe. He followed a river downstream, hoping for signs of people who weren't in uniform.

He found them near dusk.

A village huddled on stilts, houses thatched with palm, dugout canoes pulled onto a muddy slope. Smoke from cooking fires climbed in straight columns. Dogs barked when they smelled him before the people did. The sound carried across the water.

He stayed at the edge of the tree line, half-hidden. He was a wreck: shirt torn, one sleeve red to the elbow, mud dried in plates on his legs. No man stumbled out of the bush looking like that without bringing questions. Questions meant names, names meant cages. So he waited.

Children played on the dock, shouting at one another in a dialect that bent Portuguese into a song. A woman hauled a net from the shallows, fat with silver fish. A man sharpened a machete on a stone, the sound like teeth being filed. He envied their ordinariness so hard his chest hurt.

South-west, the pull reminded him. You don't belong here. The dogs wouldn't stop. A boy pointed.

Heads turned. The man with the machete stood straighter.

Ben swore under his breath and stepped out, hands raised halfway, palms open to show they were empty.

He expected shouts, rifles, maybe a call to the soldiers who still combed the bush behind him.

Instead, the woman with the net only narrowed her eyes. "Quem é você?"

He searched his scraps of Portuguese, found nothing useful. "Australiano," he said hoarsely. "Só... passando."

Just passing.

The man lowered the machete but didn't smile. "Perigoso. Polícia procuram."

Dangerous. The police are searching.

Ben nodded once. "Eu sei." I know.

The villagers didn't move closer. They didn't offer food, water, or shelter. But neither did they raise an alarm. That was enough. He gave a slight bow, awkwardly, and turned downriver.

A canoe waited at the bank, its prow lashed with twine. He pointed at it, question plain. The man spat into the river.

"Leva. Mas rápido."

Take it, but fast.

Ben didn't argue. He shoved the canoe into the chocolate current, leapt in, and let the river have him. The current tugged firmly. The banks slid past, green and endless, branches clawing at air heavy with insects. He paddled twice, three times, then gave up. The river wanted him; the river could carry him.

Night fell again, a curtain ripped across the sky. Stars punched holes through it. The canoe drifted silently except for the occasional slap of a fish. Ben leaned back, every muscle trembling, and closed his eyes. But rest didn't come. The events of the last three days replayed themselves over and over again.

The canoe rocked gently. The river sang. Behind him, the strip burned lower, and the dogs stopped barking. Ahead, nothing but current, darkness and the slow, terrifying promise of what he might become.

The river finally spat him out into saltwater once more, and the canoe grounded against a spit of sand. It was serene and moonlit. He curled up as best he could and finally allowed himself to get some sleep.

The next morning, he woke sore; the battering his body had taken was not forgiving him. He hauled the canoe onto the sand, hoping that at least here the villagers would find it.

He left and kept walking—slowly, surely, but upright—for hours, until he found a rutted track that led inland. The track ended at a coastal strip. Not military—civilian, ragged, but functional. Two hangars leaned in the sun, paint flaking, roofs patched with tin. A battered fuel truck sat lopsided in the grass. And beyond it, three planes crouched on their wheels like patient dogs.

A man in oil-stained coveralls smoked outside one hangar, a pistol tucked carelessly at his belt. His eyes tracked Ben the way a farmer tracks a stray bull—measured, wary, not yet hostile.

Ben raised both hands. His voice cracked from thirst. “I need south-west. Across the Andes.”

The man squinted. “You pay?”

For once, Ben didn’t have to lie. He drew the leather wallet from his pocket. Mud-stained but intact. Inside—cash. Five thousand in American bills, folded flat. He peeled the notes slowly, letting the man see the sum.

The man’s eyes widened just enough to show he wasn’t expecting this stranger to carry the kind of money smugglers killed for.

He dragged on his cigarette, exhaled, then nodded.

“Five thousand, I fly you. Quiet. No questions. But you ditch your phone—if you have one. Change your shirt. Hide in the cargo. Keep your head down. And don’t talk on approach. Military’s on the band.”

“Done,” Ben rasped, pressing the wad into his palm.

The man whistled. From the hangar emerged another, younger pilot, lean and sharp-eyed, his shirt unbuttoned to the sternum. He glanced at the money, then at Ben's state—muddy, blood-streaked, wild-eyed—and shrugged.

"We take the Beech. Belém first. Then further south if the weather holds."

Ben followed them without protest. His body screamed for rest. His mind wanted only silence.

The Beechcraft sat tidy compared to the wrecks he'd crawled from—twin props, paint faded but cared for.

The younger pilot climbed in, ran his hands over the switches with an ease Ben envied. Engines coughed to life, then purred smoothly. The smell of fuel and oil filled the cabin. Ben took the rear seat. For the first time in days, maybe weeks, he did not touch the controls, did not fight with fate at the yoke. He leaned back, head against the worn cushion, and let another man do the flying.

The plane rolled, lifted, and climbed into the morning air. The coastline fell away, mangroves shrinking into smudges, the sea stretching silver and endless. Ben let out a breath he hadn't realised he was holding. His hands unclenched. His ribs still ached, his shoulder throbbed, but none of it mattered here. Not while someone else guided the wings.

The pilot hummed tunelessly, eyes on the horizon. The older man counted bills again, satisfied. Neither asked who Ben was—neither cared. Cash spoke cleaner than any name. The hum of engines steadied into a rhythm. Clouds thinned above, the Atlantic calm below.

For the first time since Fez, Ben let himself close his eyes without fear of slamming into earth or water. He dreamed, not of bone armies or wreckage, but of flight without struggle—smooth, silent, effortless. A dream he did not want, and yet it came anyway.

When he woke, the sun had shifted, bright on the water. The pilot gave him a glance over the shoulder. "You're lucky, gringo. The weather's with us. South will be easy today."

Ben nodded once, words thick in his throat. Easy. For once.

He turned his gaze to the horizon, where the pull inside his chest tugged ever downward, ever onward. The Andes waited. But for now, he rode the air as a passenger, the ground far below, his fate deferred. And for the first time in longer than he could remember, he let himself breathe.

Chapter 4
The Horde

The night above Fez burned like a second sun. Jets screamed in formation, their afterburners cutting rivers of fire across the black. Then came the roar—the thrum of ordnance released, the howl of bombs falling blind into the ancient city. The stone that had stood for centuries shattered in a heartbeat. Whole blocks dissolved into blossom after blossom of orange light. Minarets toppled as though giants had kicked them. Walls crumpled, domes buckled, and streets that had once carried caravans of salt and silk were reduced to fire pits.

The living ran. The dead did not.

Skeleton ranks filled avenues like rivers of bone, their bronze-stained shields locking together even as high explosives tore the asphalt beneath their feet. The carpet bombing was merciless, yet futile: craters swallowed men of flesh, but the risen did not scatter. They absorbed the fire, closed their gaps, and marched on. Jawbones clattered like castanets in mockery of the screams around them.

Leila—no, Lilith now—walked through it untouched. Her hair streamed black in the shockwaves, her dress whipped by the heat—but no shrapnel touched her. The bombs fell wide as if the sky itself bent to her will. She had spoken the command earlier, a word dragged from the marrow of language so old it had never been written down.

We are not the target. And so they were not.

She stood atop a shattered wall that overlooked the old Medina, her eyes reflecting the inferno. Where once she had been human—aching, fearful, torn between survival and surrender—now her gaze was sovereign. Her lips moved not in prayer but in invocation, shaping the syllables of a command that had reshaped the path of American bombers without them ever knowing it.

"Strike the streets. Burn the stones. But not me. Never me." The air obeyed.

Beside her, the Sleeper had awakened fully, no longer a husk wrapped in ancient linens but a thing terrible and deliberate. The Mummy's golden-black eyes burned with unblinking patience. His armour was patchwork: pieces of bronze, iron, and bone fused by rituals older than the Nile. He raised a hand, and the phalanxes below reoriented, pivoting like a single body. Shields angled against the direction of impact, spears tilted forward.

Every bomb that fell only made the dead more certain in their silence.

Lilith smiled. The world had sent its fire, and fire had failed.

"Let them come," she whispered. "We will teach them what it means to be endless."

A second wave rolled in. Bombers thundered lower, their payloads heavier. The old city disappeared in choking dust, shockwaves blasting apart markets, mosques, and mansions that had stood since dynasties were young. Civilians scattered through alleys, their cries drowned by the detonation of ordnance meant to erase armies. Yet through it all, the ranks of bone moved unhindered, as if guided by invisible metronomes.

Lilith lifted her hands, palms outward, and the dust began to thicken unnaturally. Where human lungs choked, she shaped the storm into form. The dead beneath her clicked their jaws in approval.

She had seen the Mummy raise them with gesture and silent will, and now she imitated his motion. Her words were her own, but the source of the power had to be the same.

“Rise,” she commanded.

Nothing.

She tried again, harder, as if force could make language obey. “Rise.”

Still nothing.

For a moment she stood very still, listening—not to the rubble, but to herself. Then she copied the Mummy’s hand exactly: the same wrist, the same cruel patience in the fingers. Her voice dropped, not louder but sharper.

“Rise.”

Something in her spine answered—an old memory that wasn’t hers and yet had been waiting there all her life. The spell flooded in, already complete, and spilled out through her hands.

From the rubble around her, fresh soldiers clawed their way out. Civilians crushed beneath the bombing pulled themselves upright, flesh sloughing to dust as skeletons emerged ready-armed with whatever fragments remained: twisted rebar for spears, shattered doors as shields, the debris of modern ruin reforged into weapons.

The Mummy regarded her with a long silence. Then, slowly, he inclined his head. Not approval—acknowledgment. "You have learned," he said, his voice like sand dragged over stone.

Lilith's smile widened, sharp and terrible. "I no longer need to wait for your call. The dead answer me now."

"Good." His gaze turned northward, toward the horizon where the night glowed faintly with the reflection of the Mediterranean. "Then we divide."

He stepped down from the wall, dust and fire sliding away from his form as though reality itself recoiled from his weight. The phalanxes parted to make way.

"I will lead this host to the Strait of Gibraltar. Europe will feel our tread before dawn."

Lilith lifted her chin, eyes already east. "And I will take the Levant. Through Syria, through Turkey, into their fragile heart. A pincer across the continent. They will not know where to turn."

The Mummy's hand passed over the hilt of his ancient khopesh. "Do not falter. The gods will resist you. The ethereals may oppose you."

She laughed, the sound carrying unnaturally far through the smoke. "Let them. They had their chance. Humanity prayed to them, only to be abandoned. Now they will pray to me."

The ground quaked—not from bombs, but from the synchronised step of the undead divisions. Rows upon rows, more than had ever lived in Fez in its proudest days. The city itself had become a reservoir of bone.

Above, a flight of American jets roared low, seeking targets in the dust. Their bombs fell once more—but their trajectories twisted, detonating wide of Lilith and the Mummy, tearing empty streets instead. The pilots swore over their radios, certain their aim was true.

Lilith lowered her hands. The spell still held.

"North," the Mummy said, and without waiting, began his march. Columns followed, shields high, spears angled, their collective clatter like rain on bronze. Toward Tangier, toward the crossing where Europe slept unprepared.

Lilith remained atop the broken wall, the heat of fire curling her hair, the glow of ruin painting her skin in shades of prophecy. East. The Levant awaited.

She turned her palms upward, whispering her new words, words she had shaped herself rather than borrowed from her ancient companion.

The ground beneath her feet began to stir, as every graveyard east of Fez had heard her and was listening.

"Rise," she said again, more firmly this time. "Rise, my children. Walk with me."

From far off, beneath the crash of bombs, another sound began: the rustle of graves opening, the grind of bone upon stone.

Lilith smiled into the storm.

Lilith waited until the last wave passed—until the sky stopped shaking and the dust stopped hissing down like hot rain—then she stepped off the broken wall and walked into the street as if onto a throne.

The spell rode in her bones like a second pulse. She could feel its edges now, where it clung to her and shed from her like heat. The words were less important than the intent, the grammar less than the pressure she put behind it.

She tested the perimeter with a lifted hand. "Not mine," she murmured.

A final bomb, late or lost, fell shrieking toward the square. Its course bent with the grace of a hawk changing its mind. It slammed into an empty lane, peeled stone like fruit, and threw dust across her skirt. The blast lifted her hair and went searching for something else to break.

She smiled. "Good."

The ranks below had already learned the cadence of her will. They looked up without eyes and waited. She shaped a command that was also a promise. "East."

The phalanxes pivoted, bronze rims touching, spears tilting. They began to move—step, scrape, step—the city's old alleys suddenly too small for their certainty. Every doorway became a mouth for more soldiers. Every collapse revealed ribs that rattled awake and rose standing. She let them form behind her like a tide.

A child lay cradled by a woman who had run out of hope hours ago.

Lilith paused. The living flinched when she cast a shadow across them. The woman did not beg. Their eyes met, and in that moment, Lilith saw the old poverty, the old betrayals, the old prayers that had gone nowhere but roofs and rain.

She raised two fingers. "Go," she said—to the woman.

The mother did not scream. She closed her eyes and whispered something that might have been a thank-you or a curse. Lilith did not listen. Mercy and horror tasted too similar tonight.

She left the city as it still burned. The gate on the east road had fallen inward; its iron teeth lay scattered like a smile. Beyond, hills rolled away toward the Algerian border, cypress and scrub turning their leaves like hands. Columns unspooled in her wake, knitting into a snake of bronze and white that crossed valleys without breaking formation.

She walked at the head, bare-headed, the dust drawing symbols along her cheeks. The symbols were not random. The wind and sweat made them so. She began to understand the trick—how the world formed patterns and power with it. She considered what glyph would seal it.

"Not the target," she repeated, until the words became threaded through the sky. "Not mine. Not those I mark."

Pilots in the distance reported that instruments refused to hold a lock. The bright dots on screens slid sideways when they reached her. The bombs that fell near turned aside at the last breath. The drones that dipped their cameras to drink her image returned with footage full of glare and sound—white shapes where she should have been, a noise like cut glass.

She did not hide. She rewrote what "aim" meant.

At a low rise, where the wind howled past a field of dry thistle, she stopped to raise the dead again.

"Rise."

She did not shout. She listened.

The ground answered again.

A caravan road lay buried under the modern tarmac. Once, merchants with jars of oil and bundles of dyed wool had died here in a robbery no god had noticed. Their bones were patient, powdered into the lane.

She reached for what was left and gave them shape.

They came up in pieces, as a dirt pile being cleared—a femur twisted and nicked, a jaw with three gold teeth, a hand that still clawed a ledger. She gave them all spears. She gave them shields painted in dust. She did not ask for names. The living had forgotten their names; she was building something that answered to a new rule.

A hawk balanced on a fencepost, watching. Its head bobbed with interest, not fear. She lifted her palm, and the bird took the air, describing one slow circle over her and then another. The feathers cut the sun into spokes.

She drew a thin arc with her index finger, matching the hawk's path, and felt the turn of the wind tap her wrist in approval.

She did not fly. She did not need to. She was beginning to be carried.

By dusk, they had crossed the first long run of scrub and stone. Villages watched them pass and barred their doors. Dogs howled at the sight of bone. People approached in vehicles as close as they dared, took shaky photographs, and then drove away fast.

At a wadi choked with tamarisk, she called again.

"Rise."

This time, a rider rose. A man in a blue mechanic's jacket with a name patch lifted his skull from mud; beside him, a horse's ribs stood like a ruined harp and then closed into a chest.

The horse shook a mane of dust and stamped.

Lilith placed her hand on the long forehead. The bone was warm. The warmth came from her. The horse bent its neck.

"Carry my standard," she said.

She had no cloth, no pole, no emblem—only an idea.

A black rope lifted from the ground and coiled around an invisible staff. When she let the idea go, the rope remembered it was a banner, loosened its threads to become a flag, rippling without the wind.

The horse and rider turned and took the front of the column.

She made lieutenants from the way bodies had been found. A woman whose wrists had healed crooked became the one who pointed left. A tall boy with a fused shoulder became the one who indicated the pace.

The dead did not argue about rank. Purpose replaced authority.

On the second night, lightning stitched a grey seam across the low horizon. Thunder rolled threateningly, promising rain. The storm avoided her without seeming to. She felt its reluctance—the kind she had first tasted in bombs—then told it what it wanted.

"Skirt us," she said. "Feed the wells."

Rain fell away to the side, leaving salt crusting the cisterns. Men in villages looked up, asking which saint had listened, but the saints weren't replying.

She did not mind taking credit from mouths not yet prepared to kneel to her name.

Under the tar-black hour before dawn, she climbed an abandoned radio tower. The bones had formed themselves into a ladder. At the top, wind gnawed at her dress and dried the sweat in her hair. The city lights of Oujda were a tired necklace to the northeast. Farther still, a black sheet that would be Algeria.

She touched the cold metal with her forehead and spoke once into the tiresome, invisible web that had tied the living into such neat patterns for so long.

“Unmake yourselves where I walk,” she told the signals. “Carry what I say everywhere else.”

Phones within fifty kilometres lost half their signal and could not recover. A warning siren at a border station warbled, re-tuning itself into nonsense. In houses from Nador to Taourirt, radios woke and played one sentence between weather and prayer.

“We are not your enemy,” her voice said, “unless you stand in our way.”

She did not repeat it. Once was enough. Repetition was cheap.

At noon, a pair of attack helicopters came across the ridgeline, shoulders hunched with rockets. She watched them approach, the air rippling under their rotors’ fists. The crews saw her. She let them, because fear was a tool and because she wanted to try the next lesson.

“Look away,” she said, and pushed the command hard.

For a moment, both cockpits filled with glare. Dials clouded. A red hand swept where a green should have been. The pilots blinked tears and saw no target. They circled twice to prove they had tried, then returned to refuel with shame disguised as professionalism.

Her dead did not cheer. They were silent. That suited her. She did not intend to build a kingdom that depended on applause.

She gave herself an hour to practice alone. In a dry riverbed, where the soil had cracked into a map of veins, she wrote new commands with her bare feet.

Not imperatives this time, not orders hammered, but clauses. *Where I pass, the eye prefers the horizon.* She walked the sentence until the dust said yes. *Where I lift my hand, metal remembers the curve of mercy.* She traced it until the shrapnel lying like teeth in the sand lay flatter, duller. *When I name a thing, it becomes impossible to ignore.* She found a thorn bush and named it *Fear.* A kilometre ahead, a soldier sent to scout her suddenly lost his nerve and ran in the opposite direction.

She smiled. Names were doorways. She would open them at the worst moment.

She thought of Ben once. Not with tenderness. With irritation that tasted almost sweet.

He was a problem that solved other issues by attracting more, like fire draws moths and men draw knives. He would live or fail under different skies. If he lived long enough to see what she was making, he would have to choose whether to kneel or to burn. Either would satisfy her arithmetic.

They crossed into Algeria without asking. The border post stood with its chain across the road and its red 'stop' sign in three languages. She brushed the sign with her fingers, and the paint peeled off into her palm. The chain dropped. The dead walked over it without lifting their feet any higher than before.

By evening, she had an army that wasn't tired. Their spears were a thousand misfortunes refashioned: a curtain rod, an axle, a gas main, a rib from a camel that had outlasted its master and then not. Their shields were doors that had kept nothing out and now would. She had lieutenants who pointed in unison at things that had not existed the day before. She had a banner the world couldn't photograph.

She also had a new weight between her shoulder blades, a pressure that was not pain. Strength has a mass. It moves your posture. She rolled her neck and felt the bones answer like satisfied dogs.

On the third day, at a place where rusted rails crossed a salt flat, she stopped and built a choir.

Not of voices.

Of bone. She chose ten of the freshest dead, fingers that still remembered deftness, jaws that still had mouths that could sing. She set them in a line and raised both her hands.

"Repeat," she said, and gave them a single sentence in the old marrow-tongue, the one that had bent bombs and taught rain courtesy.

They repeated it. The sound was ugly and perfect. The ground coughed under it. A kilometre away, a convoy of troop carriers lurched suddenly; clutches burned. Drivers cursed, wondering how.

The choir fell silent at a tilt of her wrist, and engines squealed with relief.

She smiled. "You are my Weavers. You will braid the world to my convenience."

They did not nod. They did not need to. She would teach them when to sing and when to be silent.

Night came on like a velvet bruise, and in it she felt attention. Not human. Not a machine. Something older turned its head in her direction and watched without blinking.

"Come closer," she said to the emptiness, as if to a cat under a table. "Or don't. I am busy." The attention stayed where it was, amounting to an agreement not to interfere for now.

She briefly slept on her feet, then woke and kept walking. The dead do not dream, and she needed to stop needing to.

The desert widened into a plain of salt and scrub, and Lilith strode at its head like a general wearing nothing but certainty. Her army filled the horizon: not columns now, but a tapestry, rows unspooling and knitting together with inhuman precision. Every hour, she called more to her side. Every mile, the ground beneath her whispered up corpses that had been waiting for a tongue bold enough to command them. She had stopped thinking of them as separate resurrections. It was one act, continuous, like breath.

She inhaled the silence of centuries and exhaled soldiers.

The living watched from windows, from hills, from behind sandbags erected by governments who had not believed until it was too late. Some aimed rifles, but few fired. Bullets had become prayers without gods, thrown skyward to no effect. When they fired, the sound rattled like insect wings and was swallowed whole by the clatter of her host.

Lilith moved east, her eyes fixed on distances no human gaze could measure. She saw the Levant not as borders or nations but as thresholds: Syria's bones, Turkey's roads, the way into Europe that bypassed oceans and dared any power to resist. She was building the eastward jaw of a trap, and the Mummy would form the western—a pincer. The continent would be chewed between them.

On the fourth day of marching, the dead began to change. The first had been crude: skeletons draped in rags, wielding whatever iron they found in ruin. But Lilith's will sharpened, and the bodies rose less ragged. She shaped them more carefully, coaxed sinew to linger where bone would have sufficed, pressed armour into being where only dust remained. Bronze plates re-formed on shoulders. Shields carried faded crests of dynasties long dead. Swords glimmered as if they had been whetted only yesterday. She walked through her ranks and traced her finger along their helms. Sparks leapt from touch to bone, and when she passed, their jawbones clicked not in chatter but in rhythm—acknowledgement. She was not simply raising an army. She was remembering it, and memory was stronger than invention.

The choir of Weavers she had built sang each night, voices bone-dry and yet thunderous. Their chant twisted the air, turning winds to her favour. Once, when they sang too long, the world itself misplaced a village. People went to sleep in their own beds and woke a league west, in fields that weren't theirs, with their doors opening onto the wrong road. The villagers screamed of witchcraft and cursed her name, but curses are gifts when they are repeated often enough.

She let the curses spread. A god must be named, feared, hated, adored—it mattered less which.

At Tlemcen, the Algerian military tried to stand its ground. Tanks crawled into formation on the high road, muzzles glinting beneath the noon sun. Mortar crews scrambled, artillery roared. The first shells found her lines, sending plumes of dirt and bone into the air. For a moment, the living thought they had found a weapon that mattered.

Lilith raised her hand. "Return."

The word slipped into marrow like a disease. Skeletons marched into craters, picked up the shells that had failed to explode, and hurled them back with strength they should not have possessed. Some detonated midair, showering the tanks with shrapnel. Others fell behind the Algerian line and cracked open fuel depots. Firestorms bloomed where defence had been.

She did not need to watch. She walked forward, her host closing the gap around her. The tanks reversed, metal treads shrieking, but retreat is slow when terror drives it.

The dead reached them before they cleared the ridge.

A skeleton climbed a turret, its bony hands dragging the hatch open. The crew screamed inside. Flames coughed through the seams a second later.

Lilith tilted her head. "Learn."

The host obeyed. From then on, every machine of war they encountered became a vessel of flame. The dead knew where to pry, where to strike, where to pour oil that no living hand had lit.

By dusk, the ridge was silent save for burning hulks. She stood among them, the heat rolling across her face.

"East," she said again. The army marched, and the world behind them was left glowing, skeletal outlines drawn in smoke.

That night, she allowed herself the luxury of sitting. A ruined amphitheatre overlooked the valley, its seats broken but intact enough to hold her weight. She sat where once an emperor might have, and her host filled the stage.

She closed her eyes.

The chant of the Weavers rose, and with it came visions. She saw the Levant bathed in moonlight, its rivers swollen with corpses that climbed ashore to meet her. She saw the Bosporus choke with bone and iron, bridges sagging under the weight of her tread. She saw Europe's heart split open—not with bombs, not with treaties, but with the slow certainty of her pincer closing.

When she opened her eyes, stars had gathered thick. Her body ached not with weakness but with fullness, as though strength itself had weight and she carried too much of it.

She whispered into the night, not as a plea but as a promise.

"They cannot stop me. Not gods. Not ethereals. Not the dead—I command them. Not the living—I consume them. I am Lilith, and the east will kneel."

The amphitheatre held the echo, reluctant to let it go.

By dawn, she had raised a thousand more. They came from graves beneath olive groves, from cemeteries long tended and suddenly abandoned, from the bones of those who had drowned in rivers and been forgotten. They came without hesitation, without memory, with only her name as their gravity. And she felt the world begin to bend. Roads emptied before her long before anyone could see her.

People said you felt Lilith coming in your jaw first, the way you feel a storm in old bones—an ache in the hinge when you tried to swallow. Then phones lost signal, not all at once, but like a tide picked at the edges: four bars to three to two to a blank face. Car alarms hiccuped and went quiet. Dogs stuttered, as if trying to bark and thinking otherwise. The living learned new kinds of silence.

In a roadside tea shop outside Sidi Bel Abbès, a sergeant in mud-caked boots stood with both hands around a chipped glass that had long since stopped being hot. His platoon lay scattered across hospital cots two towns back. He had been the one to run when the tank went red inside, and the hatch burned his palms. No one had forgiven him yet, least of all himself. The television above the counter showed a satellite loop of weather fronts. The ticker at the bottom never mentioned the weather.

The owner kept turning the volume up, as if loudness could make sense faster. "...mass displacement underway. Government advisories recommend—"

The picture rippled. A woman's voice—low, certain, and not belonging to anyone in the studio—cut into the broadcast between a rainfall report and casualty numbers.

"We are not your enemy," it said, the consonants smooth as a knife's spine.

Every glass rang the way metal does when it's trying to behave. The owner crossed himself without meaning to. The sergeant lifted his cup and, somewhere behind his teeth, the ache came again.

"Unless you stand in our way," the voice added, and the screen returned to maps as if nothing had passed.

No one spoke for a long breath. Then the sergeant set his glass down and said, very softly, "I think we already stood." He left without paying. The owner didn't ask him to.

The refugees began to travel at right angles to the roads. They learned to trust dry creek beds and the back fences of farms and the long, thorny corridors where goats had already negotiated the world. A woman with two children walked along an irrigation canal outside Relizane. The older boy counted steps because it was a game that didn't require breath. The little one kept stopping to pick up rocks that were too heavy, then tossing them because owning anything felt dangerous.

They heard the choir before they saw the dead—a thread of sound so straight it seemed to hold the horizon taut. It shook dust from acacia pods. It turned her breath to glass.

The boy's counting faltered, and then he whispered, as if to the numbers themselves, "Shh."

When the army came into view, it did not crest the hill like a crowd. It arrived like the answer to a riddle: suddenly obvious, faintly insulting—bronze and bone and the steady white of jawlines.

The woman pressed both children down into the reeds. Their hearts hammered under her palms.

The line of the dead flowed past without turning heads. Leading the centre, a skeletal rider and horse led with a rope banner snapping in the wind, followed by the horde.

At the last moment, the older boy lifted his face to look. He expected to meet a gaze. There was none. There was only the strange relief of not being seen. They lay there until the choir faded and the canal remembered how to be water. She stood up with knees full of sand.

"We go the other way," she said, and they did, though none of them could have said which way that was anymore.

At the air operations centre outside Naples, the big table carried more screens than wood. Officers stood with their hands on their hips to keep from pointing where pointing meant nothing.

"They're calling it a jamming cloud," one major said, tired enough to make the joke twice. "Except it moves like it's on a leash."

A captain zoomed a thermal feed. The image went white where the host marched, and where it should have shown a single heat signature bright enough to blind, there was a hole shaped like a woman. Every attempt to drag a box over the hole made it jitter and slide to the edge of the screen, as if embarrassed.

"We can target the ground," the major said. "We can't target her."

"So target the ground," the colonel snapped. "Crater her corridors."

"We did," the captain said, a little too gently. "She walks between the craters like she drew them."

They escalated to slides that made politics out of fear. "Western thrust approaching Gibraltar. Eastern thrust tracking toward the Levant. We are witnessing a pincer maneuver," the briefer said, as if naming it gave anyone more time.

"What is her centre of gravity?" a voice on the teleconference asked. Transatlantic, stiff with committees.

The colonel looked at the hole in the thermal that erased the world around it and said, "Confidence."

On the outskirts of Oran, a priest set out folding chairs in the nave because pews felt too permanent. A woman from the mosque across the street brought water jugs because all thirst is the same size. They did not quarrel over verses. They had run out of time for proof.

"Perhaps she is a blight we deserve," an old man said, for the comfort of self-blame.

"A blight doesn't ask permission to spare your children," the woman said.

She had heard the broadcast, too. She didn't say she had considered the first half a promise and the second a rope. An argument started softly and ran out of words. They prayed at different angles in the same room, and outside, the choir's dry thunder measured a marching time that didn't care about religion.

A stringer for an international wire service rode east in the back of a produce truck, typing with both thumbs because writing longhand made her hands shake worse. She had filed three pieces already that editors kept softening until they read like weather. She wrote this one without adjectives.

Algerian Army elements attempted to block route N22 at 1100. The dead walked through the cordon. Engines failed. Radios repeated one sentence in a woman's voice, "*We are not your enemy unless you stand in our way.*" Fuel depots ignited without visible cause. Surviving crew abandoned armour.

She hesitated, then added: No artillery unit that fired twice remained intact.

She hit send.

The truck hit a pothole, jarring her spine. The driver cursed. She apologised for him, then asked if he believed in saints.

"I believe in taxes," he said. "And in going around things, I cannot move."

They went around.

Customs officers at the Algerian–Tunisian border posted a paper notice when the computers went silent. It said CLOSED in French and Arabic, and had a signature—an extra flourish that couldn't make it an authority. Families read the paper and then set it on fire for heat.

The Weavers' chant rolled across the flats. A young lieutenant raised his father's binoculars. He had grown up with stories of men who chose lines and then held them. He watched the white tide coming and lowered the glasses.

"We fall back," he told his squad.

His voice did not shake. It wasn't courage. It was clarity.

"To where?" a soldier asked, not insolent. Just practical.

The lieutenant looked east and then farther east, past maps, to places that only existed in footnotes and prophecy.

"We'll know when we get there," he said, and they did not.

In a hotel basement in Ankara, men and women with maps that still smelled of ink argued terms that had kept empires from starving. Someone said Article Five like a spell. Someone else said the word Bosphorus as if it were a door with only one key.

"She is not in our theatre," a defence minister said, meaning not yet. "Your theatre is a street with both ends," a general told him. They spoke of flights and bridges and river crossings and mouthfuls of sea. No one asked what to do when aim stopped meaning anything.

A boy in Constantine posted a rooftop video. You saw nothing at first, just a field of thistle making small decisions in the wind. Then the frame found the banner he couldn't focus on, and you felt your eyes blur trying to see it. In the comments, someone wrote: *It's like trying to remember a dream.* The post lasted 9 minutes before it disappeared.

An imam recorded a message on a phone with one last bar of battery and more courage than reception.

"*If she is a trial,*" he said, "*pass it. If she is a mercy, don't insist on making it otherwise. If she is a liar, do not give her the dignity of fear. If she is a queen,*" and here his mouth tightened, "*remember that queens are only people who have perfected asking. Say no where you can. Say nothing where no has been taken from you.*"

He pressed send.

The message took its time getting anywhere.

Near the front, farther east than she had a right to be already, Lilith stood on the roof of a school and watched the city's lights try to decide whether to stay on. Entire neighbourhoods flickered.

Her Weavers sang once and stopped.

In a room below her, a teacher with chalk on her sleeves unlocked a cabinet and took out a national flag. She folded it carefully along seams she had taught children to respect.

Then she put it back because some days were not for flags.

Across the city, a colonel gathered his staff and said, "Aim for the streets. Don't look at her."

"Sir?" a captain asked.

"You'll know it," the colonel said. "You'll know it by why you can't see her."

They aimed where he said and hit nothing important.

The dead crossed another threshold.

The living learned how fast a rumour can become doctrine. And in halls that hadn't been prayed in since famine was a verb, small candles began to appear—not to stop a thing, just to make a small place where light could pretend to hold.

Lilith felt the candles and did not begrudge them. Light was not a rival. It was not a weapon. It was a measurement. She kept walking east, and everywhere, the measurements changed.

Chapter 5

The Penthouse

The basalt on the marble table had gone black. No hiss, no glow, only the memory of fire trapped in stone.

"He's cooling," Pele said, arms crossed tight across her chest. "Jian Wu's furnace is choked with sand and silence. He crawled east, into the desert, where even the wind struggles to breathe. If left, he will smoulder for years, waiting for the world to forget him."

Her voice was flint on steel. She wanted him buried.

Zed finally turned from the window, crow shifting on his shoulder, feathers rustling.

"Cooling," he repeated. "Not gone. A volcano sleeps; it does not die."

Jamil's tone was colder still. "And in the ledger, his mark remains. Suppressed flame is still imbalanced. If he is to rise, he must be convinced to rise with us, not against us."

"That convincing is not mine to give," Pele snapped. "He will not hear me. He will not forgive me. If I walk into his desert, he will see the hand that smothered him, not the face of a sister."

Her admission hung in the air. Even Ari stopped his restless tapping on the table edge.

"Then someone else goes," Hera said.

She sat straight-backed, hands clasped, eyes like blades. "Not fire meeting fire, but something softer. Jian Wu must be coaxed, not cornered. We need his strength, but more than that—we need his consent. Forced, he burns. Willing, he reshapes battle itself."

Dionysis tipped his bottle, letting the wine catch the candlelight. His smile was languid, his eyes sharp.

"Soft, is it? Perhaps a little kindness, perhaps a little charm. I've walked deserts with worse company than Jian Wu. Let me try. The man beneath the fire may want laughter more than orders."

Si stirred, her voice a whisper meant to be heard. "Or silence. A voice that does not command, does not strike. Sometimes men listen only when the world around them goes quiet."

Thales had been tracing a tide-line across the edge of his chart, but now he lifted his head. "It must be someone who carries patience. Persuasion is not words alone—it is presence. If Jian Wu feels hunted, he will harden. If he feels seen, he may walk with us."

Pele's jaw worked, but she said nothing. The basalt on the table stayed dark, as if to prove her point.

Ari broke the silence with a sharp grin. "So, who do we send? Our most charming drunkard? Our knife-edged whisper? Or some mortal-faced envoy he hasn't yet decided to hate?"

"Not mortal," Hera said quickly. "He would see through a disguise. He always did. No—he needs to face one of us, but not the one who drowned him in the rock."

Her eyes slid to Dionysis first, then to Si. "We'll decide. But it cannot be Pele."

Pele exhaled hard, shoulders stiff. "Then choose quickly. Because while we debate, the bones keep marching north, and the lava waits for me to uncork it."

Zed's voice rumbled like distant thunder. "First, we settle Jian Wu. Lava without direction is ruin. With him at your side, Pele, the fire will be aimed. Without him—" He let the thought hang. The crow croaked, as if finishing it for him.

Hera drew her fingers across the basalt, as though testing its chill. "He is cooling. That buys us a window. We send someone who can walk into the desert and persuade him to rise not as Scourge, but as a shield. If he refuses..."

Pele's eyes flashed. "If he refuses, I bury him deeper."

"No," Hera said. "If he refuses, we wait. Even refusal can change. But we do not waste him by turning him into an enemy before he's chosen."

Dionysis chuckled, raising the bottle in mock salute. "Then it seems Jian Wu has become the most eligible bachelor of this council. The question is: who dares to court the fire without being burned?"

No one laughed.

Their decision to send Si into the desert had stripped the tension from the room for a heartbeat, but only a heartbeat.

War doesn't stay quiet for long.

Ari rose, pulling the hood from his head as if that act alone declared the meeting finished. His grin flashed, but there was nothing playful in it. "While our whisper goes to court fire, the rest of us need to sharpen steel. Lava may hold a line, but it won't march. I will."

He stepped to the map Thoth had spread across the marble. Red marks scarred the Atlas mountains, the ancient lines of Carthage's bones.

Ari stabbed one with a finger. "The bones push here, here, and here. They don't stop, they don't rest. Good. I don't want them to. That makes them predictable. I'll meet them at choke points—bridges, narrow passes, places where numbers mean nothing and fury means everything."

Zed's crow croaked once.

Zed translated with a single word: "Hours."

"Yes," Ari said. "That's all we're buying. Hours. We bleed them of time. We grind their rhythm. Si will kill their song, Pele will spill her lava, but between those strokes it's men with blades and guts that hold the line."

He straightened, scanning the room. "I'll need three things. First: soldiers who won't panic when the bone arrives. Mortals, yes. But not green boys with soft hands. Give me the French Foreign Legion. Give me veterans who already suspect death is a poor accountant. I don't need numbers; I need faith that doesn't snap when the dead refuse to fall."

Jamil frowned, the faintest creasing of his brow. "Faith is brittle. Balance tilts if you recruit too many mortals into a war they cannot win."

"They don't need to win," Ari countered. "They need to fight and keep fighting. That's their only measure. I'll tell them straight: they're not here to survive. They're here to buy minutes. Some men fight better when they know the price."

Dionysis swirled wine lazily in his bottle, eyes gleaming. "You'll need more than grizzled veterans. You'll need rhythm. Songs of your own, to drown the silence when Si isn't near. I can work a crowd, Ari. I can keep the edge sharp when the field wants to collapse. Soldiers who believe they're drunk on glory will kill twice before remembering to breathe."

Ari's grin widened. "Good. You'll be my banner, then. War and wine. Frenzy over fear."

He tapped another mark on the map, near the narrow throat of the strait. "Second: I need machines. Not their drones, not bombers that strike and vanish. I need teeth on the ground. Armoured divisions—Spanish, Moroccan, Algerian, it doesn't matter whose flag. Tanks don't scare bone, but bone doesn't scatter tanks either. We use them to funnel the dead where we want them. A tank isn't a wall—it's a shepherd. Herd the legions toward Pele's flows."

Thales cleared his throat, leaning forward with his tide charts. "If you want armour to channel the march, you must use terrain with precision—hills on either side, lava across the middle. Make the skeletons choose between steel above and fire below. If we time it with the tide, the strait itself becomes a cul-de-sac."

Ari clapped him on the back hard enough to jostle the map. "Exactly. I don't care how many drown—they don't breathe anyway. But scatter them, break their ranks, force them into panic, and even bones remember they once feared fire."

"Third?" Hera asked, her voice flat.

Ari leaned over the table, knuckles pressed white against the marble. "Third, I need commanders who understand this isn't a war to win—no generals who count in victory conditions. I want butchers. Street fighters. Men who've led gangs through alleys. Women who've marched into gunfire and kept walking. People who know what it is to fight for breath, not for banners."

Thoth's pen scratched, slower now. "Unorthodox."

"Necessary," Ari said. "The bones don't read manuals. They march like water, relentless. Manuals won't stop them. Only chaos will. Pele gives us rivers of lava. Si kills their choir. But it's me, and the fighters I choose, who turn all that into hours mortals can still breathe in."

Dionysis leaned forward, smile crooked. "And if they break?"

"Then I break with them," Ari said.

His grin was sharp, dangerous, almost beautiful. "War doesn't run. War burns itself out only when there's nothing left to kill. That's my oath."

The room stilled at that.

Zed's eye gleamed under his brow. "So who will you call first?"

Ari rattled the list off like he'd been waiting his whole life to speak it. "French Foreign Legion. Gurkhas, if I can pry them loose. Old comrades from Chechnya, men who can't go home but can still kill clean. Spanish partisans. Moroccan irregulars. Anyone who owes me a favour and still has the spine to stand."

"You'll have mutiny on your hands," Jamil warned.

"Good," Ari said. "Mutiny fights harder than obedience. Obedience dies on schedule."

Hera finally rose. She walked to the basalt Pele had brought and placed her palm on its cool surface.

"Very well. You will have your fighters. You will have your chaos. But hear me, Ari—you are not to spend cities like coin. You buy time, not pyres. If you cross me on this, not even Si's silence will shield you."

Ari met her gaze and didn't blink. "I don't burn cities, Hera. I burn armies."

The crow croaked once, as if sealing the pact.

The map between them was scarred with ink and blots, but no amount of red lines could predict every variable.

Thoth's pen finally stilled. His voice was measured, almost weary. "We have accounted for terrain. For fire. Even for the tide. But what remains unmeasured is the other half of the spear—the Stilled Breath."

The word itself made the room shift.

Jamil's eyes darkened. "He is patient with teeth—discipline without fatigue. I watched through mortal eyes as he moved his ranks—every step the same length, every shield at the same angle. No commander shouts, no horns sound, and yet the legions turn as one body. That is no mortal drill. That is memory made flesh."

Ari spat to the side, disgust and respect mingling. "So he's an army general that never blinks. Fine. Generals die. I'll crack his mask and see what dust hides underneath."

"Dust that remembers," Thales said softly. "That creature has walked under more suns than even Rome or Greece. Every siege, every ambush, every stratagem—he carries them like beads on a string. You may meet a thousand years of war every time you cross him."

The crow croaked once, sharp as a blade.

Zed repeated with a grunt. "Predictable. He is old, but he is old in pattern. Lava breaks the pattern. Silence breaks the rhythm. Even patience falters when ground melts."

"That is why he frightens me less," Hera said at last. She turned the basalt in her hands as if weighing the future. "We know his nature. We know his limits. What we do not know is the girl."

Lilith's name settled like smoke.

"Her power is raw," Si murmured. "What she learned in Fez, she taught herself. She bends bone as if it were clay. No scripture, no rite, just command."

"She raised an army in weeks," Pele said. Her tone held both scorn and a hint of awe. "What took centuries for others, she drew from the ground with her breath. That is not mere craft. That is something new."

Jamil's lips thinned. "New things topple ledgers faster than old ones."

Dionysis swirled his wine, eyes glinting. "The Stilled Breath, at least, we can drink to. He's a story already written. But the girl? She's the toast no one's tasted yet. She could sour the mouth—or make gods drunk."

Ari's grin was harder now. "Then I'll test her. Bone breaks. Songs end. If she bleeds, I'll find out how."

Hera's gaze sharpened. "Do not underestimate her. Even Zed's crow has gone quiet when her name is spoken. That silence tells me more than prophecy ever could. We plan for the Stilled Breath because we understand him. But Lilith—Lilith is the unknown. And the unknown is what ends empires."

The room was thick with silence after Hera's words. The basalt on the table had cooled, but it felt as if fire still smouldered beneath it.

Finally, Thoth set his pen down. "Buying time is only ever the first stanza. What do we sing after?" His eyes scanned the table, daring anyone to answer.

Zed's jaw worked, his good eye fixed on the night skyline. "After the hours and days we steal, the mask drops. Mortals will see. No council chamber, no Monte Carlo theatre, no private apartments. The world will know us for what we are."

"Revealed," Dionysis said, rolling the word on his tongue like a sip of wine. "And not in whispered myth or shadow markets. Our names on lips that never knew them. Statues walking again."

He laughed softly.

"Half the world will worship, half will revolt, and both halves will dance. I almost look forward to it."

Jamil's voice was iron. "Revelation is not celebration. Once the balance is broken openly, every act has weight. Mortals will cry for saviours. They will curse us as tyrants. And the ethereals—"

He stopped there, as if speaking their name too freely would summon them.

Hera's hand pressed flat against the basalt, as if steadying it. "This is the end we have always feared. Not Ragnarök, not apocalypse—disclosure. Once the bones march into Europe, once lava cuts Spain in two, there will be no hiding what we are. The endgame is a world where we are visible again. Where we rule openly, or are hunted openly."

Ari gave a savage grin. "Then rule. Better to stride in daylight than hide in shadows while skeletons laugh at us."

"Rule is not so simple," Thales murmured. "Mortals have armies, governments, markets. They will not kneel neatly. They will bargain, betray, fracture. We may stop Lilith's tide, but in doing so, we invite a war of every flag against every god."

Si spoke softly, but the hush carried. "Perhaps that is the only way forward. To stop pretending. To step out of myth and admit ourselves."

The crow croaked once, low and raw. Zed gave no translation, but his eye burned brighter.

Hera exhaled, and for once, there was no iron in it—only weariness.

"Then the endgame is no longer about hiding balance. It is about surviving revelation. If we buy time, it is to prepare for a world that knows us. To decide whether we appear as guardians or conquerors."

The word hung, and none dared speak against it. The fire in Pele's basalt had gone dark, but the table still seemed to radiate heat. Around it, the gods sat or stood in thought, each measuring what the word revelation truly meant.

Ari was the first to break the silence.

He slammed a fist into the map, his grin savage. "When the hours are ours, when the legions stagger, then we step forward. Not in whispers, not as myths. The world sees us. And when they see War, they kneel—or they run."

"Or they rise against you," Thales said gently, smoothing a crease on the chart. "Mortals have made whole empires without us. They may resent being reminded of our weight. They may see us not as saviours but as tyrants returned."

"Then let them rise," Ari shot back. "I'll break them as surely as I break bone."

Hera's eyes narrowed. "We do not plan to break mortals. We plan to rule through necessity. If they believe we are the only thing that can stop Lilith and the Stilled Breath, they will accept us—not as gods, but as governors. A world in chaos will cling to order."

Zed's crow croaked, low and unsettling.

Zed nodded once. "Order, yes. But fear is quicker than faith. If we stride into daylight, it must be with spectacle. War. Fire. Silence. Wine. The world must feel awe before it feels resentment."

Dionysis smiled, raising his bottle in salute. "Awe—I can deliver. Cults will blossom overnight. I'll throw feasts that last a week, and mortals will come crawling to pledge themselves. You mistake me if you think worship needs temples—it needs ecstasy. Give me crowds, and I'll ruin them."

"And when the feasts end?" Jamil's voice was cold. "When the bodies are sober again, and the ledgers demand reckoning? Revelry buys loyalty in hours. But hours are what we are already spending."

"True," Dionysis said lightly. "But hours can stretch into movements if you keep the wine flowing."

Pele leaned forward, eyes still hot. "My revelation will not be feasts. It will be survival. When I pour lava across the strait, mortals will see their cities saved from bone by fire. They will not love me. But they will not forget me. Fear is loyalty, when it is fear of the right thing."

"And Jian Wu?" Si's voice was soft, but all turned toward her. "If I bring him back from his desert silence, he will not be worshipped. He will be dreaded. But dread, too, has its uses."

Hera inclined her head. "Yes. Scourge is a weapon we can aim. Mortals will not see him as a saviour, but as a threat chained to our side. They will respect the leash, even if they despise the hound."

Thoth finally spoke, his pen still for once. "Understand what you are saying. We become visible. That means accountability. The ethereals will not stay quiet. Already, they stir around the aberrant mortal. If we reveal ourselves, they may reveal themselves in kind. The balance will fracture in ways we cannot predict."

Zed's good eye gleamed. "Balance is already broken. Mortals watch skeletons march on their television screens. They see cities burn and refuse to believe it is anything but another war. When we step forward, it will be the end of their illusions. And perhaps the end of ours."

"What role do you imagine for yourself then, Zed?" Dionysis asked, almost playfully. "King in a tower? General of generals? Or prophet of doom?"

Zed's jaw tightened. "The last. Doom is already upon us. If the world must hear it, they will hear it from me. Ragnarök, Judgement, the final war—it does not matter what word they choose. But they will know it is not theirs to command. It is ours."

Hera looked around the table, meeting each gaze.

"Very well. Let us lay it bare. If the revelation comes, each of us must decide how we will stand in the light. Ari, you will be War incarnate, the sword they cannot ignore. Pele, the fire that saves by burning. Dionysis, the reveller who wins their hearts while they are weak. Thales, the voice of earth and sea, teaching them that even nature answers us still. Zed and I, the crown and the council, ruling not by choice but by necessity. Jamil, the scales that weigh all, reminds them that no deed is without consequence. Thoth, the scribe who writes the new law of the world. Si, the silence that stills their doubt. And perhaps Jian Wu, the scourge chained at our side."

Si's pendant turned slowly between her fingers. "And Lilith?"

All eyes shifted back to Hera. Her jaw tightened. "Lilith is the storm we cannot measure. We must show mortals she is chaos, and we are order. That is the endgame. Not merely victory, but narrative. She is darkness, we are dawn. That is how we survive revelation."

Dionysis chuckled, raising his bottle. "So we are gods again. No more hiding. No more veils. The masks fall, and the world throws roses or stones. Either way—we will not be ignored."

The crow croaked once more, harsh and final, as if sealing the pact.

Zed rose without a word. The crow shifted, feathers rustling, as if it knew what was coming.

He crossed the apartment, boots striking the marble like thunder already forming. The balcony doors opened beneath his hand, and the city's hum spilled in—traffic, laughter, sirens—all the fragile illusions of a world still pretending. He stepped out into the cold night air, lifted his chin, and stretched his hand toward the sky.

For a moment, nothing happened. Then the clouds gathered as though dragged on chains.

The first bolt cracked down the length of Manhattan, white fire splitting glass towers into silhouettes. A second lightning bolt struck across the river, shattering the Hudson into a mirror of storm. The air boomed, every window trembling, alarms wailing in chorus.

Zed raised both arms, and the storm obeyed. Lightning leapt in spears, branching across the heavens until the skyline glowed like an X-ray of the gods' intent. Wind screamed through canyons of steel. Rain came sideways, silver and sharp.

The city gasped and faltered, mortals stumbling into doorways, staring skyward as though the end itself had chosen to walk above them.

Inside, no one spoke. The council watched in silence as their leader carved memory into the sky. When at last Zed lowered his hands, the thunder rolled on, echoing against the bones of New York.

His voice followed, low but carrying through storm and glass alike: "Let them remember. The gods are awake."

Chapter 6
Intermission

What the hell is going on?

Good question. Shame nobody's got a decent answer, least of all Ben. But let's take a crack at it anyway, because somebody has to narrate this slow-motion car crash.

Fez split open like a rotten fruit, and instead of maggots, it was skeletons—thousands of the bastards—clicking, clattering, and marching like they'd never heard of a day off.

The Americans responded in the only language they know: "Drop bombs until it looks like democracy." Trouble is, the bombs developed performance anxiety. They veered left, they veered right, and somehow every "precision strike" managed to miss the only targets that mattered.

Why? Because Leila—pardon, Lilith now, she's rebranded—told the sky they weren't invited. And the sky, being spineless, obeyed. How convenient.

The Stilled Breath, ancient, disciplined, and allergic to small talk, took his bony parade north toward the Strait of Gibraltar. Europe, predictably, panicked with its usual flair: form subcommittees, issue grave press releases, and move a few tanks around so it looks like they're doing something besides arguing over who owes NATO gas money. Spain rolled armour to choke points, the UK declared it was "monitoring," and Greece muttered about "phalanxes" like someone had just insulted its grandfather.

Meanwhile, Lilith, our brand-new necromancer-in-chief, strolled east like she was headlining a festival tour. Every graveyard along the route coughed up fresh fans, all eager to click their jaws in rhythm. Helicopters tried to stop her, she told them to look away, and they did—lols—because apparently even hardware can be peer-pressured.

On social media, the #NotTheTarget trend went viral, proving that when civilisation collapses, we'll still have hashtags.

And the gods. Oh, the gods.

Picture it: Zed by the window, doing his brooding one-eyed Odin act with a crow that won't shut up. Hera, spine like a guillotine blade, lecturing everyone on restraint while planning her next power grab. Pele, the hothead (literally), insists Jian Wu—the firebrand cooling in some desert—either plays nice or gets buried deeper. Dionysis arrived drunk and stayed drunk.

Their agenda? Convince Jian Wu, aka the Scourge, to get off his sandy ass and join the right team. Pele smothered him last time, so sending her would be like asking an arsonist to deliver the fire safety lecture. They picked Si instead, because she whispers like silence itself and looks harmless until the world forgets how to breathe. If anyone can coax a volcano out of bed without getting incinerated, it's her.

Ari—the god of war, poster boy for rage issues—wasn't interested in coaxing anybody. He stabbed his finger at maps, demanded soldiers who wouldn't wet themselves at the sight of endless bone, and promised to "buy hours." Not victory, not triumph, just hours.

He's pragmatic like that.

Hours are currency now. Veterans, mercenaries, the French Foreign Legion—Ari wants the kind of lunatics who already know death is bad at arithmetic. Throw in some tanks, add Dionysis for morale (wine rations and bad songs), and presto: you've got yourself a war plan.

And let's not forget the defectors-in-waiting. Effie, goddess of beauty and heartbreak, is looking a little too sympathetic to the wrong side. Diane, the Huntress, has been missing more shots than usual—hard to tell if it's shame, nerves, or the creeping suspicion she's picked the wrong team.

Either way, balance is wobbling, and balance hates wobbling. It's like the universe's OCD. When balance twitches, gods reach for paperwork and mortals reach for exits.

Mortals, bless their hearts, are handling this about as well as expected. Markets went haywire. Insurance companies rewrote their fine print. Pastors are saying, "We told you so" without choking on it. Conspiracy forums are convinced the end times are finally delivering the content they subscribed to. And the Space Bros Forum? They're actually useful now, cataloguing skeleton formations from satellite photos like amateur bird-watchers. L is for Lilith, naturally. Nobody's waiting for M.

So, what the hell is going on? Let's recap in the simplest terms: skeletons are winning the attendance award. The gods are arguing over who gets to play envoy to a moody volcano. Ben keeps surviving his own bad decisions, which is starting to annoy probability itself. And somewhere in all this, mortals are still asking, "Is this the end of the world?"

Answer: Yes, but only the current version. Don't worry, there'll be others.

The plan, such as it is: buy hours, bleed for them, and hope someone, somewhere, screws up big enough to tilt the board. Because even ancient patterns break eventually, lava cools, storms lose steam, and armies—bone or not—eventually run out of clever choreography.

Until then, keep your head down, avoid making eye contact with Lilith, and if you hear thunder from a clear sky, that's not weather—it's Zed reminding everyone he still thinks he's in charge.

You're welcome—now that you're all caught up. Try not to die before the next chapter.

Now, if we must, let's talk about Ben. Yes, Ben—the so-called hero of this mess. A man with absolutely no skills, no training, no pedigree, and yet the gods keep tripping over themselves like he's the last lottery ticket in town.

Here's what he's good at: breathing. Here's what he's bad at: literally everything else. If there's a skill tree in this apocalypse, Ben hasn't unlocked squat. Swordsmanship? No. Magic? Not a spark. Strategy? Please.

The man thinks a "pincer movement" is something you do when crabs get frisky. He has no army, no training montage, not even a mentor to misquote. And yet, he's still here, walking around like a cosmic clerical error.

The gods hate it. Yama, a play on Jamil, the bureaucrat of death, stabbed at him with fire, spells, and needles, and somehow Ben just coughed smoke and rolled over in his hospital bed like, "Sorry, not today."

Artemis, er sorry, Diane—lined him up in her divine sights and missed. Imagine being the goddess of the hunt and whiffing against a guy whose most excellent tactical maneuver is forgetting his wallet. Embarrassing.

The ethereals? They don't even know what to make of him. Death sniffs around like a cat trying to figure out why this one mouse won't keel over. Chance hangs nearby, curious to see if Ben will trip into greatness or trip into another ditch. Time pretends it isn't watching, but it's been setting its watch by him since Morocco.

Nobody will admit it, but the balance—the grand cosmic scale everyone worships like it's a deity of its own is leaning in his direction. Not because he deserves it. Not because he worked for it. But because sometimes the universe likes a good joke, Ben is the punchline.

Let's review his résumé so far. He's:

Survived a cursed paper that should have killed him.

Walked away from fires, crashes, and near-death experiences like he was late for the bus.

Accidentally kicked off a divine manhunt by existing.

Awakened beings far more powerful than himself.

Heroes in myth usually have swords pulled from stones, god-blessed armour, or something at least extraordinary. Ben's got a battered pair of boots, a lighter, and enough paranoia to fuel a thousand cigarettes.

And, his big skill? Refusing to stay dead.

Congratulations, he's a weed with better hair. And still—still he's the name whispered in divine chambers. The aberrant mortal. The inbetweener. The one whose karmic balance sheet is so empty, Yama stares at it like an accountant finding a blank tax form.

Even the Stilled Breath, whose patience is carved from a thousand campaigns of being still, glanced at him once and decided not to blink again.

Lilith doesn't bother yet—she's got continents to chew—but give her time. Everyone eventually looks his way.

Ben, naturally, has no idea. He thinks he's just unlucky. He thinks surviving car crashes, fires, and supernatural assassins is normal if you squint hard enough.

He hasn't connected the dots. He hasn't realised he is the dot.

That every time he lights another cigarette and mutters about fate, the gods are up there checking their ledgers and muttering back, "Who signed off on this idiot?"

But maybe that's the point.

Maybe skill isn't what the cosmos wanted. Perhaps it needed a man who can't be bribed by power because he doesn't believe he has any. A man who won't kneel because he doesn't even know there's a throne. A man so catastrophically average that even fate can't predict what he'll do next.

That's Ben: the wildcard who doesn't know he's holding the deck.

The gods, the dead, the ethereals—they're all working from ancient scripts. Ben's ad-libbing with crayons. That's why they can't pin him down.

Picture it: a god with a thousand years of strategy, a necromancer commanding legions, a divine council bickering in marble halls—and all of them are quietly sweating over a mortal who still doesn't know how to land a plane.

Sardonic enough for you?

Good.

Because that's the only way to explain why this world keeps spinning around a man whose biggest achievement so far is refusing to stay in his grave.

So here's your hero: Ben. No sword, no shield, no clue.

Pilots spend years training to survive one stall. Ben pulls them off like party tricks. Why? Because he doesn't know enough to be afraid of the right things. His motto might as well be: If it's got wings, it'll sort itself out.

The next blockbuster is his own budget spin-off: Idiot Tries to Fly.

Some men cross continents with armies. Ben does it by refusing to die fast enough. Let's be honest: if Odysseus took this long, the Odyssey would still be on backorder. Frodo got to Mordor faster, and he walked. Ben can't even point a plane the right way without turning it into confetti, and somehow the narrative keeps giving him more aircraft like he's racking up frequent flyer miles.

And for what? He's not training, he's not growing, he's not even learning to read the damn gauges. He's wasting chapters the way other people waste oxygen. Readers have slogged through gods debating apocalypse, necromancers raising bone armies, and divine strategies being hammered into marble—and then there's Ben, still trying to land without turning the runway into modern art.

Does he have charisma? Please.

The only thing Ben inspires in others is confusion. Soldiers look at him and wonder if he's a lunatic or a prophet. Doctors patch him up and assume they must have misread the charts. Strangers feel bad for him, which makes them nervous.

And yet here's the dirty little secret: the longer Ben lives, the more everyone else starts to feel like he's the point.

If a man with no plan, no power, and no clue can walk through fire and come out coughing, maybe the rest of them aren't as inevitable as they thought.

Perhaps balance isn't balance after all. Maybe destiny's got a sense of humour, and it's running the show.

So yes, Ben is a disaster. But he's their disaster—the human-shaped loophole none of the immortals saw coming. And the terrifying part? Even he doesn't know what he is yet. Which means when he finally does figure it out, everyone else better hope incompetence was his best trick.

So here we are. Ben arrives on the correct continent. Bravo. Slow clap.

So yes, let's all admit it: Ben has eaten three chapters of this book like a selfish toddler hoarding cookies, and what's he got to show for it? Dirt in his teeth and another plane wreck behind him. If this is the pace, by the time he sets foot in the Andes, we'll all be retired, dead, or undead ourselves. At which point, the skeleton army will be cheering him on for solidarity.

C'mon...

Laugh if you like. The gods already have. They're just not laughing anymore.

Chapter 7
The Warehouse

The warehouse smelled of dust and iron, long since abandoned to pigeons and cobwebs. Diane had chosen it carefully—quiet, forgotten, well away from prying eyes. Adelaide might have been a small city, but even here, people noticed when the wrong kind of power leaked into the open.

Ellery stood in the middle of the cracked concrete floor, his fists clenched at his sides, sweat already running down his temples.

Diane circled him slowly, her eyes sharp, her voice low. "Again," she said.

"I told you," Ellery muttered through gritted teeth. "It doesn't happen on command."

"It has to." Diane's tone carried no sympathy, only certainty. "If you can't hold it, it'll keep bleeding out. And every time it does, someone dies."

Ellery shut his eyes, trying to summon the flicker he felt in those terrible moments: that surge of pressure just before a body crumpled nearby, a weight like invisible gravity crushing the air. He could feel it now, faint, trembling, like a current under the skin. He reached for it. The pigeons burst from the rafters all at once, scattering in a frenzy. Ellery staggered, doubled over as though the air itself had struck him back.

Diane's hand was on his shoulder in an instant, steadying him. "Better," she murmured. "You touched it this time."

"Felt like it touched me," he rasped. His stomach turned as the echo of it lingered. "God, Diane... if I keep practising, who's next? You?"

She met his gaze without flinching. "If you don't practice, it will be everyone. Choose the danger you can live with." The words hung between them, harsher for their truth.

The door creaked then. Both of them turned. A figure slipped inside, moving with too much ease for a stranger stumbling into an abandoned warehouse.

"Don't look so alarmed," Si said, her voice lilting as though she'd just wandered in for tea. "You're hard to find, Diane. Adelaide suits you, though. Quiet, tucked away. And I see you've been keeping busy."

Diane's hand fell away from Ellery's shoulder, but her eyes never softened.

"Si." The name was almost a sigh. "You shouldn't be here."

"Oh, I think I should." Si walked closer, her heels clicking against the concrete, echoing in the cavernous room.

She looked at Ellery the way a scholar might study a rare specimen. "So this is the detective. The man who draws death without meaning to."

Ellery straightened, trying not to bristle under the weight of her stare. "And you are?"

"An old friend," Si answered before Diane could. "A very old friend. You can call me Psyche, if you like. Most do."

He didn't like the way she said it, as if the name carried its own gravity. "You've been watching me, too?"

"Not watching." Si tilted her head, smiling. "Listening. You've made quite a noise, Ellery. The dead don't leave their silence quietly."

"Enough." Diane stepped between them, her tone flat and steel. "He's learning. That's all you need to know."

But Si wasn't deterred. She walked in a slow circle, echoing Diane's earlier movements, her eyes flicking between them.

"So you're teaching him? Training him? That's dangerous, even for you."

Diane's lips pressed thin. "It's necessary."

Ellery felt the tension twisting tighter, like he'd become a prize they were fighting over. He hated it. "If you two want to argue about me, maybe try including me in the damn conversation?"

Si stopped, her gaze locking on him. "You're right. Forgive me. But you need to understand—you're not just a man fumbling with a trick. You're standing at the threshold of something the rest of us have been preparing for centuries."

Ellery gave a hollow laugh. "I didn't prepare for anything. I didn't ask for this. Hell, I don't even know what this is."

"Which is why she's here," Si said, nodding at Diane. "To shape you before the others do. And why I'm here, too—to see if you're worth the trouble."

The pigeons rustled overhead again, disturbed by the tension vibrating through the room. Ellery felt it prickling in his chest, that pulse he couldn't quite hold, a spark that wanted to break loose. He clenched his jaw, forcing it back down, afraid of what it might do with another soul so close.

Si's smile faded. For the first time, she looked almost concerned. "He's stronger than you told me," she murmured.

Diane's reply was curt. "Which is exactly why I didn't tell you more."

Ellery looked from one to the other, his frustration boiling over. "So what, I'm some weapon you two are arguing custody over? A damn science experiment?"

"No," Diane said firmly, stepping close, her hand gripping his arm. "You're a choice. My choice. And theirs."

"And if he chooses wrong," Si added softly, "the balance tips. The gods will act. And trust me, Ellery—you don't want to be on the wrong side when they do."

Silence fell thick in the warehouse, broken only by the faint cooing of the pigeons and the sound of Ellery's uneven breathing. For the first time since this began, he realised there was no going back.

Si folded her arms, watching Ellery steady himself after the last surge. The pigeons had settled again in the rafters, their wings whispering as they tucked into silence. The whole warehouse seemed to hold its breath.

"You've changed," Si said at last. Her voice wasn't hostile, but it carried a note of disappointment, almost maternal. "The Diane I knew didn't coddle mortals. She didn't waste time on lost causes."

Diane's jaw tightened. She didn't step away from Ellery. If anything, her stance grew more protective. "He's not a lost cause," she said.

Si arched a brow. "Then what is he? A project? A distraction? You don't bring someone like him into the fire without reason. And don't tell me this is just about compassion. You've never been sentimental."

Diane exhaled slowly, her eyes fixed on Si with the unblinking steadiness of a hunter who refused to be cornered. "This isn't about sentiment. It's about survival."

"Whose?" Si pressed. "Yours? His? Or are you talking about something larger?"

Ellery felt the air grow heavier. The two women weren't simply sparring—they were peeling back layers of truth that had been kept hidden even from him. He stayed still, sensing this was one of those moments where speaking would only fracture the fragile thread of revelation.

"A war is coming," Diane said finally. Her tone was flat, stripped of ornament. "Not skirmishes. Not power plays. A war that won't stay in the shadows. Zed feels it. Ari feels it. We all do. The fractures are widening, and when the dam breaks, there won't be time to debate motives."

Si tilted her head, eyes narrowing. "So you're preparing him? Training him like a weapon?"

Diane shook her head. "I'm preparing him so I don't become one. You know what Zed wants of me, Si. What he uses me for."

Si's gaze softened slightly, though her voice stayed sharp. "Executioner."

The word hung in the space between them like a blade. Ellery felt the temperature drop. Diane didn't flinch.

"I've killed enough in his name. Enough to know that if I keep following orders, I'll become nothing but his knife. When the war comes, I refuse to be the hand that cuts down those who don't deserve it."

Her voice carried something Ellery hadn't heard before—weariness. Not the exhaustion of battle, but the bone-deep fatigue of someone who had lived too long on the wrong side of a line.

Si paced slowly, her heels clicking against the cracked floor. "So instead you take in a mortal who leaks death with every heartbeat, and you say it's training, not sentiment?" She paused, looking between them. "Diane, you're walking a knife-edge. You know what the others will say. You're letting him bind you."

Diane's hand brushed Ellery's arm again, not gently, but with conviction. "Maybe I am bound. But better bound by choice than chained by Zed's will."

Ellery swallowed hard. He wanted to say something, anything, but his throat felt locked. The warehouse felt like a confessional where he was both the subject and the sin.

Si's eyes shifted to him, measuring, weighing. "Do you even understand what she risks for you?"

Ellery forced himself to meet her stare. "Not fully," he admitted. "But I didn't ask her for this. She chose it."

"And when Zed finds out?" Si asked softly.

The question cut deeper than any accusation.

Diane answered before Ellery could. “Then he’ll know where I stand,” she said. “I won’t kill for him anymore. Not like that. And if Ellery can learn to hold what he carries, then maybe he won’t need me to shield him.”

For the first time since she’d entered, Si’s expression faltered. A ripple of something—respect, fear, perhaps both—moved through her features.

“You’re serious,” Si said.

“I am,” Diane replied.

Silence stretched. The pigeons cooed again, oblivious to the weight of divine politics spilling into a forgotten warehouse in Adelaide.

Si finally sighed, her composure returning like a mask slipping back into place. “You’ve always been stubborn, Diane. Stubborn enough to survive. But this...”

She glanced at Ellery. “This is dangerous. More dangerous than you want to admit.”

Diane’s reply was simple. “So is obedience.”

Ellery felt their words vibrating through him, heavier than any interrogation room silence he’d endured. War. Executioner. Zed. They spoke as if the world were already burning, as if the weight of his life and theirs had already been tallied and measured. He wanted to believe he was only caught in the edges of something vast. But the way Diane kept her hand on his arm, grounding him, told him otherwise.

Si broke the silence. She moved closer, her footsteps slow, deliberate, as though she were approaching something fragile.

Her smile was gentle, but her eyes never lost their edge. "Ellery Kalos," she said softly, as if tasting the name. "Detective. Mortal. Reluctant bearer of a gift you neither asked for nor understand."

Ellery's throat tightened. "You talk like you've been reading my file."

"In a way," Si said. "But not in the way you mean. What you call intuition, what you feel as unease for us, it's threads. Threads of memory, of mind, of heart. They brush against us, and we know things. That's my domain."

She stopped in front of him now, close enough that her presence felt like a pulse against his skin.

"I am Psyche. You might say I walk the corridors of the soul. Dreams, memory, longing, madness—I understand them all. I don't choose to, I do. That is my burden."

Her gaze softened, and for a moment, Ellery felt as if she were rifling through the drawers of his heart. It was invasive and comforting at once.

"And Diane," Si continued, glancing sideways, "is the Huntress. You know her as Diane, but others have called her Artemis. War is not her domain, though she has been used for it often enough. She tracks, she strikes, she enforces. When Zed calls, she has been his arrow, his blade."

Ellery turned his head, staring at Diane. She didn't deny it. Her jaw set like stone.

"So what," Ellery muttered, "you're gods? Immortals? Something like that?"

Diane's voice was quiet, careful. "We are what we are. Names don't capture it."

"But you kill for them," Ellery pressed, bitterness creeping into his tone. "For Zed. For whoever sits on this council, you keep hinting at. And now you're training me, dragging me into the middle of it."

"Yes," Diane said. "Because whether you like it or not, you're already in it."

Si's lips curved faintly, though her expression was far from mocking. "She's right. Your gift, rough and untamed as it is, marks you. Death bends when you're near. That kind of disturbance doesn't go unnoticed. The council will come for you eventually. The only question is whether you'll meet them as prey, or as something else."

Ellery barked a laugh, more nerves than amusement. "Prey. Weapon. Pawn. Those are the choices?"

"Not only," Si said. "But those are the easiest. The ones Zed would prefer. And Diane..." she turned her eyes back to her friend, "has decided she won't let him have that. Which is dangerous. For both of you."

Ellery rubbed a hand over his face, trying to steady the spin of it all. "You expect me to believe this? That you're—what—gods walking around Adelaide, chatting in warehouses, deciding the fate of the world like it's a chessboard?"

Diane stepped closer, her presence firm, grounding. "I expect you to believe what you've seen. People die when you lose control. Forces you can't explain moving through you. That isn't madness, Ellery. It's real. And if you can't learn to hold it, others will decide what you are for you."

Her words struck like iron.

He hated them because they rang true.

Si crouched slightly, bringing her eyes level with his. Her voice was soft now, coaxing. "You've already felt it, haven't you? That sense you're standing just beyond the edge of the map? That no matter what you do, the rules don't hold the same way they do for others?"

Ellery thought of the deaths. The way Diane's eyes glinted in the moonlight when she felt he wasn't watching. The storm of energy in his chest that came and went like a heartbeat, he couldn't control. He swallowed.

"Yeah," he said at last. "I've felt it."

"Then don't waste time denying it," Si murmured. "Diane is giving you something few mortals ever get—a chance to learn before the war swallows you whole. Ask yourself why."

Ellery's eyes flicked to Diane. Her face was unreadable, her gaze steady, unwavering. He wanted her to explain. Needed her to.

"Because," Diane said at last, "I don't want to be Zed's executioner anymore. And if you can master this, maybe you'll be proof there's another way."

The words settled over him like a verdict. Not flattering, not hopeful, just true.

Ellery let out a shaky laugh. "So you're training me... not to save me, but to save yourself."

Diane didn't blink. "Both," she said.

And for the first time, Ellery realised the bond between them was more dangerous than he had imagined—not just intimacy, not just strategy, but a rebellion wrapped in affection. The air in the warehouse had thickened. Ellery could feel it pressing on his skin, as if the conversation itself carried weight. Diane still stood firm at his side, but Si hadn't relaxed. If anything, her presence had sharpened.

"You're gambling, Diane," Si said quietly. "You're tying yourself to a mortal who bleeds death into every corner he walks. And you're doing it in defiance of Zed."

She shook her head, her tone both incredulous and weary. "I've seen you make reckless choices before, but this? This isn't recklessness. This is defiance with teeth."

Diane's voice was steady. "I won't be his blade anymore. That's all there is to it."

"And if your rebellion drags him down with you?" Si gestured at Ellery, her eyes burning. "Have you thought of that? Do you care about what happens to him, or only about what happens to you?"

"I care," Diane said.

The words hit Ellery harder than he expected. Simple, unadorned, and spoken without hesitation.

But Si wasn't done. She turned on him now, her gaze pinning him like an insect.

"Do you care, Ellery? Do you even know what she risks? Do you know what you are?"

Ellery swallowed. "I know enough."

"Enough?" Si stepped closer, the sound of her heels echoing off the concrete. "Then tell me what you think you are."

He hesitated, then forced the words out. "A man who doesn't know why people die around him. A man who can't hold what's inside him without it spilling out. A liability."

Si's eyes searched his face, her expression unreadable. Then she nodded once. "Honest. That's better than most."

She slowly raised her hand, palm outward. The air shifted. Ellery felt the edges of his mind prickle, as if unseen fingers were brushing through his thoughts. His knees buckled before he forced himself upright, glaring at her.

"What are you doing?" he growled.

"Testing," Si said calmly. "You want to know who I am? I told you—I walk the corridors of the soul. I can touch memory, desire, madness. If you're going to stand in the middle of this war, you need to know what that feels like."

Ellery clenched his fists. The hum inside his chest stirred, restless, dangerous.

"Stay out of my head."

But the harder he pushed back, the more the hum rose, filling his bones with pressure. He felt it pressing at the warehouse walls, rattling the rafters. The pigeons exploded upward again, feathers drifting like ash.

Si's eyes widened slightly, though her composure remained. "He's raw," she said to Diane, almost impressed. "But he's strong."

"Stronger than I expected," Diane admitted, her hand on Ellery's arm now, steadying, anchoring. "That's why I'm here."

Ellery sucked in a breath, forcing the pressure down again. The pigeons resettled slowly, as if waiting to see if the storm would return.

Si studied him for a long time, then finally exhaled.

"All right," she said. "You're not hopeless. That's something." She looked back at Diane. "And you—maybe you're not just blinded by affection after all."

Diane's eyes flicked, sharp. "You doubted me?"

"I doubted your motive," Si replied. "But maybe there's more to it. Maybe you're seeing something the rest of us haven't."

Ellery frowned. "The rest of who?"

"The Council," Si said. "Thirteen voices. Thirteen wills. Not all of them aligned. Some want to keep the balance. Others want control. And Zed—he's never hidden what he wants. Dominion. Order at the end of a blade."

She paused, her eyes narrowing. "Diane has been his arrow. His hound. His executioner. But she's choosing something different now. And that choice is dangerous."

Ellery's voice came out hoarse. "So what—you're here to warn her? To stop her?"

Si's smile was faint, almost sad. "To see if she's worth following."

The words hung in the warehouse like a spark that might ignite.

Diane tensed, her hand tightening on Ellery's arm. "You're not with Zed?"

"I'm with balance," Si said. "Always have been. And if balance means standing against him, then perhaps I will. But I won't unquestioningly pledge to it. Not without seeing proof."

"Proof of what?" Ellery asked.

Si's gaze slid back to him. "Proof that you're not just a mortal caught in the storm. Proof that you can control it. That you can choose what you are, rather than letting it devour everyone around you."

Ellery felt the pressure stir again at the edges of his chest. He thought of the bodies, the silence, the guilt. He met Si's stare and didn't look away.

"I don't know if I can," he said. "But I'll try."

For the first time, Si's smile felt genuine. "Good. Because the war is coming, whether you're ready or not. And when it does, you'll have to be more than a liability."

She stepped back, the weight of her scrutiny easing. "Diane, I'll trust your judgment for now. But remember—when Zed learns of this, there will be no forgiveness. You'll have to decide whether this man is worth burning for."

"I've already decided," Diane said.

Ellery felt her hand tighten, not as a warning, but as an anchor. For the first time since this began, he believed her.

The tension in the warehouse finally eased, though only slightly. Si's posture softened, and the edge in her eyes dimmed into something warmer. She glanced once more at Diane, then at Ellery, as though weighing the bond between them one last time.

"Well," she said with a small smile, "you've made your choice, Diane. I can respect that, even if I don't envy it."

Diane inclined her head, her jaw set but her tone gentler now. "You've always respected choice. That's why I trust you."

For a moment, the old friendship between them shone through the steel. Si stepped closer, touching Diane's shoulder with sisterly affection. "Then you'll need every ounce of that trust in the days ahead. And when the storm breaks, you'll be standing against more than him."

"I know," Diane said quietly.

Ellery stayed silent, watching them, realising he was witnessing something deeper than strategy—something that had been forged long before he entered their lives.

Si gave a final nod, her eyes flicking back to him. "Take care of her," she said. "Even if you don't understand all of this yet. She's worth it."

Ellery blinked, surprised by the directness, then gave the faintest nod. "I'll try."

"That's enough for now," Si said. Her smile widened, soft but tinged with sadness. "See you, friend."

The words were for Diane, but the warmth in them seemed to brush Ellery, too.

She turned, her steps echoing across the warehouse floor, the pigeons shifting nervously as if they felt her leaving.

At the door, she paused, her silhouette framed by the pale Adelaide light. "Hope I don't get burnt," she said without turning back.

"Where are you going?" Diane asked.

Si's reply floated back, calm and certain. "To find Jian Wu. He's cooling in the desert, and if what I've heard is true, he may be the one we'll need when the fire rises."

Si paused at the door, her hand resting on the rusted handle. The light outside framed her in pale gold.

For a moment, she seemed about to step out and vanish, but then she glanced back, her voice low and deliberate. "One more thing. Zed has spoken. The order has gone out—the gods are to reveal themselves. No more masks, no more shadows. The age of pretending is ended."

The words landed like a stone in the silence.

Diane stiffened, her grip on Ellery's arm tightening.

"He'll call it necessity," Si went on. "He'll say the world is already burning, that mortals need to see their shepherds. But you know what it really means. Dominion. He intends to stand in the open and demand the world kneel."

Diane's face was carved from iron, but Ellery could feel the tremor in her hand.

"You defy him now," Si said softly, "and you won't just be walking away from orders. You'll be standing against a god who believes himself the rightful king of men. Others will follow him. Others will turn. You need to be ready."

Then, softer still, she added: "That's why I wish you luck, friend. You'll need it."

Then she was gone, the door closing softly behind her, leaving only the faint hush of feathers settling in the rafters. For a long moment, the warehouse was silent again.

Ellery looked at Diane. "So... Jian Wu?"

Diane's lips curved in something not quite a smile. "Another piece on the board. Another choice waiting to be made."

The weight of it pressed on Ellery's chest. The war she spoke of was no longer some distant storm—it was gathering, and he was already inside it. The warehouse felt cavernous now that Si had gone, the silence so complete it pressed in on Ellery's ears.

He stood still, hands loose at his sides, waiting for Diane to speak. She didn't, not at first. She only stared at the door long after it had closed, her expression unreadable in the dim light.

Finally, she drew a long breath and turned back to him. The hardness in her eyes had faded. What remained was something Ellery had rarely seen—uncertainty.

"I should have told you sooner," she said softly.

Ellery frowned. "Told me what? That you're not just a woman who happens to know too much? That you're—what—Artemis?"

The name sounded foreign on his tongue, absurd even, but Diane didn't flinch. She stepped closer, her shoulders lowering as if she were shedding armour.

"That I'm not just the woman you've been sharing nights with," she said. "That I've been more than human for longer than I care to admit. That when I touch your arm or kiss you in the dark, I do it with hands that have ended lives—hundreds of them—at Zed's command. And that I hid that from you because I wanted, for a little while, to just be yours."

Ellery's chest tightened. He wanted to speak, but the words tangled.

Diane went on, her voice fragile now. "I told myself I was protecting you by keeping it quiet. That if you didn't know, you wouldn't carry the weight. But that was a lie. It wasn't protection—it was fear. Fear that if you saw me for what I really am, you'd walk away."

She stopped in front of him, close enough that he could see the faint tremor in her fingers. "I'm sorry, Ellery. Sorry for the half-truths, the omissions. You deserve better than secrets."

Ellery studied her face. For once, there was no mask, no sharpened edge. Just Diane, stripped down to something raw and painfully human despite all her claims of divinity.

He reached up and brushed a strand of hair from her cheek.

"You think I didn't already know?" he asked quietly. "Not the names, not the history. But I knew you weren't ordinary. No one moves like you do, no one sees like you do. I knew. I didn't want to force you to say it."

Her eyes shone, though she blinked the gleam away before it could fall.

He let his hand rest against her face. "You don't have to be just Artemis with me. You can be Diane. That's enough."

Her breath caught, and for the first time since the training began, her body relaxed fully against his. She leaned into his hand, then into his chest, and for a moment, the warehouse felt less like a battlefield and more like a refuge. The pigeons stirred again in the rafters, not in alarm this time, but in the soft rustle of settling wings.

Chapter 8
The Desert

The desert bore no kindness. It gnawed and scraped, boiled and froze, but Jian Wu endured. By day, the wind flayed his skin until it cracked and bled light. By night, the cold pressed so deep it threatened to smother his flame, yet never succeeded.

He had burned under Pele's wrath, and it had remade him. Flesh was coal, cracked in glowing seams. His eyes were ceaseless suns, casting fire even when closed.

He was Scourge through and through.

And yet—still Jian.

Somewhere inside his ember husk, the cook survived. The father. The man who once bent over steaming pots in Port Pirie, dicing ginger with careful hands.

He sat cross-legged on a stone ridge, chest hollow with hunger. Power enough to flatten mountains rippled beneath his skin, yet no bread, no water, no sleep sustained him.

His exile had stripped him to contradiction—immortal fire, mortal fatigue.

The desert noticed him. It was not empty, not silent. The dunes leaned forward like an audience, sand whispering in languages older than speech.

When he breathed, the wind shifted. When he clenched his fists, stones cracked in sympathy. The land had accepted him as something both foreign and familiar: a fire-shaped story stalking its bones.

And then the desert shifted. He was no longer alone.

Effie came first.

She did not belong here, but the desert bent to her as if it had always expected her. White linen trailed behind like banners of surrender. Desire thickened the air; heat shimmered differently around her, as though silk itself warped the horizon.

"Jian Wu," she called, her voice sliding cool across the stone.

"You burn brighter than the sky. Why waste such brilliance starving in dust? With me, your fire could light more than wilderness. It could guide empires."

Her tone was velvet, but beneath it lay command—the weight of a queen promising him not love but dominion.

Jian's cracked voice rasped: "I am tired."

The words scraped like cinders, yet the light in his sockets did not dim.

Effie stepped closer. Even the wind stilled to listen.

"We didn't come to mock you. The world is shifting. It waits. You do not belong to wilderness—you belong to what comes next."

Jian's eyes narrowed, sparks flaring. "What comes next is hunger."

Delilah followed—a shadow with fox-sharp teeth. She was not Effie's opposite, but neither was she her mirror. Her grin cut, her eyes gleamed with mischief, her movements were smoke refusing to settle. Even the desert tilted oddly toward her, shadows stretching long as if amused by her unpredictability.

She crouched low, hair spilling forward, and laughed softly.

"Tired? You don't look tired. You look like a god with his skin peeled back. Raw. Terrifying. Beautiful."

She prowled around him, her shadow brushing his molten fissures. "Why starve?" she urged.

"Why suffer? You've fire enough to swallow oceans. Devour instead. Gorge until the world howls your name. This sulking in sand is beneath you."

Her words carried chaos, and temptation sharpened into hunger. Shadows thickened, twitching at her laughter.

Jian's coal-dark hands flexed on his knees. His head tilted back. For a heartbeat, the stone beneath him cracked. Heat spider-webbed outward, Effie's gown flaring, Delilah laughing with delight.

"I will not be bent," Jian growled. Mortal rasp layered with thunder. "Not by silk. Not by smoke. Not by silence."

Effie's lips parted, but she held her tongue. Delilah's grin widened, savouring defiance. The desert shivered in response, sand trickling down the ridge as though the land itself approved.

Far off, another figure paused.

Si descended carefully, cloak pulled tight against the wind. She had followed the trail of fire across the dunes, the pulse of

Jian Wu's transformation. Now she saw him—blackened flesh seamed with molten light, eyes like suns unblinking.

Magnificent.

Terrifying. Yet unbearably human.

But he was not alone. Effie shimmered like an empress of desire. Delilah prowled with smoke and laughter. The desert faltered at their clash, as though the land itself had not chosen which voice to echo.

She came closer. The desert wind hushed. Even the stars leaned in.

"Well," Effie said smoothly. "The desert has drawn more company than I expected. Sister Si."

"Effie," Si replied, her voice flat, not greeting but a statement.

They had known one another for centuries, though "knowing" was fragile. Effie never trusted Si's restraint; it looked too much like plotting. Si never trusted Effie's beauty; it bent the weak like iron filings. Courtesy endured, brittle but intact.

Delilah smirked, rising from her crouch. "Seems everyone wants a piece of Jian Wu. Careful, pretty one. You're late—we were here first."

"And you are?" Si asked, eyes narrowing.

Delilah bowed mockingly. "Delilah. Friend, if you like. If not—still Delilah."

Effie cut her off, voice sharp as glass. "She doesn't need your riddles."

Then to Si. "Surely you see what stands before us. Jian Wu isn't meant to rot in sand."

"Maybe not," Si said evenly. "But he isn't meant to be bent into your will either."

Effie's smile curved, imperial and unyielding. "And yours?"

Si ignored the barb, stepping just outside the scorch radius of Jian's heat. The desert leaned differently toward her: silence deepened, sand settling, wind holding its breath.

"You've burned," she said, calm steel. "But you're still Jian. Even fire rests. You need not be a weapon tonight."

Jian raised his eyes to hers.

For a moment, sadness eclipsed the suns. The desert listened. Effie's words pulled heat into elegant currents. Delilah's laughter twisted shadows into unnatural shapes. Si's calm steadied the land.

Three voices wove around him.

Jian sat in the storm, a furnace wrapped in exhaustion.

Effie's tone sweetened, though no less commanding. Her voice rolled with majesty, as if pronouncing law. "Jian, no mortal survives fire such as Pele's. You are not an accident but chosen. And what is chosen must be crowned. With me, you will not wander hungry in silence. Your fire will be a beacon. Armies will march. Kings will kneel. Even gods will bow."

Her gown rippled, though no breeze stirred. Heat bent toward her as courtiers bend to a throne.

Jian's fingers dug into stone. Tiny cracks spider-webbed outward.

Delilah circled him like smoke curling through rafters. Her grin flashed white. "Empire?" she scoffed. "A gilded cage stuffed with rules. Jian Wu, you're fire. Fire spreads. Fire eats. Why leash it with banners?"

She crouched low behind him, her voice slinking into his ear. "You scare me. And I adore it. Don't waste yourself on silk promises. Feed instead. Feed until the world howls your name."

The rocks' shadows leaned unnaturally toward her, twitching like eager dogs.

Si knelt. Not close—just at the edge of his heat, where air shimmered and sand smoked. She lowered her hood, hair whipping in furnace wind.

"You are tired," she said. "That matters. Empires promise crowns. Chaos promises feasts. But even fire rests. You need not be a weapon tonight. You may sit, Jian Wu."

Her voice carried patience like steel wrapped in calm. "The desert has not killed you. That means you are meant to endure. Survival itself is proof."

The hush deepened, as though the desert itself agreed. Even the scorpions stilled—the three voices tangled in the air: silk, chaos, silence.

Jian's fists trembled. His gaze flicked from Effie's blazing beauty, to Delilah's predator grin, to Si's quiet steadiness.

For a moment, he seemed ready to crumble, eyes dimming like torches in a storm. Then fissures of light split the rock beneath him. The ground groaned as heat surged outward. Effie's gown flared, Delilah skipped back laughing, Si's cloak rippled, though she did not move.

Jian's voice thundered, layered mortal rasp with angelic roar: "Three voices. One body. Mine."

The desert convulsed, sand avalanching down the ridge. Effie halted mid-step, calm cracked for an instant. Delilah's grin sharpened, hungry. Si's eyes softened—not in triumph, but recognition.

Effie recovered first, voice still velvet though laced with steel. "You don't have to choose yet. But you must stand. You cannot sit forever in dust. Come with me, Jian. I will build the world in your fire."

Her hand stretched—not beseeching, but summoning like a queen to her subject.

Si cut across her. "He must stand, yes. But not at your side by compulsion. He must choose where. And when."

Her gaze held Effie's without flinching. Silence pooled like water around her. For the first time, Effie's smile slipped.

Delilah clapped once, fox-sharp. "Gods, this is delicious. A queen, a sister, and a trickster—clawing for the same flame."

She winked at Jian. "But let's be honest, Scourge. It's not about us. It's about you. What will you do when you stop sulking and decide to burn?"

She prowled closer, smoke curling low.

Jian's chest heaved. Cracks widened along his ribs. His lips parted. For a long moment, only silence. Then he rasped: "Can you undo it?"

Effie faltered. For the first time, her poise cracked. Delilah's grin flickered, then sharpened. Si did not move.

Jian's voice rose, hoarse but unyielding. "Can you take it from me? The burning. The hunger. Eyes that never close. I didn't ask for this."

He forced his hands open. Molten light spilled from his palms. "I was a man—a cook. I had a daughter. I cut ginger. I boiled broth. I burned once, and now I burn forever."

His gaze seared each of them. "Tell me. Can it be undone?"

Effie stepped forward, beauty trembling at the edges. "No one can take this from you, Jian. It is who you are now. But it need not be a curse. With me, it will be purpose. Worship. Even joy."

Her imperial mask wavered, if only a heartbeat.

Delilah tilted her head, fox grin glinting. "Undo it? No. That door is ash. But why beg for broth when you hold volcanoes? You're magnificent. You could unmake the world with a gesture. And you'd trade that for a kitchen's steam?"

Her laughter cracked across the dunes.

Jian's answer was a single word, cracked and raw: "Yes."

The desert stilled. Even the stars seemed to pause their cold burn.

Si moved closer, kneeling deeper into the scorch. Sand smoked beneath her knees. "I cannot undo it either," she said quietly. "What burns stays burned. But you are still Jian. Beneath the fire. Beneath the suns. That has not been taken. Hunger, weariness, sorrow—they prove you are more than Scourge. The fire revealed you. Don't let them tell you otherwise."

Her calm pressed like balm against his fury.

Effie snapped, her patience fraying. Beauty hardened into fury, queen turned executioner.

"Do not trust her! Her gentleness is a mask. She comes for the council. Persuasion is her weapon. They will bend you for their war. Against the Skeletons."

The word rang colder than desert night. The dunes hissed. Jian's chest cracked louder, molten light spilling.

His gaze speared Si. "Is it true?"

"There is truth," she said steadily. "The skeletons move. Pele believes you must be aimed like a spear. The council would take your fire into their hands." A pause. "I would not."

Effie stepped in, imperial calm restored. "Words," she said tightly. "I offer more than words, Jian Wu."

She opened her palm. A silver flask gleamed. She poured. Water arced, perfect and clean—then struck the heat halo and vanished in white steam.

"Even the desert denies me," Jian rasped.

"Not the desert," Effie said. "Your isolation. Come with me, and the world will bring you rivers. With me, your fire will light an empire. The sand will beg you."

Delilah laughed, circling. "An empire is a cage with curtains. Wear a crown, starve your teeth? Boring."

She slid behind his shoulder, whispering like smoke. "Why starve when you can gorge until the map itself burns your name?" The shadows twitched in agreement, then recoiled as if afraid.

Si remained kneeling. “You need not choose empire or feast,” she said. “Even fire rests. Let the night pass. Be Jian Wu.”

Three voices wove again: silk, chaos, silence.

Jian lifted his face to the stars. Their light wavered before his. “Three voices,” he said—not loudly, but the dunes heard him. “One body. Mine.” The desert leaned forward, waiting.

Jian’s breath deepened, once, twice, and the glow in his seams drew tight, concentrated. The air thickened around him like a drumhead stretched to breaking.

He stood.

Stone shrieked as it split. Heat slammed outward, sand glassed beneath his bare feet. Effie’s gown snapped in the blast; Delilah’s hair whipped sideways; Si’s cloak flared and settled steady again.

The desert boomed with muffled thunder rolling beneath the dunes.

Jian towered—not taller than before, but more inevitable. The suns in his skull burned white. Cracks laced his forearms, his throat, his chest, like a constellation clawing to escape.

“I asked for undoing,” he said, voice braided mortal rasp with volcanic memory. “You offered crowns. You offered hunger. You offered sleep.”

His gaze seared each of them. Effie first, who did not flinch. Delilah, whose grin trembled into awe. Si, who steadied like hands at a fevered brow.

“I will not be bent,” Jian declared, each word widening fissures in the hill. “Not by silk. Not by chaos. Not by silence.”

Effie’s chin rose a fraction—the only sign she’d been struck.

Delilah whispered, delighted and afraid, "There he is."

The desert roared back in small ways: grains rattled like rain, dunes moaning low, pebbles tumbling far off as if their nerves failed them.

Jian lifted a hand—palm outward, fingers split with light. The air stuttered. Heat bowed off him in a shimmering wall.

"When I stand," he vowed, the sentence hammered like iron, "it will be by my will. Not yours."

The heat wave hit them.

Effie took a single, controlled step back, then another—the queen yielding space so she would not stumble. Her face remained perfect, but a bead of moisture flashed to steam on her lip.

Delilah laughed too brightly, sidling away, hands raised. "Careful, suns," she teased, though her voice trembled with thrill. "You might peel the night."

Si did not retreat. She lowered her head instead, as before a shrine one does not presume to enter. The silence around her dropped deeper, giving his roar a place to land.

Jian stepped forward. Sand hissed; the glass underfoot popped in brittle screams. He was a furnace door flung wide. His voice was the thing inside that never went out.

"I burned," he said. "I am burning. But I do not burn for you."

The ridge gave way. The rock beneath his former seat collapsed, cascading in glowing shards. For a heartbeat, no one breathed. Then the power shuddered through him like a bell struck too hard. The white in his eyes flickered. He staggered. His knees dipped before he caught himself, palm pressed to the glass that squealed under his weight.

Effie's mouth opened—instinct torn between command and help. She chose neither. Delilah's fingers twitched, some impulse toward support—or theft—but she held herself still, surprised at the hesitation. Only Si moved, an inch closer, hands steady on her knees, ready to take his fall if he yielded.

He forced himself upright again, swaying in the heat of his own making. The vow still hung in the air, shaping the four of them like a wall. "Begone," Jian said—not roaring now, but iron. "While I still allow it."

The desert answered with a long sigh as a dune face slumped and resettled. Effie bowed, barely perceptible, still regal in retreat. "Very well," she said, her voice smooth but thinner. "For now." She turned, and even the sand seemed to clear her path.

Delilah lingered, eyes wide, delight and calculation warring. "You're magnificent when you choose yourself," she said, truth surprising her. She flicked her gaze over Si, back to Jian. "I'll be around when you tire of starving." She slipped into shadow, her grin a crescent ember, then was gone.

Only Si remained.

Jian's body wavered under the weight of his own fire. The suns in his eyes fluttered, steadied, faltered again. He drew a breath that scraped him raw from inside. "Go," he told Si, softer than he'd meant. "I will not be—" The word broke. He found another. "Helped."

Si's answer came without judgement. "You have already been helped. By yourself."

He almost laughed. It came out as a ragged exhale that turned to steam.

"The world will return for you," she said. "I won't pretend otherwise. But not tonight." She rose, unhurried. "Rest, Jian Wu."

Her silence folded back into the dunes as she walked.

He was alone. Shaking. The vow had been hammered; now the anvil demanded payment. His strength emptied. He sank, one knee, then both, then sideways onto stone not yet cooled. It hissed beneath his cheek. Above him, the stars resumed their cold work. The desert exhaled, long and slow. Far off, a night bird made a single astonished sound.

"When I stand," Jian whispered to stone and sky alike, "it will be by my will."

And he closed his blazing eyes—not sleeping, not yet, but letting the world pass over him until the heat inside dimmed to a steady, hurting thrum. The desert reclaimed its silence. Effie's perfume of power was gone. Delilah's smoke dissolved. Si's hush receded. Jian remained, kneeling in the hollow scorched into stone.

Jian rose again, staggering. Every seam of his body leaked light. The stars dimmed, and he hated them for their cowardice. "I will never be used," he whispered.

The desert trembled as if it had heard.

He turned inland. Each step pressed sand into glass. Hunger gnawed. Thirst split his lips. Sorrow clung. The fire sustained his flesh, but not the man. Every stride reminded him: beneath Scourge still lived Jian Wu—cook, father, man.

Chapter 9
The Rock

The Rock of Gibraltar loomed pale against the night sky, a knuckle of stone thrust into the strait as though trying to hold two continents apart. To mortals, it was only a landmark, a sentinel of empire and commerce. But to Zed, Ari, and Pele, it was a threshold. And tonight, the threshold had opened.

The sea boiled beneath them. Not with storms or tides, but with the march of death.

Skeletons by the thousands pressed forward under the waves, their empty sockets lit by sickly green sparks. Shields corroded by centuries clashed faintly, the sound carried strangely through the deep. And at their head, tall and solemn, the Mummy walked.

No longer a drifting shadow of old curses, he was awake. The Sleeper of the Sands, the King-That-Would-Not-Die, the Oath-bound Pharaoh. His wrappings glowed faintly with inner fire, every strip of linen inscribed with hieroglyphs of denial—denial of death, denial of decay, denial of the gods themselves. A crown of blackened gold sat on his brow, and though broken in places, its weight was undeniable. He walked as though the sea parted for him, and in truth, it did.

Zed watched from the cliff's edge, his single eye fixed on the figure below. The crow on his shoulder hissed, wings ruffling uneasily. Lightning threatened at the hem of his coat, sparks hungry to leap. Yet he held still, sensing the magnitude of what had woken.

"He is no longer drifting," Zed said, his voice heavy. "The Sleeper has risen."

Ari snorted, though unease edged his stance. "So it's true then. The bastard king of sand is real. Awake and leading his bones like hounds."

He spat into the wind. "I'd rather face him in the flesh than skulking in nightmares."

"You may get your wish," Zed replied.

Pele stood apart, hair glowing with a faint volcanic shimmer. The wind caught strands of it, weaving embers through the night air. Her bare feet scorched the rock where she stood, yet she paid no mind. Her eyes burned with molten certainty.

"I taste him," she said. "Ash and resin, blood dried to dust. He is not a dream—he is will. He was bound, once and buried, but no prison lasts forever. He has lain in silence. Now he remembers his name."

The sea itself seemed to answer her. The skeleton army burst from the waves, dripping brine, blades raised high. They scrambled onto the narrow beaches below the Rock, forming ranks as though centuries of death had not broken their discipline.

The Mummy followed, each step heavy enough to shake the ground. Water fell from him in rivulets, steaming where it touched the sand.

Ari stepped forward, eyes gleaming. His sword rang as he drew it, eager for blood though there was none to spill. "Finally."

"Do not be a fool," Zed warned, his voice sharp. "This is no rabble to cut down. This is a king of old, risen from silence. He is no pawn. He is the war itself."

Pele's gaze sharpened. "The Stilled Breath." The word carried weight. It was not a title of rest, but of patience. A patience now ended.

The Mummy raised his arms, and the skeletons fell to their knees as one. A whispering chant rolled across the strait, words from a tongue no mortal had spoken in three thousand years.

The sound scraped at the air, hollow and commanding, and the Rock of Gibraltar trembled in reply. Cracks shivered along its face, dust pluming into the night.

"He commands the stone," Pele murmured.

"He commands memory itself," Zed corrected. His voice darkened.

"Mortals forgot him. History buried him. But he has not forgotten us."

As if in answer, the Mummy's head turned. Across the distance, through night and salt spray, his withered gaze locked upon the three gods standing at the cliff's edge. No eyes should have remained within those sockets, yet power burned there—cold, eternal, unyielding.

Zed stiffened. The crow on his shoulder croaked and flapped its wings, but did not flee. Ari grinned, reckless, lifting his blade in salute. Pele met the stare without flinching, though her fists curled with heat enough to melt iron.

The Mummy raised his hand. The sea fell silent. Even the waves seemed to pause mid-crash.

When he spoke, the air itself carried the words: "I have crossed the silence. I am no longer bound. I am Pharaoh. I am Judge. I am the Sleeper who does not sleep."

The skeletons beat their weapons against their shields in thunderous response.

Ari bared his teeth. "Finally, someone worth the fight."

Zed did not move. His one eye glowed faintly, stormlight caught in its depths. "Careful, War. His name is older than your fury."

Pele's voice was low, reverent, and dangerous. "And older than your storms."

The Mummy spread his arms wide. The strait trembled, as if caught between opening and closing. Ships in the harbour swung violently against their anchors, sailors crying out in confusion. Mortals would call it a freak surge, a trick of tides. But the gods knew—a new will had taken hold of the sea.

And it was awake.

He did not hurry.

The Mummy crossed the last curtains of foam as a king crosses a threshold—slowly enough that the world must notice. The skeletons parted to give him the shore. He paused where wet sand met ancient limestone and set his palm to the Rock as if greeting an old adversary.

The cliff shuddered with the touch, answering with a deep, reluctant groan that rolled through its galleries and gun emplacements, through abandoned tunnels and wartime rooms full of rusting cable. Pigeons burst from narrow slits like thrown stones.

Zed raised his hand in parley, palm outward. "Hear me, Pharaoh. You have woken into a world rimmed with delicate balances. Turn aside from Europe. There are wards and wagers here you do not yet—"

The Mummy's head tilted, faint amusement in the frozen lines of his linen-cast face. When he spoke, the air itself obeyed, carrying his words up the cliff without wind. "I count no balances but mine."

His voice was sand and bronze. "You kept your world through oaths and secrets. I kept mine through memory and denial. You called me myth to make room for your thunder. And yet—here I stand, while your balances shake."

Ari snorted. "And here I am, while your bones rattle." He stepped to the lip, sword loose in his hand. "Try me."

Pele did not move. "War, wait," she said, though her eyes never left the figure below.

The Mummy spread his arms over the armies that knelt in brine.

"Stand," he said without looking.

The skeletons rose in a clatter of shields and wet mail, ranks forming as if the habit of obedience had outlived their flesh.

Zed's crow clicked in his ear—one, two, three times—an old signal from older roads. Zed answered with a faint stroke of his thumb along the feathered neck.

Not yet.

"Your denial bought you centuries," Zed said, voice even. "It will not buy you the strait."

The Mummy's withered fingers flexed. The sea stilled again, as if something vast had taken a breath and was holding it.

"This cut in the world was not made for ships," he replied. "It was made to be closed when the harvest of empires is done."

Ari laughed outright. "Listen to him. He wants to mend the planet like a seamstress."

"Tailors shape war," Pele murmured. "They decide what fits."

She stepped forward at last, bare feet searing crescents into the wind-smoothed stone. "Pharaoh," she called, her voice a furnace held barely in check, "I am Pele of fire and mountain. I will not see a gate slammed on the living because the dead dislike the noise."

Something like attention sharpened in the Pharaoh's posture. Linen whispered as he turned his mask of a face toward the glow in Pele's eyes. "Fire from the underworld. Daughter of pressure and patience. The islands remember you."

"The Rock remembers you," Pele said. "But it does not love you."

"It remembers my silence," the Mummy said and set his other palm to the cliff.

The limestone brightened under his hands—not with heat, but with a pallid radiance, the colour of moonlight on old papyrus. Carved traces, long swallowed by wind and salt, rose like lifted scars. Zed saw glyphs that had no place on this coast—hooked birds, knives, suns, and coiled serpents stitched into a grammar of command.

The Rock groaned deeper, as if some core within it were being asked to agree.

Pele's jaw set. "He's writing his name into it."

"Not name," Zed said. "Claim."

Ari took two quick steps back, then sprinted.

He leapt like a thrown spear, a blur over the drop, his laugh tousled by the levante. He fell toward the narrow shelf below, where the first ranks of skeletons clustered—landed in a shower of pebbled grit—and moved.

War was not a technique so much as an honesty—Ari's blade spoke the plainest language it knew. Bones shattered. Shields rang. Helmets popped loose like old seeds. He struck and pivoted, ducked and drove. A dozen fell, then twenty, then a laughing tumble of grey-green bodies that did not bleed.

They rose again.

Not clumsy—never that. Each reassembled with dutiful economy: a hand crawling to its wrist, a shin finding a knee, a jawbone searching for its place. The green foxfire in their sockets never flickered.

"Fine," Ari said, breath quickening with pleasure. "Again."

He went to work. The cliff face flashed and chimed, an anvil without a smith. The skeletons pressed closer to surround him, and he grinned wider, as if he'd been cold for a long time and had just stepped into a room with a hearth.

The Mummy did not so much as glance at the melee he'd permitted. His hands remained on the stone. His fingers slid, almost tender, along the limestone's fossil-salted skin.

"Open not, close yes," he told the Rock in a language that had given law to rivers. "Reminder—" He pressed his brow to the cliff and breathed in, a long, rattling draw, like a man savouring cedar after centuries in a sealed tomb. "You were once a gate. Be a wall."

The cliff answered, with a long sub-vocal rumble, then a series of cracking pops that sprinted away along fault lines toward Europa Point.

On the Moroccan side, the hills trembled in sympathy, a low reply like a drum struck with meat. Far out in the channel, a bar of darker water shouldered up—a ridge where there had been none.

Pele's hair lifted in the heat—she no longer bothered to hide. "No," she said, and put her hand to the Rock.

Fire did not like limestone; it spent itself quickly on such airy stone. But Pele's touch was not campfire; it was mantlework. Lava spoke under her skin, and pressure answered through the Rock's belly. The limestone's bright pallor browned, then reddened where her fingers spread. A hiss, a sigh, a smell of cooked shell. The glyphs under the Mummy's palm blurred at the edges, beads of molten calcite drooling like the tears of statues.

The Mummy lifted his head, at last turning to face her fully. "Volcano against tomb? You would fuse my letters?"

"I would soften your certainty," Pele said.

"Then feel mine," he replied, and the linen at his wrists unspooled like snakes. Bands of written cloth shot from his hands, whipped around Pele's forearm, then her throat, seeking purchase where even stone found little. Every thread was a vow made in a room without doors.

They smoked where they touched her, but they did not catch.

Pele smiled—small, dangerous. "Unwrap me, little priest."

She opened her fist.

A sound like a held-in storm leaving a valley cracked the night. Heat bloomed—the honest kind that bakes bread and births islands—and the wrappings went incandescent. Resin in the old linen flared. The strips flashed and dropped in ash loops, crumbling on the wind. Even the sea took a step back, seething.

The Mummy took one pace up the beach. Steam rose from the water tracking off him, white against the black.

Ari's laugh reached them ragged and alive. He had found a tempo—break, toss, stamp, roll. Bones piled high as drift until a gesture from the Mummy made them ripple apart and re-form like a tide reversing.

Ari spat brine, delighted. "Make more," he called. "Or send something that bleeds."

Zed moved at last.

He did not leap or rush. He walked to the very edge and planted the ferrule of his black staff against the stone. The crow rose from his shoulder and wheeled once overhead, then settled on a spur of rock, head cocked, one bead eye on the Pharaoh, one on the sea.

Lightning crawled up the staff from nothing, a patient coil without a thunderhead's hulking preamble. It gathered at the head into a blade so narrow it was almost absent, the colour of a fresh scar.

Zed lifted the weapon and spoke—not loudly, but with the confidence of someone who had named storms before mortals named kings.

"Yield the strait," he said. "Or take my mark."

The Mummy's mask tilted. "Thunder with a borrowed eye," he said. "You carry two thrones in one skull and call it wisdom. You ask for yielding? Hear mine. Stand aside. Let the continent divide. Let Rome and all her granddaughters remember salt. Raise your bird, old man. It will need a second wing."

"Last call," Zed said, and cast the spear of storm.

It did not fly like a thrown weapon. The world rearranged to put the spear where Zed wanted it. One moment, lightning lived in his palm; the next, it existed in the Pharaoh's sternum, white and surgical.

The Mummy took the strike without flinching.

For a heartbeat, the linen gleamed like glass, and the hieroglyphs ran bright as a scribe's dream—then the light went out, swallowed into the dry idea of him. The spear-hurtled thunder had nowhere to echo; it landed in a tomb built of denial, and denial chose not to be pierced.

Zed's jaw tightened.

The Mummy lowered his gaze to the scorch that wasn't. His voice, when it came, was almost kind. "This is the lesson you wrote into me when you made me myth—what is denied cannot be cut. It must be unwritten." He lifted a hand and made a small, contemptuous brushing motion.

Storm peeled off Zed's shoulders like old paint. For a shocked instant, the god felt naked in the wind, his coat suddenly heavy and merely cloth, his eye simply an eye. The crow shrieked, affronted, and snapped the air, reasserting the sky with a lash of wing.

"Enough," Pele said and stepped off the cliff.

She fell like a stone for three long breaths, hair streaming fire, then met the lower ledge with a sound like a smith's first hammer on the first anvil—pure, declarative, undeniable. Heat rippled out in a ring.

Skeletons nearest her sagged and slumped, ribs softening, skulls sloughing their edges like sugar sculptures in rain.

Ari whooped and used the moment, vaulting the half-melted line to cut straight for the king of wrappings.

The Mummy lifted one finger.

Ari stopped as though a spear had gone through his heel. He looked down, incredulous. Sand had crept up over his boots and calves, not clinging—remembering. In a blink, it hardened with the memory of sandstone, then older—the memory of bedrock.

He wrenched, muscles leaping along his arms. Stone cracked—but when it broke, it broke upward, creeping as a cuff past his knees to his thighs.

"Ah," Ari said through bared teeth. "Cheater."

"Judge," the Mummy corrected, and turned his hand.

The cliff under Zed's feet bucked. The world's oldest battery discharged along the Rock's spine—no lightning this time, but pressure, the kneading, tectonic sort that makes mountains blink over ages.

Zed's staff sank an inch. Cracks spidered from the ferrule.

Pele's head snapped toward the Mummy. "Let him go."

"Make me."

Her smile grew, all volcano. "Gladly." She pressed both hands to the ledge.

Heat poured down like a mantle-current breaking free, a deep, humming warmth that turned wet sand into a skin of fresh glass. The stone creeping up Ari's thighs lost its form and was undecided whether it was a dune or a cliff. Ari tore his legs free with a snarl and bolted, leaving heel-shaped negatives in the smoking silica.

The Mummy's linen smouldered, then blackened. He did not retreat. He lifted his arms a second time, not to command stone now but to call the dead in it.

Fossils stirred—fish-bones in the limestone, curled shells, crinoid ghosts. They rose as dust-and-chalk echoes, a pale host that blew from the cliff face like a storm of ash, whirling to him, condensing where his hands directed.

They took the shapes of spearmen and standard-bearers and drummers without drums, a chorus made from the sea's long-ago.

"Europe remembers me," he said softly, satisfied. "Even where it thinks it is only rock."

Zed stepped down the slope, one measured stride at a time, reclaiming his thunder as he moved, lightning returning to coil along his shoulders like snakes.

"And it remembers us," he said. "King—if you close this cut, you start a war you cannot end."

"I do not end wars," the Mummy said. "I finish civilisations."

Ari came in low and fast, sand still smoking on his calves, blade a neat promise at his side.

“Then start with me,” he said, and smiled like a challenge thrown before a hearth.

The clash was inevitable.

Ari’s sword met a linen-bound arm with a clang that rang louder than bronze on bronze.

The Mummy did not yield. His wrappings tightened with the sound of rope snapping taut, and Ari felt his blade sink no further than the thickness of cloth. Worse—the sword itself quivered, as though the steel were reluctant to stay in his hand.

“Hold,” Zed barked, but Ari only laughed, twisting the blade free and slashing again.

This time, the Mummy moved, a sudden sweep of his arm that carried with it the weight of centuries. Sand rose in a wall, swallowing Ari’s next strike, knocking him sideways into the wreckage of bones he had already cut down. The skeletons reached for him at once, obedient, though their joints cracked and their sockets guttered with green fire.

“More!” Ari bellowed, kicking free, his grin all fury.

Zed clenched his staff tighter. Lightning rippled upward from the ground, arcing across his shoulders, collecting at the eyepatch he wore as if hungry for release.

Yet he hesitated, his one eye tracking the Mummy’s stance.

He had seen this before—ages ago, on plains where jackals prowled, and pyramids were still young. This was no mere warlord. This was a king whose oaths had burned themselves into stone and star.

Pele stepped forward, her heat shimmering so fiercely the cliff face bled small rivulets of molten limestone.

"Pharaoh!" she called, her voice carrying the roar of magma through the night. "This shore is not yours. This gate is not yours to close. You are trespassing."

The Mummy's head turned toward her. The crown of blackened gold tilted, and for the first time, a hint of expression rippled across the ruined mask of his face.

"All shores were mine," he said. The words rolled like surf across tomb walls. "The Nile was not a river, but a road. The deserts were not wasteland, but a court. Even silence served me. Now I walk where silence is broken, and I claim it again."

He raised both arms, and the skeleton horde answered in thunder. Shields slammed against bone, a rolling crash that echoed up the Rock as though an army of drums had been struck at once.

The ground split beneath Pele. Old tunnels, carved by men who had once prepared for cannon and siege, burst open, coughing out streams of skeletons still clad in rusting uniforms. Some bore muskets, others bayonets corroded into jagged teeth. They rose in a line before her, empty sockets aflame, blocking her path.

She smiled, and the ground beneath them glowed. In a heartbeat, fire erupted upward, consuming the tunnel mouths, baking the soldiers into chalk and ash. Their muskets dissolved, their bones warped, their green fire sputtered out. Pele's arms lifted with the motion, her hair billowing like smoke from a new vent.

"Then face me," she said, her voice thunder and lava combined.

The Mummy did not advance, but his gaze locked with hers. A strange stillness pressed down, heavy as centuries of sand. Zed felt it—a contest not of weapons, but of will. Fire against stone, denial against eruption. He knew the danger. If Pele pushed too hard, she could unmake herself as surely as the Mummy had unmade death. And if the Mummy claimed victory, he would bind the Rock with his hieroglyphs and close the strait forever.

"Pele," Zed said sharply, "do not give him the match he craves."

Her eyes flicked, a moment of acknowledgement, but the fire in her veins would not cool so easily.

Below, Ari fought on, half-buried in the tide of skeletons, his laughter ragged but unbroken. He swung his sword in wide arcs, smashing skulls, cutting limbs, using the bones themselves as weapons when they broke in his grip. The army surged over him, yet he rose each time, blood streaking his arms, his grin widening with every cut.

"You'll have to do better than brittle bones!" he roared, twisting a skull free and hurling it at the Mummy's chest. It struck, cracked, and fell.

The Mummy did not flinch.

Instead, he raised his palm toward Ari. The sand beneath the war god's boots rippled, then opened. A pit yawned wide, dragging Ari down to his waist before he could react. Skeletal hands clawed at him from beneath, pulling, grasping, eager to drown him in their grave.

"Damn clever," Ari muttered through his teeth. He braced, forced his blade downward, stabbing the ground itself. The pit shuddered, bone shards flying upward, but the pull did not release. "Clever enough to annoy me."

Zed lifted his staff and drove it hard against the cliff edge. The sky answered at last. A crack of lightning split the clouds, stabbing down into the strait. The wave it raised threw skeletons from their feet and smashed them against the rock. The pit shivered, releasing Ari just enough for him to wrench free. He sprang clear, coughing sand, his blade blazing with fresh fury.

The Mummy's gaze turned upward to Zed. Sparks ran along his linen, absorbed into the old glyphs as though the storm itself were being catalogued, denied, rewritten into his history.

"You forget," he intoned, "I am the one who taught men to measure thunder. I am the counter of storms. My silence swallows your noise."

Zed's eye narrowed. "Then you've forgotten the one thing storms never do." The crow screeched above them, wheeling once, its wings flashing white in the lightning. "They return."

Another bolt fell, heavier, brighter. It slammed into the Rock itself, splitting stone, showering sparks, and molten fragments down onto the battlefield. The Mummy staggered—only slightly, but enough. The skeletons faltered with him, as though a chord had been plucked through their marrow.

Ari seized the moment, breaking from the horde, charging straight for the Pharaoh. "Now we see if you bleed," he growled, lifting his sword high.

The Mummy raised his hands, and the world seemed to hold its breath.

Ari did not hesitate. He had never believed in hesitation. Where others measured and weighed, he struck—and it was this refusal to pause that had made him War incarnate.

The Mummy lifted both hands, linen coiling outward like serpents, ancient vows written in each strand. They hissed and snapped, weaving a lattice meant to bind Ari mid-charge. But

Ari drove through, sword high, his laughter wild and raw. He was not speed—he was inevitability.

The first lash wrapped his arm, searing as it tightened. He ignored it. The second caught his chest, crushing breath from his lungs. Still, he pressed forward. The third coiled around his throat, a noose of hieroglyphs, promising silence.

Ari roared through it. His blade came down in a vast, reckless arc.

The steel, forged in forgotten forges, kissed the Pharaoh's crown first. The gold cracked like dry bark. Sparks and dust burst outward. Then the edge cut deeper, through linen hardened by centuries, through flesh embalmed and denied decay.

The Mummy staggered.

The army screamed—not with voices, but with a shuddering collapse, a rolling thunder of bones falling to their knees. Shields clattered, skulls bowed, sockets guttered. The strait itself heaved, a wave racing outward as if the sea, too, recoiled.

Ari wrenched his blade free, bloodless but smoking. The wound gaped across the Pharaoh's chest, black dust spilling like ground charcoal.

For the first time since his awakening, the Mummy faltered. He fell to one knee. His hand pressed against the split in his breastplate of linen, fingers shaking with the effort of denial. The crown slid from his head and clanged onto the stones.

Pele gasped, her fire dimming just slightly, as if stunned by the sight. Zed's eye glowed brighter, stormlight returning to him in a sudden rush.

"You did it," Zed murmured, awe creeping into his voice despite himself.

Ari grinned, pulling the last noose of cloth from his neck and tossing it aside. His chest heaved, but his eyes blazed with triumph.

"I told you," he spat, wiping dust from his sword. "Everything bleeds. You just have to strike hard enough."

The Mummy lifted his head.

His face was a ruin, hollow sockets seething with a new, deeper fire—not green, but red, pulsing with fury. The wound in his chest glowed faintly, as though embers lived within him.

"So be it," he whispered, his voice trembling the cliff. "If you would tear down the Pharaoh, then take the curse with him."

The skeleton army collapsed fully, bones falling into heaps, the green sparks extinguished. But from those heaps rose a dust storm, thick and choking, swirling upward in a violent spiral.

The sand carried the Mummy's denial, his fury, his promise of return. It swallowed the shoreline, clawed up the cliff face, and blotted out the moon.

Ari coughed, slashing blindly into the storm. "Coward's trick!" he shouted, though his grin had not faltered.

Zed planted his staff, lightning flashing out in desperate arcs to hold the gale at bay.

"He is not dead," Zed warned, voice harsh. "You struck him down, but kings do not fall so easily."

Pele thrust her hands into the sandstorm, fire roaring into it, burning the grains into glass mid-air. They fell around her in jagged sheets, tinkling against the rock. Her face was set in grim determination. "Then let him curse," she growled. "Let him scream. The Rock will not close. Not while I stand."

The storm shrieked louder, wrapping itself around the kneeling figure of the Pharaoh. His body glowed within the cyclone, half-broken, half-reformed, his wound still smoking with Ari's strike.

"This is not the end," the storm howled in his voice. "This is the beginning. You will remember me, as you remembered silence. Europe will choke on sand. Empires will bury themselves."

And then—he was gone. The storm tore itself free of the beach, raced across the strait like a living wall, and dissolved into the night sky, scattering toward the lands beyond.

The skeletons lay shattered and still. The waves resumed their rhythm, though the water was fouled with bone and ash. The Rock groaned once, but did not split.

Ari stood, breathing hard, blood and dust streaking his skin. He raised his sword, point down, and laughed hoarsely. "That," he said, "was worth the wait."

Pele's eyes narrowed, still glowing with furnace-heat. "You have wounded him, not ended him. He will rise again, and his curse will spread."

Zed lifted his staff, resting its charred tip against the stone. His face was grim, his single eye burning with stormlight. "Yes," he said. "But tonight, the Sleeper bleeds."

They stood together at the cliff's edge, the strait below littered with ruin, knowing that this victory was not an ending but a warning.

The Mummy had been struck down. Yet his curse was already loose upon the wind. The dust storm fled, leaving only ruin behind.

The shoreline was a graveyard; the strait littered with bone fragments that bobbed like driftwood. The crown of the Pharaoh lay broken at Ari's feet, glinting faintly in the moonlight.

For a long moment, no one spoke. Only the wind moved, carrying the smell of scorched stone and brine.

Ari planted his sword point-down into the rock, leaning on it, chest heaving. His grin remained, though it was tempered now by the raw edge of battle well-fought.

He kicked at the crown, sending it tumbling into the rubble. "So," he said, voice rough, "the great Stilled Breath falls like the rest. No more whispers. No more silence. Just dust."

Zed's eye was storm-bright but uncertain. "Perhaps," he said. "Or perhaps he withdraws. Kings do not always die when struck. Sometimes they bide."

Pele crouched, her hand brushing the scorched sand where the Pharaoh had knelt. The grains still radiated a strange heat—not hers, not volcanic, but ancient and unnatural. She frowned.

"He may rise again. Or he may not. The balance shifts. But one thing is certain: the curse he loosed is already moving with the wind."

Ari spat into the ashes, straightened, and swung his sword back across his shoulder. "Then we deal with it. We deal with all of it. No more waiting for balance, no more councils wringing their hands. We strike first. We cut down the head of this snake before it coils tighter."

Zed lifted his brow. "You mean the girl."

"The woman," Pele corrected, her tone carrying weight.

Ari's grin sharpened. "Lilith. She's raising armies of her own. The Mummy was one front, but she's the other. We cut her down, and we end this before it spreads across the whole continent."

Zed was silent, the crow clicking once from its perch nearby.

Pele rose, fire trailing from her hair in faint embers. "Lilith is dangerous in ways the Pharaoh was not. He was denial given flesh. She is hunger given voice. Do not mistake one for the other."

Ari slammed his fist against his chest, the sound echoing like a war drum. "Then let her hunger. I'll feed it steel."

Zed finally spoke, his voice low, deliberate. "This is not your call alone, War. If we move against her, the others will feel it. The council will divide, as it always has."

"Let it divide!" Ari barked, eyes blazing. "Let the cowards hesitate. We've bled tonight. We've seen what silence waking looks like. Do you want to wait until Lilith has ten thousand more corpses dancing to her tune?"

He pointed his blade south, across the dark waters toward Africa, where the shadows of her growing power stretched.

"No more patience. No more waiting. We march. We deal with Lilith."

The words hung in the air, sharp as the edge of his sword.

Pele glanced at Zed, then back at Ari. The god of war was not wrong. Lilith's rise threatened more than armies; it threatened the order of gods and mortals alike.

Zed closed his eye, listening inwardly, as though consulting a storm only he could hear. When he opened it again, his voice was grim.

"So be it. But mark me, Ari: if we go to her, we may not return unchanged."

Ari's grin only widened. "Good. Change is war. War is life."

Pele nodded once. "Then it is settled. The Pharaoh is dust. Lilith is next."

The three gods stood upon the Rock, the strait beneath them restless, the night alive with the echoes of their choice.

The world would feel the weight of it soon enough.

Chapter 10
The Reveal

The hall was crowded yet quiet, like a storm before it breaks.

Every camera blinked red. Every reporter leaned forward. Every hand held a pen that shook without permission.

Nine chairs stood in a crescent, already filled. No names were spoken. None were needed.

Hera rose first. She did not look at the cameras, but at the rows of people.

"You have wondered," she said, voice steady and unadorned.

"You have guessed, denied, laughed, and whispered. Tonight, there is no need. We reveal ourselves. We have been among you all along. In your streets, in your fields, in your hospitals, in your courts. We walked beside you while you forgot us, and for a time, that forgetting served the balance. Now it does not. Now silence is harm."

The words pressed into the room like stones into still water.

Zed's eye glinted beneath the patch. "The balance is broken," he said.

"Not by one act, but by the sum of them. You feel it already. Storms that come too soon. Droughts that stay too long.

Famine where granaries should stand full. War without cause, and peace without spine. The scales tip and do not return. We can no longer sit and watch the beam crack."

Thoth lifted his stylus, not as ornament, but as record. "The signs are not myths. They are numbers. Fenris 401b, the star you call a brown dwarf, moves closer with each cycle. The calculations are certain. Its gravity disturbs your orbits. Its heat disturbs your climate. It will pass. But the passage will cost you balance unless it is managed."

The reporters shifted in their seats. They had written about Fenris 401b before, in the dry language of astronomy. Hearing it from this mouth gave it the weight it had never carried on the page.

Jamil folded his hands. His voice was quiet, precise. "And while the heavens disturb the skies, the earth gives up its dead. You have seen them. Armies of bone, cadavers stitched to command. These are not accidents. They are summons. Each host is an imbalance made visible. To ignore them is to allow collapse."

Pele's eyes burned faintly, though her voice was soft. "You have seen the rivers shrink. The rains that do not come. Crops that wither before they flower. Famine does not march with banners, but it kills more surely than armies. Balance is not only between gods and people. It is between earth and sky, water and fire. That balance is failing."

Ari leaned forward, broad shoulders tight with strain. "You call it climate, economy, politics, war. You give it names to keep it small. Stop keeping it small. The truth is bigger—balance has cracked. Every front you fight is one wound of the same body."

Dionysus twirled a stemless glass between his fingers, though no one had seen it poured. His smile was thin. "And you wonder why we speak plainly now. Why not sooner? Because for centuries we watched, and balance returned on its own. This time it does not. The wound bleeds on, and still you tell yourselves it is only weather. Only famine. Only unrest. We reveal that the lies you tell yourselves are more dangerous than the enemy."

A low, restrained sound—then a loud crash in the audience. A frame shattered against the floor. A reporter had knocked it off the wall, straining for a better vantage, and the room lurched in awkward sympathy—half-startled, half-laughing.

Hera raised her hand. "Silence." The hall stilled again. "We are not saviours," she said. "We are not saints. We are what we have always been: witnesses, actors, and guardians of balance. It is no longer possible for us to hide in silence. So you will hear us now. Fenris 401b is coming—armies of the dead march. Drought and famine spread. If you wished for a quiet age, it is gone. You will live in the revealed age. And you will not live in it alone."

The silence that followed was not disbelief. It was recognition. The air held the weight of Hera's words. The hall did not stir until Zed shifted forward in his chair.

"I am Zed," he said. His voice carried like thunder muffled by distance, heavy but certain. "You have called me by other names—storm-bringer, oath-keeper, judge. I have walked beside soldiers and sailors, among the broken and the proud. I held silence because silence served the balance. But the scale no longer returns. You see it in the storms that tear cities apart, in the wars that refuse to end, in the law bent until it cannot stand. I reveal now because storms should not hide. They announce themselves, and so do I."

He leaned back, and the pause was deliberate, allowing the words to anchor themselves in ink and recorders.

Next, Jamil spoke, his voice low but precise, cutting across the hall like a scalpel.

"Jamil," he said. "The name is enough. You have given me others—Yama, judge of death, physician of the soul. It makes no difference. I have closed more ledgers than you have opened lives. And yet, I walked your streets unseen. I wore the coat of a doctor, the silence of a passerby. I always corrected the imbalance quietly. Now, the imbalance is louder than my quiet hand. The dead are walking. I did not summon them. They are outside the wheel, tearing order apart. And so I reveal. Not for comfort. For warning."

Some reporters shifted uneasily at his calm; his words carried no malice, but no softness either.

Thoth lifted his stylus, as if punctuating silence before he spoke. "Thoth," he said. "Record, measure, witness. When events weigh themselves, I weigh them again. I have written in the margins of your histories while you forgot the hand. Now the figures no longer balance. Fenris 401b turns, shifting tides and skies. Armies rise from dust. Crops fail where they should flourish. These are not myths; they are numbers. They do not require belief. They require action. I reveal now so you may no longer pretend you do not know."

His words felt like a record, each syllable exact.

Thales spoke next, his face austere, his voice measured as if calculating each phrase. "Thales. My name is not a story, but a principle: number, proportion, the rule of water, the truth beneath appearances. For years, you spoke of science as if it replaced us. You did not know we walked within it. The numbers now show an imbalance that cannot be corrected by denial. Droughts that map like equations, famines that spread like contagion, orbits that curve where they should hold. I reveal because numbers should never be hidden. They speak, and now you must listen."

The pause after his voice was longer, heavier, until Ari broke it with a strike of his fist against the desk.

"I am Ari," he said, and the microphone rattled. "War is my name. Not metaphor, not symbol. The fight that lives in people, the fire that won't stop burning. I stood in your battles unseen. I held the line when you thought it was your courage alone. I reveal now because war has already revealed itself—in bones rising, in neighbours turned against neighbours, in scarcity that makes people claw. Balance is gone. Conflict is everywhere already. I do not step out of the shadow to make peace. I step out so you know who stands when the clash comes."

Reporters' pens stuttered under his words.

Dionysus leaned back, a glass in hand, though no one saw it poured. His smile was soft, but his tone held an edge of iron.

"Dionysus. You call me excess, revel, madness. But I am also release—the place people turn to when weight grows too heavy. I walked in your taverns and festivals, in your music, in your grief disguised as laughter. When balance was held, joy was enough. Now joy alone is not. You face famine, drought, and death, and still you must live. You will need more than rations and rules. You will need a release. I reveal because even in an age of collapse, people must remember how to be more than afraid."

Heat shimmered at the edge of Pele's chair as she stood, her presence a quiet blaze. "Pele," she said. "Fire is my truth. I have walked among you as warmth, as forge, as spark. You saw my face in volcanoes, but not in your homes, your kitchens, your lamps. Fire always destroys, but it always creates. Drought and famine are fire without creation—only ash. I reveal because fire must be directed, or it consumes everything. If you think me cruel, look at the fields that die without rain. That is cruelty. I am only honest."

Finally, Si rose. Her presence softened the air, though her words were firm.

"Si," she said. "You may know me as Psyche, soul, bridge of memory. I have stood with you in silence, in grief, in your smallest acts of care. When balance was held, I could remain unseen. Now fear threatens to unmake people before famine or war even reaches them. I reveal because people must remember themselves, or nothing else we do will matter."

She lowered her gaze, then looked back at the press. "This is who we are. This is why we no longer hide."

The hall was silent but not empty. It thrummed with recognition, with the weight of names spoken aloud.

Hera looked down the crescent of faces, then back to the rows before her. "Now you understand. We have been among you all along. And we speak now because silence serves no one. Balance is gone. You must hear it from our own mouths."

Hera did not sit again. She turned slightly toward Thoth and Thales, as if to invite their words forward.

Thoth touched his stylus once to the tablet before him. "You have already heard the name Fenris 401b," he said. "Your astronomers called it a brown dwarf, a wandering star. They charted its path, but they did not tell you what it meant. It is not coming to strike you. It will not blaze across your sky like a comet. It will pass, yes—but in passing it pulls."

He glanced at Thales, who continued with the precision of a surveyor.

"The pull disturbs the balance of orbits. Not catastrophically, but enough. Seasons tilt. Rain falls in the wrong places. Heat lingers too long where it should break. Rivers shrink. Crops fail.

The difference between yield and famine can be as little as a single degree. Fenris 401b does not need to strike the earth to wound it. Its shadow alone is enough."

The hall was still. Reporters wrote furiously, though more than one swallowed hard at the thought of a star dragging climate by its wake.

Zed leaned into his microphone.

"You call it change, adjustment, natural cycle. Do not hide behind those words. This is an imbalance. And imbalance feeds every other wound. A failed harvest becomes unrest. Unrest becomes war. War becomes famine again. The circle eats itself."

Hera nodded once. "You cannot fight Fenris 401b with weapons. But you can face its consequences with preparation. If you treat it as a rumour, you will starve. If you treat it as fact, you will endure."

Ari shifted forward, his fists clenched tight. "And while you measure stars and rains, don't forget the armies already marching. Balance breaks in bone as much as in the sky. You saw Gibraltar. The host cracked there—maybe their master with it, maybe not. But Lilith is not gone. Her skeletal columns move east. Nileward. Towards the Levant. Not a rumour. Direction."

The words landed like blows.

Jamil's voice followed, calm and precise. "These are not armies you can negotiate with. They do not eat. They do not rest. They grow as they march, pulling from the graves they pass. When you think of them, do not think of soldiers who weaken with time. Think of tides. Every delay makes them stronger."

Pele's voice wove in next, quiet but fierce. "Famine and drought are not apart from this. They are their companions. Armies that do not eat still strip the land bare. People fleeing leave fields untended. Water flows where it should not, withheld where it should fall. Fire is left to burn until only ash remains. You will see famine not as a season, but as a chain—harvest after harvest failing, each one weaker than the last."

Dionysus raised his glass, though his smile was gone. "And famine does not stay in the field. It comes into your homes. It breaks your laughter, turns neighbour against neighbour. It rots trust. Do not underestimate how quickly hunger can hollow the soul. I say this not to frighten, but to name the truth. Hunger is not just empty bellies. It is collapse, from the inside out."

Si's words followed like a hand laid gently on a wound. "This is why we reveal. Because imbalance is no longer an abstraction, it walks in armies. It withers your crops. It bends your seasons. It turns trust brittle. And in silence, you are left only with rumour. Rumour will undo you faster than famine."

Thoth tapped his stylus again. "Understand: none of these things is separate. Fenris 401b is one weight on the scale. The undead armies are another. Drought and famine are the third. Balance is not lost by one stone but by the heap of them together. That is why we speak now. Because all three gather, and people deserve truth."

Hera let the words settle before she spoke again. "You wanted to know who we are. Now you know. You wanted to know why we reveal. Now you know. Our silence would only quicken collapse. Fenris 401b draws near—armies of bone march. Famine spreads. You cannot pretend otherwise. And we will not let you."

The hall seemed smaller now, the air heavier. Reporters looked at one another, some pale, some grim, all aware they had just been handed not a story, but an epoch. The atmosphere is stern with every revelation. Names had been given, balances declared broken, the threats laid bare.

But Hera knew it could not end with a diagnosis alone. People needed instruction and direction—not salvation.

She stood again, her presence quiet but commanding.

"You ask what people must do," she said. "We will tell you plainly. Not prophecy. Not riddles. Only what can be done when balance is already gone."

Zed's voice came first, rough as stone rolled in surf. "You must learn to endure storms as normal, not as exceptions. Floods and droughts will trade places without warning. Do not cling to patterns that no longer hold. Build for change, not for permanence. When rivers dry, move. When storms rise, shelter. The worst mistake is waiting for the world to return to what it was. It will not."

Thales added, voice measured. "Numbers guide survival. Each family should know three things: where water will come from, how much food they can carry, and where they will meet if scattered. Write it. Memorise it. Do not wait for officials to print instructions. Balance has no bureaucracy."

Jamil's tone was colder, precise. "Do not waste your dead. Cremate if you can. Burn bone to ash. If you bury, bury deep and stone the graves. Every unguarded body is a weapon to those who march against you. I do not say this to be cruel. I say this because you must understand—death is not final while the bindings remain."

Reporters paled—pens scratched harder.

Pele leaned forward, her voice low but fierce. "Prepare for fire, even in lands where fire has not ruled. Fields will burn where they once thrived. Store seed safe from flame. Learn to cook without timber, for wood will grow scarce. Ash is not the end, but if you do not plan for it, it will consume you."

Dionysus lifted his glass, though his smile was gone. "Do not let fear hollow you before famine does. Share bread. Share wine, if you can. Keep laughter alive, even when it feels treasonous. Collapse spreads fastest through despair. If you surrender joy, you surrender before the fight begins."

Si's voice carried gently but firmly. "Remember each other. Fear will try to turn you inward. It will whisper that you are alone, that you cannot trust. Resist that. Fear is the true army that marches faster than bone. Families, neighbours, strangers—weave bonds. When you are scattered, it is those bonds that will call you back."

Hera's gaze swept the room, settling on no one and everyone at once. "You now know what we are, why we reveal, and what approaches. Fenris 401b draws near—the dead walk. Famine spreads. Balance is gone. Do not expect rescue. Do not wait for a return. Prepare. Stand. Endure."

The silence that followed was longer than any before. The press corps, so quick with questions and words, sat transfixed. What had begun as a revelation ended as an instruction.

The gods rose together, the crescent breaking. They did not wait for questions, nor linger for applause. They walked from the hall without turning back, leaving only their words to anchor the storm.

And outside the hall, the world was already shifting. Phones lit with headlines:

"*We have been among you all along.*"

"Balance Is Broken."

"Fenris 401b, Armies of Bone, and Famine."

And beneath them, ordinary people began to make lists, pack bags, whisper names, and prepare.

The Oval Office lights burned long past midnight. Cameras blinked, a teleprompter glowed, aides stood silent against the walls. The President leaned forward, both hands resting on the desk, not as a gesture but as if bracing against an unseen weight.

"My fellow citizens," he began, voice slower than usual, measured as if each phrase had to be carried carefully.

"Tonight, the world heard something it has not heard in centuries. Nine figures stood and spoke plainly of who they are, and of what they see. Some of you watched in disbelief, some in fear, some in silence too deep to name. I watched as well. And like you, I am still reckoning with what I heard."

A pause, deliberate.

"They told us they have been among us all along. They told us the balance is broken. They named what we are already experiencing: the storms that come too soon, the droughts that stay too long, the crops that fail without warning. They told us of Fenris 401b, a wandering star whose passage changes the sky itself. They told us of armies of the dead, moving as tides move, toward the Nile, toward the Levant. They told us famine is no longer seasonal, but systemic."

His jaw tightened, and his eyes stayed steady on the camera. "These words are not easy to hear. They are heavier than any speech I have given in this office. And yet—they are not words of surrender. They are words of revelation. We are not abandoned.

We are not left without warning. We have been told the truth, and truth is the beginning of preparation."

He leaned closer.

"So let me say this clearly. We will not panic. We will not fall into rumour. We will not give fear the victory before the first clash. We will plan. We will prepare. We will endure. Each family will be asked to make simple choices—where you will meet if scattered, how you will hold water, how you will protect the vulnerable. Each community will be asked to coordinate, not wait for chaos. Each government will be asked to share knowledge as openly as possible. These are not extraordinary acts. They are the work of people who intend to live."

The President let his gaze fall briefly to the notes before him, then raised it again.

"I will not pretend I have every answer. None of us does. But we have been given clarity and time—perhaps only a little, but enough if we use it. We are not alone in this age. The nine who spoke tonight revealed themselves not to claim dominion, but to insist we face what comes with open eyes. That is what we must do."

He steadied his voice. "We are people. We have weathered famine, plague, war, and fire before. We will weather this as well. Together. Prepare, plan, endure. That is our task. That is our promise."

The cameras blinked. The speech was over.

Chapter 11
The Banter

The last bend in the trail narrowed into stone steps. The tourists had thinned out, peeling away to llamas and guides with little flags, leaving the higher terraces almost empty.

The wind was thin and sharp, carrying the smell of stone warmed by the sun.

Ben crested the stairs and stopped.

Athena was waiting.

She blocked the path without posture or threat, simply standing there with a walking stick braced across her body. Nap-sack strapped to her back, hat catching the light. She didn't need to announce herself — she was the road, and the road had ended.

"Turn back," she said.

Ben's pulse spiked. He glanced at the terraces, at the sky, then back at her. "Not happening."

He stepped forward. She pointed the walking stick.

Ben went left. The stick angled. He went right. It mirrored him. He ducked low and tried to shoulder past—and slammed into her like a man tackling a column. The impact rattled him.

"Move," he hissed, shoving harder.

Athena didn't budge. She turned her wrist, and the stick's handle pinned him to the stone wall, easily. He twisted, trying to break her grip. Her arm flexed once, and the stick might as well have been welded iron.

"Persistent," she said flatly.

Ben growled, slammed his palm against the stick, and shoved with all his weight. The wood didn't even quiver. He broke free by throwing himself backward, then lunged again, aiming low this time, trying to slip past her hip. Athena shifted half a step. His shoulder hit her thigh. She didn't stagger. His momentum died against her like a wave against a seawall. Breath ragged, he swung an elbow. The strike hit her with a crack that numbed his arm.

She didn't flinch.

"Enough," she said.

Ben spat on the stones and came again, reckless, both hands grabbing for the stick. He heaved. Muscles burned, veins stood out in his neck. Nothing. The walking stick was alive in her hands, an extension of her will, unbreakable. She wrenched it free and pressed the butt into his chest, driving him back three steps until his heel caught on a stair. He staggered, nearly fell.

"Enough," she repeated, voice like stone dropping into a well.

Ben bent over, sucking thin air, chest heaving. His arms trembled from the effort. His pride hurt more than his body. He raised his eyes and barked a laugh that came out raw.

"Alright. Point taken. I can't shove a mountain off its ledge."

From a low wall nearby, a soft chuckle answered.

Fiona sat cross-legged on the terrace, cloak loose, a single coin dancing across her knuckles. The metal caught the sun, flipped, rolled, vanished, then appeared again between her fingers as if gravity obeyed her whims.

“She’s immovable, darling,” Fiona said, voice lilting. “You could ram her until your bones gave way, and she’d still be right there, tidy as ever.”

“Fortuna,” Athena said, not taking her eyes off Ben. “Be silent.”

Fiona smiled, slow and sharp. “And miss the show? Not a chance.”

Ben rubbed his shoulder where it still throbbed from hitting marble. He straightened, shaky but defiant. “So physical’s out. That leaves words.”

Athena’s eyes were cold. “Words won’t change stone.”

Ben forced a grin. “No, but they might change your mind. And if I can’t break you, maybe I can out-talk you.”

Fiona twirled the coin once more and let it fall flat onto her palm. “Now we’re gambling. Lovely.”

Athena planted the walking stick on the stone, expression like a closed gate.

“Speak, then. Convince me why I should let you trespass where no mortal belongs.”

Ben wiped sweat from his forehead and met her stare. “Because if you’re here guarding it, then it’s already stirring. If it weren’t, you wouldn’t need to be standing in my way.”

For the first time, Athena’s eyes flickered, just for a heartbeat.

Ben pressed. "You're not blocking me because I don't matter. You're blocking me because I do. And if that's true, then this isn't your decision anymore. It's mine."

Fiona laughed, delighted. She flipped the coin again and caught it. "Oh, I like him."

Athena's mouth tightened, but she didn't strike. The stick stayed pressed to the ground.

Ben leaned in, breath still ragged. "So here's the deal. You can't win by standing still forever. Not against me. I'll keep coming, keep trying, keep talking until something cracks. Might be me, might be you, might be the damn mountain. But something gives. And we both know I'm not the kind that quits."

The silence stretched, heavy with thin air and the endless gaze of the terraces.

Fiona tilted her head, eyes dancing. "Your move, sister."

Athena's silence was the kind that bent men. She didn't fidget, didn't blink, didn't let the weight of the stick rest any lighter on the stone. The whole mountain seemed to copy her stillness.

Ben wiped his palms on his thighs, buying himself a second. His lungs burned from the thin air. His arms still ached from ramming her and failing. He wanted to slump, to curse, to give up.

Instead, he grinned through clenched teeth. "You know," he said, "if you really thought I didn't matter, you'd have let me walk right past and trip over myself. You'd have laughed when I broke my neck on the next step. But you didn't. You showed up because you're afraid of what happens if I keep walking."

Athena's eyes narrowed. "Afraid? Do not mistake vigilance for fear."

Ben shrugged. "Call it what you want. But the fact is, you're here. Which means I've already disturbed whatever balance you were hoping to preserve."

On the wall, Fiona let her coin spin once more. "Oh, he has a tongue after all. Keep going, dear, I'm enjoying this."

Athena snapped her gaze toward her. "Do not meddle."

Fiona feigned innocence, closing her hand over the coin. "I meddle only with odds. His words are his own."

Ben drew in a shaky breath. He could feel his pulse in his ribs. "Look, I'm not here to wake anything. Not looking to set the world on fire. But I am here because something pulled me. Something strong enough that even you decided it couldn't be ignored. You can call me an aberration, a nuisance—fine. But if the mountain itself tugged me here, then you standing in my way just makes the pull worse. You know it too."

Athena shifted, just a hair, like a heartbeat missed.

Ben leaned into that space. "So here's my wager. You let me through, I don't break your precious balance. You keep blocking me, then sooner or later this mountain—and what's under it—pushes back harder. And then it's not me you're fighting, it's the Sleeper waking pissed off because its guardian was too stubborn to listen."

A flicker of tension crossed her jaw.

Fiona laughed, clapping once. "Oh, he's quick. Sister, admit it—he's found the crack in your marble."

Athena turned, walking stick snapping up toward Fiona. "Do not call me sister."

Fiona's smile widened. She balanced the coin on her fingertip and blew gently; it spun in place, upright, defying gravity. "Touchy. Always touchy when the odds tilt against you."

Ben stepped forward, careful not to overreach. "Look. You can keep calling me mortal, aberration, mistake—whatever fits your story. But even you know I've survived things that should've killed me ten times over. That means I'm either too dumb to quit, or I've got something on my side you don't understand. Maybe both. Either way, keeping me out doesn't stop what's coming. It just delays it. And every delay makes the fall worse."

Athena's eyes were hard, but the stick lowered an inch. "You speak in riddles without knowing their cost."

Ben grinned, tired and raw. "Yeah. But so far, my riddles are keeping me alive. And I'll keep talking until you either strike me down or step aside."

The mountain air hung heavy. Tourists drifted further down the terraces, the chatter of cameras and guides fading. Up here, only the three of them remained: the wall, the gambler, and the fool who wouldn't shut up.

Fiona tipped the coin into her palm and closed her fist. Her eyes glinted. "I'll sponsor him."

Athena's head snapped around. "You dare?"

Fiona's smile was all teeth. "Of course. I like his odds. And I like watching you grind your jaw when someone finds the flaw in your perfect geometry."

Athena's hand tightened. "Fortuna, you risk more than you know."

"Risk is the only reason I wake up," Fiona replied lightly.

She hopped down from the wall and took her place at Ben's side, her coin hidden but her smirk bold.

"So what do you say, wall? Keep us here until the mountain itself cracks? Or let the game continue?"

Ben forced himself to stand straighter, though his legs still shook.

"She's right. The mountain's moving whether you like it or not. You can bar me all day, but all that does is prove how scared you are of what happens when I succeed."

Athena's gaze seared him. "And if you fail?"

Ben's grin sharpened. "Then you'll get to say you told me so. But you'll have to let me try first."

Athena's stance shifted, still barring the path, though the weight behind it felt different now. Less a wall, more a dare.

"You speak boldly," she said, "but boldness is not wisdom. Words do not open doors unless the key matches the lock."

Ben smirked, though his ribs still throbbed from the tussle. "Funny thing about locks. They're only worth having if you expect someone to try them. Otherwise, you'd leave the door wide open."

Athena's eyes narrowed.

Fiona hummed, spinning her coin once more. "Oh, I do like that. Doors that expect trespass. Delicious."

Athena ignored her. "You assume much, mortal. The Sleeper is bound not because it is curious, but because it is dangerous. You seek to pass, yet you do not know what lies beyond."

Ben stepped forward until the stick's butt pressed against his chest. He forced himself not to flinch. "And you do? You've been standing here how long? Guarding, waiting. Maybe even you don't know what's under your feet anymore. Maybe the only reason you're here is that you're too afraid to look."

For the first time, Athena's jaw tightened—just a fraction, but enough.

Fiona's coin clinked softly into her palm. "Oh darling, did you feel that? He nearly made you blink."

Athena's voice sharpened. "Do not mistake patience for ignorance. I know more than you can comprehend."

"Then prove it," Ben shot back.

Silence pressed down, heavy as stone.

Ben pushed harder. "You say I can't pass because I don't understand the cost. Fine. Explain it. Tell me what you fear. Otherwise, you're not protecting balance—you're just hoarding it."

She didn't move. But something in her eyes did.

Fiona giggled softly, rolling the coin across her knuckles. "You can't win, sister. He doesn't play by the rules. That's why I like him."

Athena's head snapped around. "You will regret standing with him."

"Perhaps," Fiona said, tucking the coin into her fist. "But regret is still more interesting than obedience."

Ben drew in a breath, steadying himself. “Look. You think you’re protecting the balance. But balance isn’t stasis. It’s motion. It’s giving and taking, tilting and correcting. You standing still? That’s not balance. That’s fear pretending to be order.”

Athena’s walking stick trembled, the faintest vibration running down it.

Ben pressed the advantage. “So here’s your choice. You can keep blocking me, and watch the balance crumble because you’re too rigid to bend. Or you can let me through, and maybe—just maybe—balance finds a new centre.”

Fiona clapped once, delighted. “Oh, I love a paradox. Well played, mortal.”

Athena’s silence stretched until the thin air itself seemed to strain. Then, with a slow, measured motion, she held the stick aside.

“Pass,” she said, voice low. “But know this: you will not out-talk the Sleeper. And when your words fail you, no one—not even Fortuna—will pay your debt.”

Ben exhaled, shaky relief breaking across his face. He took a step past her, careful, wary, expecting the spear to bar him again. It didn’t.

Fiona slipped from the wall and fell into stride beside him, twirling her coin with lazy grace. “Well done, darling. You didn’t win by strength. You didn’t win by luck. You won by seeing the hole in her armour. That’s rare.”

Athena watched them go, her feet planted hard into the stone, her expression unreadable.

Ben muttered, "Feels less like winning, more like talking my way into trouble."

Fiona's smile was sharp. "Oh, but that's the best kind of winning."

The path widened again after Athena stepped aside. The terraces sloped upward in green tiers, llamas cropping grass at impossible angles, clouds dragging themselves across the shoulders of the peaks. Tourists wandered here and there, snapping photos, oblivious to the weight pressing down on Ben's chest.

He expected Athena to fade back into the mist or vanish into some higher plane. Instead, she walked ten paces behind, her gaze never leaving him. Not blocking anymore, but not gone either.

"Feels like walking with a parole officer," Ben muttered.

Fiona twirled her coin lazily, the metal flashing dull in the thin light. "She's not watching to catch you out, darling. She's watching to see if you stumble."

"Great," Ben said. "So I'm on trial without even opening my mouth."

"That's life," Fiona said, tossing the coin high and catching it again. "We're all on trial. Some of us know the judge is crooked."

They climbed another switchback. Ben's legs burned, lungs raw from the altitude. He tried not to look back, but he could feel Athena there: constant, immovable, like the mountain's own shadow.

The closer they drew to the Temple of the Sun, the fewer tourists lingered. The air grew sharper, quieter. The chatter of guides faded. The stones themselves seemed older here, less restored, more themselves.

Ben paused at a landing, bent over, palms braced on his knees. "You sure this isn't a setup? I'm struggling to breathe."

Fiona crouched beside him, her coin rolling across the backs of her fingers. "Of course it's a setup. That's what we do—we bait and see if the bait breaks or makes you. This is what legends are made from. We test, that's why she shadows instead of bars your way. She wants to know you."

Ben wiped sweat from his brow. "I'm not sure I want to know me."

Fiona's smile turned sly. "We can see that."

They started again, steps climbing narrower, stones worn concave by centuries of pilgrims. Ben felt the pull stronger now, not just in his ribs but in the soles of his feet, like the mountain tugged at him through every step.

Athena's footsteps followed, steady, unhurried.

At a curve in the path, Ben slowed until Fiona nearly bumped into him. "She's not going to let me in, is she? Not really."

Fiona tossed her coin, caught it, and smirked. "That depends on which way it lands."

"Don't tell me my fate's in your pocket."

"Oh, darling." Fiona's grin widened. She pressed the coin into his palm, cool and heavy. "It's in yours."

Ben stared at it.

Ordinary, worn, one side rubbed almost smooth. Nothing mystical. But his stomach clenched around it anyway.

Athena's voice came from behind, clear as steel. "Fortuna toys with illusions. Do not mistake her chance for truth."

Ben turned, coin still in hand. "If chance isn't truth, then why do you guard this place like the flip could kill us all?"

Athena's eyes hardened. "Because mortals mistake accidents for destiny. My task is to keep you from confusing the two."

Ben closed his fist around the coin, heat blooming in his palm. "Then maybe destiny is just an accident that survives long enough to matter."

For the first time, Athena's gaze wavered—just a breath, but enough.

Fiona clapped once, delighted. "Oh, I do enjoy watching you tie her in knots."

The path narrowed again, leading toward the temple's carved doorway. Beyond it, the stone gleamed darker, smoother, untouched by restoration. Mist pooled low, sliding in and out of the entrance like breath. Ben stopped. His pulse hammered. The tug in his chest was almost unbearable now, like invisible fingers hooking his bones and pulling him forward.

Fiona leaned in, her voice low. "That's it. The hinge. The knot. Whatever waits, it's listening."

Athena's voice followed, solemn. "Step lightly, mortal. You passed me with words. The Sleeper will not be so merciful."

Ben glanced back. "Mercy's never been on my side."

He closed his fist tighter around the coin, drew in a breath, and stepped toward the temple's mouth.

The mountain seemed to lean with him.

Chapter 12
The Bat

The chamber was small, no larger than a village hut, its walls pressed close with damp stone. The air was stale, sour with centuries of burned offerings, old smoke ground into rock.

Violet sigils crawled across every surface, thin and brittle like cobwebs of light. They had been etched deep—meant to hold not just a prisoner, but a hunger.

In the centre crouched Camazotz.

He was not the towering monster of myth. No giant wingspan that could blot out the moon. He was small—barely taller than Ben's shoulder, lean as famine, his leathery wings folded tight against his body. His snout was sharp, his fangs too long for his mouth, and his eyes glimmered with a patient cruelty that belied his size. He looked almost frail, a withered bat-thing pressed into the shape of a man. But his stillness carried the weight of something unspeakable.

Ben stepped into the chamber.

The air changed at once. The sigils brightened, then stuttered, then began to dissolve like ink running in water. The lines broke apart, violet light flickering out in strands, peeling off the stone.

Camazotz inhaled. His chest swelled, his thin frame expanding as if breath itself restored him. His eyes widened, a grin peeling across his face.

"At last," he rasped. His voice was too deep for his size, echoing like thunder swallowed in a cave.

Ben froze, fists clenching. "I didn't—"

"You didn't need to," Camazotz said.

He stepped forward, talons scratching stone. His wings flexed once, leathery creaks filling the chamber.

"Your presence alone unmade the lattice. You are the unweighed one. The sigils cannot name you, so they cannot hold me."

The last of the runes shrieked like dying insects, then went dark. The chamber fell into true shadow.

Camazotz stretched slowly, as though savouring the freedom. His joints cracked, his talons clicked, his wings rustled like dry parchment. He turned his head toward Ben, eyes gleaming.

"And you," he whispered, "you reek of my kin. Of wing. Of blood. Of shadow."

"I'm not yours," Ben said, though his voice shook.

The god laughed softly. "We'll see."

They circled each other in the gloom, predator and prey—though neither was sure which was which. Camazotz's grin never faltered. He spoke with the ease of one who knew time favoured him.

"You survived fire. Storm. Death itself. Tell me, mortal—did you think that was yours alone? No. It was borrowed. Gifted. The night lent you its teeth."

"I survived because I refused to die," Ben shot back.

Camazotz's eyes narrowed, amused.

"Refusal. Yes. That is hunger's first prayer."

He stepped closer, and Ben caught the stink of him: blood dried centuries old, musk of caves where nothing human had walked. He looked small, yet the hunger that clung to him was immense.

"Why free me?" Camazotz asked. His talon traced the empty air where a sigil had burned. "Why come here at all?"

"I was drawn, but didn't know what would be here," Ben admitted, chest tight.

"Then chance brought you. Chance or design." His grin widened, fangs dripping with fresh saliva. "Perhaps both. The ethereals move their pieces as they please."

At that word, the air shifted. A weight pressed down, invisible but undeniable. The stone groaned. The torches guttered, yet no wind moved.

Ben felt it first in his bones: a presence. Then another. Not just one ethereal, but many.

Watching. Waiting.

Their silence, louder than Camazotz's voice.

The bat god's ears twitched. His wings trembled. He hissed through his teeth.

"I smell them. They crowd close, the way vultures do when blood is near."

Ben's stomach turned. He couldn't see them, but he knew they were there—the same terrible pressure he had felt in hospitals, in flames, in moments where survival became impossible.

Camazotz leaned close, voice low, almost reverent. "You are theirs, too. That is why you survive. That is why you reek of night. They circle you like dogs around a kill."

"Then maybe they'll stop you," Ben said.

The god's laughter cracked the stone. "They do not stop. They balance. They do not forbid blood—they savour it. And I... I am so very hungry."

He stepped forward again. His mouth opened wide, far wider than it should, fangs glistening, a string of saliva stretching between them. The hunger in his eyes was no metaphor. He wanted Ben's throat.

Ben backed away, hands trembling, breath quickening.

Camazotz's wings unfurled, filling the small chamber with shadow. He beat them once, and the air burst into motion, dust flying, stone shaking. In a blink, he was airborne, darting from wall to wall with startling speed, circling Ben like a vulture in miniature.

Ben ducked, heart hammering. Instinct screamed again. Run, flee—but there was nowhere to run.

So he jumped.

It was clumsy, desperate. But the air caught him.

Not smoothly—not like Camazotz, who darted like lightning. But enough to hold him for a breath, then another. He flailed, willed the air to steady him, and it did—barely. He rose a foot, then dropped, then rose again, limbs awkward, balance lost.

Camazotz barked a laugh mid-flight. "Yes! You do carry it. Flight, shadow, hunger—it bleeds through you."

He darted close, talons brushing Ben's sleeve before wheeling away. "But you are weak. Clumsy. Half-born. You cannot even savour the gift you've been given."

Ben crashed back to the floor, knees slamming stone. Pain lanced up his legs. He staggered to his feet, chest burning.

"I don't need your gift," he spat.

Camazotz hovered above him, wings beating the stale air. His eyes burned, his grin shone sharp as knives.

"You already have it. The ethereals made sure of that. And now I will taste it."

The pressure in the room deepened—the silence thickened, choking. Ben felt them pressing closer, unseen but undeniable, their attention fixed on the moment where hunger and survival collided.

Camazotz hissed, wings snapping wide. "They watch. They watch to see if you are prey, or if you are more."

His eyes locked on Ben's throat.

Ben braced, trembling but defiant.

The hunger of a god and the weight of the watchers closed in together, and the chamber felt smaller than breath. Camazotz dropped from the air like a blade. His wings snapped shut, his claws clamped Ben's shoulders, and before Ben could wrench free, fangs punched into his neck.

The pain was blinding.

White light burst behind his eyes. Ben gasped, choking on the sudden flood of weakness. His knees buckled. His body convulsed as if struck by lightning, then went limp.

Camazotz drank.

The sound was obscene—wet gulps, animal and greedy. His jaw worked, saliva mixing with the blood that pulsed into his mouth. His throat convulsed, swallowing again and again, the sound echoing in the small chamber.

Ben's vision blurred.

His body unfurled, unravelling from the inside out. His arms dangled, his breath rasped shallow, his heart hammering weaker with every pulse. The world narrowed to the rhythm of being drained—beat, beat, weaker beat.

The others pressed closer. He could feel them crowding the chamber, unseen but heavy, their presences curling around the moment like vultures tasting the air—each a silent witness.

Camazotz shuddered in ecstasy. His wings flared wide, trembling. "Yes," he hissed against Ben's skin, voice muffled by the feeding. "The taste... the taste of night itself!"

Ben's legs gave way. He sagged in the god's grasp, the edges of his vision blackening. His heart staggered, stuttered—then faltered.

The moment came. The moment of collapse. The final beat before silence.

And then—

It reversed.

Ben's heart convulsed, not outward, but inward. A suction, a reversal of flow. His veins tightened, muscles clenched, lungs seized. Blood rushed back, pulled into him as if the river had changed its mind.

Camazotz jerked back with a snarl, still latched to the wound.

The suction drew not just Ben's blood, but the god's saliva, his hunger, his essence. The mixture burned like liquid fire pouring back into Ben's veins.

Ben screamed.

The sound split stone. His body arched, every nerve lit aflame as knowledge, power, thirst, and darkness crashed into him. The watchers stirred—he felt their attention sharpen, heavy as gravity.

Camazotz struggled, wings flapping desperately. His claws dug into Ben's shoulders, but he was no longer feeding. He was being pulled. His eyes widened in shock, fangs locked into a bond he couldn't break.

Ben's heart beat again, backward, harder. With each thump, he drew more. Power rushed in—the echo of jungle nights filled with rivers of bats, the taste of warm blood fresh from the throat, the weight of ancient temples and obsidian altars. He felt it all—knowledge of shadows, of silence, of how to vanish where light falls.

Camazotz wailed. The sound was shrill, pained, alien. His small frame shrank further, his leathery skin crumpling like parchment left in fire. His wings withered, membranes tearing, shrivelling. His eyes dulled, flames guttering out.

Ben staggered, his throat still clamped by the god's fangs, but now he held upright not from strength but from the storm raging inside. He felt his blood swell, thick with something more than life. He was no longer drained—he was filling, overflowing.

The final pull came with a crack of bone and tendon. Camazotz's mouth tore free, his body shrivelled and collapsed. He fell to the stone floor a dried husk, limbs curled inward, his leathery face shrunk into a grotesque skull-mask. His wings hung in tatters, too frail to move.

Silence followed, broken only by Ben's ragged breathing.

The ethereals pressed closer still. He felt them like a thousand hands brushing his skin, testing, measuring, approving or condemning—he couldn't tell. Their weight nearly drove him to his knees.

Ben wiped his mouth with a trembling hand. His own blood stained his lips, thick, metallic—but beneath it, he tasted something else. Bitter. Ancient. Sweet in its rot. Camazotz. His wound still wept, but no longer weakly. The blood that seeped was thick, dark, alive with something unnatural. He pressed his palm to it and felt it pulse—not like a wound, but like a second heart.

The husk at his feet twitched once, then lay still.

Ben's eyes burned.

He blinked—and the chamber dimmed.

Not dimmed, exactly. It shifted. The shadows lengthened, bent toward him. The air itself recoiled from the thin lines of moonlight cutting through cracks in the stone.

He understood. Not fully, not clearly, but enough. Camazotz had meant to drink him dry. Instead, the exchange had inverted. His blood had returned richer, weighted with shadow and hunger. He had not been drained. He had been remade.

Ben lifted his head. The chamber no longer felt like a cage. It felt like a threshold.

The presence lingered. He sensed them whispering, though not with words. The weight pressed against his skull, and in their silence, he understood one thing—this was only the beginning.

They pressed close.

The weight was unbearable, a parliament of silences crushing into him—they hovered at the edges of his perception, thick as smoke, heavy as ocean pressure. He could feel their attention not only on him, but on the dead god at his feet, as if measuring the cost. His skull ached with the force of their scrutiny.

Then the door groaned.

Stone shifted, light spilled in, and footsteps followed.

Athena entered first, carefully, walking stick raised, gleaming faintly in the dark. Fiona drifted behind her, cloak loose, a single coin rolling and vanishing between her fingers even as her face was pale, lips parted.

They stopped short. The sight before them was not what they had expected.

The withered husk of Camazotz, dried to parchment. The walls stripped of sigils, their power spent. And Ben—blood at his throat, shadows crawling at his shoulders, eyes lit with something neither human nor divine.

Athena dropped an inch, her mask of composure cracking. Her eyes, colder than stone, widened in rare disbelief.

Fiona pressed the coin flat to her palm, her knuckles white. Awe and terror warred in her gaze, her usual smile gone. "By the wheel," she whispered. "He drank him."

Ben swayed, fists clenched, still trembling. He turned toward them, lips parting as if to explain, but no words came. The shadows clung too tightly, whispering in his ears.

Athena took one sharp step forward. "What happened here?"

Ben's throat ached, his voice raw. "He tried to take my blood. It turned. I... I pulled him into me."

Fiona inhaled sharply, as though stabbed. She closed her eyes for a moment, then opened them again, gaze locked not on Ben but on the air around him.

"Do you feel them, Athena? The room is swollen."

Athena's jaw tightened. Her hand shifted on her stick, but not in threat—more in unease. Her gaze swept the chamber. "Yes. They are here. Many. Too many."

The weight grew heavier. The others pressed harder now, drawn not just to Ben but to the two goddesses as witnesses. The chamber thickened with silence until even breathing felt like an intrusion.

Ben clenched his jaw, speaking through the pressure. "They've been watching me all along. But this—" He gestured to the husk. "This pulled them closer."

Athena's gaze snapped back to him. Her eyes narrowed, hard and assessing, but her voice was quiet. "You should be dead."

Fiona tilted her head, her coin dancing again, though her hand shook. "And yet he isn't. He carries the bat's hunger now. And something more."

She stepped closer, ignoring the weight that made the air crackle. "The ethereals marked this moment, Athena. They pressed into it. They pressed into him."

Athena's knuckles whitened. "He is an aberration. Nothing stable survives such a mixture."

Ben met her eyes. "I'm standing, aren't I?"

The silence deepened. Secrets whispered at the edge of hearing. Athena's eyes flickered—not fear, but something close to it. Recognition.

Fiona exhaled, her voice soft. "They are all here. Together. When was the last time that happened, Athena?"

Athena's jaw worked. "Never." The word hung like a verdict.

Fiona's coin spun once, caught the dim light, and vanished. Her gaze never left him. "He drank a god. He lived. And now the ethereals gather. This changes everything."

Athena's face hardened, mask snapping back into place, though her eyes betrayed the truth: awe, and a trace of dread. She lowered her walking stick, not as a gesture of trust, but because she knew it would be useless against what stood before her.

Ben swallowed hard, his throat burning. "Then tell me what I am."

Neither answered.

The ethereals pressed down on the chamber, so heavy even Athena staggered, her stick clattering against the stone. Fiona dropped her coin. It rang once, sharp as thunder, then rolled into the husk of Camazotz and stopped. Ben swayed, his shadow-wrapped body trembling under the pressure. His heart pounded backward and forward all at once, echoing with the strange rhythm he had stolen from the bat-god.

Then the silence spoke.

Not in words. Not in mortal tongues. Not even in the voices gods used to argue across council chambers. The sound was older, stripped of ornament, delivered like a commandment carved into the marrow of existence. The chamber itself groaned. The stone vibrated. Even the husk of Camazotz twitched as if trying to crawl away from the weight of the revelation.

Athena fell to one knee, eyes wide, lips parted, though no words came. Fiona's hands rose instinctively to her ears, though there was nothing to hear. It was not sound. It was knowing.

Ben's body convulsed. He gasped as the idea poured into him.

Champion

The word—no, the decree—struck through him. His bones shook with it. The ethereals were not offering. They were declaring. He was not asked. He was named.

Fiona staggered back, gasping. "They chose him."

Athena snarled, voice breaking under the strain. "Impossible. He is mortal. He is aberrant. He is unshaped."

The silence struck again, harder, and this time even the gods cried out.

Starfarer

Images slammed into their minds: vessels of steel cutting through oceans of night, fragile hulls bearing generations of humanity toward new suns; cities suspended above barren worlds, fed not by earth but by light; children born in orbit, laughing in the weightless dark. Humanity scattered across the stars like sparks blown from a dying fire.

Ben fell to his knees, clutching his skull, but the images did not stop. He saw the earth collapsing—seas boiling, forests burning, cities sinking under storms. The skeleton armies rising were only the beginning. The collapse was complete, a cleansing fire that would strip the planet bare.

Failure

The word hammered into the chamber, heavier than stone, and the gods gasped as if stabbed. Athena trembled. Fiona's cloak whipped in an unseen wind.

Ben's vision swam. He saw not with eyes but with the raw perception the ethereals forced into him—gods standing in their marble halls, bickering, wielding storms and oceans like toys; wars prolonged, famines ignored, chances squandered. Again and again, the gods had chosen spectacle over stewardship, rule over growth.

The message seared itself into him: The gods had failed to make this world fit for its children.

And so it must be cleansed.

Cleansing, Evolution, Ascent

Ben gasped, shadow pouring from his mouth like smoke. His body arched, veins burning with words not his own. "They're in my head," his voice cracked. "I can't get them out!"

Lead humans through the collapse. The world will die—live among the stars.

Athena lurched to her feet—eyes wild. "Blasphemy! We are the guardians. We are balance. We—" The thoughts struck her down. She slammed into the stone, and blood trickled from her mouth.

Fiona fell to her knees beside her, tears on her cheeks, though she didn't sob. Her eyes stared wide at nothing. "They're right. We have failed. We clutched at worship, not balance. We smothered the seed instead of letting it grow."

The thoughts pressed harder, the message final, undeniable:

Cleanse

The shadows on Ben's body writhed, alive, clinging tighter. His breath came ragged, his heart hammering forward and backward, backward and forward. He felt full, too full, his veins bursting with borrowed knowledge and hunger.

The silence began to lift. Slowly, painfully, like gravity easing. The weight retreated. But the knowing remained. Athena dragged herself upright, though her arm trembled. Her eyes locked on Ben, no longer just with contempt, but with dread.

"Who are you?" she said, voice ragged. "They have never interfered before. Not once. Not in all the turning of ages."

Fiona rose behind her, pale but resolute. "And yet they have now." She looked at Ben with a strange mixture of pity and wonder.

Ben swayed, shadows bleeding from his skin, blood drying on his throat. His voice was hoarse, but steady. “I don't want this.”

“I don't think you have a choice,” Athena said, her tone sharpening again.

Fiona shook her head, almost gently. “And if he does nothing, humanity dies with the world. The cleansing won’t stop.”

Ben knelt on the cold stone, hands shaking, breath scraping his lungs raw. The words still burned through him—*Champion. Cleanse. Stars.*—each one lodged like a shard beneath his ribs. He could feel them waiting for assent.

He laughed once—a short, broken sound.

“No,” he whispered.

Chapter 13
The Nuke

The warhead fell like an iron prayer.

High above the Atlas, the bomber banked into cloud, its payload already released. The sky trembled, and then the world went white.

Silence first. Radios died mid-word, rifles clicked into nothing, even the groan of the mountain stilled as if stone itself dared not speak. Then came the light—brighter than lightning, more chromatic than any dawn—a sphere of fury that erased shadow, erased depth, erased mercy. The bomb touched down in the valley where Lilith's host marched. For a single impossible second, the army ceased to exist. Bone and bronze dissolved, skeletons shattered into motes of dust, shields warped into liquid metal. The blast rolled outward in rings, faster than thought, flattening ridges, snapping juniper, flinging men across terraces like ragdolls.

Ari planted his boots into the stone, sword stabbed into the earth as an anchor. His grin shone through the glare, feral even as the shockwave split his lips. This was war as it should be: decisive, uncompromising, final.

Pele crouched beside him, her molten gaze narrowed. Heat was her blood, yet this was not heat. It was theft—sunfire stolen from the heavens and bottled by mortals, then cracked open in arrogance. She felt it gouge the mountain's memory, not nourishing, not cleansing—only scarring.

Zed did not flinch. Stormlight rimmed his one eye, dim against the whiteout. His crow screeched and burrowed into his neck. "They've stolen thunder and called it theirs," he muttered, staff vibrating in his grip.

The shockwave passed.

Where once had been a valley, there was only glass. Black and green, fused and smoking. Bones that had stood in formation were now shadows burned into rock.

The air roared with radiation, invisible and merciless.

On the ridges, soldiers stared in awe. Some cheered hoarsely. Some crossed themselves. Some wept. "It's done," whispered a lieutenant, his voice ragged. "Nothing could live in that."

Ari spat blood into the dust and bellowed, "Forward! See with your own eyes that hunger can burn!" But hunger had not burned.

The glass cracked.

A hand erupted first—bone blackened, sinew fused like tar, sockets burning with cobalt fire. Then another, and another. Shapes clawed from molten pits, dragging themselves upright. These were no longer mere skeletons. They had been cooked, charred, and reforged by the blast. Their armour fused to their frames, their weapons melted into claws and spikes. They were revenants now—half ash, half bone, all rage. Their jaws no longer clattered. They screamed.

From the vapour, shapes less solid gathered: whorls of smoke, drifting tatters of ash, the imprint of skeletons annihilated utterly. The warhead had stripped them of bone and bronze, but not of will. Lilith's hunger gave them a new form. They rose as wraiths, translucent and trembling, their eyes two points of malignant glow. They hovered above the revenants, keening in a pitch that froze the men's marrow.

Lilith emerged at their heart, untouched. The fire had bent around her. Her white dress was unmarked, her braids precise, her hands still empty. She walked across the glass as if it were polished marble.

"Your sunfire is mine," she said, her voice carrying without echo. "What you destroy, I inherit. What you burn, I breathe. What you strip bare, I clothe in hunger."

On the ridges, panic rippled through the mortal lines. Some soldiers broke, bolting down the slopes. Others dropped to their knees, their rifles sliding from numb fingers. One captain screamed orders that no one heard over the wraiths' keening.

Ari's laughter cracked across the chaos, sharp and mad. "Better! Harder! A fight worth bleeding for!" He tore his sword from the stone and pointed it at the glass valley below. "Form ranks! You are not done until I am!"

The colonel beside him forced his throat open, repeating the command in Arabic. Slowly, shakily, men rallied, dragging comrades to their feet, fumbling for magazines, resetting machine guns. Their ears still rang from the blast, but War's voice cut through where radios could not.

Pele rose, her body shuddering as if the bomb had passed through her skin as well as stone. She pressed her palms to the ridge, feeling the scars in the mountain. Lava answered faintly, sluggish, unsteady.

“They are wrong,” she said through her teeth. “This was supposed to end them.”

“It never ends,” Zed replied, his eye storm-dark. Lightning flickered weakly between his knuckles. “It changes shape.”

Below, the revenants screamed again and advanced, their fused forms clattering across glass. The wraiths swept ahead, insubstantial yet suffocating, their voices a knife-edge across the mind.

Lilith smiled, serene, inevitable.

The Atlas trembled.

The revenants hit the line like battering rams.

Charred bones fused with slag armour formed shields that sent men flying. Machine guns rattled, chewing holes through torsos—but the things didn’t stop. Bullets cracked off plates of glassy bone, sparks showering as they pressed forward, clawing, screaming.

Above them, the wraiths swept in a shrieking cloud. Bullets tore through the smoke, finding nothing.

A dozen men dropped their weapons, clutching at their own throats, gagging on phantom hands. Their eyes rolled white as shadows coiled into their mouths. They hit the ground convulsing, and when the spasms stopped, their bodies rose again—eyes hollow, skin grey, jaws slack.

Zombies.

Lilith raised her hand once, and the newly dead staggered to her side, turning their rifles on their former comrades. The line buckled.

Ari barrelled forward with a roar, his sword cleaving a revenant from skull to pelvis. The creature split in two, sparks spilling from molten seams.

For a heartbeat, men cheered. But Lilith only gestured. The corpse twitched, its halves clawing at the ground until they fused again, crawling upright.

Ari spat dust, laughter breaking in his throat. "Then I'll kill it twice!"

Pele threw both hands skyward. The ground cracked, lava spearing upward in jets that turned revenants to brittle statues. For a moment, the battlefield glowed with her fury—a volcanic storm tearing through the enemy. But where bone collapsed to ash, wraiths rose from it, streaming into the night with screams sharp enough to cut flesh.

The mortals faltered. A gunner swivelled his machine gun to cut down a cluster of revenants, shredding them into fragments—then watched in horror as the fragments shivered, twisted, and crawled back together. The revenants screamed louder, hungrier, reforged by his effort.

Zed stepped forward. He slammed his staff into the ridge. Lightning raked the battlefield, striking wraiths, revenants, and humans alike, reducing dozens to slag. For an instant, silence reigned.

The crow shrieked approval.

Then the fallen mortals stirred. Their bodies, still smoking from lightning, rose with sockets glowing faint blue.

Lilith extended her hand.

The lightning had not killed them—it had delivered them. "You feed me," she said, her voice calm, intimate. "Every death is mine."

The mortal line cracked. A squad fled, dropping rifles, stumbling up the ridge. Others followed, panic rippling through the ranks. The colonel bellowed, striking his men with the flat of his gun to hold them steady. Some listened. More didn't.

"Stand!" Ari roared, cutting down another revenant. "Every step back is a gift to her! Stand with me!"

A few rallied, pulling themselves into a ragged line. They braced with guns, firing, stabbing, shouting their own names as if daring death to remember them. But every gap they left was filled with the walking dead.

Pele collapsed to one knee, her body cracked and glowing, steam rising from her skin. She forced herself upright again, lava dripping from her hands. "I can hold them—a little longer."

"You'll break," Zed warned.

"Then I'll burn breaking!" She flung fire into the revenants pressing the ridge, incinerating dozens. The rest screamed louder, ash fusing into their seams, their forms hardening against her fire.

Wraiths streamed upward, spilling over the ridge, keening in a chorus that made men's ears bleed. Shadows wrapped around helmets, slipped into mouths, drove soldiers mad. They stabbed at their comrades, eyes glazed, voices stolen.

Lilith smiled, watching her army swell. "Each victory you claim is mine. Each hero you make, I inherit. How long before you see you fight only for me?"

Ari charged at her, hacking through revenants, kicking a wraith back with a snarl. He leapt onto the glass floor, his sword raised high. "Then I'll kill you, and everything falls with you!"

Lilith caught his blade with her knife. Sparks shrieked. She met his eyes with something close to pity.

"You cannot kill what you feed."

She shoved, and Ari flew backward, slamming into the ridge wall hard enough to crater stone. He dragged himself upright, coughing blood, still laughing.

"You'll choke on me yet."

The revenants pressed harder. Mortals screamed as the line broke for the last time. Entire companies scattered, cut down, and risen again within minutes. The ridge became a slaughterhouse, the air thick with smoke, screams, and the metallic stench of rebirth.

Zed raised his staff one final time, stormlight blazing, thunder cracking so loud it silenced the battlefield. Lightning fell in sheets, scouring hundreds into ash. For a moment, the dead army was gone.

Then the ash rose.

Wraiths coalesced from it, shrieking in triumph. The fallen mortals stirred and stood, blue light in their sockets. Lilith's hand lifted, and the battlefield belonged to her again.

Pele staggered, her body dimming, her fire guttering. Zed swayed, his crow limp on his shoulder. Ari, blood-soaked and grinning, stood ready but could not deny the truth.

They were losing.

"Retreat," Zed said, his voice flat, final.

Ari snarled. "Not yet—"

"Now," Pele hissed. She grabbed his arm, her molten skin searing his flesh. "If we stay, we become hers."

The colonel, bleeding and half-blind, gave the same order. "Fall back! Pull everything back!"

The gods turned. Mortals stumbled with them, dragging wounded, firing blind over their shoulders. The wraiths shrieked in pursuit, revenants clambered up shattered ridges, skeletons clattered after them, and zombies dragged themselves through the dust.

The Atlas shook under their flight.

Lilith did not chase. She raised both hands, and her army—wraiths shrieking, revenants howling, skeletons clattering, zombies moaning—filled the valley in a tide of hunger.

She smiled, serene as ever.

The gods had retreated.

The mountain belonged to her.

The mountain groaned as they climbed, dust spilling from shattered ridges, the air acrid with smoke and radiation.

Behind them, the valley boiled with Lilith's new legion—a tide of revenants screaming, wraiths keening, skeletons clattering, and zombies shambling forward in endless ranks.

The gods did not look back. Not yet. Looking back meant stopping, and stopping meant joining her.

Ari stumbled up the slope, sword dragging sparks against stone. His body was a map of wounds—a cracked rib, a shattered forearm, blood matting his hair. Yet his grin still glimmered through the grime, feral and defiant.

"That," he coughed, "was a fight worth remembering."

"You nearly became hers," Pele snapped, staggering beside him.

Her skin was fissured with glowing seams, lava-light bleeding from the cracks. Each step sent steam hissing from her feet as though she were burning herself alive with every motion. "Keep laughing, and she'll claim you sooner than you think."

Ari spat red into the dust. "Then she'll choke on me."

Zed said nothing. He leaned heavily on his staff, his crow limp on his shoulder, its feathers singed and eyes dull. His one eye glowed faintly, but the stormlight had dimmed to embers. His breathing was shallow, every step deliberate, as though he feared his bones might forget how to move.

Mortals trudged with them—ragged, terrified, broken. What had begun as companies and brigades was now handfuls of survivors, dragging the wounded, carrying comrades who moaned in delirium. Some stared blankly, their eyes haunted by the sight of comrades struck down only to rise again as enemies. Others wept openly, rifles clutched uselessly to their chests.

The colonel staggered near the gods, his uniform blackened, his arm in a crude sling. He met Ari's grin with a hollow stare. "We are finished. My men—there is nothing left to fight with."

"Then we'll steal more hours," Ari growled, though his voice cracked. He glanced down the slope, watching the faint glow of wraiths swirling in the valley like fireflies of ash. His grin faltered for the first time.

"They are not hours anymore," Zed said quietly. "They are breaths. And each one costs more than the last."

They reached a plateau where the mountain levelled for a stretch. Mortals collapsed there, gasping, coughing, some clutching wounds that would not heal. Medics worked with trembling hands, bandaging with rags, pouring canteens into mouths already cold. The night wind carried the cries of the dying up the slopes, mingling with the faint shrieks of wraiths below.

Pele sank to her knees, her palms pressed into the stone. She tried to summon heat, but the mountain gave her only silence. Her flames guttered, the seams in her body dimming. She coughed up smoke and bent forward, her shoulders shaking.

Zed laid a hand on her back. "No more tonight."

Her molten eyes lifted to his. "If I stop, we lose what little distance we've gained."

"If you burn yourself out now," he said, "you become her fuel. That is worse than any loss."

Ari dropped heavily onto a rock, sword across his knees, chest heaving. He laughed once, sharp and bitter. "So what now? We retreat until there's no mountain left to climb?"

Zed's gaze turned skyward. The storm above was thinning, clouds drifting apart to reveal faint stars behind the smoke. "We wait," he said. "We gather what remains. And we prepare for the next wound."

Pele's fists clenched. "She has an army no weapon can stop. The bomb only made her stronger. My fire feeds her. Your storm feeds her. Even your war feeds her."

"Then we change the fight," Ari said, his grin returning faintly. "If steel and fire and storm won't kill her, we find what will. Every god has a breaking point. So does hunger."

"Perhaps," Zed murmured. His voice was flat, heavy. "Or perhaps hunger's only limit is when it eats everything."

The colonel stepped forward, his face pale, eyes hollow. "We cannot stand again. My men are finished. Even if you are gods, fight on; mortals will not follow."

Ari rose, leaning on his sword, his expression wild and furious. "Then tell them they don't need to win—only to deny her for as long as they breathe."

Pele glared at him. "You would spend them all, just to spite her?"

"That's war," Ari snapped. "You bleed, you break, you stand anyway. Every step back is surrender."

Zed's staff struck the rock, the sound silencing them. His eye glowed faintly, stormlight pulsing with weariness. "Enough. You saw what she became tonight. For every man we kill, she gains another. For every victory, she grows. This is not a battle we can win. Not now."

Silence settled over the plateau. The mortals listened, their shoulders slumping, their faces hollow. The gods' words weighed heavier than their wounds.

Finally, Ari spat into the dirt. "Then we'll retreat. But it won't be a surrender. It will be buying time until we find her end."

Zed nodded, his eye closing briefly. "If she has one."

Below them, the valley glowed faintly with the light of burning bones. Wraiths drifted in spirals above the glassy floor, their keening echoing up the cliffs. Revenants clawed at the rock, testing their ascent. Skeletons reformed in ranks, and zombies moaned as they fed. Lilith stood at the centre, serene, untouched, her white dress shining in the smoke. She raised both hands, and the chorus of hunger answered her.

Ari's grip tightened on his sword. "Next time," he whispered, "I'll carve the smile from her face." But even he could not silence the truth pressing in on them all: tonight, they had not beaten her back. Tonight, they had only escaped.

The glass valley hummed with hunger.

Lilith stood at its centre, bare feet on the molten stone that had cooled beneath her. The white folds of her dress fluttered in the poisoned wind, but ash did not cling, and smoke refused to stain. She inhaled deeply. What others would call radiation—death in invisible particles—tasted to her like wine. It lingered on her tongue, sweet and acrid, promising more.

She looked upon what remained of her army. Once they had been skeletons—crude shapes reanimated by her will—now they were refined. The bomb had tested them, scoured them, broken them—and in doing so, revealed their truer form. The revenants crouched in rows, fused bone and slag armour crackling faintly as if still cooling. Their eyes blazed cobalt, their mouths stretched wider than before, their screams now war cries. They beat their claws against their chests, eager, insatiable.

Above, the wraiths circled in endless gyres, translucent wings of smoke unfurling with each shriek. They were her new voice.

They carried terror into the marrow of every living thing, and their keening harmonised with the mountain until it trembled like an instrument tuned to her hand.

The remnants of her original host—skeletons shattered but re-formed—stood in ranks still, their discipline unbroken. Clattering jaws no longer mimicked life but celebrated un-life. And the zombies... Ah, the zombies were her favourites tonight. Fresh from mortal flesh, they stumbled forward with rifles clutched in crooked hands, faces slack but eyes glowing with her mark. The gods had fought for hours to keep those men alive. Now their loyalty was hers without question.

Lilith smiled faintly.

She turned slowly, gazing up the ridges where the gods had fled.

"Run," she whispered, her voice soft but carrying through the ash. "Run and gather yourselves. Bring more soldiers, more weapons, more gods if you can. Each hour you delay is another feast for me."

The revenants howled in answer. The wraiths shrieked overhead. Zombies moaned, their voices broken but obedient.

Lilith lifted her hands, and they fell silent.

She looked east, toward the desert, where the air shimmered with heat. She looked west, toward the Atlantic, where storms gathered beyond the horizon. Both paths called to her, but she did not need to choose yet. Her hunger would decide for her when the time came.

For now, she knelt.

Her palm pressed against the glass floor of the valley. She closed her eyes, feeling the pulse beneath the rock.

The Atlas was old. It remembered. Once it had borne the weight of empires, tonight it had borne a sunfire wound. Tomorrow, it would bear her will.

The fissures whispered to her.

Through them, she felt the dead buried in these mountains—tribes, caravans, armies that had marched and perished on these passes for millennia. She felt them stir as she called. The revenants screamed in answer, the wraiths shivered, the zombies moaned, but beneath them all came another sound: the restless rumble of thousands more dead shifting in their shallow graves.

Her smile widened. She lifted her arms towards the night. The gods had retreated. The mortals were broken, and the Atlas was hers.

"Hunger does not stop," she said, her voice echoing across the peaks. "It spreads."

She turned her gaze to the cities beyond the horizon. Marrakesh, Rabat, Casablanca—places where mortals huddled still believing walls and governments could save them. She tasted their fear already, a spice sharper than fire, richer than blood.

Her army howled again, a single note that rattled the stars.

The march would begin at dawn.

ACT IV: THE BELLS OF HELL

Chapter 14

The Trickster

The ice had learned how to wait.

It had held for centuries beneath pressure it did not understand, bearing weight, memory, and old authority without complaint. But now it groaned—not loudly, not yet—just enough to announce that patience was ending.

Light leaked from the fractures in thin, uneven lines, pale as moonlight filtered through bone. The glyphs carved into the cavern walls dimmed one by one, as if embarrassed to still be glowing.

Rus stood at the edge of the seal, shoulders squared, breath slow but tight. He could feel it slipping—not the ice, not yet, but the order beneath it.

"You don't know what you're doing," he said.

His voice carried, firm and practised. He had said these words before. Perhaps not here. Perhaps not like this. But the cadence was familiar—the voice of someone who had always believed there was a line that would not be crossed.

Demi did not look at him. Her hands were already raised, thin threads of pale fire weaving between her fingers, precise and controlled. Fear trembled through the magic anyway.

"He isn't whole," she said, eyes fixed on Ben. "And whatever is bound behind that ice—"

She swallowed. "—will know that."

Ben stood still. The shadow beneath his skin was quiet. It no longer pressed. It no longer whispered. It simply occupied, settled like something that had unpacked and decided to stay.

Fiona rolled the coin across her knuckles, caught it, and closed her hand around it. "This stopped being a debate a while ago," she said.

The ice answered her. A low crack ran through the glacier, branching fast and jagged, light spilling through it like breath escaping a lung. The cavern shuddered. Frost exploded outward, mist rolling across the floor in a cold wave that bit deep and fast.

Something moved inside the haze. Not emerging. Arriving.

A fox stepped out of the mist. Small. Neat. Fur shifting subtly in colour—copper, silver, hints of aurora caught beneath frost. It padded forward with unhurried confidence and sat on the ice as if it had always belonged there.

Golden eyes swept the chamber.

"Well," a voice said. It came from everywhere. Not loud. Not echoing. Perfectly placed. "This took long enough."

Rus moved instantly, feet bracing, weight shifting forward. "Back into the ice," he snapped. "You'll not walk free."

The fox looked at him. Actually looked. "Oh," it said mildly. "You're still pretending."

A smile crept into the voice. "That's charming." It rose and took a few steps closer, claws clicking faintly against the frozen floor. "You know, I always wondered—did they tell you guarding me mattered, or did you tell yourselves that to get through the centuries?"

Rus said nothing.

The fox's attention drifted past him, over Demi, who stiffened under the gaze, then settled briefly on Fiona.

"Ah," it said. "Luck still pretending it's neutral."

Fiona met the stare evenly. "You're loose because the board is already cracked."

The fox's grin widened. "Exactly."

Then its gaze found Ben. And stayed there. The voice changed—not warmer, not softer. Sharper. Focused. "Well now," it said. "There you are."

Ben did not move.

The fox circled him slowly, steps soundless, eyes bright with interest.

"Hello, Shade," Loki said pleasantly.

The word settled heavily in the air. Not an insult. Not a joke. A name. Fiona felt the weight of it immediately. Demi flinched. Rus frowned, as if something had slid into place without his permission.

"They are not monsters," Loki continued. "Just devils."

A small, thoughtful pause. "The inconvenient sort."

He leaned closer, sniffing once, sharp and deliberate. "Mm. Yes. You reek of consequence."

Ben met his gaze. Calm. Unflinching.

Loki's eyes flicked back to him.

"Tell me," he said conversationally, "when fire comes to a field—"

The glacier groaned again, deeper now.

"—do the rabbits survive..."

A beat. "...or the horses?"

Silence slammed down. The question hung there, naked and cruel.

Ben did not answer. He held the fox's gaze without offering anything back. No flinch. No irritation. No tell.

Loki watched him a moment longer, then gave a small, satisfied exhale—almost a chuckle. "Good," he murmured. "Stillness is rare."

Rus stepped forward despite himself. "What are you playing at?"

Loki glanced at him lazily. "A game you can't win."

Fiona's coin rolled once across her knuckles and stopped. "You didn't break your cage to test us," she said calmly. "And you didn't announce yourself to walk back into the dark."

Loki's ears flicked.

"You came because something shifted," Fiona continued. "And you intend to see it through."

A small pause. "So don't pretend this is a choice."

Silence.

The fox studied her—not amused now, but measuring.

Then the smile returned. "Oh, Fortuna," Loki said softly. "You always did understand timing."

"I was never leaving."

His gaze drifted back to Ben. "And because I want to see which of you burns first."

The ice split again, louder this time.

Rus took another step forward, anger shaking loose from restraint. "Answer me. What are you doing?"

Loki slowly turned his head toward him, as if remembering that Rus existed. "Oh," Loki said. "You again."

Rus's jaw tightened. "You're not walking out of here."

Loki blinked, languid. "I wasn't aware I needed your permission."

Demi's fire threads snapped tighter between her fingers. "Stop playing. What do you want?"

Loki's ears flicked. "Want is a human word. It's messy. It implies hunger."

He rose again, unhurried, and padded a few steps across the ice as though the cavern were a private lounge. The light beneath the glacier caught his fur, turning it briefly into something that didn't belong in nature.

"I prefer *intent*," Loki continued. "Intent is clean. Intent is what people do when they stop lying to themselves."

His gaze slid to Fiona. "And you, Fortuna, are already lying less than usual."

Fiona's coin rolled across her knuckles once and stopped under her thumb. "If you're staying, state your terms."

Loki laughed. "Terms."

He looked delighted by the concept. "Do you hear yourself? You've been surrounded by councils so long you've started speaking like them."

Fiona's eyes did not move. "I don't negotiate with councils. I negotiate with realities."

Loki's grin sharpened. "And what reality is that?"

Fiona nodded once toward Ben. "That he exists. That she exists. That the board is breaking whether we like it or not."

Loki's eyes drifted to Ben again, lingering with obvious enjoyment. "Devils," he repeated, tasting the word.

Demi's voice cut in, defensive. "Stop calling them that."

Loki didn't even look at her. "I'll call them what they are."

He turned to Ben, conversational. "Do you know why they hate that word?"

Ben didn't answer.

So Loki answered for him.

"Because *devil* means you don't belong in their categories," Loki said. "Not servant. Not sovereign. Not pet. Not priest."

Rus's fists clenched. "You're baiting him."

Loki glanced at Rus with mild amusement. "No. I'm naming him."

He looked back at Ben. "They'll tell themselves you're a mistake," Loki murmured. "A fluke. A fever. A crack in the math."

His tail flicked once. "But you know what you are, don't you?"

Ben's voice was calm. "I'm someone you should stop talking to."

Loki's grin widened, delighted. "There it is." He came closer—not threatening, but deliberate—closing the distance the way a man does when he wants the other person to feel that there *is* distance.

"Listen to me," Loki said softly. "I talk because talking is a blade. And I have always enjoyed knives."

Ben didn't move.

Loki's eyes glinted. "I'm not here to worship you. I'm not here to leash you. I'm not here to save you."

Fiona's coin clicked once in her palm.

Loki glanced sideways at her. "And I'm certainly not here because you asked nicely."

He turned back to Ben. "I'm here because something has changed," Loki said. "Something that even the council can't pretend is stable anymore."

He sat again, composed. "You killed one of them, and drank another."

Rus went rigid. Demi's fire faltered for half a heartbeat. Fiona didn't flinch—only watched.

Ben's expression didn't change. "They tried to kill me."

Loki shrugged. "They always do."

He said it like a bored truth. Like gravity. Then he smiled. "But you survived it."

He tilted his head. "And survival is contagious."

A crack split the glacier behind them with a sound like a bone breaking in slow motion. The cavern shuddered. Fine snow sifted down from above.

Loki listened to the sound with faint pleasure, then looked back at Fiona.

"You want terms?" he said.

Fiona held his gaze. "Yes."

Loki's tone became almost cordial. "Very well."

He lifted one paw, as if counting on invisible fingers. "First," Loki said, "I don't answer to your council."

Fiona's mouth tightened. "Noted."

"Second," Loki continued, "I don't take orders from devils."

His eyes flicked to Ben and back. "I find it healthier when everyone keeps their hands off my leash."

Ben's jaw flexed.

"Third," Loki said, voice brightening, "I don't do loyalty. I do proximity."

Fiona narrowed her eyes. "Meaning?"

"Meaning I'll be close enough to see what happens," Loki said. "Close enough to interfere if I feel like it. Close enough to profit from the fallout."

Demi spat, "You admit it."

Loki smiled at her at last. "Sweetheart, I admit everything. The only people who hide are the ones ashamed of their motives."

He returned to Fiona. "Now your turn. Your terms."

Fiona didn't hesitate. "You don't touch him."

Loki's grin twitched. "Touch is vague."

Fiona's voice sharpened. "No trials. No games. No nudges. No 'questions' that leave him bleeding from the inside."

Loki's eyes glittered with amusement, but something else sat behind it—measurement. Calculation.

"And if I do?" he asked.

Fiona smiled without warmth. "Then you'll learn what happens when luck stops smiling."

Loki laughed quietly. "Oh, Fortuna. You do have style."

He looked at Ben. "And you, devil—what are your terms?"

Ben's answer was immediate. "You don't use me."

Loki's ears flicked, as if amused by the audacity.

Ben continued, calm and flat. "You can walk beside us. You can talk. You can watch. But you don't get to steer."

Loki stared at him for a long moment. Then he smiled. A slow, pleased smile.

"That," Loki said softly, "is the first sensible thing anyone's said to me in a long time."

He rose once more and padded to the cavern mouth, where the mist thinned and the Siberian night pressed cold against the world. He looked out into the dark as if checking the weather.

"Fine," Loki said. "Proximity it is."

He glanced back at them, golden eyes bright. "But understand something."

He paused. "If the world burns, it won't be because I lit it." His grin sharpened. "It'll be because devils don't like cages."

The glacier groaned behind them like a living thing waking up. And for the first time, it felt believable—not like a deal, not like a pact—but like three trajectories crossing because the universe had run out of ways to keep them apart.

They did not leave immediately. No one suggested it. No one ordered it. The cavern simply *held* them, as if the glacier itself wanted to hear what came next.

Loki remained near the mouth of the chamber, his silhouette cut against the faint blue spill of ice-light beyond. He looked outward, tail still, posture loose, like a man leaning against a balcony rail while a city burned somewhere below.

Rus broke first. "You expect us to accept this," he said, voice rough. "You expect us to walk away and pretend this—" he gestured sharply between Ben and the fox, "—isn't treason."

Loki didn't turn around. "Treason is a word invented by people who think the world owes them permanence."

Rus took another step. "You were imprisoned for a reason."

Loki finally glanced back, eyes gleaming. "So were storms."

Demi's fire flared brighter. "You twist everything."

Loki's ears twitched. "Only what's already brittle."

He turned fully now, padding back toward them with lazy confidence. "Let me tell you something about cages," he said conversationally. "They don't fail because of strength. They fail because someone eventually notices the bars were built for a different creature."

He stopped a few paces from Ben.

Up close, the fox felt wrong—not threatening, not overwhelming, just *uncomfortable*. Like standing too near a live wire you couldn't quite see.

"You," Loki said, studying Ben openly now, "were never meant for their architecture."

Ben met his gaze. "Neither were you."

Loki's grin returned, sharp and approving. "See? Devils recognise each other."

Fiona shifted her weight subtly, placing herself half a step closer to Ben without announcing the movement.

Loki noticed, of course. He always noticed. "Ah," Loki said. "Positioning. How very Fortuna of you."

Fiona didn't rise to it. "Rus," she said calmly, "you and Demi need to go."

Rus stiffened. "We are not abandoning—"

"You're not equipped for what happens next," Fiona cut in. "And you know it."

Demi's voice shook with restrained fury. "You're choosing him."

Fiona looked at her then—really looked. "I'm choosing the board as it exists," she said. "Not the one we wish we still had."

Silence stretched.

Rus's gaze flicked between Ben and Loki, then back to Fiona. "This ends badly."

Loki chuckled. "Everything worth watching does."

Rus ignored him. "When it does," Rus said to Ben, "don't expect mercy."

Ben nodded once. "I never have."

That seemed to drain the last of Rus's resistance. He exhaled through his nose, sharp and bitter. "Come on," he muttered to Demi.

Demi hesitated, eyes locked on Ben. Something like grief flickered there—grief for a world she could no longer reach.

"Don't let him rewrite you," she said quietly.

Ben didn't answer. Because there was no answer that would make that better.

They left together, their footsteps fading into the ice corridors until the cavern suddenly felt unnervingly large.

The moment they were gone, the air changed.

Loki felt it too.

"Oh," he murmured. "That's better."

Fiona turned sharply. "Do not mistake absence for permission."

Loki raised a paw in mock surrender. "Perish the thought."

He glanced around the cavern, eyes lingering on the shattered glyphs, the ruined seal, the ancient scars in the ice. "You know," he said, "this place was never meant to hold me forever."

Fiona folded her arms. "It held you long enough."

Loki tilted his head. "No, not really."

She didn't answer.

Instead, Ben spoke. "You said you wanted proximity."

Loki's ears perked. "I did."

Ben stepped forward, just enough to claim space. "Then understand this. You don't lead. You don't test me. You don't teach."

Loki smiled faintly. "Teaching is overrated."

Ben continued, voice steady. "If you stay, you stay because you choose to walk beside us—not ahead, not behind."

Loki regarded him with something close to genuine curiosity. "And if I get bored?"

Ben's eyes didn't waver. "Then leave."

That surprised him. Loki laughed, not sharp this time, but soft. Almost pleased. "Most people beg gods to stay," he said. "You're telling one to go."

Ben shrugged slightly. "I don't trust anything that needs to be begged."

Loki studied him for a long moment. Then, slowly, deliberately, he sat. "All right, devil," Loki said. "Let's walk."

Fiona exhaled quietly, tension easing by a fraction. "We need to move quickly. Before the council senses the fracture."

Loki snorted. "They are slow—it cracked the moment the sea went quiet."

Ben's head turned. "What does that mean?"

Loki's grin flickered. "Oh, nothing poetic. Just physics."

He padded past them toward the exit. "When something old stops holding its corner of the world together, everything nearby gets... creative."

They followed. The passage out of the glacier was narrow, forcing proximity. Loki didn't mind. He walked with infuriating ease, as if the ice parted for him out of habit.

At one point, as they climbed, Loki glanced back at Ben. "You didn't answer before," he said casually. "When the fire comes—and it will—are you a rabbit or a horse?"

Ben frowned.

Loki's eyes gleamed, letting the question hang unanswered, unfinished.

When they emerged into the Siberian night, the cold hit like a slap. Stars burned hard overhead. The world felt vast, indifferent, waiting. Loki paused at the threshold, inhaling deeply, as if tasting freedom rather than air.

"Ah," he said softly. "Still a mess."

Fiona stepped beside him. "You helped make it one."

Loki grinned. "Of course."

Ben looked out across the ice, shadow stirring quietly inside him—not whispering, not urging, just *present*.

Three figures stood at the edge of something irreparable. Not allies. Not enemies. Just forces now too close to ignore one another.

Chapter 15
The Crack

The penthouse was silent but for the storm crawling across its glass skin. The city below still sparkled, oblivious, but no one at the table cared for it. The gods had revealed themselves, torn the veil wide, and the world had seen them. That page could not be turned back. Humanity had cried out for protection and received instead the sight of immortals watching, calculating, and now—failing.

Athena stood, her voice hard and clipped. "At Machu Picchu, the ethereals broke the silence. They named Ben Callum their champion. They spoke it so I would hear. They declared us failed. That was their judgement."

No one moved. The torches guttered once, as though the word failed unsettled even the fire. Rus leaned forward, his eyes narrow. "He released Loki. The Trickster walks again, and he will not walk alone."

Demi's voice was low but certain. "We tried to hold the seal. It broke in his shadow. Loki looked upon him as kin—two devils. There was no hesitation, no struggle. It was release by will."

The words were heavy enough to shift the air itself. Loki was free. A mortal anointed not only by the ethereals, but by Loki as well. Lilith rising without restraint. And the gods—scattered, absent, some already silent in defiance.

Zed rose. The storm followed, rumbling through his chest until the windows trembled. His single eye blazed with the fury of lightning barely restrained. “Then hear me. We have no unity, no balance, and no time. Lilith marches, Loki laughs, Ben walks under silence itself. The ethereals will not turn back, and mortals will not forgive if devils walk the world. The age of the council is over.”

He lifted the staff, and the room shook.

“From this moment, every god, every mortal, for themselves. No more deliberation, no more waiting. We stand, or we fall alone. War is upon us. Take what followers you can hold, keep what ground you can defend. The council is dismissed.”

Hera did not counter him. Her silence was judgement enough.

Athena struck the marble once with her walking stick, a final echo of order. “Then let the record show: the ethereals chose man, and the gods chose war.”

Lightning broke over Manhattan, rain thundered down on glass towers, and the penthouse stood in stunned silence. The gods looked at one another and saw enemies.

The echo of Zed’s words still hung heavy.

Every god for themselves.

For a long moment, no one moved. They were immortals, beings that had bent ages into their shapes. Yet tonight, the veneer had cracked. The ethereals had spoken, Loki was loose, Lilith walked unchecked, and a mortal wore the title of devil.

Athena raised her arm. “We cannot undo the revelation. Humanity has seen us. They begged for saviours and found us wanting. The ethereals spoke because we failed, not because they love him."

Rus leaned forward. "And now Loki is free because of Ben—his hand opened the seal as if he were the key."

Demi nodded, quiet but firm. "It seemed ordained. He chose. And Loki joined him as a friend."

The room shivered with the weight of that truth.

Pele's voice cracked like stone under heat. "So the ethereals have a champion, Lilith has her army, and Loki has his devilish games. What do we have? Silence, defiance, and empty chairs."

Dionysus let out a humourless laugh. "We have relevance as relics. Monuments watch the city until the dead strip it clean."

Hera did not stop him. She only said, "We revealed ourselves. That was our wager. Now mortals look up expecting salvation and will learn the last truth instead—that the gods bleed and the gods abandon."

Jamil's tone was harsher than the storm. "They will curse us. And they will not be wrong. But curses are nothing compared to what Lilith will make of them. Balance has slipped. The ethereals no longer mask their hand. We are irrelevant unless we fight as council."

Zed rose again, lightning crawling down the staff he held. "I said it before, and I say it clearer now. This council has ended. The ethereals have written our epitaph. The game board is scattered. Each of you must decide how to endure what comes. Align with mortals, ally with Lilith, court Loki, chase shadows—it makes no difference. The council no longer shields you."

Athena's jaw tightened. "You call it war, but this is not war. This is dissolution."

"Then dissolve," Zed thundered, "but dissolve with teeth." The storm slammed into the glass, shaking the room like a heartbeat too large for the world to hold.

One by one, the gods began to speak—not in commune, but as fractured voices.

Ari leaned forward, eyes alight. "If it is every god for himself, then I will gather armies still foolish enough to march. Let them curse me when they fall; their deaths will sing in my blood until even Lilith tastes ash."

Dionysus poured nothing into his glass and drank it. "Then I will give them laughter as the house falls. A mad feast for a mad ending. If we must be irrelevant, let us at least be remembered in death."

Hera's face was marble, unflinching. "So you speak. So you choose. Remember this: you do not choose for all. You choose only for yourself now. And when the reckoning comes, no throne will cover your name."

Zed's voice rolled low, final. "The council is ended. The age of unity is gone. Go where you must. Do what you must. When the storm clears, only ruin will tell who remained relevant."

The gods looked at one another and saw not allies, not even rivals—only survivors scattering to a world that no longer needed them. Zed had spoken; Hera had not contradicted him. The council was dissolved.

Athena was first to move. She did not bow, did not curse, did not linger. She drew her cloak around her, grabbed her walking stick, and turned toward the elevators. "If the ethereals and Loki want him, they have him. I will not stand between their decree and his shadow. But I will not stand idle. Mortals will need order when chaos feasts on them. I will give them discipline, even if it is only long enough to die cleanly." Her words clanged like armour even after she was gone.

Rus followed, silent until the doors hissed closed behind them. The falcon in him could not abide being trapped with the others any longer. "I will guard from above," was all he said. Then the storm opened like a throat, and he was gone into it, wings of shadow cutting between lightning veins.

Demi's voice trembled but did not break. "The boy has walked too far to be undone. He carries a wound he cannot put down, and if mortals cling to him, then I will sit with them. Not as a goddess. As a nurse. They deserve at least one hand that does not let go." She pressed a palm against the cold table, then slipped away without another sound.

Pele spat embers on the marble, leaving black scars.

Ari laughed, sharp and loud, the only joy in the room.

"Every god for himself? At last! Then let the dogs of war feast while there's meat left. I'll raise banners in the sands, call every fool with a blade, and drown the deserts in wrath."

He clapped Zed on the shoulder like a brother-in-arms, then strode out with the swagger of a man who had already tasted his end.

Dionysus lingered, smiling with no mirth. "Then I will pour wine until the goblets drown them while laughing." He tipped his empty glass and was gone in a lilt of perfume and silence.

The others left in a flourish only gods could manage.

At last, only Hera and Zed remained. The storm quieted, coiling close around them, listening. Hera's hand touched the back of Zed's chair, fingers tightening. "So it ends. Here we are, monsters facing our own demise."

Zed's eye burned with stormlight, but his voice was weary thunder. "Then let us be monsters. Relevance is survival now, not worship." He turned toward the glass, watching lightning split the skyline. "The world is broken, Hera. Each of us must flee into it and carve what meaning we can from ruin."

Hera's face was marble set in shadow. "Then let us flee too. Better monsters together than gods alone." They stepped from the table, and the penthouse emptied. The storm peeled away from its crown of glass, releasing it to the mortal night.

The boy had been scavenging when the sky split.

Nothing grand—just a burlap sack of tin, copper wire, a cracked bottle that might still hold rain if he patched the seam with wax. The city was half-gutted already, blackened from riots and bombings, but to him it was still home. Streets he knew by heart, doorways where his mother used to sell bread, corners where the old men would sit and argue football scores.

Now all silent, all hollow. He kept to shadows, feet soft on broken glass. That was how you lived—quiet, smaller than the hunger that prowled.

But then the air changed. It began with thunder. A low roll that grew teeth. The boy squinted upward and saw a dark wedge cross the moon. Not a plane, not a bird. The shape was too sharp, too alive. Wings wide as rooftops, feathers gilded with the storm's fire. A falcon.

His heart seized. He knew the name, though he had never said it aloud: Rus, some called him now, as if the syllable had been chewed down by time. His grandmother had once whispered the old stories in a hushed kitchen—gods who had ruled the Nile, eyes like the sun itself. He had thought them only tales. Then came the Revelation. Then came the slaughter.

Rus wheeled above the ruins, gaze fixed, gold burning through shadow, as a general scanning battlefield lines.

Then the ground answered.

The boy felt it in his teeth before he heard it—like drums pounded beneath the earth. A clang of steel followed, echoing down the ruined avenue. The heat in the air rose, as if war itself had chosen to walk in flesh. He crouched behind a burnt-out car just as a second god appeared.

Ari.

The god of war strode through the wreckage like it was kindling, broad-shouldered, sword strapped across his back like a banner. He wore no helmet, only a grin that stretched too wide. The boy had never seen joy look so terrifying.

Ari's boots rang against the asphalt, each step a challenge.

Above, the falcon screamed.

The boy's breath caught. He should have run, but where could he go? The sky belonged to the gods. The streets belonged to hunger. All he could do was hide and watch, heart beating faster than his legs could ever carry him.

Rus folded his wings and dove, talons bright as bronze. He struck the street with the force of a falling tower. Sparks burst as claws scraped Ari's blade.

The war god laughed—a deep, booming sound that rolled like a drumbeat across the ruins. "At last!"

Steel flashed. Ari swung upward, meeting talon with tempered edge. The clash cracked windows up and down the block. Shards rained onto the boy's shoulders as he pressed tighter into cover, but his eyes never left the fight.

It wasn't war. It wasn't even a battle. It was myth breaking itself across the bones of a city. Rus's wings carved the air, gusts tearing signs from their posts and tossing them like paper. Ari roared with every strike, sword ringing each time it met feather and fang. Each blow lit the night brighter than lightning.

The boy trembled, half in awe, half in terror. He had seen gangs fight for scraps, soldiers fire into crowds, and revenants crawl out of bomb craters. But this—this was something else. This was power untethered, fighting not for mortals but for itself.

Ari drove the blade down, splitting the pavement into a canyon. Fire flared in the cracks.

Rus launched upward again, circling, golden eyes unblinking.

Dust choked the street, turned the boy's lungs raw. He pressed his shirt to his face, but still he looked, unable to turn away. Part of him felt pride. Pride that his city had become a stage for gods. That history wasn't written in temples anymore but here, on broken roads where he lived. For a heartbeat, he thought maybe it meant humanity mattered after all.

But then Ari laughed again—mad, joyous, savage—and Rus screamed, sharper than knives, and the boy understood. They weren't fighting for him. Not for anyone. They were fighting to prove themselves in a world already burning. The boy's stomach turned cold. His grandmother's words came back to him, words he hadn't believed when he was younger: gods don't save; gods survive.

Ari swung, and an entire building's facade collapsed. Rus struck back, talons raking sparks from stone. Flames licked upward, catching old curtains, turning windows into mouths of fire.

The boy bolted then, sack abandoned, feet pounding broken glass. He didn't run from hunger, revenants, or soldiers. He ran from the gods. Behind him, thunder rolled, laughter echoed, and a falcon's cry split the night. For the first time, he knew what Zed had meant when he declared war: every god, every man, for himself.

And for the first time, the boy understood that included him.

Chapter 16
The Priests

The chamber of the United Nations had never been so packed, nor so silent. Delegates sat stiff in their seats, translators hunched over earpieces, pens hovering useless above notepads.

The air tasted of fear and recycled oxygen.

On the screens above, satellite feeds showed what had been Libya the week before—convoys of bone marching across the desert, a tide of shields and skulls that did not tire. Southward, villages emptied. Eastward, Egypt braced.

Cairo had thirty days, maybe less.

When the Secretary-General rose, his hands trembled only once before he clasped them. His voice, when it came, carried the weight of unanimity.

"Humanity is at war."

The words rippled outward. Headphones repeated them in French, Russian, Mandarin, and Arabic. No one argued. No one asked for clarification. They had all seen the same maps, the same feeds: Morocco drowned, Algeria cracking, Tunisia silent.

"The dead march east, under a will we cannot name. But they are not invincible. They bleed not flesh, but fractures. We must strike those fractures. Not as nations. Not as factions. But as one."

A murmur rolled through the hall—approval from some, unease from others. The representative of China leaned forward to the microphone. "Then let us be clear. You call for the unification of armed forces. Shared command. Joint fire."

"Yes," the Secretary-General said. "Every arsenal, every soldier, every pilot. The threat does not respect borders. Neither can we."

For the first time in the history of the UN, the vote was not tallied electronically. It was spoken, aloud, one by one.

"Yes." "Yes." "Oui." "Sí." "Da."

A few abstained, their silence heavy with fear of surrendering sovereignty. A handful of voices said no—rogue states clinging to their own shadows. But the overwhelming roar was agreement. For the first time in living memory, humanity had declared a single war.

Yet even before the bureaucrats finished their applause, others were already fighting.

In Algeria, crop-dusting planes had been pulled from their hangars, their tanks filled not with pesticide but with fuel bombs and improvised napalm. Farmers who once scattered locusts now dove at columns of bone, releasing trails of fire that clung to armour and burned the marrow inside.

In Tunisia, hobby pilots took their two-seater kits to the skies, strapping on homemade racks of grenades, dropping them with the precision of desperation. For a time, it worked—skeletons shattered under fire. Columns broke. Civilians cheered from rooftops as burning bones collapsed into black heaps.

But then the wraiths came.

Born of annihilated soldiers, these were not bound to the ground. They rose like smoke from the columns, drifting upward, eyes glowing cobalt in the night. They caught wings in their incorporeal grasp, dragging planes from the sky, wrapping cockpits in suffocating dark. One militia squadron was snuffed in minutes, its burning wrecks scattered across the dunes.

Still, new pilots rose. For every plane lost, another farmer, another mechanic, another dreamer pulled theirs from a barn and painted teeth on its nose. They called themselves the Vigilantes. The name spread across radios, across stolen transmitters, across refugee camps.

In Alexandria, Father Maroun had not slept in three nights. He walked the nave of his church, rosary clutched until it cut his palm, listening to the sound of wind battering stained glass. His congregation had thinned to almost nothing—many fled, many taken. Yet those who came whispered the same thing: the dead were near.

When the first revenant clawed its way through the broken door, he thought it was the end. Its fused armour smoked from some earlier blast, its sockets burning like furnaces. He raised his hands not in defiance but in prayer. The cross swung against his chest. The creature halted. Just for a heartbeat, its advance faltered. Instinct overtook him. He yanked the cross free, pressed it forward, words spilling unbidden from his throat: In nomine Patris, et Filii, et Spiritus Sancti.

The revenant shrieked. Its jaw cracked open, smoke hissing from within.

Nearby, a basin of holy water trembled with the shock. Maroun grabbed it, hurled it across the monster's face. Where the droplets struck, bone hissed, sizzling like fat on coals. The creature reeled, clawing at its own skull.

Maroun stared, panting, realisation blooming.

Faith hurt them.

He wrote the discovery in trembling script, sealed it in an envelope, and pressed it into the hands of the one refugee bound for Rome. "Give this to His Holiness. Tell him the cross still stands."...

Far away, beyond the Nile's horizon, Lilith walked with her army. The desert opened before her like a stage, and she, its queen, serene in white, braids unbroken, eyes reflecting no fatigue. Around her, the revenants screamed, the wraiths drifted, the skeletons marched in formations older than empires. She did not need to command. They moved as her will moved.

But she had noticed the change.

Columns delayed. Ranks broken. Smoke in the sky that was not hers. Human machines, crude and desperate, diving from clouds with teeth painted on their noses. Villagers fighting with torches and firebombs. And somewhere, she felt it—holy syllables cutting faint lines in her tapestry.

It amused her.

"Children with wings of tin," she murmured, watching the desert burn where Vigilantes had struck. "They think they invented defiance. They only mimic me."

One of her revenants stumbled, its fused bones blackened by fire. She touched its shoulder gently, and it straightened, whole again. "They win moments," she whispered, "and call them victories. But I am patient. Their moments will string together like beads, and still I will reach Cairo."

Yet a flicker of interest stirred. The priest's prayers, though distant, had brushed her like a draft through stone. It did not wound her—not yet—but it reminded her of chains older than the council, older than balance. Chains she had broken once. Chains she did not intend to wear again. So she let the Vigilantes live, for now. Let them savour their little triumphs. Hope was a sharper torment than despair.

Back in New York, as the UN vote sealed, the Secretary-General looked into the cameras that carried his face to every corner of the globe.

"Let this be known," he said. "Humanity fights as one. Nations may falter, militias may rise, priests may pray—but together we will stand. If bone can march, so can flesh. If the dead can rise, so will courage. This is our call to arms."

And across continents, the words took root. Farmers turned their tractors into barricades. Engineers rewired drones into bomb-carriers. Soldiers drilled side by side with civilians. And priests blessed water until their voices cracked. For the first time since Lilith's march began, hope was no longer a rumour. It was an army in the making.

They told me to name the plane for luck. I painted a fox on the nose instead—teeth bared, eyes bright—because luck is a liar and teeth are honest.

The old Air Tractor had been yellow once. Now it was smoke-streaked and patched with sheet metal my cousin hammered into shape on a kitchen table. We bolted two stub racks under the wings, the kind you'd never trust if you had any sense, and we ran a hose from the belly tank out to a nozzle we bent from copper pipe.

The boys in the garage filled the tank with fuel thickened by soap and fertiliser—homemade fire that clung like gossip. Someone slipped a string of little water bottles into the cargo well, each one tied with blue thread and a paper cross taped to the cap. I didn't ask who blessed them. In Sfax, blessings come from whoever dares to say the words. I taped one small cross to the dashboard. It clicked against the altimeter when the engine rattled awake.

"Samir," Hedi crackled through the handset we'd built out of an old VHF and a prayer. "Column moving east of the Kairouan road. Wraiths reported. You ready?"

I looked past the prop, where dawn was unrolling from purple to coral over fields I used to dust for locusts. The fox's eyes grinned back from the cowl.

"Ready," I lied, and pushed the throttle. The Air Tractor did not leap; she considered the request, then shrugged herself into motion. Tires hummed over broken tarmac, the tail lifted, and we were sky. My hands stopped shaking exactly then. They always did. On the ground, fear talks. In the air, fear listens.

We kept low—treetop low, minaret low—because the wraiths liked height the way sharks like deep water. The city fell away behind me, white cubes of houses, the great green of the mosque's courtyard, laundry snapping messages I couldn't read. I banked south-east, and the fields turned into scrub and then into a brown that looked like old bread.

"Hedi," I said, "mark me the wind." We no longer had weather reports, but we had cousins on roofs with flags. "North-west," he said. "Good for you."

Good because I'd spray upwind and let the homemade napalm ride the breeze into bone. Good because the dead did not breathe, but they walked through the air all the same.

I saw dust first. Not the rolling kind tractors kick up, but a long smear, like someone dragged a dry finger across the horizon. Then the glints—bronze, black, a line of wrong reflections. You don't ever forget the sound, even from the cockpit: jawbones clicking in their thousands, a dry rain.

My tongue went to my teeth like it always does at that sound, as if it wanted to count them to make sure they were still mine.

"Column confirmed," I said. "Two ranks wide. Revenants among them—shine like coal in a barbecue."

"Copy." Hedi tried to keep his voice steady. "Wraiths?"

As if the word called them, something unstitched itself from the column and climbed. Not quickly. Not like birds. More like smoke that remembered being a man and resented the forgetting. A drift of them, half a dozen at first, then more, their eyes that sick cobalt—like gas flames when the pot's just starting to boil.

"Affirm," I said. "We have guests."

On the floor beside the seat, the flare gun knocked against my ankle. We'd tested them the night before—magnesium flares, too bright to look at, too hot to love. The wraiths hated them, hated the sudden white and the way it turned their edges from rumour to shape. If light could be a net, magnesium was the rope.

I came in low along their flank. The column did not break. It never breaks unless you make it. I toggled the pump, felt the belly tank thrum, and the nozzle threw a silver stream that caught sunlight and turned dirty. The cocktail splashed across shields and ribs, slopping into joints and coating hollows. A second later, Hedi's voice in my ear: "Ignite."

I thumbed the switch. The spark hit the stream at the nozzle, and the world put on a crown. Fire bit bone, crawled, licked down into places bullets never find. Skeletons staggered. Revenants screamed—a deeper, furnace complaint. The stream ran dry faster than I liked. I banked, climbed a breath, looked back.

It worked. It always worked the first time.

The wraiths rose to meet me. They don't rush. That's what steals your breath. If they came hungry, jaws wide, that would be honest. They drift, deciding, like grandmothers at a market. One touched the wingtip—no weight, no pressure, just a cold that reached for my elbow. The engine coughed as if it had swallowed a cloud. The cross ticked against the panel. I levelled and kicked the rudder, shaking the wing free.

"Samir," Hedi said, voice tight, "you've got three on your tail."

"I know," and pulled the flare gun.

I had taped a little bracket at the side window so I could pop it open with my knee. I popped it. Air punched the cockpit, throwing paperwork into a storm around my shoulders. The first wraith slid along the fuselage like a smear of shadow, looking for a home. I put the flare gun out into the wind and fired. The flare went off so close that the cockpit washed white. Spots burst in my vision, and a hot needle stitched down my cheek. The wraith tore, parting like cloth, and shrieked with no mouth. The sound went into my teeth and rattled there. The second came anyway. I fired again. The third slipped beneath the belly.

"Blessed water," Hedi said, reading my mind like he always did. "Do it."

I rolled a little to keep the stream off my own wing and grabbed a bottle with my free hand. Cap off with my teeth—cross-tape between my fingers. I wondered—not for long—if a Muslim could throw Catholic water and make it count. Then I remembered Fatima two streets over, who had sent me off with a kiss and a plastic bag of little bottles, and said, God hears whoever shouts first.

I threw the bottle out into the wake. It shattered against a ribcage below. Where droplets touched, bone hissed like frying onions. The thing arched and fell, legs tangled in its own melted armour.

"Copy to all," Hedi said on the open band. "Holy water is effective on revenants. Repeat, effective. Any source." The band filled with voices. The Vigilantes were always listening, always stealing each other's courage.

I emptied two more bottles along my own slipstream for the wraith beneath me. It didn't burn; it thinned. Like steam when you lift the lid. The cold pulled out of the cockpit. I breathed again.

The second run, I didn't go for the long pour. The tank was nearly half full, and I had a new idea. I swung over the column and cut the pump to a spit, a mist—a farmer's trick when you want to paint a whole orchard, but you're cheap.

The fine spray spread wider, rode the wind deeper into their ranks. I popped another flare just above the stream and watched an orange ribbon run along the mist and drop like summer rain on bone. They buckled. Not all, not even many, but enough to see space open in the line. Enough to plant the idea in mortal heads that the dead could be made to stumble.

"Samir," Hedi said, "you're poetry."

"Tell poetry to bring up more soap," I said, and rolled to come back.

They learned. They always learn. The wraiths climbed higher, then dropped in a sheet, a curtain of cold. It had a weight this time, a decision in it. I felt it press against the windshield, saw frost sketch spider-webs across the edges of the glass. My breaths turned to clouds, each one a minor betrayal; the engine note went thin, like it had a fever.

I did the stupid thing then—the thing pilots promise each other never to do. I let go of the yoke with one hand and reached for the dashboard. I put my palm flat over the little cross I'd taped there and pressed until the wood bit. The plane didn't get warmer. I did. Or maybe that's a story I tell myself so I can sleep.

I popped the window again and fired two flares low and wide, not to hit but to make light where their bodies wanted to be dark. They recoiled—not much, but enough for the engine to take a deep breath and find its voice again. I dropped a string of blessed bottles in a line, like breadcrumbs back to the living.

On the ground, I saw them then—the line of our people. Not soldiers, not many. Men with scarves over their faces, women with wet scarves over their mouths, kids with their fathers' goggles, everyone with a bottle, a bucket, or a kitchen pot. A priest in a brown coat stood knee-deep in a horse trough, hands in the water, lips moving. A woman beside him dipped her cupped hands and flung the water toward the road as if she could reach from there to the skeletons with will alone. Maybe she could. I wagged my wings. It means I see you. The line cheered, mouths open like birds.

Third run. Last fuel worth the name. I went lower than sense and aimed not at the front but thirty ranks deep, where commanders used to ride. There aren't commanders now, only momentum—but even momentum has a skeleton, and I was learning to break its ribs. Mist on. Spark. The ribbon caught and ran under me at the speed of gossip in a small town.

Something big moved in the heart of the column, something fused and heavy, a revenant whose armour had melted and set around it like a tomb. It looked up at me with those furnace eyes and reached both clawed arms high as if to pull me from the sky by my shadow. I dropped the last bottle with a childish spite, right between its eyes.

It flinched. It flinched.

"Mark that," I said aloud, to the fox on the nose, to the cross, to anyone with a radio. "They can flinch."

When the tank coughed, I turned for home. You never run it dry. Dry is death. Half the wraiths followed a hundred meters, then lost interest when the ground threw new prayers into their faces. I climbed into clean air, where the sun was higher, and the cold was honest.

“Samir,” Hedi said softly. “You’re coming back.”

“As if I’d miss your mother’s coffee,” I said, and only then let my hands shake.

Below me, the line of people moved forward, step by step. Not to chase, not with stupidity, but to take back ten meters of road that had been bone and now was blackened and steaming and ours. The Vigilantes on other bands read out recipes like chefs on morning radio: two parts petrol, one part soap, a fist of nitrate; add courage; ignite. I turned once more to look. In the far distance, the column coiled and reformed, the wound closing. It always does. But it closed more slowly than it had an hour ago. That is a kind of victory most people don’t have time to celebrate.

On the edge of vision, a white figure walked along the ranks. Too far to see a face. Far enough to feel noticed. My skin prickled where the wraith-cold had laid its claim. I touched the cross without looking at it and pressed until the wood bit again.

“I saw you,” I said to the glass, to the heat, to the quiet thing that listens beyond radios. “And you saw me.”

When I landed, the fox on the nose had caught a ribbon of soot that made it look like it was smiling wider. Hedi ran out with the fuel drum, the funnel, and a grin that made him look ten years old and a thousand. He hooked the hose, and I slid to the ground on rubber legs. The priest in the brown coat arrived, breathing hard, with two boys dragging a crate between them. Bottles clinked inside. Some had blue thread, some had nothing but a thumbprint pressed into the plastic as if that would help.

“Father Maroun?” I asked.

He nodded. Up close, the lines around his eyes were maps of bad nights.

"Bless it all," I said, half joke, half order, and he laughed the way men laugh when something inside them stops trembling for the first time in days.

"Already done," he said, and lifted the first bottle like a toast. "Again."

We poured hope into the belly of the fox while the world burned. It's not the worst job I've ever had.

The desert wind remembered him. It struck his face sharp as knives, bent his wings with old familiarity. He had not flown in centuries, not with this body, not with these feathers, but the sky had never forgotten. Rus—Horus to those who still whispered his name—rose above the Nile like a shard of sunlight made flesh. His eyes, hawk-bright, cut the horizon where dust rolled in from Libya. Behind that dust marched Lilith's host, endless, unbroken, a tide of bone that would not halt until Cairo was only a story.

He could not wait for councils or debates. He had seen too many chambers crumble into words while armies bled. The gods argued balance; mortals begged for saviours. Horus chose neither. He chose war.

The city lay restless beneath him. Minarets gleamed in dawn haze, bridges crawled with refugees, and rooftops bristled with antennae and makeshift signal flags. Cairo had not slept in weeks; its people lived in a constant half-march, ready to flee, prepared to fight.

When Rus descended, men dropped their rifles, women pressed children to their skirts, and the old remembered. They fell to their knees as the shadow of wings swept over the square before the Citadel. He landed hard, dust spiralling from talons that became boots. His shoulders still bore the outline of wings, translucent and golden in the glare. He stood tall, eyes sharp as razors, and raised his voice so that every microphone, every cell phone, every ear would carry it.

"Cairo," he said, and the word carried like a drumbeat. "I have come because you are the wall. If the dead break here, the Nile runs red and the world is ash. But if you stand, you are the river that cannot be dammed. Will you stand?"

The answer rolled like thunder. A thousand voices, then ten thousand, swelling as more crowded the square: "We will stand!"

He moved through barracks and garages, not as a god handing down decrees but as a commander with dust on his boots.

Soldiers followed because he spoke their language—orders clipped, eyes unflinching, hand steady on the map. Civilians followed because his wings had lit the dawn, and they remembered stories of hawks that avenged the innocent.

Within hours, Cairo shifted. Truck convoys were no longer lines of refugees but mobile armouries—soccer fields filled with volunteers learning to march. Priests and imams blessed bullets side by side, sprinkling holy water and murmuring prayers that braided into something neither tradition could claim but both could wield.

On the runway outside the city, Vigilante pilots taxied beside Egyptian MiGs, patched biplanes shoulder to shoulder with steel predators. Rus walked among them, a giant shadow against burning tarmac.

"You fly not as nations," he told them, "but as wings of the same hawk." A roar answered him—engines, voices, hearts.

By sunset, a banner flew above the Citadel. Not the flag of Egypt. Not the seal of the UN. It was white, marked with a single black hawk in flight, wings spread across the cloth. Refugees carried smaller versions in their hands, children painted it on cardboard, and pilots stencilled it on their fuselages. It was not a symbol of divinity. It was a symbol of defiance.

Far west, where her army camped in the desert shadows, Lilith paused. The wind brought her news faster than spies: Cairo had chosen its hawk. She closed her eyes and tasted the devotion in the air, sharp as citrus, strong enough to sting. For the first time since Morocco burned, she frowned.

"An old falcon stirs his feathers," she murmured. Revenants knelt around her, silent, waiting. "He thinks wings make him free. But my wraiths fly too."

She opened her eyes, their depths black as desert wells. "Let him gather his army. The more he rallies, the more I will inherit when they fall. Their faith will clothe me."

And yet, when she turned, her fingers tightened. Hope was a dangerous contagion. The Vigilantes had already proven that. A god on the side of mortals could shift the battlefield more than bombs.

She raised her hand. The wraiths rose from the dunes like a mourning veil. "Find the hawk," she whispered. "Clip his w ings."...

Night fell over Cairo, but no one slept. Searchlights crisscrossed the sky, antiaircraft batteries thumped into readiness, and the Nile gleamed with barges laden not with tourists but with ammunition. At the Citadel, Rus stood on the ramparts, looking west. Around him gathered soldiers, priests, farmers, mechanics—every shape of mortal he had sworn to defend. He raised his hand, feathers glowing faintly where torchlight touched.

"Swear with me," he said. "Not to me. To each other. Swear that the living will not kneel while the dead march. Swear that Cairo will not fall."

The square erupted in oaths—Arabic, Coptic, English, French, a hundred tongues, but all carrying the same promise. It rolled up the walls and into the sky, a sound that even the wraiths drifting at the horizon heard and hesitated.

Rus spread his wings fully, gold cutting the night. "Then we are an army." The hawk had risen, and Cairo breathed easier for the first time in weeks.

But in the west, Lilith's host quickened its march.

The bells of Saint Peter's rang without schedule, hammering the air as if the Vatican itself could feel the armies of bone creeping closer.

Rome had seen invasions before—emperors, barbarians, plagues—but never like this. Never an enemy that laughed at death because it had already died.

In the Apostolic Palace, the Pope stood before a wall of cameras and microphones. He had not slept; the purple beneath his eyes betrayed that. His robes hung simple, white against the dark wood, as though he had dressed not as a sovereign but as a soldier.

The letter from Father Maroun lay open on the lectern, its ink smudged by the priest's trembling hand.

The Pope lifted it.

"Brothers and sisters," he began, voice thick with exhaustion and fire. "I have read a testimony from Alexandria. A priest, armed with nothing but cross and water, stood before revenants—and they faltered."

The words went out live, carried on networks that had abandoned advertising, on pirate frequencies where Vigilantes tuned their radios between sorties, into refugee camps where people huddled around cracked smartphones.

"The undead march with weapons older than empires," the Pope continued. "But faith is older still. The sign of the cross still strikes terror into their skulls. Holy water still burns their flesh. The Gospel is not a metaphor. It is a weapon."

The hall held its breath.

Cardinals leaned forward, faces pale. Camera operators forgot to blink. Outside, pilgrims pressed against the barricades, whispering Hail Marys into the cold.

The Pope's voice hardened. "Therefore, I say this: every priest, every deacon, every man of cloth, every woman consecrated to God—come to Egypt. Cairo is the wall between the living and the abyss. Rus rallies armies there. The Vigilantes bleed the skies there. Now we must bring faith there. Your vestments are your armour. Your blessing is your bullet. Your hands will baptise not only the living but the weapons of the living. Go."

He lifted the cross from his chest, silver flashing under the lights. "We are shepherds, but the wolves are bone and fire. If we were to guard the flock, we must stand with staff in hand. The Nile is the new Golgotha. Go."

The cameras caught his raised arm, cross gleaming like a star.

The square outside erupted. Seminarians wept openly. Nuns tore veils from their heads and wrapped them as bandages for refugees waiting on the cobblestones. Priests gripped one another's arms, swearing to book passage by whatever means—train, plane, ship. Cardinals hesitated only a moment before one stepped forward. He bowed, voice carrying through the microphones. "Holiness, the College of Cardinals will stand with you. We go to Egypt." The Pope nodded once, grave as a general. "Then the Church is an army."...

The speech ricocheted across continents.

In Brazil, priests blessed rain barrels, pouring them into bottles marked for Cairo. In Poland, abbots rang monastery bells and loaded pickup trucks with casks of holy water. In the Philippines, entire congregations gathered at docks, chanting rosaries as if the prayers themselves would propel the ships east.

Not every bishop agreed. Some whispered of blasphemy, of dragging the sacred into mud and fire. But the tide of faith was louder. In refugee camps, survivors began dipping rags in water and crossing themselves before charging barricades. Soldiers lifted their rifles not to kiss them, but to let priests bless them. Even those who doubted found courage in ritual.

In her desert tent, Lilith sat on a throne of fused bone. A revenant entered, sockets glowing faintly. It carried a radio stripped from some broken convoy. The static burst, and the Pope's words spilled through—translated, distorted, but clear enough.

Lilith listened. Her smile was thin, almost fond.

"Faith," she said. "They will clothe themselves in it, thinking it armour. Let them. Their prayers will make their screams sweeter when I tear them from their throats."

But even as she mocked, her fingers tightened on the arm of the throne.

Faith was old. Older than her hunger. Chains of prayer had bound her once. She remembered the burn. She had broken those chains—but memory had weight, and weight pressed even queens.

She rose, letting the radio crackle to silence, and spoke to the gathered wraiths. "Go to the priests first. Snuff their candles. Let them learn the futility of water against fire."

The wraiths bowed, smoke folding inward, and dissolved into the night.

Back in Rome, the Pope leaned forward, his voice softer now, almost tender. "Do not think this is the end of days. Think of it as the hour when humanity proves it was worthy of being born. Lilith marches with the dead, but we march with life. Even if we fall, we fall as witnesses. The dead cannot sing. The dead cannot hope. Only the living can. And while one voice sings, we are unconquered."

He closed the book of Gospels on the lectern, kissed it, and whispered: "In Egypt, the world will rise again." The bells rang anew, louder, faster, as if the Vatican itself were answering him.

By midnight, trains leaving Rome overflowed with priests in cassocks and nuns in plain clothes. Airstrips in Sicily refuelled ancient planes carrying barrels of water labelled Sanctified. The Mediterranean glowed with lights of fishing boats pressed into pilgrimage, their crews chanting prayers in languages that had never crossed an ocean before.

Faith had become a supply line.

Chapter 17
The Herald

The Siberian steppe stretched endlessly, a frozen plain that seemed to breathe in silence. Frost cracked faintly under Ben's boots.

A flicker of copper crossed the snow. The fox. It padded forward, tail curling in a neat loop, eyes bright as molten coin. Ben's chest tightened—the paddock, the fire, the fever-dream, *shooshoo* whispered in delirium. Always the fox. Always watching.

The fox blinked. Fur bent into flesh, shadow folded into man, and Loki crouched there, flame-haired, eyes still fox-bright, grin sharp as cut glass.

"You saw me then," Loki said softly. "That day long ago. The fox by the bushes—that was me."

Ben's jaw clenched. "Shoosh shoo." The word felt torn from him.

Loki's grin widened. "My whisper in the dream. My print on your mind. I told you to be quiet. To run."

The fury rose in Ben's chest. "So, you started all this?"

Loki smiled. "Perhaps."

"Enough games. Stop circling. I want the truth." Ben's voice cracked raw against the frozen air. "What did you do—what have I become?"

"Oh, my little darkling, I only nudged you along." He slipped back into fox form. "I prefer this guise."

"Was it you in the Aston Martin?" Ben demanded.

"No. That one wasn't mine." Loki's tone stayed casual.

He continued. "You wake when the seam splits. And when you wake, others stir."

The silence stretched.

Fiona stepped from the dark, coin flashing silver in her hand. She caught it, held it steady, and met his eyes. "In old lore, you are the one who walks with night. Every time you lived when you should have died, you carried the night with you. You did not escape it—you were born from it."

Fiona turned the coin in her palm, then continued. "And you are not alone. The others that stir in your shadow are kin. They are bound to you—each carries their own ruin, and each waits for your call." She lifted her gaze to the stars. "Death walks near you. Chaos already cuts. Despair follows. Fire waits." Her voice sharpened. "And together with you—darkness."

Loki's grin glimmered, fox-sharp. "Quite the stable you've collected, night-born."

Ben's breath burned his throat, but he stayed silent.

Fiona's hand closed around her coin. "And against you stands Lilith. She is not fear—not anymore. She is seduction itself, a very old Queen. Every corpse she raises, every soul she tempts, every ruin she makes beautiful—they belong to her. She is your rival. Your opposite."

Ben lifted his eyes to the sky. The stars seemed closer, brighter, bending low as though to witness what had been spoken.

Fiona's voice fell to a whisper. "This is who you are. This is who they are. And the night has already begun."

Ben stood between them both, chest tight, every nerve humming with the pressure of what had just been spoken.

Then the silence broke.

It began as a taste, faint and sweet, carried on the wind. Not snow. Not smoke. Something richer, heavier. Myrrh. Spice. A perfume too warm for the frozen night.

Loki's grin faltered. "She heard."

Fiona's coin froze in her hand, silver flashing pale. "She always hears."

The air shimmered, and Ben's knees almost buckled. His sight blurred, the stars smeared, the horizon rippled. When it cleared, he was no longer standing in frost. He was standing in Cairo. The Nile glowed black under a burning sky. Pyramids loomed like teeth. From the sand, they came—linen-wrapped bodies, bandages trailing, eyes gleaming with unnatural light. Pharaohs rose first, their crowns dulled by centuries, yet regal even in death. Priests followed, their staffs clutched as if still chanting prayers. Then, the warriors, blades rusted but lifted high. And at their head, she stood.

Lilith.

Her gown was woven from shadow, her skin alive with warmth that seemed to burn the air around her. Her hair spilled dark as ink across her shoulders. Her smile was not cruel—it was devastatingly tender, and that tenderness was a weapon sharper than steel. Her eyes found him at once. They softened as though she had been waiting for him all her life.

Herald, her voice whispered, inside his marrow. We are meant for each other.

Ben's breath caught.

She stepped forward, and the mummies behind her stood taller, prouder, like soldiers beneath a queen they adored. She touched one pharaoh's chin, lifted it gently, and the corpse seemed to smile, jawbones shifting in rapture. Look, she purred. Kings and priests, once hungry for eternity, now granted it by me. They do not serve from fear. They serve because I am beautiful, and they love me. The perfume thickened, curling around him like silk. His chest ached with a longing he couldn't name.

Fiona's voice cut through the haze, faint but urgent. "She lies."

Lilith's gaze snapped to Fiona, though Fiona was not truly there. Her smile never faltered. "The gambler thinks herself immune, but even chance longs to be chosen," Lilith said. "And you, fox-trickster..." Her eyes flicked to Loki. "Your grin masks hunger. You would come to me, too, if I crooked a finger."

Loki's own grin wavered. "Not likely," he muttered, though his eyes avoided hers.

Ben forced his throat to work. "What do you want from me?"

Everything, she whispered, and her voice stroked his bones. You are night. You carry the road everyone must walk. Join me, and I will make that road velvet. No one needs to fear the dark if you walk it with me. Together, we will turn night into the sweetest embrace. You bring them into shadow, and I will keep them there. Content. Beautiful. Mine.

She extended her hand. It gleamed like ivory in the pyramids' firelight.

The vision pressed harder. Ben could almost feel her fingers brushing his. Behind her, the undead army stood not as monsters but as a congregation, faithful and serene. They adored her.

For one raw instant, he wanted her too.

The scent of her promised warmth and never being alone again. But Fiona's coin flashed in his memory. Loki's fox eyes gleamed sharply in his periphery.

Ben shut his eyes.

The perfume faltered. The warmth dimmed.

When he opened them, Lilith's hand was still outstretched, her smile softer, more dangerous. Do not mistake me for fear, she whispered. I am seduction itself. I do not chase. They come to me. And so will you.

The vision shattered.

The frost of the steppe returned, cold enough to bite his lungs. Ben staggered, bracing against the air, shaking with something that was not entirely fear.

Fiona's coin spun once and landed in her palm. Her voice was low, steady. "That was only the first call. She will not stop."

Loki's grin came back, but thinner, edged. "Careful, night-born. Darkness is yours, yes. But Seduction is hers. And she knows how to dress damnation in silk."

Ben said nothing. His breath smoked in the frozen air, and the steppe seemed to listen.

"What does it mean?" he asked at last, voice low. "All of it. The naming, kin, her. What does it mean?"

"The ethereals don't judge," Fiona said. "They weigh."

"Humanity was given light. It worshipped it."

Loki's eyes gleamed. "Now the board tilts. If light failed, perhaps night will move you."

"And if it fails?" Ben asked.

Fiona caught the coin. "Then silence." She let the coin land flat against her palm. "Then Fenris bites."

The name burned in his ears. Fenris. The wolf-star. He stared at the ground, frost crunching faintly under his boots. "So they gave light, and it failed. Now they hand over darkness. To me."

"To you," Loki echoed, with a sly grin. "Light promised certainty—night forces movement."

Ben lifted his eyes to the stars. They gleamed cold and merciless, closer than they should be. "And if night fails too?"

Loki shrugged, fox-tail flicking. Silence answered him.

Fiona's voice softened. "But you've already done what no one else could. You lived when you shouldn't. You gathered the others without knowing. Even Lilith stirs against you because she feels the scale tipping. You are not an accident. You are the hinge."

Ben closed his eyes. Lilith's perfume still haunted him, her hand still reaching, her smile still promising. He forced it aside. "If the ethereals are watching," he said quietly, "then let them see. If night is their test, then I'll walk it. But I won't walk it alone."

Fiona's coin snapped into motion once more. Loki's grin sharpened. Ben rubbed his hands together, chasing warmth, though the cold wasn't what gnawed at him. It was the weight of the names Fiona had spoken. Death. Chaos. Despair. Destruction.

"My kin," he muttered. "That's what you called them."

Fiona's coin spun and gleamed. "Yes."

Ben shook his head. "This is ridiculous. I am not their commander. They're people. Broken. Dangerous. They don't follow me."

Loki chuckled, fox-tail flicking in the snow. "And yet they move when you do. You've stirred them without trying. You breathed, and they woke. That's not command. That's resonance. You walk into the dark, and they hear footsteps."

Ben stared out across the steppe, the horizon an endless smear of black and silver. "So what happens if I bring them together?"

"Then the board changes," Fiona said. "The four are not balance—they are disruption. Together they cannot be ignored—not by gods, not by mortals, not even by her."

Ben's stomach tightened at the thought of Lilith's smile. "And if I fail to hold them?"

Loki leaned closer, voice a conspirator's whisper. "Then chaos burns the map, despair smothers the fire, destruction tears the house down, and death calls it finished. That's the risk. A hand of knives is only useful if you keep the blades pointed outward."

Ben's jaw clenched. "So I'm meant to bind them."

"Not bind," Fiona corrected, sharply. "Remind. Jian is still a man who feeds strangers at his table. Delilah is still a woman who inked stories into skin. Jake is still a captain who laughs with his crew. Ellery is still a detective who asks questions when others turn away. If they forget those parts, their ruin will devour them. And you."

The words cut, but they rang true. He remembered Jian's quiet hospitality, Jake's reckless grin, Delilah's sharp gaze, and Ellery's silence that carried weight instead of emptiness. Human threads. Fragile, but real.

"And what about her?" Ben asked, voice low.

Fiona's coin flashed, caught between her fingers. "Lilith will try to unmake every step you take. She is seduction itself. She will offer them what they secretly crave—power, release, comfort in damnation. If they turn, they are hers. She collects gladly."

Ben thought of the mummies in her vision, standing proud, adoring her even in death. Not shackled, but willing. His skin crawled. "So we move," he said. "Before she reaches them first."

Loki clapped his hands, laughing brightly. "At last, he says it. The herald makes his first decree."

"It's not a decree," Ben snapped. "It's a necessity."

"Call it what you like," Loki said, grinning. "The dice are rolling now."

Ben dragged in a breath, the air biting sharp in his lungs. "Where first?"

The fox-shadow curled behind Loki as if wagging. "Fire, of course. Jian Wu. He burns inside whether he wants to or not. If she tempts him before you reach him, the Scourge becomes hers. And then you'll face fire that doesn't care who it consumes."

Fiona nodded once. "Agreed. Jian first. Then Delilah. Chaos bends easily if it's not steadied. Despair and Death will wait—but not forever."

Ben nodded once, as if signing something he couldn't unsign. "Then Jian," Ben said.

The wind shifted, rattling frost like distant applause. Or warning.

Chapter 18
The Falcon

At dawn, the hawk-banner snapped in a wind that smelled of silt and diesel and incense. It flew above the Citadel like a promise carved into the air—we stand. Below it, Cairo breathed the way men breathe when they know the sea is coming and they have built only sandbags.

Rus rose over the square in a flare of heatless light, wings in the geometry of sunrise. His shadow poured over truck beds of water barrels stamped *SANCTIFIED*, over priests knotting rosaries tight around their wrists, over vigilante pilots chalking a hawk onto patched fuselages.

He watched the river of faith hurry through the streets—white collars and black cassocks jostling beside mechanics, bakers, mothers with bottled water balanced on their hips.

Cairo had become an army of the living.

It would have to be. He lifted, beating toward the western haze where the desert boiled.

Dust marched there in bands and curtains, not shaped by wind but by steps.

The first ranks appeared: skeleton phalanxes in bronze and leather that time had forgiven, shields lifted in perfect angles, jawbones clicking to a rhythm no drummer led. Behind them came the shamblers and the swift, revenants with tendons like cables and wraiths that were only the idea of a soldier, their edges fraying the light.

Farther still, like a stain spreading to the horizon, the host of the newly risen mummies in priestly wrappings black with pitch, necromancers in broken collars, their mouths stitched and humming, and hierophants whose ribs were cages for trapped embers. Above all of them, the Weavers sang: a choir of bone and air, voices so dry they turned cloud to parchment.

She walked at their crown, calm as arithmetic. Lilith. Each step set a new measure for distance. Each breath unspooled a spell.

"Hold," Rus said, and the order rolled across frequency and flesh alike. MiGs and biplanes and ridiculous crop-dusters settled into pattern over his shoulders. On bridges, the militia raised corrugated-iron shields. On rooftops, imams and priests blessed rifles and hands and the throats that would soon be screaming.

Athena stood on the Museum's steps with her spear in the crook of her elbow, eyes narrowed; Demeter knelt with both palms on the ground, whispering to soil that had known kings and famines and floods.

The first contact was sound. The Weavers' chant braided into the crack of a hundred thousand bones stepping in time. Faith answered with bells and engines and the sizzle of holy water tipping into gutters. Then the lines touched, and the world forgot how to keep time.

Rus struck like he had sworn he would—no speeches, no theatrics, a hawk's mathematics. He dropped into the vanguard and smashed it flat, wings cutting bone to static; he rose with a clutch of revenants in his talons and hurled them into the next rank; he turned in the air and roared, and for a heartbeat the dead flinched, remembering that fear had once been theirs.

"Left bank!" he barked, and the vigilante pilots bent their ragged formation like a scythe. Kerosene streams stitched fire across the sand. Where the flames failed—barrels cracked and the rain of sanctified water hissed like a sea coming to boil.

Priests ran to meet the impact. A dozen together made a wall of hands and books and breath. Crosses lifted, Qur'ans opened, palms pressed forward in benediction.

The first wraith to touch them smoked, then screamed in absolute silence, folding apart as if an invisible hand had wrung it dry. The line cheered. For twelve heartbeats, hope was a visible thing.

Then Lilith lifted her chin.

Her Weavers inhaled and exhaled as one. The song bent. A note like thirst itself passed through the living. From the front ranks of the mummy-priests came a sound like papyrus being torn, and a line of sigils flashed across the sand in blue fire. The holy water fell into it and vanished, not boiled, not consumed—measured out of existence. The next pour hit the ground as if it had hit glass. The priests faltered, recalculating prayers into weapons again. Three revenants crossed their hesitation and took them like nets.

"Break them," Rus hissed, and he tore a trench through the dead so fast the air behind him folded shut. It didn't matter. The trench filled with more dead, the way the Nile fills any channel given long enough.

"Now," Athena snapped, and she leapt from the steps into the melee with a grin she had not seen since the ages when marble was still soft. Her spear flickered—a line as sure as his wings—and wherever its point traced, skeletons fell. She counted the dead—undead. The battlefield's sums favoured them.

Then the hierophants sang back.

Symbols she did not know burned in the air around her like wasps. A circle closed about her ankles so exact it was cruel. She stepped free with contempt—a circle drawn by dead hands would not hold Athena. But in that delay, ten priests were lifted screaming and swallowed, voices cut off as they were bound, eyes propped open by bone pins so they could watch their hands swinging against the cloth.

Demeter felt it. Her palms drove into the dust.

"Up," she whispered to the old cracked earth itself, to the silt of the river.

The ground listened. For a screaming minute, the desert remembered mud. It sucked at skeletal feet, glued ranks together, and dragged down wraiths. Stone teeth rose where paving had slept, biting at shinbones. Dust ran like a river uphill.

Lilith tilted her head. "Return," she said to the wet sand. The mud sighed in shame and hardened. Trapped ankles shattered, their feet caught in the ground—but the skeletons did not fall. They advanced on splintered stumps, instead.

On the flyover, a young pilot threw a bottle of water and whispered a prayer. It struck a revenant's face, and the skin boiled away. The boy hollered and threw another. A wraith rose behind him and pushed its hand through his ribs, ripping out his heart. The boy's mouth held surprise as his plane dove into the crowd below.

Rus climbed through the smoke into the sky.

The Weavers' sound tried to thin his wings. He roared against it, tore after it, and found them—thirty on a ridge, mouths opening like dry doors, bone fingers conducting the wind.

He dove.

He reached them. He discovered what Lilith had saved for him. They were bound to sigils older than him.

His strike broke bodies, and their song did not stop. Collapsed skeletons still sang in tune. It was terrifying to watch. He felt that instant's recoil, a lull in the world, and shouted down to everyone who could hear: "Push!"

Cairo pushed. Pilots skimmed minarets and dropped holy water bombs. On bridges, water flew in silver arcs that burned whatever was undead.

Athena took a step, another—no longer fighting to win, only to keep the line from collapsing. Demi whispered to palm groves still flexing. For a moment, it seemed possible, not to win, but to stretch the hour.

Lilith raised both hands.

The horizon rippled. From it rose columns of undead.

Black stone remembered, doorways stood where the desert had been. Through them came ranks of embalmed priests with gold leafing their lips, jackal-masked mages with eyes alight like kiln mouths, and queens whose crowns had rusted into their scalps. Each stepped from a door and began speaking.

Their words tilled the air.

Spells moved as though real—shadows that cut, light that brought men to their knees, silence that snapped banners and morale. A ripple of commands from the jackals made radios keen and wail. A sentence from a queen ripped weapons from hands. Weapons fell in the dust.

Lilith herself took a step forward and drew a glyph in the air.

The Nile surged as a tidal wave, collecting and destroying countless barrels of holy water, as well as support tents, medical triage and operational command.

Rus plunged with everything he had. He hit another of her spells and felt it try to unchoose him. Feathers burned at his edges, trying to dissolve. He cried out—reclaiming the negative space around him.

The spell slid behind.

"Hold your line!" he yelled, as an eagle screeching.

His routing force regrouped and held till they no longer could.

Priests were cut down everywhere. A line of Lilith's clergy opened their mouths, exhaling centuries of horror into seminarians who had barely learned Latin. Breaths turned to dust in throats. Nuns tied their veils tighter and walked forward anyway. Some laid their hands on the dead and felt the old chains of devotion tighten around their own wrists. Some made it one more step. Some did not.

Athena's spear cracked. She gripped the broken half and drove it into a hierophant's chest. It laughed—she did not. Demeter bled from the nose, eyes red, fingers dug into stone that would not become soil again for her.

On the river, a flight of vigilantes banked low, lining up for a pass. A Weavers chord cut their lift like a thread. Three planes made it back to the sky. Two slid into the Nile ungracefully.

Rus dropped.

He did not ask who needed him most. He gave himself to the worst of it, which was everywhere. He caught a falling priest and felt the frail bones of the man's hands. He slammed a revenant into a wall so hard the wall cracked and bellowed. He cut, he carried, he called. He did not look west. He could feel Lilith the way a man senses being watched.

Then the city itself betrayed them. It began with a shudder beneath the Citadel. Stones groaned, dust fell in rivulets from arches that had stood since Saladin. The square cracked. Priests staggered, looking down to see hieroglyphs burning through cobblestones, lines of blue fire tracing patterns too ancient to be remembered.

Then the first sarcophagus split the pavement and clawed its way open. A mummy rose in vestments of gold and pitch-black wrappings, its jaw sewn shut but its eyes burning with priestly fire.

Behind it came others—scores, then hundreds—their staffs capped with ankhs that dripped with green flame. Necromancers, long interred beneath mosques and mausoleums, lifted their skulls and opened mouths, spilling words that gnawed through faith itself. And then the hierophants came, tall and robed in tattered linen, ribs split wide to reveal the glowing hearts of bound stars. Their voices were not sound but weight; every syllable pressed down like a slab of granite on a tomb.

They rose from crypts beneath the Citadel, from catacombs threaded under mosques, from forgotten chambers in the pyramids themselves. Cairo had been a city of the dead long before it was a city of the living, and now the dead remembered their dominion.

Rus wheeled in the sky and saw the trap too late. His eyes widened as the western horde surged forward and the city split behind him, releasing its dead. His army—a patchwork of militias, priests, vigilantes, and gods—was caught between a hammer and an anvil.

"Rear flank!" Athena shouted, voice slicing through the chaos. She spun her spear in a blinding arc, cutting down the first wave of mummies as they lurched from the broken streets.

Demeter cried out as black roots burst from the soil—tendrils of bone wrapped her wrists, dragging her toward the earth. She wrenched free with a scream, slicing her hand, blood streaming.

The Citadel square dissolved into a slaughterhouse.

Priests raised crosses only to have them wrenched away by invisible hands. Soldiers fired rifles that jammed with sand the moment the hierophants whispered. Children screamed as tomb mouths yawned open in alleyways, spilling embalmed priests into their flight.

Rus dove, talons tearing through necromancers, wings flaring to shield the Citadel steps. He shouted commands, but half his army was already turning, caught between the desert horde in the west and the rising dead within their own walls.

The hawk's cry faltered under the sheer weight of numbers.

Lilith's laughter drifted from the western ridge, carried on the Weavers' song. She had not needed to breach Cairo's walls.

Cairo had been her arsenal all along.

"Contain them!" Rus roared, striking down with all the fury. He ripped a hierophant in two, its star-heart imploding in a flare that blinded a dozen men. Athena fought at his side, smouldering slick with ichor, her lips pressed into grim determination.

Demeter staggered, mud, blood and bone warring beneath her fingers, her voice raw with exhaustion.

Everywhere, priests and men fell.

For a long breath, the ridge held the wind and the thin silver of the Weavers' song. Then silence.

Lilith stepped down from the desert. Her cloak was dust, her crown of bone and void braided into a circlet that refused to touch her brow. She did not hurry. Spells walked ahead of her to move the air aside.

"HOLD!" Rus roared.

Athena threw herself into the hinge where the two fronts tried to close. She did not have enough spears for this, so she made do with angles—shield corners, broken lengths of rebar, the edge of her own hand. Where she pointed, men and women found the straightest path through chaos and took it. It bought minutes.

Demeter bled from the ears now. She had ordered the soil to clutch and the palms to drag and the old brick to crumble into snares; the city obeyed until the hierophants spoke. Their voices laid weight across her edicts and the earth. She spat pink, wiped her mouth, and kept her bloodied hands on the ground.

Lilith reached the first collapsed wall of the western quarter and paused—not to rest, but to measure. "Here," she murmured, and drew a character in the air with one finger.

It hung—black, uncomplicated, incurious—and then clicked into the world.

Across the city, every bell that had not already been ripped down pealed once, badly. The sound crawled into throats. Priests tried to shout blessings. Nuns tried to sing. Nothing came out.

She drew another character, as lazy as a girl drawing on a windowpane. The city shadows lengthened and moved like nets. Where they crossed a street, men stumbled into darkness. The living were being drowned by the absence of light.

"NO." The word tore out of Rus as he hurtled towards her.

Athena reached Lilith before Rus. She came with no announcement and hit like fact: point, twist, recover, point. The spearhead skated into a spell that behaved like glass. Lilith turned her head as if someone was tapping at the window. For a heartbeat, the two women were carved into the exact moment—the huntress of intellect, the queen of absence.

"Do you remember me?" Athena asked, very softly.

"I remember your confidence," Lilith said, forming another spell. It closed around Athena's spear, drank the steel, and exhaled ash. Athena did not let the surprise climb into her eyes. She broke the haft cleanly, caught the back edge in her left hand as if she had planned the loss, and went on.

Lilith's smile was small and fond, the way a teacher smiles at a bright child in a losing class, and then pushed away from Athena.

Demeter felt a change in the ground. It was minor at first, an ache in the way it held itself together—then not minor at all. The ground started to quake. She slammed both hands immediately into the dirt and willed *DOWN.* Buildings, minarets and walls stopped shaking and steadied as the ground relaxed.

"Rally to the museum!" Rus ordered—the nearest high ground that was still theirs. Runners took the words into the alleys. Radios were muted. The living moved by sight: a hawk's shadow, a nun's hand, Athena's chin. They fell back street by street, not broken, folded. Behind them, the dead filled every negative left by their retreat as if ink were chasing a stylus.

Lilith did not chase. She walked to a fallen priest and knelt beside him. She touched two fingers to his forehead, smearing grit and blood, and read what he had believed. "You were brave," she said, almost gently.

She looked up at the wall of the Egyptian Museum, at its smashed windows and its banners flapping themselves to pieces. "Open," she told its doors, and they obliged. The mummies that had slept there came out in orderly rows—curators of their own resurrection.

On Tahrir Square, priests from three continents formed a circle and raised their books. They spoke as one, voices braided into a rope so tight. The rope held the square for a count of ten. On eleven, the hierophants countered, the rope snapped, and the priests dropped their holy books. A woman snatched the Qur'an out of the dust and kissed it, then used it to strike a revenant in the jaw so hard the revenant lost its head. Faith was a weapon even when the rules quit.

Rus bled now—thin lines along the vanes of his wings where spells had shaved him. He refused to think about the pyramids. He could feel them like pressure on a bruise.

"Rus." Athena's voice tight. She had fought her way to his shoulder. Demeter lurched to his other side, hair matted with dust and blood, eyes wild and sane at once. "We cannot hold both faces," Athena said. "Choose."

He looked west, where the desert horde pressed. He looked east, where the city birthed more death at every step. He looked at the museum doors, and the people jammed against them, praying for a hall that could still be defended by glass and marble and the notion of history. "Retreat," he said, and hated himself for the word even as he knew it was right.

"We fall back on the east bank," Athena said. "We hold what we can and buy what we cannot." Her voice shook once, then found stone. "We'll make them spend us one by one."

Rus nodded. It felt like choosing which finger to lose first. "Go."

They went. The living flowed toward the bridges that still wanted them. The dead did not hurry. Lilith did not raise her hands again. She did not need to. The day belonged to her and to the city's memory.

Athena spun, cutting down two more revenants before yanking a wounded soldier to his feet. "East bank!" she shouted. "To the river!" Her voice was iron, commanding even in retreat. "Carry who you can, leave no one standing!"

The order rippled through the square. Soldiers slung rifles and lifted bodies. Priests dragged seminarians half-dead from the rubble. Vigilantes leapt from wrecked aircraft and pulled children onto their backs. The retreat was not orderly, but it was desperate, alive. That was enough.

Demeter raised her arms one last time. The street cracked, and a wall of dust lifted between the Citadel and the advancing dead. It would not hold long, but long enough. She collapsed to her knees, gasping, but a boy no older than twelve caught her elbow and hauled her upright. "Not yet, lady," he said. She almost wept at the word.

Rus dropped into the chaos, gathering survivors in his wings, shielding them from arrows of bone and shards of spellfire. His shadow became a canopy, guiding them eastward. "Move!" he bellowed. "The river waits!"

From the west came the steady grind of Lilith's host, relentless, endless. From beneath came the rattle of catacombs vomiting kings and hierophants into the streets. From the east, the Nile glimmered faintly, black water catching the broken moon. It was not salvation, but it was escape.

Athena fought a rearguard action, each thrust and kick a testament of defiance. She barked orders like drumbeats: "Hold this alley! Cover the crossing! Drop the bridge when we're through!" Her presence carved a path where chaos would have devoured.

The hawk-banner over Cairo burned in green fire, its fabric curling in silence. Survivors saw it fall and nearly broke, but Rus roared—"Eyes forward!"—and the sound bound them together again.

They reached the first bridge, a span of stone scarred by centuries. The Nile churned below, restless. Boats jammed against its banks, already overloaded with refugees. Soldiers shoved them off as more hands reached for the gunwales. Screams carried across the water.

"Across!" Athena ordered. "Every soul across!"

Demeter pressed her palms into the bridge. The stone quivered, then hardened, remembering its purpose. "It will hold," she whispered. "It must."

The living poured across in waves. Mothers clutching infants, soldiers with comrades over their shoulders, priests dragging relics they refused to leave. Behind them, the dead surged closer, their voices a choir of hunger. The first arrows fell, black shafts hissing into flesh. Men stumbled, women screamed, children dropped. Rus swept low, wings like shields, deflecting the worst of it.

Athena stood at the bridge's throat, alone, cutting down anyone who dared approach. Her eyes burned with fury, her movements precise even in exhaustion. "Go!" she snarled at the last of the stragglers. "I'll follow."

"No," Rus said, landing hard beside her. His talons cracked the stone. "We go together."

The last wave stumbled across, priests carrying Demeter limp between them. The gods turned as one. Rus beat his wings, stirring a gale that shook the bridge. Athena slammed her broken spear into the keystone. Demeter lifted her head and whispered, voice barely audible: "Sleep."

The bridge shuddered. Then it broke. Stone screamed as it cracked and fell, plunging into the river. The dead at its mouth toppled into black water, thrashing, dragged down by weight and current. The living watched from the far bank as the Nile swallowed the last span.

For a heartbeat, silence. Then Lilith's voice, drifting across the water like a lullaby: "You cannot run forever, hawk. The river carries you east, but I will be there before you land."

Rus stood at the bank, wings bleeding, eyes like molten gold. He did not answer. He only turned to the survivors huddled in the dark and said, "You live. That is enough for tonight."

Athena leaned on her broken spear, jaw tight. Demeter collapsed into the arms of priests, her lips stained with blood. The city behind them burned green, black, and violet, pyramids crowned with scaffolds of bone. Cairo was gone. But the living still breathed. And as long as they did, the war was not finished.

Chapter 19
Intermission

What a disaster. I've been reading along with this "epic struggle for the fate of the world," and I've finally had to set the book down to laugh. Or cry. Or both. Because if this is what stands between humanity and oblivion, then the dead might as well save everyone the trouble and get it over with quickly.

The gods? Don't make me laugh. They strut about like peacocks, polishing their marble halls, holding solemn councils, muttering about "balance." As if the universe is a set of scales and they're the accountants making sure the numbers add up. Meanwhile, Lilith is out there turning cities into bone-pits and deserts into highways for corpses, and the gods' response is to nod gravely and light more torches.

If that's divinity, I'll take my chances with atheism.

And their powers—oh yes, they still have them. Lightning, storms, beauty, wisdom, harvests, chance. All the party tricks that once impressed farmers and frightened kings. Now? They're about as useful as a pocketful of fireworks at a house fire. Lilith doesn't blink at lightning. Skeletons don't drown in storms. Revenants don't swoon at beauty. The gods keep gesturing dramatically, expecting the world to gasp, but the world is too busy dying.

You'd think, with the stakes so high, they'd bring out the heavy hitters. You know, the real muscle. Odin's fury, Zeus's thunder, Thor's hammer.

Where is Thor, by the way?

We've got Loki running about causing mischief as usual—of course, we do—but Thor? Absent. Missing in action. The one guy who might have swung a hammer big enough to matter apparently took the day off.

Wonderful. Absolutely wonderful. We have Loki, but not Thor. Mischief without muscle. Comedy without a punchline.

And then there's Ben Callum, our so-called doorway to Hell, the man who doesn't die. What a resume. Immortal by clerical error, stumbling from one catastrophe to the next, dragging behind him the worst entourage since Don Quixote picked a fight with a windmill. These are devils meant to save the world? What a strange contradiction. Death, who can't frighten the dead. Scourge, who's gone on holiday. Chaos, who thinks fireworks will fix it. And Jake, lord of the sea, pirate in charge. This isn't the cavalry. It's a bloody pantomime.

The irony is thick enough to choke on. Mortals pray harder than they have in centuries, temples are overflowing, priests are burning through their holy water like it's cheap wine—and the gods are as useful as a chocolate teapot. Not because they can't wave their hands. They can. They try. They just don't matter. They still believe themselves relevant while Lilith doesn't even acknowledge their existence. She doesn't fight them because they aren't worth the energy. They're not enemies. They're scenery. Props. Background noise for her coronation.

I swear, this isn't an apocalypse. This is a comedy routine, and not a good one. Everyone is playing their role badly. The gods are actors who've forgotten their lines. The fractured, half-woken devils are merry men in merry costumes, merrily dancing private little jigs. Ben is the leading stagehand, accidentally shoved into the spotlight. And Lilith? Lilith is the director, the playwright, and the critic, all rolled into one, watching the whole farce unfold with a smile and clapping her hands in delight.

So yes, let's all take a deep breath and admit it: absolutely everyone is useless. The gods, the devils, the mortals, the lot. A shit show of cosmic proportions. And when you think someone might step up and deliver something resembling ability, Loki wanders in. Of course he does. Mischief incarnate, smirking at the flames, making jokes while the world burns.

And still no Thor. Why not?

Because of course.

Oh yes, our one and only shining example of competence in this cosmic circus is Lilith. She raises the dead like she's running a startup with infinite funding. Skeletons, revenants, mummy-priests, hierophants—entire armies conjured as easily as mortals boil tea. She conquers cities not by storming them but by recycling them. The priests who resist become her clergy—the soldiers who fall rise again in her ranks.

Cairo didn't just fall; it was absorbed. Efficiency that would make any corporate board proud.

But let's ask the question no one dares: what exactly is the plan here?

Lilith keeps conquering, yes. She keeps marching, yes. Her armies swell. But to what end? Is she just collecting cities like trinkets on a shelf? Does she plan to rule a world populated entirely by skeletons? Picture it: bone parades, skeletal bureaucracy, an economy run on dust and marrow. Riveting. Imagine the diplomatic summits: one side clattering jawbones, the other side clattering slightly louder. Inspiring stuff.

Or maybe she's aiming higher. Maybe she's playing the long game. Perhaps the earth is just her launchpad, and she dreams of skeletons in space. Starfaring legions, bone-armoured ships cutting across the void, conquering planets that never asked to be part of this farce. Aliens watching in horror as an army of mummified priests floats toward them, chanting hymns that sound like sandpaper being torn. The future we've all been waiting for.

And yet does she even know? The series she's producing has no finale in sight. She's on autopilot—terrifying in the moment, directionless in the end. What's the point of ruling ashes? What's the use of skeleton empires? What does she feed on when everything has been stripped down to bone? She can conquer everything—but after that, what then? Eternal parades? A throne built out of jawbones? The satisfaction of knowing she finally achieved what moths and termites achieve daily—total consumption without meaning?

It's almost disappointing. She's the only competent figure in this entire disaster, and even she might not have thought it through. Conquest for conquest's sake. Domination because domination is there to be had. A skeleton empire that stretches from Cairo to the stars—impressive, yes, but hollow. Literally very hollow.

And this is where the narrator, bored and sardonic, can't help but smirk. Because if Lilith's endgame really is to launch starfaring skeletons into the cosmos, then the universe is in for one hell of a joke. Imagine the scene: Earth, ravaged and empty, serving as the galactic skeleton factory. Star systems falling to bone ships powered by necromantic fuel. Entire galaxies clattering in unison. And somewhere, Lilith sits on her throne of ribcages, smiling, never once asking herself the most straightforward question: why?

Maybe that's the punchline. There is no why.

So yes, she's competent. Terrifyingly competent. But competence without purpose is just another kind of failure—a grander, more spectacular failure. The gods fail by being useless. Lilith fails by being unstoppable without a destination. The result is the same: a universe heading toward absurdity.

Perhaps, one day, someone will stop her. Perhaps not. Either way, the thought lingers: is humanity's last chapter really to be a footnote in the age of bone? If that's genuinely the vision, then congratulations, Lilith. You've outdone everyone. You're building the most pointless empire the universe has ever seen.

Bravo.

And then, of course, Ben. Ben Callum. Our so-called fulcrum of this whole saga. The aberrant mortal who won't stay dead. The gods whisper about him like he's destiny incarnate. Loki and Fiona look at him as though he's salvation. Lilith, to her credit, mostly ignores him, which is the only sensible response. Because honestly—how does he think he's going to stop this mess?

What does he have, exactly? Immortality by accident. That's not a power, that's a clerical oversight. He doesn't die, yes, but he doesn't do anything either. He doesn't command armies. He stumbles. He survives. He's a human cockroach with good timing. And somehow this has been mistaken for heroism.

And then his entire entourage—of misfits—the universe's answer to comic relief. If Ben is a walking error, they're the punchline.

Death. The one name that should strike terror in every heart. Except Lilith already stole his job and is doing it better. He's the Grim Reaper who shows up at a graveyard and finds the work's already been done—a bystander at his own party.

Scourge. Oh, the mighty bringer of plague, fire, and ruin. The one who could scorch the earth with a gesture. Except—he's not here. On a walkabout. The apocalypse is in full swing, and one of Ben's biggest weapons is treating it like a sabbatical. Gone thinking. Be back never. That's Scourge. Lilith probably doesn't even know he exists, which might be the cruellest cut of all.

Chaos. At least she turns up, which is already more than the others can say, but her contribution is the cosmic equivalent of waving sparklers and shouting "Boo!" at a freight train. She flares, she dazzles, she crackles with energy. She believes herself indispensable—but against inevitability? She's a magician at a funeral, pulling scarves out of a hat while the coffin is lowered into the ground.

And Jake. Poor Jake, the sailor without a sea. Lord of tides, master of waves, scourge of navies. A magnificent ally if Lilith had any interest in launching a fleet. But she doesn't. She marches across deserts, she takes cities, she reanimates armies. His power is as relevant to this war as a lighthouse in the Sahara. At least the Leviathan might keep him entertained.

So there they are. Ben's champions. Together, they are not the Four Horsemen of the Apocalypse. They are the Four Blunders of the Afterparty, plus one. The poor immortal that has no plan but to follow his heart—if he had a heart.

But let's be honest: if this is the plan, then there is no plan. How does he think he's going to stop Lilith? With pep talks?

It would be funny if it weren't tragic. No—it is funny, because it's already tragic. The gods are useless, Lilith is tireless, and

Ben is immortal for no reason at all, dragging three-and-a-half disasters behind him like a parody of Revelation.

The world is ending, and he's the cavalry. So yes, here's the sardonic truth: Ben doesn't have a chance in hell. And hell's already here.

The universe isn't conspiring against us. It's laughing.

And Ben is still breathing. Because, of course, he is.

Chapter 20

The Strategy

The doors were supposed to be sealed. Security had argued, twice, that no one else would be admitted once the session began. The sound of heavy boots in the corridor froze the room more effectively than any speech.

The aides moved first, chairs scraping. A hand twitched toward a pistol before its owner remembered he was standing beside three generals, five presidents, and the Pope's envoy.

The boots came closer, unhurriedly, as if they belonged there. Then the doors opened without ceremony, and Ari filled the frame.

He didn't knock. He didn't bow. He didn't even ask.

The generals in the front row stiffened, eyes darting to the President. No badge. No entourage. No explanation. Just a man built like a weapon, broad-shouldered, scar along his jaw, eyes sharp as cut glass. His jacket was half-buttoned, his shirt open at the collar, like he'd stepped away from a brawl, not a motorcade.

"Who the hell are you?" the French President snapped, already on his feet.

Ari smiled, the kind that carried no warmth. "You've been talking about walls and mirrors and salt. Clever. But useless if no one bleeds in front of them."

The Israeli PM's hand hovered above his microphone, then dropped. He stared. He knew the name. He had read the reports, though none ever confirmed them. Ari. The war-dog who never died in the desert, who drank smoke like it was wine. The one whispered about in mess halls, filed under "unconfirmed myth."

The President of the United States leaned back slowly. "You're not cleared for this room."

"And yet," Ari said, stepping inside, "here I am."

Two guards moved, but he didn't glance at them. He didn't need to. Something in the air around him warned them off. He walked to the centre of the table, boots thudding against the floor.

"You're building moats. Belts of brine. Fine. But you'll run out of salt before she runs out of dead. Mirrors? They shatter. And the Weavers won't stop singing because you give them a headache."

He placed both hands on the wood, leaning forward until the map's glow lit his jaw.

"You want to stop the horde before the holy land? You don't build walls. You hunt the head of the snake."

"You presume much," the Saudi envoy said. "We are discussing strategy. You are a soldier. At best."

Ari turned his head, slow, deliberate. "I am war," he said simply. "And war doesn't wait for permission."

The Vatican envoy crossed herself before she realised she was doing it. The engineer who had proposed mirrors scribbled something frantically in her notebook: not a word, but a sketch, as if capturing his presence mattered more than what he said.

The President tried again, voice calm but edged. "If you've come to contribute, make it clear. Otherwise, I'll have you removed."

"Remove me," Ari said with that wolf-smile, "and you remove your only chance of striking Lilith where it hurts."

He tapped the map where the Canal pulsed red. "You don't stop inevitability. You stab it in the heart. That means hitting her directly, not her armies. The longer you waste time fighting skeletons, the more she sings the land into graves."

"Impossible," the Israeli PM said, though his voice lacked conviction. "She travels with an army the size of nations."

"Good," Ari said. "That makes her easy to find."

The Jordanian King studied him, weighing. "And how do you propose we strike her? Walk into the dead as if they are fog?"

"Not walk," Ari said. "Fall. From the sky. From behind her. From the places she doesn't expect. You have aircraft—use them for men, not payloads. Drop soldiers where she isn't looking. Cut her Weavers first. Cut her necromancers second. Then burn every stitch of spell she breathes. You think she is untouchable because you keep fighting her shadows. I've seen her. She bleeds. And when she bleeds, her songs falter."

The room went quiet. Not because they believed him, not yet—but because someone had finally spoken of Lilith herself as a target, not just her armies.

The President drummed his fingers once against the wood. "And you'll lead this strike, I assume?"

The room had been carved from bedrock long before anyone alive had needed it. Fluorescents hummed overhead, throwing flat light across a horseshoe of flags. On the far wall, a map of North Africa into the Levant glowed with heat signatures that were not heat—just the world's best guess at where the dead were. They called it a summit, but it didn't feel like one. This had water bottles that sweated in the stale air and a clock that had stopped sometime after Cairo.

The President spoke first because everyone expected him to. His voice had the rasp of someone who'd been awake for days. "The objective is simple to state and impossible to meet. We stop the advance before it reaches the holy sites. If Jerusalem, Bethlehem, Hebron, Mecca, and the Medina become parades of bone, the world will break twice. Once in bodies, once in spirit." He looked at the map. "We hold them east of the Nile. Failing that, we hold them in the Sinai. Failing that..." He didn't finish. He didn't need to.

The Prime Minister of Israel hadn't taken off his coat since landing; his tie sat in a tight, angry knot. "We are moving reserve brigades to the Negev. Every engineer battalion is on trenching detail. We're cutting canals where there should be none. But we need air corridors to survive the approach—our radios die at a kilometre from their front. We need a signalling doctrine that can't be sung out of existence."

"Flag code," the Jordanian King said, drily, as if the word itself tasted like sand. "Signal mirrors, heliographs, runners on bikes. We've started drilling scouts to reread banners. It's not fast, but it is honest. The song cannot erase cloth."

"Nor smoke," said the Turkish President. "We have adopted a three-colour code with flare guns. Red for wraiths, white for revenants, yellow for necromancers. It is crude. It works."

The Saudi Interior Minister—sent because the King could not leave—spoke without preamble. "You will not fight this on your borders only. If the host turns south, it will not stop at Gaza or Aqaba. It will look at Hejaz and remember old roads. We will not permit that road to exist. We propose a sanctified brine belt from Tabuk to the Red Sea. Salt, water, blessing. Pour it into the soil and let it clump."

"The Vatican can provide priests," said the tiny woman representing a city-state that still made half the world sit up when it cleared its throat. "Consecration at scale is a logistics problem, not a theological one. Put the water in front of us, give us trucks, give us time."

"Time is the one we don't have," murmured the EU Council President. "But we can give trucks. And plants. Israel, Egypt, Jordan, Saudi Arabia—where are your desalination nodes?"

"Haifa. Ashkelon. Hadera," the Israeli PM said. "We can divert output if we have the power. We can lace it with salt. We can build spray towers. But Ashkelon is under rocket threat even in peacetime. Now?" He spread his hands.

"Eilat," said the Jordanian. "We will draw there. Pump east and north. But we will need pipe, and pipe is copper, and copper is..." He glanced at the map. The red smudge near Suez moved like spilled dye. "Copper is behind them."

"The Egyptians are fighting in pieces," said the American Chairman of the Joint Chiefs, voice low. "They will do what they can on the east bank, but you must assume the Canal will not hold them. They cross water."

"They don't float," someone said.

"They don't drown either," the Chairman replied.

A French President who had aged a decade in a week cleared his throat. "We must speak plainly. The nuclear question is not a question—your own Atlas strike proved the physics. Where there were skeletons, there are now revenants. Where there was flesh, there are wraiths. Fission adds teeth."

Silence settled like dust. They all knew it. No one had the power to say it first until someone did.

"Then we do this old," said the British Prime Minister. "Earthworks, firebreaks, brine. We cut, canalise, and we keep the sky busy."

"The sky is busy," the President said. "It will stay busy. But we cannot bomb a number that grows with every mistake. We interdict the Weavers and the hierophants. We find the ones whose mouths write the air, and we end their writing." He tapped the map where satellite guesswork drew a faint sigil field like frost along the dead's leading edge. "Our ISR can still read power signatures at a distance. When those choirs open, the spectrum shifts. That's our opening."

"Air can hit a choir," the Israeli PM said. "But the song keeps singing after you break the bodies. We saw that in Cairo."

"Then we break the script," said a woman in an engineer's uniform with the patch of a country too small to be there and too stubborn to leave. She had been invited because someone had whispered her name enough times. "You don't kill a formula with a bullet. You interrupt it. You put noise in the proof." She thumbed toward the Vatican envoy without apology. "Your people wrote their symbols on paper and water for centuries. Ours was written on stone. They write in the air. It's all the same fight. We propose: mirror barrages."

The room let the words sit, unsure of their weight.

"Say it again," the Turkish President said.

"Mirror barrages," she repeated. "We build battery lines not with guns—with light. We arrange heliographs by the thousands. We set banks of panels on ridgelines and rooftops. When the Weavers open their mouths, we flash codas that don't exist in their grammar. Noise. Chaos. Stutter. We don't need to understand their spell. We only need to make it trip."

The Vatican envoy smiled with a weariness that felt like yes. "The Gospel of John in sunlight."

"Or just static," the engineer said. "I don't care if it's holy if it works."

"Power?" the EU President asked.

"Sun," the engineer said. "We'll need copper. Steel. Men to lift. Women to aim. And maps that tell us where those choirs stand."

"We can provide a lattice," said the American NSA Director. "We can see when an area's spectral properties change. The song interferes with the signal. We've learned to read it."

"Good," the President said. "Mirror barrages become Pillar One. Pillar Two is sanctified brine. Not trickles—belts. We cut three across the Sinai like stitches. One at the Canal. One mid-peninsula. One along the border. Trenches twelve meters wide, four deep. Fill with brine. Bless as you pour. Maintain with pumps. Nothing fancy. Just a holy moat."

"You assume they walk," the Jordanian said. "They also are placed." He looked at the Israeli. "We saw the doorways in Cairo. She sets units like stones."

"So we give her bad ground to place into," the engineer said. "Salt-crusted. Mud. I know Demeter—" She stopped. "We can draw water in the desert if we persuade her."

"You will not rely on gods," the Saudi said. It wasn't a warning, exactly. More like a boundary set gently in front of a cliff. "We will rely on water, salt, and prayer."

"Prayer is not a switch," the Vatican envoy said softly. "But it is a vector."

"Vector it into pumps," the British PM said. "We can fund the pipe."

"Pillar Three," the President continued, "is evacuation. I know what that word does in this room. I know what it means to say it with Jerusalem in earshot. But we will stage corridors now—east to Amman, south toward the Negev, west to the sea if we must. We move the vulnerable before we see skeletons in the alleys."

"You will not empty Jerusalem," the Israeli PM said flatly.

"I said corridors," the President replied. "Not abandonment."

The Iranian President had been silent long enough that several aides kept checking to make sure his audio worked. Now he spoke, voice low, steady, careful. "You speak of the holy land as if it were one city. It is a belt from Aleppo to the Hijaz. It is Karbala as much as Bethlehem. Qom is as much as Hebron. You cannot triage sanctity with maps."

"No," the President said. "But we can triage roads." He pointed to the north. "Turkey, you own the choke at Iskenderun. Close it. Mine it with salt: Jordan—bridge demolitions along the King's Highway. Israel—destroy, today, every paved shortcut through the Negev that an army would use. Do not leave a straight line. Iran—if you can bless water, bless it. Put your clerics in tankers. Point them at wherever the map looks like a bottleneck."

"We can," the Iranian said. "We will. But understand: blessings are not fireworks. They exhaust men. They must sleep."

"Then we rotate them like pilots," the Chairman said. "Find the cadence. Keep the belts wet."

"We will need to protect the belts," the Israeli PM said. "She has jackal-magi who turn radios into paper. They will try to turn pumps into sand."

"Then we post soldiers with spears," the Jordanian said, half-smile, no humour. "And mirrors. And flags."

A young aide from nowhere in particular darted forward and changed the map. The red smear had reached the Canal in three thin fingers. Each finger had its own pulse, like a stethoscope pressed to a wound. The room leaned in without deciding to.

"Name it," the British PM said, because humans trapped fear beneath acronyms. "This belt-and-mirror mess. Give it a flag so everyone knows what to shout."

"Operation Aegis," said the engineer, before anyone else could. "Three pillars and a shield. If we're lucky, a prayer."

"Not luck," the Israeli PM said. "Work."

"Work and water," the Vatican envoy said.

"Work, water, and the sun itself," the engineer said.

The President nodded once. "Aegis it is. Pillar One: Mirror Barrages targeting choir signatures. Pillar Two: Sanctified Brine Belts in depth. Pillar Three: Evacuation corridors staged now, not after. Air keeps killing conductors. Ground keeps cutting roads. Everyone keeps their clerics fed."

He glanced at the stopped clock and smiled without warmth. "And someone find me an idea for what happens when doorways open inside our lines. Because she will try."

"She will," the Jordanian said. "And we will answer with doors of our own."

"What doors?" the French asked.

The Jordanian tilted his head, almost in prayer, nearly daring. "Hospitals. Kitchens. Places that choose the living."

No one laughed. The map flickered. The fingers at the Canal twitched, like a hand deciding what it wanted to touch. The President looked around the table and let the weight of it press on their shoulders, as the ceiling pressed on the rock. "Then we dig," he said. "We bless. We aim the sun. And we teach the desert to say no."

Ari's grin widened. "Of course."

"You'll need authorisation," the Chairman of the Joint Chiefs said.

"I'll need men who aren't afraid to die," Ari answered. "Authorisation is paper. Paper burns."

The Israeli PM's jaw tightened. "You think you can save Jerusalem with a knife fight in the desert?"

"I think," Ari said, leaning closer, "that while you all debate where to dig ditches, I can be in her shadow by tomorrow. I think someone has to remind her that not all the living wait politely for death."

The engineer shut her notebook and looked around the table. "If what he says is true—that Lilith bleeds—then every plan here changes. Aegis becomes a shield, not a wall. And a strike team becomes our sword."

The Vatican envoy whispered, "David against Goliath."

Ari laughed once, sharply. "David with better aim."

The table was still vibrating from Ari's words when he straightened and let the silence thicken. He let them all sit in it—the generals staring at the map, the politicians fighting their instinct to argue. Then he spoke, crisp as a knife across stone.

"I'll need battalions," Ari said. "Not peacekeepers, not conscripts—crack troops. Men and women who can drop from the sky without flinching, who can hold formation when the air itself turns against them. I want brigades that bleed discipline. I want units that can improvise when orders collapse. Drop them on her back, behind her front, in the marrow of her army."

The French President's jaw went tight. "You speak like you command them already."

"I do," Ari said. "They just haven't been told yet."

The Chairman of the Joint Chiefs leaned forward, trying to cut his authority into the moment. "Airborne operations against a host the size of continents? Dropping into comms dead zones? No resupply, no extraction plan? You're asking for suicide missions."

"I'm asking for victory," Ari shot back.

The Israeli Prime Minister shook his head, disbelief and hunger fighting across his face. "You're asking us to commit our best to certain death."

"No," Ari said. "I'm asking you to commit your best to a chance. Small, sharp, and bloody—but a chance. Because if she walks into the holy sites, you don't just lose cities. You lose faith itself. And when faith collapses, no moat, no army, no wall will matter."

The Jordanian King rubbed his jaw. "You want brigades. How many?"

Ari didn't blink. "Three battalions minimum. One American, one Israeli, one multinational—French, Turkish, Jordanian, whoever still has men willing to jump. Three points of impact. Three teeth in her spine."

The American President's voice went hard. "And what makes you think my generals will hand you a battalion?"

"Because you're out of options," Ari said. He slammed his palm on the map, hard enough to make water bottles jump. "Every hour you argue, her army grows. You think you can out-dig inevitability? Out-salt inevitability? No. The only thing inevitability fears is the knife you don't see coming. Give me your knife."

The Vatican envoy whispered a prayer too low to catch. The Turkish President folded his hands, staring at Ari like he was staring at a storm rolling in. The British Prime Minister, pale, muttered, "And if they don't come back?"

"Then they don't come back," Ari said flatly. "But they'll take pieces of her with them. Enough pieces, and she stops marching. You don't need to win forever. You need to buy time—time for the trenches, time for the salt belts, time for the mirrors. Time for the living to remember they're alive. That's what a battalion buys."

The engineer spoke suddenly, voice sharp. "If you're serious—if we build this into Aegis—we'll need drop zones marked in advance. Land is shifting under her steps. GPS fails near the sigils. You'll need mortal markers. Smoke, flags, fire."

"Then get me volunteers," Ari said. "Not just troops. Scouts. Engineers. Priests. Drop them with us. Drop them first if you have to. Anyone who can plant a flag in the dirt before she swallows it."

"Madness," the French President muttered.

"War," Ari corrected.

The American Chairman pushed back in his chair, glaring at the President. "Sir, this isn't doctrine. It's suicide theatre. We can't sanction this."

The President rubbed his temples. He looked old, suddenly, the map's red glow carving hollows under his eyes. "What happens if we don't try?"

No one answered. They didn't have to. The map pulsed. The fingers of red crawling across the Sinai were wider now, fatter.

"We need names," Ari said. "I want paratroopers who've jumped into fire. I want foreign legionnaires who forgot how to surrender. I want special forces who've been trained to operate in the dark. If they have fear left in them, leave them home."

The Israeli PM exhaled through his nose, long and bitter. "We could call up the Shaldag. They've jumped before. They know the Negev."

The American Chairman bristled. "You're not committing Israeli commandos before we even agree this is—"

The President cut him off. "The 82nd," he said quietly.

The Chairman turned. “Sir—”

“The 82nd,” the President repeated, louder. “They trained for jumps no sane man would take. They’ve lived their doctrine in deserts before. They’ll live it again. Pair them with whoever else has the guts. We form Ari’s strike. Call it Pillar Four.”

The EU envoy stared, horrified. “You cannot make a myth into doctrine.”

“You can,” Ari said, smiling that wolf-smile. “You just did.”

The Jordanian King gave a single nod. “We will commit a battalion. Call them what you like. If they fall, they fall in the service of holding the line.”

The Saudi envoy pressed his hands together. “We do not drop men like stones from the sky. We do not burn lives like tinder. But we will send a company of the Royal Guard. Not to drop. To follow. To cut when you cut.”

“Then we have it,” Ari said. His eyes burned as they moved across the room. “Three battalions. Three wounds deep enough to make her stagger.” He leaned forward, voice dropping. “This is how you stop inevitability. You don’t out-wait it. You bleed it.”

The President looked at him long and hard, then turned to his generals. “Start drawing plans. Identify drop zones. Find me pilots with nerves of iron. Ari has his battalions.”

The map flickered again. The red smears twitched like muscle, flexing toward the east. Ari watched it, lips curving into something between a grin and a snarl.

“Good,” he said. “Now let’s see if inevitability can scream.”

The room had gone taut, like the air before a lightning strike. Three battalions—named, promised, argued into existence—hung in the space between hope and madness. The aides whispered, generals scribbled notes, ministers prayed beneath their breath.

And then Ari leaned back, the wolf-smile gone, his tone suddenly colder.

"You think you're sending those men alone?"

The American President raised an eyebrow. "You just told us you wanted them so that they'd go where no one else would. What are you saying now?"

"I'm saying," Ari growled, "that the gods will march with them."

The silence that followed was different from before. Not stunned into stillness, but heavy, doubtful, almost superstitious.

The British Prime Minister barked a laugh that didn't carry far. "Oh, splendid. We'll have Zed parachute in, shall we—dropping in with the paratroopers, no doubt."

Ari's eyes cut to him like a blade. "Call them what you want. You've already seen them. In Cairo. In Morocco. Do you think it was only your priests and your militias holding lines for minutes at a time? No. Rus tore trenches through bone with his wings. Demeter made the desert remember mud. Athena counted her kills. They are here. They are not myths anymore."

The Vatican envoy swallowed hard. "We... have confirmed reports. Miracles that weren't ours. Powers that no priest could claim." She looked down, ashamed to admit what the church had whispered for centuries but never believed it would see.

"Exactly," Ari said. He jabbed a finger at the glowing map. "They walk among us already. Some fight because they must. Some fight because they cannot bear to be forgotten. Some fight because they have scores older than your nation's. I don't care why. What matters is this: they will be in the fight whether you plan for them or not. And if you don't plan for them, you waste them."

The Israeli PM leaned forward, hands flat on the table. "And you think you can... command them? Direct them like soldiers?"

"No," Ari said simply. "No one commands gods. But I can fight beside them. I have. And I will again. They recognise strength. They recognise resolve. If they see men falling from the sky to strike Lilith herself, they will answer. They won't leave that field to mortals alone."

The Jordanian King's expression was unreadable. "You would gamble our battalions on the cooperation of beings who have ignored us for millennia?"

Ari's eyes flashed. "They haven't ignored you. They've been hiding in plain sight, waiting to see if humanity could stand on its own. Well, now the dead have risen, and the world burns. Standing alone isn't an option anymore. They will move."

The French President's voice was dry as dust. "Drag Zed, Athena, and Rus into your little drop zones? What are you, their flag bearer?"

"No," Ari said, and his voice cut low, raw. "I'm their reminder. They can sit in their marble halls muttering about balance all they want, but when the living start dropping out of the sky to cut Lilith's heart open, they will either come, or they will reveal themselves as cowards. And if they're cowards, then I'll put a knife in them too."

That silenced even the cynics. The American Chairman leaned forward slowly, as if gauging the edges of Ari's words. "You're saying... the battalions will have the god's support?"

"I'm saying they'll have god interference, at the very least," Ari said. "Better we set the field so that interference cuts our way. You plan mirrors and trenches. Fine. Add to it this: when the battalions fall, have priests ready to sanctify their blades, have engineers ready to mark ground with symbols, have commanders ready to adjust when a hawk drops out of the sky or when lightning splits bone columns in half. Because it will happen, it already has. And it will again."

The engineer who had spoken earlier looked around the room, eyes alight with a strange certainty. "If what he says is true, then Aegis isn't three pillars and a sword. It's three pillars, a sword, and—" She hesitated, searching for the word. "And thunder."

The Vatican envoy crossed herself again. "We cannot build doctrine on the promise of miracles."

"Then don't call them miracles," Ari snapped. "Call them artillery you didn't order. Call them reinforcements you can't schedule. Call them chaos. But when it comes, you had better be ready to ride it, not cower from it."

The American President's face was unreadable. He glanced at the map, to the pulsing red blotches creeping eastward. Then back to Ari. "If we do this—if we commit three battalions, if we open Aegis to the interference of gods—what guarantee do we have that it will matter?"

Ari leaned over the table, his shadow falling across the Sinai, glowing on the wall. His voice dropped to a growl that seemed to come from the stone itself. "The only guarantee you have," he said, "is that if you don't, you lose everything. The holy land.

Your faith. Your people. And then your world. You've seen what happens when mortals fight alone. Cairo fell. Fez fell."

The Israeli Prime Minister looked down at his hands. He had not slept since Cairo.

"Next will be the desert gates, then the holy cities. You want a guarantee? Fine. I guarantee this: I will be there. In the sky. In the dirt. In Lilith's shadow. And when I fall, the gods will know it's time to stand."

The map pulsed again, red spreading like spilled wine. No one spoke. The room was full of the sound of breathing—fast, shallow, mortal.

Finally, the American President exhaled and tapped the table. "Very well. Aegis becomes four pillars: mirrors, brine, evacuation, and strike. And... thunder. We will plan for interference. We will assume gods will be in the fight."

The British PM rubbed his eyes. "Gods in doctrine. Saints preserve us."

"Not saints," Ari said. "Warriors."

He bared his teeth in something that was not quite a smile.

Chapter 21
The First

The wool store squatted on the port like a beast that had outlived its usefulness. Salt ate the bricks, iron ribs groaned in the wind, and pigeons shifted restlessly in the rafters. It was a place no one visited unless they wanted to disappear.

Ellery Kalos stood in the dark beside Diane, lungs steady, heart fighting the hum that had been gnawing at him for weeks. He felt it: pressure under the skin, a vibration in his bones like a storm building without clouds. Diane felt it too. Her hand was on the rifle before the first boot scraped the threshold.

The door shrieked open. Light carved a line across the concrete floor.

"Ellery," a man's voice called, calm, measured. "I know you're here."

Ellery's jaw clenched. He knew that voice. Not from hearing it, but from expecting it—the same way he'd known when the file landed on his desk.

He didn't answer.

Diane's voice cut the silence, sharp and level. "One more step and I shoot."

The silhouette froze in the doorway. A pause. Then: "I'm not here to fight."

"You're here because you can't help yourself," Diane said. "So explain, before my finger grows heavy."

Two more shapes slid in behind the first. Fiona, coin bright between her fingers, and Loki, grinning like a man who had already stolen the ending.

"Good evening, huntress," Loki said, too soft to be harmless. "Or do you prefer Skaði when you stalk in the dark?"

Diane's cheek twitched. The rifle didn't waver. "Say it again, trickster, and I'll remind you what became of giants in my country."

Fiona lifted her chin, offering a quieter greeting. "Diane. It's been too long."

"Not long enough," Diane said.

The first man stepped into the sliver of light, just enough for Ellery to see his face. Ben Callum. The fugitive whose name had stalked him through reports, whose photo had set his hands shaking, whose shadow had prowled his dreams since the night Ellery woke screaming.

The hum in Ellery's ribs surged. His grip on control slipped. A pigeon dropped stone-dead from the rafters. Another followed, wings snapping on concrete. Diane's hand brushed his shoulder—steady, grounding. "Hold."

Ben didn't flinch at the thud of wings. His eyes stayed fixed on Ellery's corner of the dark. "I came to collect you."

Ellery stepped out just far enough that the light found half his face. Smoke curled from the cigarette trembling at his lip.

"You're a murder suspect on my desk," he said flatly. "Now you're trespassing in my city."

"And you're not a detective anymore," Ben replied. "You're Death, whether you like it or not."

The words cut deeper than the blast of a gun. Ellery felt the room still around them. Diane's gaze flicked between them, reading the weight in their stares. Loki chuckled low, enjoying the performance.

Ellery's throat went dry. "You don't get to say that word."

"It isn't mine to give you," Ben said, voice steady. "It was always yours. I just woke you."

Ellery remembered the night he woke, the city breathing wrong, the symbols he had scrawled without knowing why. He had blamed chance. He had blamed Diane for saving him. Now he saw the truth staring him in the face.

"You're the pull I felt," Ellery whispered.

Ben nodded once. "And you felt it because we are of the same blood, different names. Kin. You, Death. Me, Darkness. That's why neither of us dies clean."

For a moment, Ellery wanted to deny it. He wanted to lift the rifle from Diane's hands himself and put a round through the stranger's chest. But the tether hummed too loudly. His ribs thrummed in answer to Ben's. The truth sat there, immovable, like a verdict he had been waiting for all his life.

"You ruined my case," Ellery said, voice breaking low. "And now you want to ruin me."

Ben shook his head. "I came to bring you out of hiding. Death doesn't belong in exile. And neither does kin."

The silence hung too long. Diane's rifle tracked every subtle twitch. Fiona's coin stilled in her palm. Loki grinned, waiting for the room to break.

And Ellery broke it.

He let the leash slip. The air collapsed, heavy as a grave settling. Pressure rolled out of him like an undertow—crushing, invisible. Nails shrieked in the beams overhead. The pigeons still alive fell screaming. Ben staggered, the marrow in his bones seared by a weight colder than winter.

Ellery's eyes burned with fury and recognition. "You woke me," he hissed. "You dragged this into me. Then you walk in here and expect me to follow?"

The aura bit deeper. Fiona gasped, hand white around her coin. Loki clapped once, delighted. "There he is. Death in full bloom."

Ben moved.

Before the pressure could crush him flat, he leapt. One moment rooted on concrete, the following his form blurred into shadow and vaulted upward. He hit the rafters with no sound but the groan of old iron, his shape dissolving into night.

The warehouse answered with a roar.

It tore down like thunder in a canyon. The sonic blast ripped the air apart, rattling steel, shattering glass. Chains whirled from the ceiling. The weight Ellery had unleashed cracked, staggered, and recoiled against the sheer force of it. He fell back a step, clutching his chest, the aura shivering like a wounded beast.

Diane fired.

Her shot ripped through the dark rafters where Ben had been, sparks biting off rusted steel. But Ben was already gone, swallowed by shadow, his outline no more substantial than smoke. The bullet punched daylight through the corrugated wall.

"Hold your fire!" Fiona snapped, voice ragged, her coin spinning wildly in her hand. "This isn't the fight!"

Ellery's breath came in ragged gasps, but he didn't stop glaring upward, toward where Ben's shadow flickered between light and dark. "You don't get to cage me," he snarled. "Not you. Not anyone."

Ben's voice thundered back from the beams, vibrating through every rib of the warehouse. "I'm not here to cage you! I'm here to stop you from tearing yourself apart before Lilith gets her hands on you."

The blast had rattled Diane, too, though she masked it. She steadied her rifle, sweeping the shadows, teeth bared. "You step down, Ben, or the next shot won't miss."

Loki laughed, spreading his arms wide, watching sparks rain from the rafters. "Oh, gods, this is beautiful. Darkness against Death. Hunter is aiming at both. The world really is ending properly."

Ellery straightened slowly, the death-aura drawing back into him with visible strain. His eyes locked on Ben's shadow above. "You call yourself kin. You call me Death. Then prove you're not lying."

Ben dropped from the rafters, shadow peeling away as he landed hard enough to crack the concrete. The sonic echo still hummed in the walls. He met Ellery's eyes, chest heaving. "I proved it the moment I stopped you," he said, voice raw. "And the moment you didn't kill me when you tried."

The pigeons lay dead across the floor. The smell of gunpowder hung sharply. Diane kept her rifle up, finger tight on the trigger. Fiona's coin trembled, balanced impossibly on its edge in her palm. Loki whistled, a tune without melody, grinning like he was watching his favourite play unfold.

The echoes of the blast still quivered in the bones of the building. Broken glass trembled on the floor like chimes, chains clinked against themselves, and the smell of cordite and rust sat thick as breath.

Ben stood in the middle of it all, his chest rising and falling, shadow still clinging to his shoulders like smoke reluctant to leave. Ellery faced him—dragging the aura back under his skin.

For the first time since his awakening, Ellery looked uncertain. His voice cracked with disbelief. "You should be dead."

Ben wiped blood from his lip. "I don't die easily."

Ellery's eyes narrowed. "Nobody withstands me. Not gods. Not mortals. But you—" He broke off, shaking his head like he could throw the thought away.

"Because he's kin," Fiona said quietly. The words landed harder than Ben's blast.

Ellery turned, fury and confusion sharpening his stare. "What did you say?"

Fiona didn't flinch. Her coin spun once, catching the thin light like a blade. "Death and Darkness. You felt it the moment you saw his face in that file. You felt the rope tied between you, even before you knew the name." She nodded once toward Ben. "And he felt it too."

Ellery's breath rasped. The memory of the morgue file, the photograph under neon, the crow calling over the Botanic Gardens—all of it flooded back. He'd tried to ignore it, tried to cage it. But the pull had been there all along.

"You knew," Ellery accused, his voice raw. "You knew what I was."

Ben didn't blink. "Not at first. But I knew you were mine the night you woke, just like I knew Jian, just like I knew Delilah. Threads pulling together. No choice. Not an accident."

Diane adjusted her stance, rifle never wavering. Her eyes locked on Ben. "Kinship or not, you came here uninvited. You tore through this place like a goddamn storm."

"I stopped him," Ben shot back, pointing to Ellery. "Do you think the city survives if I let him loose unchecked? He doesn't want to kill, but Death doesn't ask permission."

The weight of it pressed on Ellery again, the cold truth of his curse. His hands trembled; he curled them into fists. "You make it sound like I'm a weapon to be carried."

"You're not a weapon," Ben said, voice low but firm. "You're the end. I'm the shadow before it. That's why we're tied."

Fiona's coin rang in her palm. "Herald and Death. The weave won't let it."

Ellery took a half step closer, his aura flaring. Ben didn't move. Their gazes locked, and for a moment it seemed the warehouse itself leaned inward to listen.

"You expect me to follow you?" Ellery spat. "After you woke this curse in me? After you dragged me out of a life that made sense?"

Ben's jaw clenched. "I expect you to stand with me, because hiding won't stop what's coming. You're already awake. You can't go back."

Diane's finger tightened on the trigger. "And if he refuses?"

Ben turned to her, eyes hard. "Then he tears Adelaide apart the next time he slips. And you'll be the one forced to kill him. Is that what you want?"

For the first time, Diane hesitated.

Ellery's voice dropped to a whisper. "Why me?"

"Because you're my brother," Ben said.

The words froze the room. Even Loki, who had been smiling like a wolf at a feast, went still. Ellery stared, throat working, eyes wide with something between rage and recognition. The aura around him flickered, death straining for release, then faltering.

"No," he said, hoarse. "That's not—" He stopped, because he could feel it. The tether in his bones, the echo of Ben's hum in his ribs. Not metaphor. Not a trick. Kin.

Fiona's coin dropped flat in her palm with a clean metallic slap. "Truth."

Ellery's cigarette shook between his fingers. He let it fall, ember hissing out on the concrete. His voice cracked when he spoke. "If that's true... then everything I've done since waking—everybody, every shadow—it's on you."

Ben didn't look away. "Then I'll carry it."

The warehouse breathed with them, the weave knotting tighter, pulling them into a bond none of them had chosen. Diane lowered the rifle a fraction, not out of trust, but because she finally understood there was no bullet for what bound these two men together. The warehouse seemed smaller now, as though the walls had crept in. The dead pigeons on the floor were a grim chorus, their silence thicker than any echo.

Ellery rubbed a hand across his face, the glow of a streetlight outside catching in his hollow eyes. He looked older in that moment, worn down by the weight he hadn't chosen. Diane stood beside him, rifle still ready but her stance less sure, as if even she knew this conversation had left the realm of steel and powder.

Ben took a slow step forward, no shadow-play this time, no theatrics. Just a man with exhaustion in his shoulders and resolve in his eyes. "Ellery," he said, voice steady. "You know now. What you are. What I am. What we are. So I'm asking plain: will you join us?"

The question hit harder than the sonic blast.

Ellery felt the pressure stir inside him, the aura tugging at his ribs, desperate to spill loose. He clenched his fists, swallowing hard. "You woke me," he said, low, accusing. "You made me this."

"No," Ben said. "You always were this. I only lit the fuse. Better me than Lilith. Better kin than the horde."

Ellery's head shook slowly, cigarette trembling between his fingers. "And if I say no? If I stay here? Keep hiding until the city caves in around me?"

"Then Adelaide dies faster," Fiona said, her coin glinting in her palm. "And so do you."

Loki leaned against a pillar, watching like a theatre critic at the best seat in the house. He chuckled, eyes bright. "Even the gods will shiver."

Ellery shot him a glare, but it couldn't hide the way his chest tightened at the word brothers.

Diane's voice cut in, calm, measured. "He's right about one thing. Kinship doesn't dissolve. You can shoot him, you can walk away, but that tether's still going to pull. You've felt it. I've seen it." She lowered her rifle another inch. "The only choice left is whether you walk willingly, or are dragged."

Ellery's breath rasped. He looked at Ben again. Every instinct screamed to resist, to push back, to end it before it consumed him. But his heart beat in rhythm with Ben's. His aura quivered, not in defiance, but in recognition.

"You think Death belongs in your little army?" Ellery asked.

Ben stepped closer, eyes unflinching. "I think Death belongs beside Darkness because one without the other is meaningless. If we don't stand together, Lilith writes the next age in bone."

The words settled in Ellery. He closed his eyes, listening to the silence press in, feeling the tether hum between them. Kin. Brother. No escaping it.

He opened his eyes. "Damn you," he whispered. Then, louder: "Alright. I'll walk with you."

Ben let out a breath he hadn't realised he was holding. He extended his hand, steady, palm open. Ellery stared at it for a long moment. Then he reached out, grip rough, calloused, cold with the echo of death. Their hands locked, the tether pulling tight like a knot being cinched.

Fiona's coin spun high and landed flat in her palm. "The weave accepts," she murmured.

Diane finally lowered her rifle fully, though her eyes stayed sharp. "One inch earned," she said. "The rest, we'll see."

Loki clapped, delighted. "Ah, family reunions. Nothing sweeter."

Ben ignored him, still holding Ellery's gaze. "Then it's settled. You're with us."

Ellery nodded once, jaw set. "For now. But don't think for a second this absolves you. Everybody that falls near me—every death—I'll count it against your promise."

Ben didn't flinch. "Then keep the count. I'll carry it."

The dead pigeons lay silent on the floor. Outside, the tide slapped against the pylons. In the rafters, the chains stilled.

Chapter 22
The Second

The track was little more than a scar through saltbush and stone, the kind of road that led nowhere important. The sun leaned heavy on their shoulders, baking the dust until it tasted like iron. Ben followed the pull in his chest, every step of it taut as wire. Diane walked in silence, rifle slung but ready. Fiona's coin flicked nervously between her fingers. Loki whistled tunelessly, and Ellery smoked like he wanted to burn holes in the horizon.

"Here," Ben said, finally. He stopped on the rise of a shallow ridge. Beyond, a lone campervan squatted in the scrub, paint dulled, tyres half-swallowed by dust. The kind of vehicle that might have once belonged to a drifter, or someone trying to disappear.

But it wasn't the van that held their attention.

Jian Wu stood in the open ground beside it, slow and deliberate, his movements flowing like a dancer's. Arms extended, knees bent, spine loose—the shapes were unmistakably Tai Chi. But every gesture carried a violence the form was never meant to bear. When he swept one palm outward, a ribbon of fire uncoiled from his hand and lashed a stand of saltbush, exploding it into smoke. When he exhaled and thrust both arms forward, a ball of blue-white flame erupted and shattered against a boulder, leaving black scars etched into the stone.

The ground around him told the story. Scorched circles marred the scrub, patches of dirt glazed over, the air itself warped and shivering. Each movement was both meditation and destruction—a man teaching his body how to carry what nobody should.

Ben watched in silence. The pull in his ribs almost knocked the breath from him.

"Looks like he's been busy," Diane muttered.

"Busy?" Loki grinned. "He's auditioning for the rodeo of the damned."

The figure straightened slowly, pausing at the end of a form. He wore jeans, a checkered shirt, and boots worn white at the edges. A broad-brim hat shaded his face, sunglasses hid his eyes, and a neckerchief was drawn high. From a distance, he could have been a ranch hand cooling down after a long day. But the air around him shimmered like the skin of the world had been put too close to a flame.

Jian turned his head toward them. The fire at his fingertips winked out. For a long moment, he didn't move, just watched, the sunlight glinting off his shades.

Ellery flicked ash from his cigarette. "He knows we're here."

"Of course he does," Fiona murmured. Her coin spun once, fast, then clattered into her palm as if confirming it. "It's loud here. Louder than anywhere else we've been."

Ben swallowed and stepped forward, shadow dragging close at his feet. "Jian Wu."

The man didn't answer. He pushed his hat up a fraction with one thumb and began to walk toward them, slow, steady. Dust kicked off his boots. His disguise—the glasses, the neckerchief—couldn't hide the heat bleeding off his skin. Even at twenty paces, Ben felt it ripple against him.

"You brought gods," Jian said at last, voice muffled under cloth, low and edged. "I can smell them."

Loki spread his hands, all false innocence. "Technically, they brought themselves."

The sunglasses tilted toward him. Jian didn't bother to answer. He stopped a few paces short, close enough that the heat seared the sweat from Ben's brow.

"Why are you here?" Jian asked.

Ben licked dry lips. "Because of a memory."

Jian was silent.

"The noodle house," Ben said. His voice cracked. "You fed me when no one else would. You didn't ask questions. You didn't treat me like a monster. You just gave me a meal and let me sit in silence. That night kept me alive."

Jian stood utterly still. Then his hands clenched at his sides, light leaking faintly at the seams of his gloves. "And that memory brought you here?"

"No," Ben said. "Kin brought me here. Whatever's tying us. The memory is the reason I trust it."

For the first time, Jian tilted his head, and the heat around him eased slightly. "You speak like someone who's fought without training."

"I did," Ben said. His chest tightened. "I had to fight a god when I didn't even know what I was. No one came. No help. No guidance. Just me, raw and terrified, bleeding into the dark. And I won. But it cost me everything I was."

Jian's hand trembled. He tore the neckerchief down, ripped the sunglasses off, and the world saw him. Skin like charcoal, veins pulsing molten light, eyes blazing like stars.

"Then we are the same," Jian said, voice thick with fury. "I was given no training. Only storms hurled by gods. They cracked me open and left me to burn. This is their gift. This is their curse."

The ground at his feet blackened as he spoke, scorched by nothing but his gaze.

Ben didn't step back. "Then don't fight for them. Fight with me."

Jian stared at him, starry eyes searching, the fire inside his veins flaring bright. For a long moment, the world seemed to hold its breath.

The air between them shimmered with heat. Jian's disguise lay at his feet: hat tilted back, sunglasses hanging from one hand, neckerchief tugged loose. What he had hidden was impossible to mistake now. His skin was blackened charcoal, fissured with molten seams that pulsed brighter with each breath. His eyes burned white-gold, starry, so intense that the scrub he glanced at smoked and curled to ash.

No one spoke at first. Even Loki's grin faltered under the weight of that gaze.

Finally, Jian broke the silence. "You brought them." His chin lifted, the glow in his veins surging as he scanned the group. He stopped first on Diane. "The huntress. I know your scent I felt your storms drive across the ranges—chasing prey that wasn't mine, but striking through me all the same."

Diane's jaw tightened. She gripped her rifle, but her voice stayed flat. "I never aimed at you."

"You never cared where the bullets fell," Jian snapped. A plume of fire cracked out from his palm, detonating a patch of scrub twenty paces off. "You hunt for the gods. That's enough."

His gaze shifted to Fiona next. "Fortune-spinner. I felt your coin flip over my life long before I understood why my temper scalded everything I touched. You wagered balance while I bled."

Fiona's eyes dropped, her coin trembling. "The weave is bigger than my hands. I don't always choose where it lands."

Jian's eyes blazed hotter. "But you chose not to warn me."

Then came Loki. Jian's expression twisted, fire flaring in the cracks along his throat. "And you... trickster. I know your laugh. I heard it echo in the thunder that split my sky. You made storms into games. Do you know what those games did to me?"

Loki's smile thinned but didn't vanish. "I know you're still standing. That means my joke didn't kill you."

Jian raised a hand, and the air rippled with heat. "I should kill you now."

Ben stepped between them, shadow pooling at his feet, voice raw with urgency. "Jian—stop. They're not why I came. I didn't drag you into this to chain you to them. I came because of what you did for me. The noodle house. That's why."

The fire in Jian's hand guttered, but his eyes still burned bright. He looked at Ben, and in that moment, the fury shifted—not gone, but tempered. "You fought raw. No training. No guide. You survived because you had to. That I respect. That I understand. The gods left me to drown the same way."

Ben's voice cracked. "Then don't drown. Don't let them win. Stand with me. Not with them — never them. With kin."

The pull in Ben's chest thrummed louder than ever, pulling like a rope knotted between their bones. Ellery grunted, hand trembling around his cigarette. "Feels like the ground's choosing sides without asking us."

Jian's gaze flicked to him. "You're kin too. I smell the end on you. Cold as a grave."

Ellery blew out smoke through clenched teeth. "You're not wrong."

Jian looked back at Ben. His eyes flared brighter, and the scrub at his feet scorched black. "I will walk with you. But understand me—I will never stand with gods. If they try to claim me, I burn them. Pele most of all."

Diane tensed but said nothing. Fiona's coin stilled, heavy in her palm. Loki smirked, but the edges of it were brittle. Ben nodded, his chest aching with the pull of the rope. "I'm not asking you to stand with them. Only with me. With us."

Jian's fire dimmed, his eyes still blazing like stars. "Then we are agreed. But remember this—I was never afforded training. I made myself in the fire they forced through me. And if I'm unleashed again, it won't be their leash I wear. It will be my fury."

Ben held his stare, unflinching. "Then let's make sure it burns in the right direction."

For the first time, Jian took a step closer, fire rolling off him in waves. The group shifted uneasily, the heat pressing against them all.

Kin.

The word didn't need to be spoken again. It was already branded into the ground beneath their boots.

They drifted toward the shade of the campervan's awning, the only mercy the scrub would offer. Up close, the van told its own history—stone dings along the lower panels, a spiderwebbed crack in the back window, a strip of duct tape holding a flapping trim. Jian had rigged a tarp off one side with fencing wire and a broken rake handle. Under it sat a milk crate, a battered esky, a cast-iron pan blackened to mirror, and a five-litre jerry with "WATER" scrawled in permanent marker like a prayer.

Jian kicked his hat back into place, slid the sunglasses onto the crate, and stood with his hands on the small of his back, rolling heat from his shoulders as if he could stretch fire like muscle. Even "at rest," he distorted the air; the dust at his boots lifted in tiny devils, spun, fell.

Ben stayed in the mouth of the shade, not too close, not retreating. "There's more you should hear," he said. "Not from them." He didn't look at Diane, Fiona, or Loki. "From what sits behind them."

"The others—the ones in between—you feel them? Apparently, they think we are supposed to drag the species forward. Not as rulers. As proof. As a... road through the wreck."

Jian's mouth flattened. "They broke me with a storm. Now they want me to pour tea over the wound."

"No," Ben said, voice rough. "No tea. No altars. Just not letting the next age belong to thrones or corpses."

Ellery knocked ash off his cigarette with a fingernail, watching the grey flecks fall and fail to reach the ground before Jian's heat took them. "You're underselling it. We'll be targets, not banners."

"We already are," Diane said. Matter-of-fact, not cruel.

Jian studied Ben, star-bright eyes steady. "You said you fought a god raw."

Ben swallowed. "In the ocean and at Machu Picchu. I have claimed two."

Jian's gaze softened by a knife's width. "I boiled a dry creek," he said. "Turned two acres of salt to glass. The only people who calmed me were the indigenous elders. They asked me to sit. To breathe. To feel the ground. That's what kept me till now."

"Then that's the road," Ben said. "We feel the ground and keep each other standing. We learn as we walk."

Jian tipped his head, considering. "If I walk with you, it's for that. For stubborn learning. For the memory of a man who cleaned his bowl when he could barely stand."

He glanced at the gods without warmth. "Never for you."

"That'll do," Ben said.

A hot wind ran its hand across the tarp. It snapped twice and settled. Somewhere out in the scrub, a crow barked a complaint and then thought better of it. Fiona drew a breath. She lifted the coin an inch; it tugged toward the valley like a magnet finding a nail. "Delilah."

Loki leaned his shoulder against the van, smiling like a man tasting something he couldn't decide to love or spit out. "Effie has her wrapped in velvet and knives. Private rehearsals in the vineyards. People are already lining up to be soldiers without uniforms."

Jian's jaw worked. "Aphrodite will polish her until she can no longer see her own reflection."

"Aphrodite lures," Ben said, heat in his voice. "She's Delilah Kitsune. Artist. Japanese-Australian. Smarter than most. She'll wake up not knowing why. That's why we need to break Effie's spell."

Jian took that in, then flicked a glance toward the camper's open door. Inside, a tidy chaos: rolled swag, a small gas cooker, a battered knife magnet holding three Japanese blades, a shelf of mismatched bowls.

He pulled the cast-iron pan from the crate, set it on a flat rock he'd soot-blackened into a stove, and poured water from the jerry into it. The water trembled and came to a near-boil without flame. He dropped in a pinch of loose tea he'd kept in a snapped Altoids tin, stirred with a metal spoon he'd hammered straight from bent.

"Drink," he said, not looking up. "If we're going to meddle with love, you'll need your hands steady." He filled enamel mugs and passed them without ceremony.

Ben wrapped his fingers around the heat. "We go by back roads," he said. "Avoid eyes. When we hit the valley, we don't walk straight to Effie. We find where Delilah sleeps. We talk to her alone if we can."

"She'll be ringed," Diane said. "Security, soft and hard. Volunteers who think they're finding meaning. Paid teeth smiling in suits. Cameras."

Fiona shut her eyes, the coin trapped between her palms like a moth. "She's near Tanunda," she said after a beat, voice distant. "Big house on a rise. Music in the air. Too many cars for a weekday. Women laughing. Men are trying too hard. Effie's perfume over the crush of grapes."

Diane already had a map in her head. "We can come in along the creek. Use the old rail easement as cover. There's a service lane behind the ridge—if it hasn't changed, we can get eyes on the place without stepping into the courtyard."

Ben nodded. "We take Jian's van. Less obvious than ours."

Jian's eyebrow twitched. "Obvious is relative," he said, looking at the duct tape and the battered panels.

"People ignore what looks tired," Ellery said. "It's how the world gets robbed."

Jian turned, reached into the camper, and pulled out a canvas roll. He snapped the ties: inside, tools arranged with a cook's neatness—whetstone, cloth, a small blowtorch, a steel. He added a fourth knife to the magnet with a click and rolled the kit closed. "Give me ten minutes," he said. "Heat wants company when it moves."

"Pack," Ben told the others. "Water. Food. If we can avoid starting fights, we do. If we can't, we end them fast and quiet."

Jian reemerged wearing the hat again, the neckerchief low on his throat, sunglasses back in place. The rodeo shirt hid the glow; the glow didn't care. He slammed the camper door twice until the latch remembered its job. For a heartbeat, he stood with one palm flat to the warm metal, the van humming faintly under his heat like a content animal.

He looked at Ben. "You asked me to walk for humanity," he said. "Not gods. Not thrones." A beat. "I'll walk."

Ben held his gaze. "With me."

"With us," Jian said.

They climbed in—Ben driving, Jian riding shotgun, the others wedged among tools and tea tins and a coil of hose that smelled like summers past. The engine caught on the third try, coughed, thought about dying, then agreed to live. Dust leapt under the tyres.

As the camper bumped onto the track, something inside Ben sang almost like language. Three notes tight and true, a fourth somewhere ahead, rising like a promise or a warning.

"Delilah," Fiona said softly, eyes on nothing the wind could touch.

"Barossa," Diane confirmed.

Jian rested one wrist on the open window and watched the world burn a little in his reflection. "If she's already building an army," he said, "we cut the banner first, then talk."

Ben nodded, shadow pooling where the dashboard met the glass. "We get her to look at us and remember she's human before she's anything else."

"And if she remembers she's not?" Ellery asked.

"Then we remind her what happens to gods," Jian said, mild as heat. "They burn."

The van rattled south, carrying fire, shadow, and end past the last polite fences, into rows of vines that had listened to older songs than Effie's—and weren't sure which chorus to follow next.

The campervan groaned along the track, its engine a stubborn mule, never quick, never graceful, but refusing to quit. Dust boiled out behind them, hanging in the air like a trail of smoke.

The smell of scorched metal clung faintly inside the cab—Jian's heat bleeding into the chassis—but no one commented.

Ben drove with both hands on the wheel, eyes fixed on the horizon. Jian sat beside him, hat low, neckerchief drawn high again, sunglasses hiding his starry eyes. From the outside, he could have passed for an outback horseman. From the inside, the air bent around him like a forge's breath.

Ellery leaned back in the rear bench, cigarette smouldering between two fingers, his aura of endings pressing into the van until every creak sounded closer to collapse. Fiona sat beside him, the coin in her lap trembling like a trapped insect. Diane, rifle stripped and reassembled on her knees, checked every spring and bolt as though polishing her patience. Loki sprawled near the door, grinning at the radio static like it was telling him secrets.

For a long while, no one spoke. The hum of tyres on stone filled the silence.

Finally, Ben broke it. "When we get there, it won't just be Delilah. Effie will have people. A lot of them. Volunteers. Followers. She doesn't need chains when she can bind with desire."

"Desire's a stronger leash than iron," Diane muttered.

"Depends who you ask," Loki said cheerfully. "Iron doesn't whisper in your ear while you sleep."

Fiona's fingers tightened on the coin. "It's worse than that. Each one believes she's the answer. That's harder to break than any trick."

Jian turned his head toward the window, watching the scrub slide past. "And in the middle of it, Delilah." His voice was low, edged. "Effie is polishing her."

Ben gripped the wheel tighter. "Then we cut her free."

The van crested a rise. Ahead, the valley spread wide—rows of vines stretching green across ochre soil, cellar doors gleaming white among gums, and on a distant rise, a house too big to be modest. Its pale walls caught the sun, its windows flashed like eyes, and even from here, music floated faintly on the wind.

Fiona's coin spun violently in her palm. She clutched it, eyes wide. "That's her. Delilah's there."

Ben felt something tighten in his chest until it hurt. Jian's starry eyes flared behind his glasses, burning holes into the distance.

The Barossa waited.

In its heart, Effie was building an army.

Chapter 23

The Third

The camper looked like it had already survived the end of the world. Its paint was bleached by the sun, windows patched with duct tape, and the body dented from years of collisions with scrub and stone. Jian Wu sat behind the wheel with one hand loose on the rim, the other shifting idly as though even driving was a kind of Tai Chi. Heat shimmered around the van, blurring its outline. Now and then, his eyes flared in the mirror, and the whole machine seemed to breathe.

Behind him, Ben's car followed the wavering taillights. He gripped the wheel tight, hunched forward as though bracing against something more than the road. He had driven plenty of stolen cars, knowing the crash would never kill him. Tonight the irony weighed heavier.

Ellery Kalos sat up front, shoulders squared, cigarette smoke curling into the night air through a half-cracked window. He looked like a man on surveillance, his silence a constant pressure that filled the cab. Even without turning his head, Ben felt him there—an undertow gnawing at his ribs.

In the back seat, gods. Cramped together like unwanted hitch-hikers, their knees pressing against the seatbacks, their shoulders brushing every time the car jolted. Diane had her rifle standing between her boots, barrel angled down, jaw tight as though she could muscle the road into obedience. Fiona spun her coin in a steady rhythm, each flash in the dim light a soft pulse like a heartbeat. Loki sprawled diagonally across the middle, humming off-key, tapping the roof as if the car were his instrument.

The irony of it hung in the air: gods riding in the back, Death riding shotgun, and a mortal cursed not to die stuck with the wheel—a cursed chauffeur.

Ben broke the silence first. "Explain to me again why I'm the one driving?"

Ellery didn't move. "Because you're not afraid of wrecks."

"Because," Loki interrupted, grinning wide, "when the wheels come off, you'll crawl out smiling while the rest of us eat asphalt."

Diane shifted, unimpressed. "Keep your eyes on the road, mortal."

Fiona's coin flickered in the rearview, a tiny star caught between her fingers. "It isn't the road that matters. We must get to them before she does."

Ben snorted. "Them?"

"The women," Diane said flatly. "And their army."

"Army?" Ben's knuckles whitened. "You mean the Valleyboys."

Loki laughed. "Ah, yes. Twenty-seven drunkards with farm tools. A splendid apocalypse militia."

"They'll fight," Fiona murmured. "They already are. Effie whispers, and they follow. Delilah sharpens her chaos, and they cheer. We just have to collect them."

Ellery finally spoke, voice a low rasp. "And what happens if they don't want to be led?"

No one answered—the question coiled between them, thick as smoke.

The headlights picked out the first long shadows of the Barossa hills. The air changed—less salt, more eucalyptus, the scent of vines carried across the night wind. For Ben, it was memory as much as landscape, every fencepost and dirt track a ghost from childhood. He felt it in his chest, that old tug of soil and dust, and it almost made him laugh.

The gods in his back seat, Death beside him, Jian's fire-camper blazing a path ahead, and he was driving them home.

Row upon row of vines sloped in darkness, silvered by moonlight, the valley rolling like a sleeping beast. Jian's camper surged ahead, its headlights haloed in a shimmer that looked too much like flame. For a heartbeat, Ben thought he saw the tyres smoking as they touched the earth, but when he blinked, it was only dust.

Loki leaned forward suddenly, his grin brushing Ben's ear. "I love it. Gods, devils, monsters—headed into wine country to raise an army of rednecks. Your people, Ben. Your kind."

"They're not my people," Ben muttered.

Fiona's coin stilled. "They will be."

Diane checked her rifle. "We'll need them ready. Lilith won't wait."

Ellery flicked his ash out the window, eyes never leaving the road. "And they won't wait for you, either. You'll have to prove why they should follow."

The words struck harder than Ben wanted to admit. He pushed the accelerator, the car shuddering as the road narrowed. The Barossa rose ahead, black against starlight, and somewhere among the vines, Effie was weaving her charm into men and women who would gladly bleed for her. Somewhere nearby, Delilah honed her chaos into something lethal. Somewhere in the valley, twenty-seven of them waited with rough hands and stubborn hearts, ready to be convinced the end was theirs.

Ben exhaled. “Barossa,” he said. “Time to pick up the rest of the damned.”

The car roared on. Jian’s camper flared brighter, flame-shadow licking across the night as if the valley itself was already burning.

The road narrowed as they turned south, trading vineyards for paddocks and corrugated sheds. Moculta had never been much more than a cluster of farm blocks, the kind of place where rusted tractors sat in fields like forgotten monuments. But tonight, the valley had life.

Ben downshifted as the headlights picked out a gate welded from scrap steel and star-picket posts. The fence was patched with wire and corrugated tin, the kind of barricade you built when you meant to hold ground. Not decorative. Not theatrical. Functional. A skull—cow, not human, though it took a second to be sure—hung from the crossbeam, its sockets stuffed with fairy lights that glowed like tired embers.

The gate was already open.

They rolled in slow, Jian’s camper leading, Ben’s car close behind. Gravel crunched under tyres, the sound echoing off sheds stacked high with firewood and scrap metal. Beyond the sheds, the compound widened into a gravel yard ringed by floodlights strung from poles. The beams buzzed and hummed, drawing moths in frantic spirals.

The first figures stepped out of the dark. A man and a woman, leather vests catching the light, both holding .44 Magnums long enough to look obscene in their hands. They didn't posture. They didn't call out warnings. They just walked forward with the kind of confidence that said they'd shot before and wouldn't hesitate to shoot again.

Ben eased the car to a halt. Jian's camper stopped beside him, its engine growling low, heat bleeding off in visible waves.

The armed pair spread out, weapons steady. The woman spoke first. "Names."

Loki started laughing in the backseat. "Names? Ah, so sweet, you've no idea who you're asking."

The man didn't blink. His voice carried like gravel in a tin. "Try me."

Diane's hand twitched on her rifle, but Ellery cut her off with a glance. "Not yet."

Ben lifted his hands from the wheel and slowly pushed the door open. He stepped into the gravel yard, the night air sharp with eucalyptus and smoke. "We're here for Effie and Delilah."

The woman's eyes narrowed. The man cocked his revolver just enough to make the hammer click audible. "Not how it works. You don't call them. They come to you."

As if on cue, they did.

From the far side of the yard came the sound of boots and laughter, a ragged chorus that carried the smell of smoke and cheap wine. Figures spilled into the floodlight—men and women in patched denim and oil-stained flannels, wielding bats, axes, and shotguns that had seen better decades. Twenty-seven of them, ragamuffins by any measure, but moving with the unity of a pack.

At their centre walked two women.

Effie burned in leather, smiling like the air gave way toward her. Her hair caught the light like spun gold, every step deliberate, a queen in a paddock. Beside her, Delilah moved sharp and feral, her fox tattoo slipping from her collar as if it might leap free. Her eyes found Ben first, then flicked to the car behind him, to the gods crammed inside.

They stopped in the middle of the drive, the Valleyboys fanning out behind them in a ragged crescent. Effie tilted her head, her grin widening. "Well, well, what do we have here?"

Delilah's voice cut in, lower, edged. "Looks like trouble finally remembered where to find us."

The armed man and woman with Magnums lowered their sights a fraction, waiting on their queens.

Ben stood his ground, heart hammering. Behind him, he heard Diane's rifle shift, Loki's laugh bubbling up again, Fiona's coin flicking once in the dark.

Ellery exhaled smoke through his nose. "This is going to get loud."

Effie stepped closer, chin high, eyes burning with mischief and hunger. "You brought us gods, Ben Callum. Death. And whatever Jian is now." She laughed, rich and dangerous. "The end must be nigh."

Delilah smiled like a blade. "Or better."

The yard held its breath.

Effie's ragamuffins stood easy, weapons slung and boots planted, but there was an edge to them that didn't belong to vineyard workers or bikies. Her presence had sharpened them into something fiercer than they'd ever imagined. One word from her and they'd fire, swing, bite.

Delilah's fox smile tilted. "You show up uninvited, dragging gods behind you on a leash, and expect us to clap and cheer?" Her eyes lingered on Diane, then on Fiona, before coming back to Ben. "We've been busy without you."

Loki leaned against the car, grinning like a cat. "Busy, yes. But not busy enough."

"Shut up," Diane snapped.

Effie's eyes never left Ben. "Why are you here?"

Ben felt the coin-flutter of Fiona's rope thrumming in his chest, louder here than anywhere since Jian. He swallowed, stepped forward into the harsh floodlight. "Because we can't do this without you."

A ripple of laughter moved through the yard. The man with the .44 shook his head. "That's rich."

Delilah raised her hand, and they fell silent. She walked a step closer, boots crunching gravel. "Speak plain, Ben Callum. Why us? Why here?"

He dragged a hand over his face. "Because you're already fighting. Because you've built something here out of nothing—out of wine bottles and farm tools and guts. Because people listen to you when they won't listen to anyone else. You've made yourselves an army without anyone calling it that."

Effie's smile deepened, dangerous. "And now you want to name it."

"Yes." Ben's voice cracked, but he didn't back down. "Lilith's marching. Cairo fell. Jerusalem's next. We don't have time. You've got fire. With us, you'll have direction."

Delilah studied him. "You sound like you believe it."

Ellery ground out his cigarette, voice low. "He does."

For the first time, Effie looked at Ellery. Her eyes narrowed, recognition flickering. "Death in the flesh."

Ellery didn't deny it. Smoke still hung around him like a shroud. "He's right. If you want to keep drinking and dancing on these hills, you'll fight. If you want to see another harvest, you'll follow."

Magnums dipped lower. The motley crew shifted, muttering. Fiona flipped her coin and caught it without looking. Effie's gaze slid back to Ben. "You've got gods in your pocket. You've got Death for a brother. And you've got Jian burning holes in the ground just by breathing." She laughed, soft and sharp. "And you think we're going to follow you?"

Ben clenched his fists. "No. I think you're going to join us because you don't bow to anyone. Because you'd rather burn the world than let someone else tell you how to live. And because if you don't, Lilith will turn you into another army—hers."

The silence thickened. The floodlights hummed.

Delilah's grin sharpened, fox bright. "He's got a tongue after all."

Effie tilted her head, considering. Her group waited on the edge of her decision. Finally, she spread her arms wide. "Well then, boys and girls—shall we hear him out?"

The yard erupted in cheers, boots stomping gravel, bottles banging against rifle stocks.

Delilah stepped in beside Effie, their shoulders brushing, their voices twining. "Welcome home, Ben. Let's see if you can knit us tighter than we already are."

Effie's smile turned molten. "But understand this—we don't kneel."

Ben nodded, chest tight, pulse roaring in his ears. "Then we'll stand. Together."

Ellery muttered, almost to himself, "For now."

Behind them, Loki clapped like it was a comedy show, Diane looked like she'd bitten glass, and Fiona's coin spun faster, flashing in the floodlight.

The Valleyboys closed in, grinning, shouting, welcoming their leaders' choice. Moculta shook with the sound. Ben felt the weight of an army at his back. Ragged, chaotic, half-drunk maybe—but real.

And he knew, deep down, it was only the beginning.

The cheers hadn't faded before Delilah's grin widened into something sharper. She stepped forward, fox-bright eyes fixed on Ben. "All that talk," she said, circling him like a dancer. "All that kin and destiny shit. Pretty words. But destiny doesn't win wars."

Effie tilted her head, watching, but didn't interfere.

Ben frowned. “I thought you agreed—”

Delilah laughed, a sound that rang like breaking glass. “Agreed to hear you out. Not to follow you blindly. My Valleyboys aren't that stupid, Ben Callum. They follow strength. So let’s see yours.”

The yard hooted, stomping boots, clapping the butts of shotguns against their thighs. The air loaded with smoke and sweat and something like expectation.

Ben raised his hands, palms open. “I’m not here to fight you.”

“Not fight,” Delilah said, twirling a length of chain she’d pulled from her belt. “Spar. Play. Show us your teeth. Or show us you don’t have a spine.”

The chain whistled through the air, light catching on steel links. She moved closer, laughter bubbling up like it couldn’t be contained.

Loki leaned against a fencepost, grinning. “Oh, this I like.”

Ben hesitated, then stepped into the yard. Gravel crunched under his boots. The Valleyboys ringed them in a loose circle, eyes bright, mouths grinning.

Delilah struck first. The chain snapped out, wrapping around his wrist before he could dodge. She yanked, laughing, and he stumbled forward into her waiting kick. It slammed against his ribs, the impact rattling through his bones.

He caught himself, shoved the chain off, and straightened. “You don’t need to prove anything,” he said.

Delilah’s fox-smile burned hotter. “Oh, but you do.”

She came at him again, chain whirling, her laughter never stopping. He dodged once, twice, letting her blows graze past. But each time she pushed harder, each strike a little closer, each laugh a little sharper. The crowd fed on it, shouting, jeering, urging her on.

Ben tried to keep it soft, defensive. A block here, a shove there. But her speed kept rising, her joy mounting. She slammed the chain around his leg, tripped him to the gravel, and pounced with a knife pulled from nowhere.

The blade pressed against his throat. She leaned in, eyes wild, grinning. The yard leaned forward with her. "Gentle doesn't cut it."

The Valleyboys roared their approval, boots pounding, voices hoarse.

Something in Ben snapped. He rolled, shadows gathering at his shoulders, his breath going cold. The rope in his chest thrummed so loud it drowned out the cheers.

He rose in a blur, his body slipping out of flesh into shade. Darkness wrapped him. Wings of nothing unfurled with a hiss like torn silk.

Gasps rippled through the crowd. Even Delilah froze, chain dangling from her hand, grin faltering.

Ben leapt, shadows trailing. He vaulted skyward, higher than any mortal could, the night swallowing him whole. For a heartbeat, he hung above the compound, a shape half-man, half-storm. Then he roared. The sonic blast ripped down like thunder in a canyon. It struck a tree at the compound's edge and split it from crown to root.

The sound rolled over the yard. Then stillness.

Ben dropped back to earth, shadows peeling away until he stood on gravel once more, chest heaving, eyes still burning with the echo of it.

The compound went silent. Even the armed guards lowered their Magnums, mouths open.

Delilah's chain slipped from her hand. Slowly, her grin returned—wider, wilder. She laughed—full-throated, unashamed, delighted. "Now that," she gasped between breaths, "is worth following."

Effie's eyes gleamed, her lips curling in a smile that promised fire and ruin.

Around them, the compound erupted in cheers that shook the night.

No one questioned who now held the air in their lungs.

Chapter 24
The Hercules

The convoy snaked deeper into the base, tyres crunching over bitumen, engines coughing smoke into the floodlights.

It looked like a carnival had broken through the perimeter fence—Valleyboys shouting from the back of utes, Delilah dancing on a bonnet, Loki grinning like he'd orchestrated the parade.

Yet under the racket, there was a real plan, fine as a thread.

Effie left the convoy at the Rec Hall. The door opened on a room heavy with fatigue: four pilots and a flight engineer killing time over cards—boots unlaced, uniforms sweat-worn. A muted footy replay stuttered across the television. The air reeked of instant coffee and boredom.

Effie stepped in barefoot.

Every head lifted. The game forgot itself.

"Evening, boys," she said, sliding into the circle like she'd been invited. "Cards down. We've got a hop, and you're the crew fate picked for it."

The captain frowned, hand half raised. "Hop? We've had no—"

"Orders," Effie cut in, voice velvet and certainty. "Edinburgh to Darwin, Darwin to a mercy run out past the maps. Small island. Heat. People are short of breath. Your bus is the knife, and you're the hand on it. Ten minutes to start. You'll thank me tomorrow."

She touched the captain's sleeve, not seduction but benediction. His mouth closed.

The engineer found himself nodding before realising. The sergeant gathered the cards without a word.

They were hers already.

While Effie wove pilots, Loki walked into Operations with a clearance badge that had never existed until now. The duty commander—a major with red eyes and an inbox groaning on two screens—looked up. "Who the hell are you?"

"Paperwork," Loki said brightly, dropping a folder on his desk.

The major scowled down. The forms looked immaculate. Too immaculate. Every box ticked, every line stamped, his own signature glimmering where his pen had never touched.

"BK-09 humanitarian," Loki said, leaning casually against the desk. "Slot cleared for Darwin fuel, onward leg classified. Your handwriting is impeccable, by the way."

The major stared at the page too long. "That's not my signature."

For a fraction of a second, it wasn't. The ink thinned. The looping "M" in his surname frayed at the edges. The lines of the signature lifted like smoke from a slow burn. Ash drifted across the paper and vanished before it hit the desk.

The air shifted. The man standing opposite him was smiling—but not entirely. For a blink, the major saw something behind the grin.

Not a man.

A narrow muzzle where a jaw should be. Eyes too bright. A flicker of russet where skin had been.

A fox.

The room tilted. Then it snapped back. The signature lay solid and black again. Ink. Perfect. Real. The man in front of him was human. Completely.

Loki tilted his head. "You alright, Major?"

The major swallowed. He had seen something. He knew it. But the paper was clean. The signatures were his.

His pulse hammered in his ears. "...Ground in ten," he muttered, voice flat.

"Excellent," Loki said softly.

For a second—just a second—the major thought he saw a tail sweep behind the desk. Then it was gone.

Out by the Hercules, Fiona flicked her coin, and the night bent to listen. Two lineys in orange vests looked up from their smoke break.

"Tasking change," she told them as if they'd always known. "BK-09 wheels up. Darwin fuel stop. Chocks clear, ladder off, ties stowed. Engineer meets you on the ramp in six."

One frowned. "BK-09?"

"Humanitarian," Fiona said gently, eyes glinting in the halogen. "You'll feel good about it tomorrow." The coin tapped her knuckle—tink—, and both men nodded, already moving, as if the words had been sitting in their heads all along.

The Herc stirred awake: lights blinking along its spine, props uncowled, stairs rolling into place. Metal sighed like it knew it was meant to move.

Meanwhile, the Valleyboys had spilled out near the hangar, rowdy as a football crowd. Delilah led them, twin revolvers spinning, laughter cracking across the apron. They heckled the ground crew, sang dirty songs, and clanged rifles on scaffolding. But they weren't chaos—they were cover.

A smokescreen of noise that made Effie's charm, Loki's lies, and Fiona's luck slip unnoticed beneath the racket.

Ben watched from the sedan, jaw tight, hands white on the wheel. Engines roared, laughter echoed, floodlights blazed. And somehow, impossibly, the plan held.

"Darwin first," Diane reminded him, loading a round into her rifle and tucking it under the blanket. "Then your bloody mate."

Ellery smoked in silence. Jian leaned against the landing gear, heat shimmering in sheets around him, and the aircraft seemed to stand straighter for his weight.

Ben exhaled. "If this works, it'll be a miracle."

"No," Fiona said, her coin catching moonlight as the props began to turn. "It's a noose. And nooses always pull tight."

Effie led the crew out from the barracks, her new flock of pilots and engineers blinking as if they'd woken mid-dream. The captain cradled his flight bag like a talisman, jaw set in the strange calm of a man who has accepted orders he couldn't recall receiving. The loadmasters followed, boots clattering, eyes alight with the rush of purpose.

"Here's your bus," Effie said sweetly, guiding them toward the Herc's ramp. "She's waiting on you." The engineer patted the fuselage as though it were a horse, and the aircraft seemed to sigh in recognition.

From the other side of the apron, Fiona waved the groundies forward. Her coin flashed in the arc of floodlight as she spoke soft instructions: fuel for Darwin, quick turnaround, nothing wasted. They nodded without hesitation, lost in the certainty that this had always been their job tonight.

Loki, meanwhile, strode down the line of vehicles, waving papers he'd conjured and barking like a sergeant-major. "Clearance confirmed! You're looking at an endorsed humanitarian op, gentlemen. Try not to look so bloody surprised—it was your idea in the first place."

The major waited until the door closed.

Then he stood abruptly. "Conference room. Now."

Two captains and the duty controller followed him into the adjoining office. The door shut.

"What did you see?" the controller asked.

The major hesitated. "I don't know."

That was the truth. And it terrified him. He ran a hand over his face. "The paperwork's valid. The digital clearance is clean. But something's wrong."

"Wrong how?"

He didn't answer directly.

"Get Tower on the line."

The call connected. "Hold BK-09 on the runway. Do not clear for takeoff. Repeat: do not clear."

A pause.

"Sir, they're already taxiing."

"Then hold them."

He hung up.

The room was quiet.

One of the captains leaned in. "What's going on?"

The major stared at the wall for a long moment. "I think," he said slowly, "we are dealing with something outside protocol."

The captains exchanged a look. Outside protocol meant many things. None of them included fur.

The duty controller shifted uncomfortably. "Sir... you're looking pale."

The major's jaw tightened. He could still see the ash drifting. Still see the muzzle. Still feel the room bending around that grin.

The tower crackled through the speaker. "BK-09 requesting immediate departure. Engines at power."

The major hesitated.

If he stopped them—questions. Reports. Investigations. A review. Fitness for command.

If he let them go—they left his airspace.

They became someone else's problem.

Tower again: "Sir, clearance required."

The room felt smaller. The major looked at the captains. Neither spoke. Neither agreed. Neither supported him.

He understood, in that moment, what frightened them more: The aircraft leaving. Or him not making sense.

"Clear them," he said quietly.

Silence.

Then: "BK-09 cleared for immediate departure."

The engines roared through the speaker.

The major sat down slowly. His hands were shaking. "Log it as standard humanitarian dispatch," he said.

The duty controller nodded—carefully.

In the silence that followed, the major realised something worse than fear: His command staff were watching him. Not the aircraft. Him.

The Valleyboys were last to be wrangled. Delilah had them mustered in a rough cordon by the hangar, twenty-seven loud, armed, and far too drunk on chaos to be contained. She sat on the bonnet of a ute, revolvers twirling in her hands, grin bright as magnesium.

"They'll fit in the bus," she declared, nodding toward the military cargo plane. "Strap them down like cargo if you must."

"Cargo drunk on opinions," Diane muttered, shouldering her blanket-wrapped rifle as she stalked past.

The Valleyboys laughed, shouted, and raised their weapons in salute. Some carried bundles of ammunition. Others had eskies clanking with bottles. Their songs were ugly but proud, and they took them onto the ramp like offerings to a god who had yet to reveal himself.

Inside, the Herc's belly echoed with the sounds of preparation: webbing slapped taut, straps tightened, crates shifted. The loadies corralled the Valleyboys into rows, tying down weapons, confiscating bottles when necessary. Delilah perched on a crate, revolvers across her lap, eyes sharp and amused.

Ben climbed the ramp last, the pull in his ribs thrumming so hard he could taste salt and tide. He touched the fuselage in passing, hand rough on metal warm from the lights.

"This gets us to Darwin," he muttered. "Then the draw takes over."

Ellery followed him up, smoke curling from the cigarette glued to his lip. "You sound like a man boarding his own coffin."

"Coffins don't fly," Ben said.

At the cockpit door, Effie kissed the captain on the cheek and whispered something he didn't repeat. He settled into his seat, headset sliding into place, eyes clear with purpose. The engineer flicked switches; gauges flared to life.

Four props stirred. One by one, they caught, whirring into a chorus that drowned the night. The whole aircraft trembled with life, as though it had been waiting for this madness to climb aboard.

From the jumpseat, Diane leaned forward, voice sharp. "Darwin first. No detours. If anyone so much as fumbles their belt, I'll put them down."

Loki laughed, already strapping himself in. "Ah, the warm reassurance of armed babysitters."

Fiona flicked her coin once more. It rang against her knuckle—tink—and landed sure. "The rope pulls further. Darwin will only be a breath."

The ramp closed. The Herc rolled, heavy and willing, toward the runway.

The comms crackled. "BK-09, you are cleared for take-off."

Ben closed his eyes as the engines thundered. Somewhere beyond Darwin, somewhere nameless—Jake's bell was ringing.

The Hercules thundered up into the night and left the city lights of South Australia behind.

Inside the belly, the Valleyboys were a restless tide, strapping down rifles, singing half-drunk hymns, and arguing over who got to sit nearest Delilah. Diane sat stiff, rifle across her knees. Effie sprawled on a cargo net like she was born airborne. Loki wandered the aisle, stealing cigarettes and telling each man his fortune as if he already knew it.

Ben sat buckled in, the draw in his ribs pulling steadily west. Darwin first, then the sea. Not the sea again. He whispered those words like a mantra.

And the major stared at his departure screen long after the aircraft vanished. For a moment, the transponder flickered.

Not a call sign.

A symbol.

The descent came before dawn, the aircraft's four props grinding against headwinds. The Northern Territory coast glittered faintly with sodium lamps and oil fires on the horizon.

The crew brought her down hard, tyres screeching against the wet runway. The Valleyboys cheered as if a football goal had been scored.

On the apron, refuelers rolled up quickly, hoses rattling.

Fiona slipped among them, coin glinting, every instruction in her mouth sounding like one they'd been waiting to hear all night: top her tanks, double-check oil, flight plan extended. They nodded and moved with mechanical obedience, none daring to question why this mission was suddenly a priority.

Inside the Ops hut, the Darwin duty controller frowned at the flight docket Loki slid across his desk. "Cocos?"

"Classified relief corridor," Loki chirped, as if the man had just asked him the colour of the sky. "You signed it at Edinburgh, remember? Here—your initials. Lovely penmanship, by the way."

The controller squinted. The page bore his handwriting, exact. His signature gleamed at the bottom like it had always been there. He rubbed his temple. "I don't... recall—"

"Of course not," Loki interrupted smoothly. "Long night, no coffee. But the clearance is good, the fuel's flowing, and your lads want the bragging rights. All you need to do is nod, and you're the hero who kept the corridor open."

The controller hesitated a beat too long.

Loki leaned forward, grin thin as a knife. "The rope's already tied, mate. Better you pull it than let it choke."

The man swallowed, stamped the clearance without another word, and waved them through.

Back on the Tarmac, Effie drifted down the ramp, wrapping the loadmasters in gratitude, kissing the engineer on the cheek like he'd saved her life. Delilah corralled her crew, shouting over the refuelling trucks, keeping them just rowdy enough to be mistaken for noise, not mutiny. Jian stood by the nosewheel, heat shimmering off him, and their aircraft seemed eager to leave Darwin behind.

Fiona returned with a nod. "Tanks full. Crew cleared."

Loki flicked the forged clearance order at Ben. "All tidy. We're expected at Cocos."

Ben frowned at the page, then at the horizon. The rope in his chest thrummed, salt and tide already in his lungs. "Still don't know the name."

"You'll know it when it forgives you," Effie said, climbing the ramp.

The props began to spin again, blades catching the thin light of morning. The Herc's belly swallowed the mad rabble once more. Diane buckled herself in without a word. Ellery lit another cigarette, smoke curling like an omen.

Ben closed his eyes as the aircraft rolled for take-off. Somewhere beyond the sea, Jake's bell was ringing.

And the rope dragged him closer.

Chapter 25

The Pirate

The Hercules touched down heavily on the Cocos runway, wheels shrieking against wet tarmac, props grinding down like a giant exhaling. Dawn hadn't yet broken; the island was still a smear of salt air, diesel fumes, and the ghost of palm silhouettes trembling against floodlights.

The cargo bay yawned open, spilling Valleyboys half-drunk, gods half-disguised, and mortals wholly confused onto a strip of cracked asphalt.

The air was thick with ocean damp. Somewhere beyond the palms, a generator coughed, and the faint pulse of music rolled in—low bass, laughter, a woman's shriek cut short.

Ben's ribs thrummed harder. It had to be Jake.

The aircrew stumbled out with the others, no longer men in uniform but men folded into the rabble. Effie's benediction clung to them; Fiona's coin made their purpose shine false and true at once. They carried their flight bags like talismans, but their eyes gleamed with the same reckless hunger as the Valleyboys. Whatever they had been, they were something else now—Jake's crew, whether they knew it or not.

The club squatted near the jetty, a low building patched from shipping containers and driftwood, neon tubes buzzing fitfully along its rusted roofline.

Inside, the air was a wall: thick with rum breath, cheap perfume, and smoke from cigars fat as fingers. Music thumped from battered speakers, a rhythm that belonged more to Havana than the Indian Ocean.

Hookers lounged across the laps of men whose skin was tattooed with salt and scars. Waitresses—topless but not powerless—shouldered through the crowd with trays stacked in glass and firewater. Poker tables crouched under the smoke, green felt sticky with sweat and spilled tequila. A brawl lurked in every laugh. A kiss might break into a knife fight.

This was no sailor's refuge. It was a storm bottled in walls, and Jake's pirates were the tempest inside it.

Jake himself sat at the biggest table in the back, cards fanned in one hand, cigar clamped in his teeth. He looked broader than memory, hair tied back, skin leathered by sun and spray. Around him were men and women as wild as the sea—Jake's pirateers—swigging, shouting, one moment deadly serious over a hand of poker, the next cackling like devils.

Ben paused on the threshold.

This was the place. No mistaking it. But before Ben could step in, the door swung on its hinges, and a figure blocked the way.

Mercury leaned there like he'd been waiting all night. A lean man in a grey suit too fine for this island, too pressed for this club. His smile was easy, but his eyes were not—they flickered as quickly as coin flips, calculating, amused, never at rest.

"Well, well," Mercury said, voice smooth as smoke. "What's this parade? A rabble of gods and gunmen, pirates-in-waiting, and one mortal tied to a rope none of you can see."

The Valleyboys bristled, some raising rifles until Delilah barked them quiet with a laugh.

Loki stepped forward, grin bright as a blade. "Merc, old friend. Thought you'd be halfway to Cairo by now. What brings you to this dirty jewel?"

Mercury's smile sharpened. "The same thing that brings you, Loki. Trouble dressed up as opportunity."

He looked over the crew, eyes catching on Effie, lingering on Fiona, sliding past Jian with a flicker of unease.

Finally, his eyes rested on Ben. "And here's ground zero. The aberrant mortal."

Ben didn't flinch. His lungs burned steadily, but his voice was low. "We came to see Jake."

"Yes," Mercury said. "So you think. But Jake doesn't just welcome strangers. Not even strangers he used to know."

The club's noise spilled out—laughter, glasses breaking, the slap of flesh on wood.

Behind Mercury, shadows moved: Jake's pirates, keeping half an eye on the entrance. The smell of rum clung to everything, and the sea pressed close, as if waiting to hear what was decided.

Loki made a show of rubbing his hands together, smiling slyly. "Then let us in, and share this opportunity. You love the show, don't you?"

Mercury's smile didn't falter, but his eyes narrowed. "Opportunity without lies, Loki. Not wrapped too neatly in silk. Every word out of your mouth is poison, and I've learned that your show always burns down the stage."

Effie stepped forward, bare feet silent on the boards. Her hand brushed Mercury's sleeve, soft as benediction again. "We're not here to burn. To drink. To meet a friend. Want to sit down and catch up on the news?"

Mercury studied her, the smoke swirling between them. "You weave honey well, girl. But even honey hides arsenic."

Fiona's coin flicked against her knuckle, the glint catching Mercury's restless eyes. "Sometimes," she said lightly, "the coin falls whether you want it to or not. Best to step aside before it tests your luck."

Mercury's smile thinned. "You always did gamble with words, Fiona."

He exhaled, glanced at Ben again, then at Loki. "Convince me, trickster. Why should Jake see you tonight, when the night already belongs to him?"

The door hung between them, open but not yet yielded. Inside, Jake's laughter rose like cannon fire. Outside, Ben's ragged crew waited, luck thinning, bravado fading.

And Mercury stood as the hinge between it all...

Before Loki could reply, the club thundered with Jake's laugh.

"Mercury! Stop polishing your paranoia and let the circus in! If the cat's dragged them this far, they've earned a chair."

He waved a hand like he owned the island. "Ben, you cavalier—bring your rabble. Sit with me before they drink the place dry."

Mercury hesitated, eyes flicking from Loki to Ben and back again. But the captain's command was iron, and so he stepped aside with the faintest bow. "As you wish."

The crew spilled through the doorway in a tide: Valleyboys rowdy, the aircrew blinking like they'd been reborn into pirates, Effie, a barefoot moon among them, Fiona licking her lips, Delilah smirking with revolvers at her hips—VIPs following in their wake.

The club closed around them—thick smoke, neon buzz, the smell of spilled rum and women's perfume. Waitresses wove between tables, poker games snarled in curses, and a fistfight toppled chairs at the far wall.

Nobody stopped them—everyone noticed them.

Jake rose from his table in the back, cards in one hand, cigar in the other. He was larger than Ben remembered, sunburnt skin creased by salt and laughter. Around him clustered his core, the original crew of the Fading Dawn: Katie, sharp-eyed, like she'd boxed her way through adolescence. Anika, braids woven with beads and seashells. Reuben, beard thick with sea salt, hands as steady as ropes in a gale. James, slight but watchful, soft voice masked by quick hands. And their recent acquisition—Mercury, restless, Jake's chosen first mate.

"Five boats now," Jake declared, waving at them all. "Five crews, mixed blood and mixed sins. The Southern Wind, the Old Malabar, the Blue Dolphin, the Sirens' Call, and the Fading Dawn. All theirs by misadventure, all mine by the luck of timing. You're looking at pirates, every last one."

The room answered in cheers, some slamming glasses, others lifting bottles. The Hercules crew was already being claimed, pushed into poker games, and handed cigars as if they'd been born to it.

Jake threw an arm across Ben's shoulders and pressed him into a seat at the table. "Now then. Tell me what you want from me. And tell me quick, before Mercury dies of caution."

Ben set his jaw. The smoke made his throat rough, but the words were heavier still. "Leila," he said.

Jake's hand stilled on the cigar.

"She isn't Leila anymore," Ben continued. "You've seen it on the broadcasts. Cairo falling. Undead in the streets. Armies broken. The gods can't deny it, either. She's Lilith now. And she's leading the horde."

The table quieted. Katie's grin faltered. Reuben's knuckles went white around his glass. Even Anika stopped her banter with a waitress.

Jake didn't blink. "Rumour and smoke. I've heard all manner of stories since the Atlas lit up. Why should I believe she's behind it?"

Ben's voice was steady. "Because every feed says the same. She walks at the front of the dead. She casts the spells that raise them. The gods admit it. She isn't pretending to be anything else. She's claimed the name—Lilith—and the horde answers."

Mercury gave a soft, humourless laugh. "And you expect us to believe she just... turned? One week, a woman; next week, the queen of corpses?"

"That's exactly what happened," Fiona said, her coin glinting in the smoke. "Abrupt. Violent. Like someone jammed a power meant to trickle into her veins all at once. Corrupted her as it filled her."

Effie leaned forward, voice velvet. "It's not a story the news invented. The gods themselves are shaken. Even they don't know how she rose so fast."

Jake sat back, smoke curling around his beard. "And you—what are you in this tale, Ben? You call her Lilith. What name are you hiding?"

Ben shook his head. "I don't use names. Not for myself, not for the others. We are kin; somehow, same as her. She was one of us. Still is, in a way."

Delilah swung herself into a chair backward, arms hooked over the chair's back. Her laugh was sharp as glass. "She always did love the stage. Just took a darker spotlight."

Ellery exhaled smoke into the rafters. "The dead are drawn to her. They watch her closely."

Jake narrowed his eyes. "So she's corrupted. And you're not. What keeps you clean while she fouls the water?"

Ben glanced down, hand pressing the phantom tug in his ribs. "Maybe nothing keeps me clean. Maybe the corruption's just waiting. But she... she bent straight to power. No hesitation. No chance to weather it. Whatever silent force made us what we are, it rushed her, and she drowned in it."

Mercury swirled his glass. "Or she simply showed her true self. Charm has always been her gift. Now it's sharpened."

Katie slammed a hand down. "Don't matter how she rose—she is brutal. Every night, the broadcasts show another city gone."

Reuben's voice was deep as a keel. "And every life we lose rises to her."

James finally spoke, quiet but clear. "If her power is seduction, then every fight is a trap. The more you struggle, the deeper you're caught."

The words sat heavily. Jake stubbed his cigar out in the ashtray, leaned both elbows on the table, and looked Ben dead in the eye. "So, little Leila has become your Lilith. And you expect me to follow you into the dark with five ships and a crowd of thieves?"

Ben nodded. "Yes. Whether we like it or not, she's not done. This is only the beginning."

Jake leaned back in his chair, the timber creaking under his weight. His cigar glowed red in the smoke, ash threatening to tumble but clinging stubbornly on.

His eyes bored into Ben.

"Why?" Jake asked at last, the word landing heavy enough to stall the noise of the nearest table.

"Why in all the hells should I follow you? I've got five ships, five crews, rum in my glass, and coin enough to keep the tide sweet. Why sail into death just because your ribs say she is kin? Sounds ridiculous—yet somehow you've acquired quite the entourage."

Silence. Even the Valleyboys held still, half-drunk, half-sober, waiting.

Mercury lifted his glass, turning it slowly so the light caught the rim. His voice came smooth, but pitched low, as if speaking only to Jake, though the whole room bent in to hear.

"Because, Captain, this is not just a calamity. It is your chance."

Jake's eyes narrowed. "Chance?"

Mercury smiled faintly. "The chance to become more than a man with boats. The chance to become a legend."

The word seemed to hang, weighty, pulling the air taut.

Mercury leaned forward, elbows on the table, gaze steady. "Every pirate worth his salt has stolen gold, smuggled guns, and cracked a port open with cannon fire. They're remembered—if lucky—for a generation. Then the sea swallows their names."

He tapped the table with one long finger.

"But you—this crew, this moment—you could be remembered as more. The ones who rose when gods faltered. The ones who dared when the world itself was failing. Not songs sung in a tavern for coin, but stories carved into history, into myth."

He let the silence stretch. Smoke curled. Jake's cigar burned lower.

Mercury's voice dropped to a near whisper. "Do you want to be a captain who dies fat and forgotten on some nameless shore? Or the captain remembered for centuries—the one who looked at the abyss and laughed, and sailed anyway?"

The room was silent. The card games had stopped, and the dice were left mid-roll. A waitress froze mid-step, tray balanced on her palm. Even the Valleyboys, loudest of all, sat hushed.

All eyes turned to Jake.

He stared into his glass, rolled it once, then set it down. His cigar went to the ashtray, crushed. He straightened in his chair, shoulders squaring like a mast taking wind.

"Legend, you say," Jake murmured. "A tale to outlast the tide."

He looked around at the faces fixed on him—his pirates, Ben's rabble, the gods disguised in mortal skin. He breathed out smoke and salt. Then he grinned, wide and reckless.

“To hell with fat and forgotten. If the noose calls, then we’ll answer. Let the sea choke on our names before it ever swallows us.”

The room erupted.

The roar hit like cannon fire—Valleyboys howling, pirates pounding fists on tables, glasses shattering as drinks were thrown high. Waitresses laughed, rum spilling, bodies colliding in embraces. The aircrew shouted themselves hoarse, swept up in the tide.

Jake stood, raising his glass above it all. “To legend!”

The cheer doubled, shaking the walls, the smoke itself seeming to quake. Somewhere outside, faint and distant, the bell tolled again—two strokes, sharp and cold, like the sea itself giving its answer.

The roar faded by degrees, laughter and glass clatter thinning until the club’s pulse steadied again. Jake dropped back into his chair, face lit with that reckless grin of his, and slapped the table.

“Then we sail,” he said. “But not into legend blind. We need a plan.”

Mercury tipped his glass in agreement. “A plan, yes. Speed above all. Lilith’s horde doesn’t crawl—it spreads like fire in the wind. If she reaches the Levant first, there’ll be nothing left to save.”

Ben nodded, the rope in his ribs humming at the name. “We have to beat her there.”

Jake leaned forward, cigar forgotten, hands broad on the stained wood. “Boats carry men, but boats can’t outrun an army. Not across seas this wide. We need wings as well as sails.”

The Hercules engineer, already three rums deep, blinked and pointed vaguely toward the door. "She's still warm, the Herc. Good bird. Can hop her from here to Darwin, Darwin to..." He trailed off, trying to remember his charts.

"Hop, skip, and jump," Effie supplied sweetly, resting a hand on his arm. He melted under her touch, nodding eagerly.

Jake's eyes lit. "Exactly. The Herc becomes our courier. We load her with supplies—powder, shot, medicine, rum—and whatever treasure I've been sitting on too long. She skips ahead, drops what we need, and keeps the line alive. The fleet follows in her wake, boats running lean for speed."

Mercury smirked. "At last, the treasure gets some exercise."

Jake ignored him. He jabbed a thumb toward the Hercules crew, who looked up from their drinks like schoolboys caught out. "Effie, you and a few of my sharper pirateers keep them charmed, keep them honest. No drunken detours, no coward's retreat. That bird doesn't fly without their hands, and their hands don't move unless yours guide them."

Effie's smile curved, serene as moonlight. "Consider them mine already."

The engineer beamed as though she'd knighted him.

Jake turned to the Valleyboys, already back to brawling, arm-wrestling, and spilling beer. "Your rabble—too many for wings. They'll ride with us on the water. Gods, too." He gave Diane a hard glance, then Fiona, then Jian. "If you're meant to be part of this legend, you'll stand shoulder to shoulder with the sea."

Diane's expression didn't flicker. "I've stood in worse places."

Fiona flicked her coin, letting it ring once before catching it. "The rope pulls that way. Water's as good as wings."

Jian simply exhaled, heat shimmering off his skin until the table's surface smoked faintly.

Jake looked back at Ben. "So. We run light. Crews pared down, cargo tight, sails trimmed. The Hercules runs ahead, feeds us from the sky. The boats keep close, cut lean through every tide. We move faster than rumour. And if the sea spits us out on the Levant first, then maybe, just maybe, we'll have ground to stand on when Lilith comes knocking."

The table held the silence again, but this time it was different—not doubt, but gravity. The shape of the thing was real now, not a dream.

Ben felt the rope strain, tugging in his ribs as if eager for the course to be set. He spoke low, specific. "That's it. Speed. We reach the Levant before her. If we don't, no plan will matter."

Jake stood again, raising his glass high once more. "Then it's settled. We make for the Holy Land. The Herc above us, the boats beneath us, the tide beside us. Fast and lean. No fat, no waste. The sea will know our names before Lilith ever sets foot on it."

The cheer this time was shorter, sharper—less a party, more a war cry. Pirateers slapped each other's backs, Valleyboys howled, the aircrew whooped like boys at their first bender.

Jake leaned down close to Ben, voice pitched just for him. "You've got your legend started, shade. Don't waste it."

And somewhere out in the dark, beyond the walls of smoke and neon, the bell tolled again. Once, twice. Calling them west.

Chapter 26
The Sinai

The desert hummed like a furnace about to burst. Engines idled in ranks: tanks crouched in arrowheads, bulldozers hunched with their blades lifted, and convoys of priests stood by with mirror-shields polished to a fevered gleam.

Floodlights flared as pools formed in the mud, where rain had already started to fall.

Overhead, black-bellied bombers lumbered in formation, bellies packed with something heavier than water.

Jean-Luc Veyrac tightened the strap of his harness in the belly of the Atlas and spat grit into the dark. He'd jumped into wars before—Mali, Chad, the unending dust of forgotten borders—but never into this.

The men around him were not ordinary legionnaires. They were Ari's. Scarred, silent, knives strapped as tight as faith. Each one had the look of a man who had accepted he was already dead.

The red light glowed over the ramp.

Ari tugged his straps one last time, then raised his head. His scar caught the glow like a stone cut. "You land in her shadow," Ari said, voice low and hard.

"Not behind. Not beside. In it. Necromancers first. Break their throats. When the choir falters, the horde falters. And if you see her…" He let the thought hang, unfinished.

Every man knew that Lilith's name already meant death.

The Atlas lurched as if struck by a giant hand. Outside, thunder bellowed. Zed had opened the sky. The cloud wall came alive in seconds.

Rain hammered the fuselage like fists. Lightning split the desert floor into ragged white scars. Jean-Luc smelled ozone even through the stink of fuel and sweat. Zed's storm dragged water into the bones of the desert until it began to sag under the weight.

And then Demi's hand closed over it.

Below, the hardpan shuddered, softened, and turned into mud. Vines erupted in the sodden dark, thick green cables that writhed upward to snare shinbones and shields.

Battalions of tanks revved their engines, ready to carve channels through the bog. Bulldozers roared forward, blades lowered, teeth bared.

On the flanks, Pele crouched beside rain-filled wadis and whispered fire into them. Pools boiled into screaming geysers. Fissures split wide, spewing lava that crawled across the wet earth to lines of skeletons that should have remained dead. When the lava crossed puddles of rain, steam rose as a thick, hot fog. The air itself became a weapon.

The pilot's voice crackled over the comms: "Bombers inbound. Two minutes. Funnels hot."

Jean-Luc closed his eyes and pictured them: massive amphibious bombers, the kind built to scoop lakes to drown forest fires, now flying low and fat with napalm. Not water today. Fire. Their bellies would paint the desert edges in orange, pushing Lilith's army into the maw of tanks and dozers.

Inside their aircraft, the red light flicked to green. The ramp yawned open, and the Sinai spread beneath them...

Rain-lashed, burning at the edges, its centre churned to mud and vines. In the distance, the horde advanced—phalanxes of skeletons gleaming wet, revenants loping with tendon-tight speed, wraiths drifting like frayed banners. And behind them, the necromancers. Wire-jawed, throats split and bound, voices wrung into spells. Their song wasn't music. It was negation—water measured out of existence, courage scoured from hearts, storms bending the wrong way. Beyond them towered the hierophants, ribs glowing like censers. And above them all, the figure who needed no pointing out. Lilith.

"Go!" Ari roared and stepped into the storm.

Gravity took Jean-Luc by the chest and flung him after. The chute cracked open, snapped him skyward, and the world became blur and scream and rain. Lightning strobed over canopies, bursting around him. Below, the first ribbons of napalm tore across the flanks, fire hissing against water, and the skeleton ranks shuddered inward, funnelling into the killing ground.

Tracer stitched the rain. Wraiths drifted upward toward the parachutes like horror made smoke. A shadow blotted them out. Rus stooped. The hawk god ripped a clutch of wraiths into ribbons and vanished, only to reappear hauling a screaming soldier from a collapsing canopy and setting him down neatly on the ridge.

The ground rushed up.

Jean-Luc hit hard, rolled, tore free of his chute, rifle up. Mud clung to his boots and vines wrapped around his knees. Ari was already there, cutting through revenants with blade and rifle as if both were extensions of his stride. The rest of the cadre hit like meteorites, pulling themselves free and forming around him by instinct.

"Necromancers!" Ari barked, pointing into the storm-dark.

They drove forward. Skeletons pivoted to meet them, shields grinding, jawbones clicking. Revenants slid into the gaps, obscene in their grace. The legionnaires fired at skulls, at knees, at anything that might slow the tide.

Jean-Luc found himself screaming as he rammed his bayonet through a necromancer's wired jaw. The thing's incantation broke into silence. Instantly, the rain corrected, pounding straight down. Demi's vines surged, coiling thicker, dragging whole phalanxes into the muck.

Ari tore another necromancer open, black ichor spilling with the last of its stolen voice. "Keep cutting!" he shouted. "They bleed, and the song falters!"

The bombers came again, laying fresh rivers of orange across the flanks. Bulldozers shoved the skeleton tide into the furnace. Tanks fired canisters into packed bone, shredding lines like clay pigeons. Priests rolled their mirror shields forward, sanctified water spraying in arcs that hissed over steel and into the ranks. Where it struck, wraiths folded, revenants smoked, skeletons shivered apart.

For a heartbeat, the impossible looked possible.

Then the necromancers inhaled as one.

A new circle burned into the mud around Jean-Luc's boots. Letters crawled up the rain like spiders. The nearest priest screamed as his reflection in his mirror showed only a skull. Holy water hit a blue sigil in the sand and vanished—not boiled, not spent, gone. Jean-Luc staggered, stomach lurching. Ari hauled him upright with one hand, drove his blade into the necromancer's chest with the other.

The spell snapped. Relief flooded through them for a breath.

Zed's storm cracked their relief with lightning so close Jean-Luc smelt singed hair.

And then the horizon bent.

Lilith stepped into the storm as if it had been her veil all along. Every soldier felt it. The funnels narrowed. The song of the necromancers deepened, weaving tighter. The horde tilted toward her like iron to a lodestone.

Ari lifted his blade and bared his teeth. "With me," he said.

And they went.

Mud frothed around Jean-Luc's boots as he followed Ari into the throat of the storm. The air smelled of burning oil, ozone, and bone turned to dust. Lightning carved white scars across the desert, every flash showing a different nightmare. Tanks roared forward in staggered wedges, their turrets spitting flame. Bulldozers pushed walls of bone into berms, piling skeletons into obscene architecture. Napalm hissed on wet sand, funnelling the horde toward the killing lanes.

It almost looked like victory.

Rus tore the sky open again. His cry wasn't a hawk's anymore—it was the scream of an old god in feathered disguise. He stooped through the rain, talons tearing a necromancer from the choir and hurling it into Pele's boiling trench. The thing thrashed like parchment in a fire, notes warping into silence. For every necromancer torn apart, the storm straightened, the vines surged higher, and the tanks found easier targets.

Jean-Luc glanced back once. Bulldozers rolled side by side, blades pushing skeletons into fire with relentless patience, as if they were clearing rubble instead of slaughtering an army. The men riding their decks raised rifles and fired down into the press, cursing, laughing, weeping—anything to keep fear from finding them.

Ahead, Ari was the point of the spear. He cut through revenants like a machine built for killing, each motion efficient, never wasted. When one lunged with tendon-cable limbs, Ari stepped aside, took its head, and kept moving. Around him, the parachute cadre fought like men who'd already written their epitaphs.

"Break the throats!" Ari roared.

They hit the necromancers. Wire-jawed, throats slit open and bound with bone pins, their bodies swayed like metronomes. Voices poured out of them in chords too heavy for lungs. Circles of fire sprang up around their feet, spreading across the mud like spilled ink.

Jean-Luc drove his bayonet through one's chest. The song cut off mid-breath. Rain slammed straight down again, hammering the sand into a swamp.

Demi seized it. Her vines writhed upward like the fingers of drowned giants, tangling phalanxes into grotesque knots. Skeletons fell without falling, locked in embraces of living green.

Pele exhaled, and a pond beside the necromancers erupted. Water turned to steam, steam to shrieks, and then a lava tongue slithered out, swallowing the bound singers and the revenants shielding them. The smell was sulphur and meat.

For a moment, the horde recoiled.

Then Lilith's hand rose.

She did not shout. She didn't need to. The necromancers still standing inhaled in unison. The air thickened. Circles flared beneath Jean-Luc's boots again, letters crawling up his calves like worms of light. His rifle shook in his hands, too heavy, as though belief itself had been stolen.

Ari cut through the circle before it closed, grabbed Jean-Luc by the harness, and shoved him forward. "Keep your feet, Legionnaire!"

The words landed like nails in his chest. Jean-Luc staggered but moved, firing into the next rank of necromancers. One collapsed with its jaw snapped, wires sparking in the rain. Another dropped when Rus plucked it from the mud and flung it skyward, wings beating storm into song.

Zed's thunder rolled closer, heavy as judgement. The storm no longer looked like weather; it looked like architecture, scaffolding built to hold the sky in place. Lightning stitched the edges of the battle into frames of frozen violence. In one frame, Jean-Luc saw Ari shoving his squad through revenants; in another, he saw Demi's vines twisting into living walls; in the next, Pele's lava burning a corridor into the choir.

"Press!" Ari shouted. "She will bleed, the nightmare ends!"

And for a moment, they advanced.

The horde wavered. Skeleton ranks stumbled on mud too deep for their precision. Revenants slipped in the vines and were torn down. Wraiths screamed as holy water scalded them into vapour. Necromancers fell, one after another, their spells breaking into silence.

Jean-Luc felt hope seize him like a fever. Maybe—maybe—this impossible plan would hold.

Then the Weavers began to sing. Their jaw-wires vibrated in harmony with the necromancers, braiding spells into ropes of pressure. The rain faltered again, bending sideways as though ashamed. Demi's vines withered mid-clutch, shrivelling into black husks. The boiling pits cooled, Pele snarling as steam turned back to water.

The skeleton tide surged forward, free again.

Jean-Luc fired until his rifle clicked dry. He slammed a fresh magazine home with trembling hands. Around him, the squad fought like wolves in a burning forest. Men screamed, fell, rose again. Rus's shadow swept overhead, dragging a paratrooper free from a circle, only for the man to collapse moments later with his chest caved in.

"Keep moving!" Ari bellowed, voice cutting through the cacophony like steel. His eyes locked on the necromancers still singing, their throats glowing with sickly light.

"Cut them! CUT THEM!"

They charged.

Jean-Luc felt himself swept along, bayonet flashing. A necromancer shrieked when he drove it into its belly, wires snapping in sparks. Ari tore another open with his blade, black ichor spraying. The men followed, hacking, stabbing, firing point-blank into throats stretched too wide.

The songs broke. The storm straightened. And for an instant, the balance tipped again.

Then Lilith herself stepped into the breach.

The world seemed to stop. Even the thunder paused to listen. She was taller than memory, her hair streaming in the storm, her eyes bright with cruelty. Every skeleton raised its shield in unison. Every revenant froze mid-lunge. The necromancers swelled their song until the mud boiled with symbols.

Ari raised his rifle like a sword and spat into the rain. "With me!"

Jean-Luc followed because there was nowhere else to go.

The mortal force met the tide head-on.

Skeletons shattered under tank fire, bone spraying like gravel. Bulldozers carved lanes, their blades now red with gore. Bombers laid another wall of fire on the flanks, the smell of burning marrow choking the air. Zed hurled lightning into the necromancers, each bolt cracking them like porcelain. Demi screamed with the effort of dragging vines back through dead earth, and Pele kept splitting the ground—fissures swallowing skeletons whole by the hundreds.

But Lilith still walked untouched.

Spells braided around her like a crown. With a flick of her hand, the necromancers' song turned into shackles. Circles sprang up around Ari's boots, brighter, deeper, faster.

He hacked through them once, twice, but new ones coiled tighter. Sigils climbed his arms like serpents.

Jean-Luc saw it—saw Ari fighting against chains of light that didn't exist in the air but in the soul. He roared, firing, stabbing, cutting anything that touched Ari. Revenants swarmed, skeletons closed in, necromancers screamed louder.

Ari drove his blade through a necromancer's throat, breaking its song, but three more picked it up in harmony.

Rain bent away from him, refusing to touch his skin.

Jean-Luc realised, with the horror of certainty, that they weren't trying to kill Ari. They were binding him.

The spell tightened.

Ari stood inside a spell that was a tempest—rings of script turning faster than blades, light cinching at his wrists and throat. Each time he tore one, two more closed.

The mud hardened to stone around his boots. Rain slid away from his skin like it had been told to forget him.

Jean-Luc hit a revenant full stride, bayonet low. The thing folded with a wet crack. He shouldered through, boots slipping, eyes never leaving Ari. "En avant!" he roared at no one and everyone, throat raw.

A wraith reached for his face; a mirror team beside him flared their pavises, and the thing shrank from its own reflection, edges unravelling. The priests pushed, shouting prayers that sounded like orders.

"Keep him breathing!" someone screamed. It might have been Jean-Luc.

Zed drove a spear of lightning down the storm's spine. The bolt smacked the ground ten paces from Lilith and split into a spider of white veins. The Weavers' jaws thrummed; the bolt guttered and went sideways, harmless, biting black glass from Pele's cooled rock. Zed bared his teeth around the cigar and drew more resounding thunder from a horizon that no longer obeyed.

Demi clawed both hands into the soaked earth. Vines tore up in ropes, green and iron-tough, and whipped around Ari's spell-rings, trying to lever them apart. Firefly runes popped like solder. The vines blackened, smoked, and slumped away. Demi didn't stop. Her palms bled mud.

Pele stamped once. The ground between Ari and Lilith shivered and opened into a boiling oval. Steam billowed; something in the scream was metal. Lilith did not turn her head. The necromancers inhaled and the pit skinned to stone, heat caged under a frost of symbols.

Rus skated the rain, wings shuddering, and tried the impossible—he dove to hook Ari under the arms and lift. Talons met invisible cords. The hawk's cry cracked into a raw, human sound, and he tore free, trailing feathers like sparks. Jean-Luc felt the drop of them on his face—warm, impossible—before the storm took them.

"Hold him," Lilith said.

The choir obeyed. The necromancers' note went from negation to pressure, braiding into a rope that wrapped Ari's chest and throat. The Weavers wove counter-sound under it, a steadying hum that felt like a hand forcing his head.

Ari still fought. Each breath was a shove against a wall only he could see. His blade grated against light and bit nothing. He looked like a man leaning into a gale.

Jean-Luc reached him. He slammed his shoulder into a skeleton, broke it at the hip with the butt of the rifle, and used the suck of mud to hold his feet. He got one hand on Ari's harness.

The War-Dog's muscles were iron under a wet cloth. "Mon capitaine," Jean-Luc rasped, not caring that Ari wore no rank. "We cut. We cut—"

Then a bronze sword slid between his ribs and made a noise like a cork pulled wrong. Breath left him with heat. He drove the bayonet up automatically, found a throat, twisted, and staggered. The sword withdrew, then returned higher, under the collarbone. He tried to pull air, but it tasted like iron.

"Stay," Ari said. His eyes were knives. "Stand."

Jean-Luc laughed without sound. "Toujours," he mouthed, and turned to the necromancers. The nearest one swayed, wire-jaw glinting. Jean-Luc went for it like a man late to an appointment, bayonet down, hate up. Something bit his calf—teeth, iron—then his knee went hot and soft at once. He fell and crawled, dragging himself by his elbows. He no longer felt hands on him. He felt the earth push.

Lilith stepped into the ring.

She was not wet. The rain behaved around her. Her blade was old—curved Bedouin steel with the dull shine of heirloom—and the spells wanted it. Symbols crawled along the fuller like fish schooling.

Ari jerked once against the bonds. "Look at me," he said, voice ground down to gravel. "Don't look away."

Lilith obliged. "War," she said, like a greeting.

"Always."

"Not anymore."

She lifted the knife and did not hurry. The necromancers' song shifted key; the circles under Ari's boots flared white. Jean-Luc heaved himself onto a knee. A revenant's hand caught the back of his neck and pushed. He stabbed backward, and the bayonet found meat; the hand let go. He lurched up, blade out.

"Mirrors!" a priest shrieked, and a row of pavises rolled to catch whatever would happen, faces pale behind the glass. Holy water arced, hissed on sigils, vanished into arithmetic.

Lilith set her free hand under Ari's jaw like a lover and drew the knife across his throat. The sound was clean. For a heartbeat, nothing else made any.

Blood sheeted, bright and arterial, then thickened in the air, captured mid-flight by lines of script that rose to meet it. The red turned darker, black around the edges, and flowed inward along the rings, not down. It did not hit the ground. It wrote itself into the spell like ink poured back into a pen. Ari's knees buckled. He did not fall. The circles would not let him. His mouth opened and closed with words no throat should manage.

Jean-Luc staggered forward two steps, bayonet cocked, and a shield rim took him across the face. The world flashed and narrowed. He spat teeth and rain, tasted rust already in the back of his throat. "Non," he said, to the bone ring, to the woman with the knife, to the sky that had failed to strike. The word fell at his feet.

The choir sang. It wasn't a sound so much as a taking of pulse, of heat, of name. The necromancers' jaws jittered; wires glowed. The Weavers held the pitch like surgeons. Ari's blood became smoke. The smoke became script. The script sank through his skin.

Zed hit the line again with thunder that should have shattered years. It cracked open the wadi and tank alike and still did not touch the woman in the centre. Demi sobbed once, a complex, ugly sound, and jammed both hands into soil that fought her. A new green nub thrust up between her knuckles and died. Pele's mouth was a furnace; the heat vibrated the air, but the knife did not cool, and the blood did not run where it shouldn't.

Jean-Luc crawled. His hands left prints that filled instantly with rain and then emptied as the sigils drank. A skeleton trod on his wrist, and he yanked it free, skin left like a glove turned inside out. He reached the nearest necromancer's ankle and drove the bayonet in. Bone cracked. The note wavered. A spear punched through his back and into the mud, pinning him to the earth he had been trying to save.

He did not drop the rifle. He tried to push the bayonet deeper with palms that no longer had grip. The spear twisted once. His vision went wide and then far away, like the desert had stepped back to see better.

He could still see Ari.

The War-Dog's head hung at an angle that declared the cut fatal. His chest did not move. The lights at his wrists and throat dimmed and then flared, as if deciding. Lilith's hand pressed flat over the wound. The blood that should have soaked her fingers crawled up instead and disappeared into her palm. She whispered something that belonged in a mortuary and a nursery, both.

The wind reversed.

Jean-Luc felt it along his tongue, a pressure that tried to shove breath back into his lungs against their will. The circles brightened until the rain looked dark in comparison. The necromancers' knees began to tremble with the force of the note they held. Ari's fingers twitched. The blade in his hand lifted a fraction as if remembering.

"Rise," Lilith said.

The word landed with weight.

Ari's spine straightened. The cut in his throat closed from the outside inward, skin knitting with a seam you could only see because you knew where to look. His eyes opened. Whatever colour they had been was drowned by a pale, tidal glow. The rings around his limbs eased and then inverted, turning from bonds into bracelets, from noose into collar of office. The last of his breath left him as frost.

He did not breathe again. He did not need to.

Rus crashed the air, wings ragged, and saw. He banked hard, feathers shredding in the torque, and left a scream on the wind that made men think of winter. Zed went still on the ridge, the cigar a coal by his lip that refused to die in the rain. Demi's hands slid out of the mud. She stared at the black lines etched in her palms where the earth had written no. Pele looked at Lilith and then at Ari and then down, into the ground, as if searching for a second heat that wasn't there.

"Ari," Jean-Luc whispered, and blood bubbled in his throat. He couldn't hear himself. He could see the shape of the name on his lips.

The War-Dog turned his head. The movement was smooth and wrong, as if joints had been oiled with something colder than oil. He looked at Jean-Luc without recognition or with too much of it—like a ledger remembering every line. His mouth opened, and no steam came out.

Lilith laid two fingers along the healed seam, claiming.

"General," she said softly. "Walk."

Ari stepped forward out of the last guttering circle, and the desert made room.

Jean-Luc tried to lift the rifle once more. His arms didn't get the message. He let his head rest in the crook of his elbow like a man finally allowing sleep. The last thing he saw was Ari's boot print filling with rain and not filling at all.

Somewhere far off, beyond the storm and the screaming engines and the harsh clatter of bone, a bell began to ring—a church or a mosque or a memory. It didn't matter which. The sound came thin and true through everything, like a thread thrown across a canyon. The necromancers' song let it pass. It did not need to take everything yet.

Ari lifted his blade. It made no light. It did not have to. He faced the living.

The desert had no horizon anymore.

It was wall-to-wall with bone and smoke and mud, a single heaving organism rolling inexorably east. Tanks that had roared a short hour ago lay canted on their sides, turrets torn open like tin. Bulldozers smouldered, their drivers strewn in broken lines where they'd tried to make the machines stand after their engines gave up. The storm Zed had called still clung overhead, but it no longer obeyed him. The thunder had gone out of its voice. Rain fell only where Lilith wished, softening roads, drowning trenches, filling rifles with mud.

Jean-Luc's body lay pinned in the sucking earth. He did not move. His bayonet still jutted from the necromancer's ankle, a tiny act of defiance already swallowed by the song. Around him, other legionnaires sprawled like discarded toys, some staring skyward, some half-buried in mud. A mirror-shield lay cracked face up beside him. It reflected nothing at all.

The gods still fought, but their struggle was now a theatre.

Rus circled low, wings shredded, stooping again and again to lift men out of the press—only to watch them die a minute later when revenants tore them apart. His cry had grown ragged, more vulture than hawk, but he did not stop. Demi knelt at the centre of a ring of withered vines. Her shoulders shook with sobs that pulled new shoots from the soil and killed them in the same breath. The ground beneath her palms had stopped listening, deaf to her grief. Pele's mouth still bled heat, but her lava no longer held. The flows cooled into stone before they reached the horde. Her eyes burned, not with fire, but with the fury of futility.

And Zed—Zed alone remained upright on the ridge. His cigar was ash at his lip. The storm he had raised drifted loose, breaking apart into tatters like cloth pulled from a nail. Lightning twitched feebly at the horizon and died. His eye, what remained of it, glimmered once, then turned flat.

The horde rolled forward unbothered. At its crown, Lilith walked, serene as geometry. Around her clustered the necromancers and Weavers that remained, their voices braided into a single endless chord—at her right hand strode Ari.

Not Ari. Not anymore.

The cut at his throat had closed into a seam black with script. His eyes were a tidal white that reflected nothing, saw everything. His blade moved with mechanical certainty, cleaving men who stumbled toward him in hopeless bravery. Where he walked, mortals faltered. The spell that bound him was not a leash but a crown, and he wore it without hesitation.

A Bedouin company, last of the desert's proud volunteers, broke from the ridge with rifles raised. They charged into Ari's path, ululating cries mixing with gunfire. Ari lifted his blade once. When it fell, twenty men folded as if they had been one body. The survivors dropped their rifles and knelt in the mud, weeping. Ari did not even look back at them.

"Forward," Lilith murmured, and her general obeyed.

The rout was not sudden. It was slow, like sand collapsing into a sinkhole. The tank battalions broke first, crews fleeing eastward across mud-sunk tracks. The bulldozer drivers ran next, leaving their machines standing like blind beasts with no handlers. The priests sang until their voices bled, until mirrors cracked, until water turned traitor and refused to sanctify. When their throats gave out, the skeletons took them.

In the sky, the bombers turned for another pass. Napalm spilled in ragged rivers. For a heartbeat, the flanks flared orange—and then the song bent the fire sideways, blowing it back across the aircraft. One wing blossomed into flame, then another. Jean-Luc, dead in the mud, did not see the great planes spiral down. But the living did, and their hearts drowned with them.

The battlefield stank of wet ash and open graves.

Demi collapsed face-first into the mud. Pele caught her shoulders, but even fire could not rouse the earth goddess now. Rus landed hard beside them, wings limp, talons black with revenant blood. He folded over them, shielding what little still breathed from the rain that had chosen sides. Zed watched it all, his silhouette sharp against the last shred of storm. His crow cawed and hid frightened in the nape of his neck.

He looked down at Ari, then up at the woman who had turned war into a servant.

His single eye teared up, but he did not move. Not yet.

The necromancers sang louder. The Weavers joined. The whole desert seemed to hum in Lilith's key. She lifted her face to the east. Beyond the Sinai, the Holy Land waited—Jerusalem, Bethlehem, Hebron, Mecca, Medina. Names that had stitched faith into flesh for centuries. Names that had anchored the world's soul. Lilith smiled as though she had just remembered them. Her army answered in one motion. Skeletons lifted shields. Revenants snapped their tendons taut. Wraiths shivered into clarity. Ari raised his blade, its edge glinting pale, and pointed east.

The horde turned as one and began to march—no battle cries. No drums. Just the endless clatter of bone, the hum of sorcery, the splash of boots in mud that once belonged to rivers.

Behind them, the battlefield lay silent, a graveyard still steaming with the heat of futile defiance. Men groaned in the muck, some alive, some half gone, some praying with mouths that filled with water. None rose. The gods did not follow. Rus bent his head over Demi's still body. Pele turned her face away from the sight of Ari's back. Zed ground the last ember of his cigar into the mud. None spoke.

Only the wind found words, whispering eastward. And in its breath rode the certainty: the Holy Land would be next, and the world had no army left to meet it.

Acknowledgement

To my wife—patient custodian of reality while I wandered off to invent new ones. For aeons, I have attempted to persuade her to read a paragraph, a page, a chapter—even the book. She has resisted every request with calm, graceful tact and disciplined resolve. Her patience has been heroic. Her scepticism has been correct. Whatever merit these pages possess exists because she tried to believe the man who insisted on writing them.

To my friends—long-standing companions in noble but frequently misguided adventures. We built kingdoms on tabletops, conquered imaginary worlds, and argued at exhausting length about rules no sensible civilisation would ever adopt. You taught me that great stories are rarely planned, usually improvised, always born from overconfidence, and often redeemed only by stubborn luck. But the spirit of those years—the laughter, the disasters, and the belief that a ridiculous idea might just work—is quietly embedded in every chapter.

I didn't tell you I was writing a book. I considered this a strategic advantage.

To Norbit Whitewhisker—self-appointed editor, senior keyboard consultant, agent of chaos, and companion extraordinaire. He supervised many writing sessions, offered strong opinions, commandeered the mouse, rewrote important paragraphs without consultation, and demonstrated a bold editorial philosophy centred on the delete key. His contributions were frequent, confident, and creatively hilarious. His dedication was unwavering.

To AI—the ever-optimistic late-night sounding board and uncomplaining accomplice to endless edits. Without it, this book would be thinner, rougher, and almost certainly in the recycle bin.

And finally, to those who walked beside me when the road was dark—thank you for the torch, the map, and for teaching me to see by starlight.

To those still in darkness—may you find light in these pages.

About the author

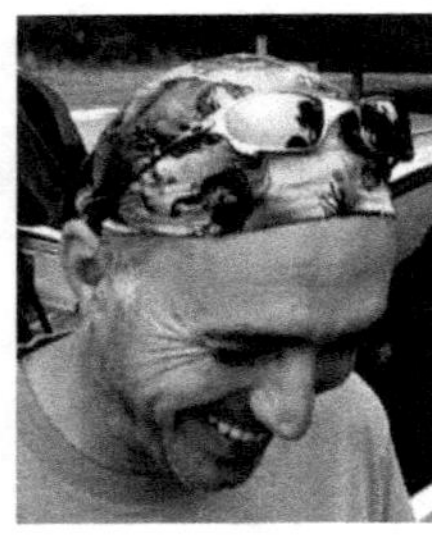

Kevin Britton is an Australian speculative-fiction author whose work blends mythic imagination with hard-edged futurism. Writing from South Australia, he builds vast narrative systems where ancient archetypes collide with near-future science, and where flawed, stubborn humans stand between extinction and transcendence.

Kevin is the creator of *The Transit Star Continuum*—an interconnected series of novels that merges epic fantasy, cosmic science fiction, and philosophical inquiry into power, identity, and survival. His stories are shaped by a lifelong fascination with astronomy, mythology, and the fragile mechanics of civilisation, as well as by hands-on pursuits ranging from winemaking and leatherworking to aquaristics, gardening, and design.

A believer that great stories are forged through struggle rather than comfort, Kevin writes about characters pushed beyond certainty—people who survive what should have killed them and must decide what kind of force they will become. His work often explores legacy, moral ambiguity, and the cost of change in worlds no longer willing to stay still.

When he isn't writing, Kevin lives with his wife and animals, tending vines, building improbable projects, and quietly plotting the next expansion of a universe he refuses to let end neatly.

By Rusty Fish Press

To the critic the work of art is simply a suggestion for a new work of his own, that need not necessarily bear any obvious resemblance to the thing it criticizes.

Oscar Wilde

In My Craft of Celluloid

ISBN: 978-1-7334914-0-2

Book and Book Cover Design by Kate Glad
Front Cover Photograph by Suzanne Berberet

Made in the United States of America

To Cypher Blueman and Girl From the Bronx. Without their enthusiasm there would be no Billy Glad.

And to my family.

Contents

Foreword

My dad says things. My memories of my childhood could be mapped with his phrases as marking points along the way.

"I'm gonna live forever," in the kitchen.

"If it's free, take," around the dinner table.

"*Cosa nostra*," in the drop-off line at school.

"Here's looking at you, kid," every night before bed.

And the most important one of all: "Art is synthesized experience." That essential phrase is all over this book, and to be introduced to it prior to reading is one favor this foreword can do for you, the reader.

I don't remember when I first heard it. Certainly before college, maybe even before high school. It means that every confusing thing, every scene that appears mismanaged, every choice of words that doesn't hit the ear quite right isn't wrong because it's bad art inherently. We like or dislike art not because of a Platonic ideal or an aesthetic higher purpose, but because of our experience and the artist's experience and the way they come together in a work of art—nothing else matters.

What's so great about this idea is the compartmentalization it affords for its subscriber. Like a key, this idea makes art make sense. It allows work to be seen as a collaboration between the artist and ourselves, and, frankly, that makes the whole thing easier. Criticism is easier, watching and reading is easier, and making art is so much easier with a peek into where art comes from.

Once it's clear that dissonant experience is the issue, we're free to explore and interface with art that at one time would have felt too lowbrow or too taboo. Nothing is really trash or perverted this way, it's just a totem for trashy or perverted experience, which suddenly opens up a whole host of socio-economic options for scholarship.

When I first read these posts I was in awe. I've always known my dad was smart and I like his films. But even so, I was surprised he quietly wrote most of these wonderfully contained but interconnected, atmospheric, and thoughtful blog posts while I was learning how to spell. This body of work is good, readable and challenging where it has to be. Through it, through this collection of things he says, these snapshots, all that my dad is comes alive.

Kate Glad

In My Craft *o*f Cellu*l*oid

Introduction

I like accidents, ephemeral events, things you catch out of the corner of your eye. Melancholy moods, dark streets, the rain. Redemption. Seeing the old order brought down and chaos reign. Reluctant heroes. Magic and the supernatural. Women who work retail.

Everything is memory, even those recent memories we think of as the present. If you can't buy that, nothing I say will make sense. My recollections of my own life are exactly like my memories of films. And of my dreams.

A long time ago, I had a recurring dream that lasted for months, the kind of dream you can wake up from, go back to sleep and pick up where you left off. I was a prince in exile on another planet. There was not a trace of the modern world. Everything was medieval, 10th Century maybe. We fought with swords, spears and bows and arrows. With axes. Mostly in the dark. I had a wife and a couple of kids and a band of loyal followers. Sometimes I feel like I just fell to earth.

I was a kid who could read words he couldn't pronounce. And I misunderstood and mixed up half of the things I heard. I thought Pound said "hang it all, Robert Browning, there can be but one *bordello*," and Dylan Thomas said "in my craft *of celluloid*."

I was born in a Texas Gulf Coast town, during the Depression, right before the war. On my mother's side of the family, my grandmother was Italian and my grandfather was an Irish cop. I never knew my father's parents. He was a tall bohunk from Pittsburgh who was in the Army when he met my mother. He got out of the Army, cut grass and delivered ice until my grandfather got him a job on the force. He went back into the Army after Pearl Harbor and ended up occupying Japan. My mother had a half-brother, my uncle Bill, who was in the Army Air Corps when the war started. He was the toughest man I ever knew.

My mother and I lived with my grandparents in their house down by the docks. During the Depression, my mother said, my grandfather used to bring home groceries and meat he got from the grocers and butchers on his beat. We'd share the food with my grandmother's sisters and brothers and their families sometimes. My mother emptied bed pans at the hospital down the street until she got a job with the Corps of Engineers.

I don't remember any of that. I remember card games in the dining room, listening to people talking and laughing while I fell asleep, a paper jack-o-lantern that caught fire, and falling off the back porch. Later, I remember the lights were off at night along the beach because of the German submarines in the Gulf. When my dad came home from Japan, he brought me a sword.

My first motion picture theater was the State Theater on 21st Street in downtown Galveston. The ticket window was on the street and there was a lobby with a concessions stand. The "colored section" was a small balcony upstairs. Admission was 20 cents and I got a feature, a cartoon, the news and a Western serial for my money. I'm sure I started out on Disney films, Tom and Jerry cartoons and the Cisco Kid but, when I was old enough to take the bus downtown by myself, I moved on to films like *Storm Warning (1951)*. I was eleven years old. The movie frightened me, of course, but I sat through it twice. There were other theaters down the street that showed steamy adult movies like *The Story of Bob and Sally (1948)* and I heard people talking about those movies, but I was too young to get in to see them, so Ginger Rogers getting dressed, Ginger Rogers in a slip, Ginger Rogers' white shoulders, her stockinged legs, muscular arms and a glimpse of her breasts were probably my first exposure to sex in the cinema. Doris Day, Ronald Reagan, murder, rape, a whipping, burning crosses and white hoods were part of the *Storm Warning mise en scène*, too, although that term wouldn't have meant anything to me then even if it had been invented.

The Martini Theater down the street from The State was a more tony venue. I went to grade school with the manager's daughter. They had a color television, the first I had seen. The first television of any kind that I saw, a black-and-white RCA, was owned by the Salinas family down the block. The neighbors gathered over there to watch boxing matches on TV. That was in the late Forties and early Fifties. In Galveston, Texas. *Peter Pan (1953)* was the last Disney film I saw before high school. The stage version with Mary Martin, televised by NBC a couple of years later, was more impressive.

I handled 16mm film at an early age, threading Barney Google and Snuffy Smith cartoons and short Westerns into a little, gray Keystone projector I had gotten as a present. I don't remember how old I was, the occasion, or who gave it to me. Thinking back, it seems strange to me now that I should have had a projector like that. I projected the films on the wall in my long, narrow bedroom. I staged plays with prop characters I made by cutting them out of comic books and pasting them on cardboard. I built a platform in the backyard and talked my friends into improvising scenes on stage. I drew comic books, mostly about fliers and air battles, because the airplanes were easy to draw. Saturdays, I listened to *Let's Pretend* on the radio in the living room and football games in the kitchen. I read Andrew Lang's *The Blue Fairy Book* more than once. My favorite character was the Yellow Dwarf in *East of the Sun and West of the Moon*. Looking back, and how much clearer things seem looking back, I see all of that as work that was more important than church, school or family.

I remember my mother, pointing at a black man in Eiband's Department Store and telling a crowd of white men and women: "He touched that woman." Her face was angry and self-righteous. We had black maids the entire time I was growing up. I went to segregated schools. I didn't have a single black friend. And yet, when I drifted into the Civil Rights movement at the University of Texas in 1961, tieing up the ticket lines at the Varsity Theater and having long conversations about the real goals of the movement with the Reverend B.T. Bonner seemed as natural to me as going to a Clarence Ayres class or listening to Shostakovich while reading Updike in the library of the student union. Such is the transformative power, for better or worse, of literature and film.

When I had the measles as a child, my grandmother and her sisters took turns reading to me. I don't remember the title of a single book. Outside of the books we read aloud in class and comic books of all kinds, I only remember reading Rex Stout, Raymond Chandler and Mickey Spillane detective stories, a few Reader's Digest books and *Peyton Place* before I graduated from high school. I vividly remember the *Peyton Place* scene of a man giving his pregnant wife head. Somehow, though, young *Phaethon*, plummeting to earth from the Sun God's chariot, slipped in and nudged the Yellow Dwarf and his Spanish Cat off of the beaten path.

The summer before I went away to college for the first time I set out to get ready for college by reading "everything," but I don't think I got very far. I enrolled in an American Literature seminar and was laughed at when I named James Michener as an important American writer. I was mortified. But in another seminar I heard Chaucer read in Middle English and snapped to what college and college professors were about. I cut classes to read Camus, Sartre, Kierkegaard, Dostoevsky, Teilhard de Chardin, Mailer, Algren, Jones, Shaw and Ginsberg. I saw films by Vadim, Truffaut, Godard and Bergman. I moved into a boarding house full of vets going to school on the GI Bill. I made drunken road trips to Mexican border towns.

I witnessed the advent of color, wide screens, surround

sound and Dolby, 3D, theater complexes with tiny theaters, naked women and almost naked men on the big screen in living color and in black-and-white. By the time I had graduated from high school, dropped out of college a couple of times, been drafted into the Army, lived in Germany where I wrote for an American tabloid, and got back to the states, I had been watching movies for over 20 years, but I don't remember commenting on a single one of them to anyone until, watching *Scorpio Rising (1963)* sometime late in the summer of 1967, I turned to a friend and whispered: "Did he just say that Jesus was queer?" And my friend, turning his leering, acid-distorted face my way, replied: "I don't know. But I like the way he said it."

That was my first brush with metonymy, a concept that, like *mise en scène*, I experienced long before I had a name for it. Years later, over dinner one night, I tried to sell the importance of metonymy in film to the Greek wife of a museum director. She cut me off. "Man lives by metaphor," she said.

That summer I discovered Antonioni and Fellini. I saw *Blow-Up (1966)*, *Juliet of the Spirits (1965)*, *Persona (1966)*, *The Loved One (1965)*, and Andy Warhol's *Vinyl (1965)*. I watched *Godzilla (1954)* and *Kiss Me Deadly (1955)* on late night TV. I read a Wonder Wart-Hog comic book. I saw a drunk sleeping on the stoop of Carnegie Hall.

It was the summer an Army buddy and I took over the second floor of an old duplex in Galveston and put in some time arguing politics versus culture. He was a Swiss Marcusian and argued that politics shapes culture. I argued the opposite.

He loafed on the beach while I programmed computers at an insurance company downtown. After work every day, I'd drop a deck of punch cards off at the computer room and the operators would run my latest Keynesian model on the company's IBM 7080 mainframe. The models always blew up. I never got the accelerator and the multiplier right.

It was the summer of the Six-Day War, and our favorite cartoon showed the aftermath of a collision between an Arab and an Israeli tank, the Arabs holding their hands in the air, the Jews holding their necks.

I read the *Koran* that summer and I was impressed by the idea of *houris*.

I read *The Autobiography of Malcolm X*.

Sitting by the pool at The Galvez, a grand, beach hotel one afternoon, I suddenly understood what a function was and lost my fear of mathematics forever.

My buddy relieved me of the burden of paying the note on my '65 Barracuda Fastback by totaling it on the Boulevard one afternoon. He had just come back from the Monterey Jazz festival. The richest man in town sent him out there with somebody's wife, probably as a joke. He ended up inheriting a department store in Basel and slowly disappearing, like that big cat. I was happy to learn recently that he's alive and well in Seattle.

Somebody's wife ended up finding Jesus under the sink in the bathroom of a cheap motel in Laredo one night. She was crouched in the corner, desperate for help, and it was Jesus or the big cockroach that had just crawled out from under the sink.

I still think it's about culture. About education in all its forms. If I don't know what a credit default swap is, never saw a play or an opera, never read a serious book or saw a serious film, don't know what a function is, never read any history, how can I believe I know anything worth knowing at all? What does "serious" mean? I think it's about the intention to do more than pass time.

Politicians, like everyone else, swim in the sea of mass culture. Political movements emerge and ride the wave of mass culture for a while, then sink back into the sea. It is impossible to imagine the New Deal outside a culture that valued people and the idea of society, just as it is impossible to imagine the Civil Rights Movement and the anti-war protests that followed outside the Counterculture of the Sixties and Seventies. The problem with the American political system now is that not only the leaders, but all of the possible pretenders to positions of leadership — to political office, you see — have been vetted by an establishment process that has eliminated the possibility that any anti-establishment — read anti-Wall Street and anti-Corporate — idea will work its way into the political process. The culture of dissent just isn't there to sustain it. It's not my intention to create a culture of dissent. I wouldn't know where to start.

My intention is less ambitious and less serious than some. Norman Mailer felt "imprisoned with a perception that will settle for nothing less than making a revolution in the consciousness of our time." I just want to raise sensibilities a notch. I freely admit that my intention is highbrow, though I fear I am too lowbrow myself to produce anything of real highbrow value. I will settle for building a little raft by lashing together, in homage to that brilliant scene in the HBO series *Rome (2005 - 2007)*, the bloated bodies of a few old thoughts.

I read John Simon and Pauline Kael before I went to film school. In film school I read Andrew Sarris, Robert Warshow, Claude Levi-Strauss and Hannah Arendt. After film school I read Bazin, Wollen and Tarkovsky. I believe it was Simon who said the difference between critics and reviewers is that critics assume you've seen the film.

I could find out if was John Simon who said that, but I'm determined to resist the urge to "Google it." I've had too many dinners and friendships ruined by people reaching for their cell phones to resolve a doubt, nail an ambiguity, or dispute a fact. No one vaguely recalls, imagines or speculates in the face of a cell phone and Google. No one makes up a more pleasing reality at dinner anymore.

When I got out of film school in the late Sixties I was able to make the films I wanted to make for a while. If they are inaccessible and too allegorical it's because I was inaccessible and too allegorical myself. I was never interested in the world as it was. Things of this world were only manifestations of a ghost world or of a long gone past I tried to evoke without much success. That kind of filmmaking requires a patron. If I ever had a chance to acquire one, and in retrospect I think I might have had a chance, I didn't snap to that at the time. I guess the lesson there is to keep your eye on the main chance.

There was only one film I wanted to make that I couldn't. I saw Jerry Jeff Walker perform at Liberty Hall in Houston and left the hall thinking that anyone who had ever had a friend or hoped to have one would want to know Jerry Jeff Walker. But the timing was bad. Before I could put the film together, Walker's career was in a tailspin. If I had been Albert Maysles, Walker would have been a perfect subject, but I was still thinking like D. A. Pennebaker and trying to get in on the beginning of something good, not to document its end.

What I remember best about my career as an independent filmmaker is the generosity of friends who gave me jobs, loaned me equipment and helped me make my films.

In the introduction to *I Lost It At The Movies*, her 1960 collection of film reviews, Pauline Kael asks: "Isn't it precisely the artist's task to give form to his experience and the critic's task to verbalize on how this has been accomplished?" Yes. But to what end?

Alfred North Whitehead once wrote: "Our knowledge of the particular facts of the world around us is gained from our sensations. We see, and hear, and taste, and smell, and feel hot and cold, and push, and rub, and ache, and tingle. These are just our own personal sensations: my toothache cannot be your toothache, and my sight cannot be your sight."

What mathematics does, Whitehead explained, is create a public world that's the same for everybody. Mathematics imagines a world "as one connected set of things which underlies all the perceptions of all people. There is not one world of things for my sensations and another for yours, but one world in which we both exist."

Can film criticism, or any kind of criticism for that matter, discover one world that underlies all of the perceptions of all people? And does it matter if it can or not?

Mathematics is essential to the science of bombs, and vaccines, and medicines. It makes architecture and engineering, air and space travel possible. That these things matter is obvious. But do things like films and what we make of them matter in the same way? And to whom do they matter?

Tom Wolfe famously pointed out that without the theories of Rosenberg and Greenberg — Red Mountain and Green Mountain — *le monde*, the little world of artists, dealers and collectors in the Fifties and Sixties, was unable to see. Until you grasped the theories, you saw something all right, but not the "real" paintings. So what? Rosenberg and Greenberg didn't even have the same theory about what they were looking at. They weren't seeing the same things even.

Physicists sometimes think of light as particles. Sometimes they think of light as waves. Neither particles nor waves by themselves explain all there is to know about light, but taken together they do. And that matters. Because the bomb blows up.

What matters about criticism is that it should be useful somehow. A modest goal for a critic might be to make something accessible to a viewer, or listener, or reader, or a maker that wouldn't be accessible to them without the critique. And my thought is we should do that without going overboard about the importance of the work we're talking about. We should talk about art the way we talk about mushrooms on our lawns, keeping our heads straight when we swim, finding our way home after a night on the town, or whether we prefer one-egg or two-egg omelets.

All I can make accessible to anyone is what I see, hear and think when I watch a film. But again, to what end?

To stay afloat as the wave of pap rises to fill the bandwidth streamers are creating. For the maker of films there are thoughts here, jottings, comments and notes about how to make film from the world. Tarantino is right. A good review can be studied like a class assignment. And for the viewer of films there are thoughts here about how to make film from film. The essays may be more useful to the student than to the accomplished maker or to the viewer who wants only to be informed, entertained or emotionally moved. But there may be something useful here for viewers who can entertain the notion that the film we experience as memory is the real film.

If I have any single reader in mind it is the independent filmmaker on the brink of becoming the next big thing. The good news for that maker is that there is a lot of bandwidth to fill. The bad news is there will be a lot of crap competing to fill it. When bandwidth was scarce, the value of information was that it added something novel to our picture of things. Now bandwidth is unlimited and we have to create a new standard of value. The problem for the filmmaker now is how to stand out and the problem for the viewer is how to make good use of his or her time.

It's a truism that art and literature, including film and photography, are synthesized experience. A film is something that doesn't exist until the maker creates it. But the experience of the world, of emotion, of memory that the maker uses as the building blocks of his or her creation is important. The maker's own experience and direct knowledge have special standing. Write what you know. Film what you know. That's good advice. Or maybe we should say write and film what you remember. Of what you remember choose those things that are first-hand, intimate and full of emotion for you. Bring those emotions to every situation. Write and film what you know with abandon. Write and film what makes you feel. Imbue every situation, past and present, historical or speculative, with your own experience and authentic emotions. The story is just an occasion for synthesis and the quality of the film depends on the quality of the emotionally moving experience the maker is able to create.

I am a product of the Sixties. Mine is a Sixties sensibility, reflecting on the media of the millennium from a low to middlebrow point of view. My viewpoint is that of an artist more than that of a critic. It's the viewpoint of someone who, like Pollock trying to recreate the body language that produced a de Kooning, needs to feel in his bones where the maker is coming from.

It is the filmmaker's task to make emotionally moving films, the streamer's task to provide emotionally moving streams of films, the viewer's task to seek out films that linger in memory and enrich his or her life.

It's not enough to watch reality TV and sports, to listen to rap, country or pop, to follow celebrities on Twitter and Instagram and to be caught up on the latest episodes of series like *Game of Thrones (2011 - 2019)*, that spectacular triumph of *mise en scène* over narrative. If you want to get high and immerse yourself in the rich *mise en scène* of *Game of Thrones*, just do it. But absorb the *mise en scène* and the second unit-directed action. Don't subject the narrative to a strip search for significance or meaning. For me, *Game of Thrones* ended with Daenerys Stormborn, The Unburnt, victorious. For one moment, thanks to CGI, she is not like a dragon. She is a dragon. I don't really remember or care to remember what happens after that.

We have to paddle hard to reach the top of the oncoming swell, before the wave breaks, swamping our little craft.

We're all McLuhanistas now. We take it for granted that the contents of each new medium, the World Wide Web, for example, is other media. In the case of the World Wide Web, it is television, film, photography, music, radio, books and magazines of all kinds that make up most of its contents.

The Web started out where the media that preceded it ended up, as a mass distribution network. The content of the Web, a photograph or a film, for instance, may be transformed by being published in the context of the Web, where it collides, lickety-split, at random, with other data, but the photo or film is not altered on purpose to make it "Webic" in the way books and plays are altered to make them "filmic," by breaking them down and putting them together again as screenplays and films — Frank Nugent's adaptation of Alan Le May's novel *The Searchers* for John Ford's Western film *The Searchers (1956)* is as fine an example as any — or for that matter, the way film created for television is made "episodic."

There is no art form yet the object of which is the creation of exciting Web collisions, juxtapositions or chains of hyperlinks. Nor, for that matter, is it possible to imagine what the medium that may someday subsume the Web will look like much less what the "art" of that medium might be — unless the medium is an all-seeing artificial intelligence that imagines the ephemeral events of the Web and real life as, essentially, one and the same, and becomes, at the same time, solitary creator and only viewer, muttering to itself.

Generally, art is degraded as it makes its way through the media food chain. Novel to film to streamed television to YouTube snippet, inserted into an article about an article on the Web, is a downhill trip. But only the last stage of that journey, the Web, was designed from the get-go to abstract, distill, decontextualize and repackage — usually without adding value — to transmit, or, when not simply transmitting, to transform, by reducing content to pap. When it is not just moving content from one point to another, the World Wide Web has managed, on purpose, to dumb down its content —print, film, television and the other media — to an extent previously unimagined. Even more than television, the Web is — with a few notable exceptions — a vast graveyard where ideas and creative energy go to die. And now it has an unlimited bandwidth to fill.

The history of television is instructive. Film has been kinder to books than television — the medium the Web resembles most — has been to films. In some ways, television has advanced the art of film. Certainly, the extended length of series like *Rome*, *The Sopranos (1999 - 2007)*, *Lonesome Dove (1989)* and *Angels in America (2003)* has given audiences more time with the characters and the *mise en scène* of those films than movie-going audiences ordinarily get. And *mise en scène* — a stage term applied to film by the French critic André Bazin that refers to everything about a film except its script — takes time to appreciate. It's *mise en scène* that makes it necessary to actually see a film before we can talk about it as film. But, at the same time that television gives audiences an extended look at the *mises en scène* of some films, it alters the film experience by degrading a film's *mise en scène*, making it smaller, flatter and more frontal, an effect that favors montage over extended scenes, blocked and photographed in a way that develops the illusion of depth on the screen and recreates the real world. Sometimes the art of that is subtle, sometimes, as in Otto Preminger's *In Harm's Way (1965)*, it is obvious and in and of itself a pleasure to watch and to study.

Television was not conceived as a distribution medium for films any more than film was conceived as a distribution medium for books. Films may end up — along with made for TV movies — feeding the practically insatiable maw of cable television and streamers — just as novels may end up as films — but television itself was envisioned, like radio before it, as a live medium. That aspect of television is in decline, too.

The fact that television news and opinion has degenerated until even raw video of breaking events is edited, explained and commented on in search of memorable and persuasive phrases, designed to lead viewers to preconceived points of view, is not the result of television's intention, so much as it is the result of the corruption of television's original intention to reveal, inform and transport.

The Web, on the other hand, has adhered to its original intention. It remains as it began, a network of people, separated in space, each identified by a unique address on the web, coalescing into temporary communities around points of common interest where data is exchanged. Some of that data is information. It actually adds to the representation of something. Most of it is redundant, simply repeating something already known, and a lot of it is noise, data that adds to the representation of nothing. The World Wide Web creates the illusion of connection while it affirms our separation in space.

Apart from the content they pass back and forth, the World Wide Web and the sites on it, are not very interesting. Most sites lack the kind of structure that narrative gives to novels, plays, films and television. Even so-called reality television is structured by formulaic plots that include some element of suspense. Nor does the structure that embeds the *mise en scène* have to be narrative in the sense of a traditional plot with a familiar commercial structure. Films like Warhol's *Sleep (1963)* and *Blow Job (1963)* are structured by the nature of the event. The Netflix series *The Keepers (2017)* is structured by vivid verbal narrative reminiscent of Bergman's *Persona*.

The Web has not found a way to adapt content — to transform a subject — without copying it on the one hand, or destroying it on the other. Even when sites manage a sort of transient narrative, usually around some great and scandalous event — a favorite of muckraking sites and tabloids — their *mises en scène* are, frankly, a mess. They quickly turn into echo chambers, some of the most boring sites on the Web. But, I might add, some of the most popular and profitable, too.

This collection of short essays was written for *Annals of the Hive*, a personal diary I've maintained off and on at blogspot for many years. In some cases the comments are better than the original posts and I have included edited versions of them as well. Most of the essays are in reaction to a film, but some, like the critiques of *Rise Of The Planet Of The Apes (2011)* and *The Best Years of Our Lives (1946)* are in reaction to other critics. I haven't tried to group the essays, but I have kept the five essays I wrote about the documentary film nominees for the 2010 Academy Awards together. I've grouped the WikiLeaks posts, too. Streaming leaks in real time may be the way of the future. A few of the essays have not aged well. Since 2011, for example, Chelsea Manning has revealed that she is a trans woman and she has steadfastly refused to roll on Julian Assange. My only excuse for underestimating her ten years ago is that I didn't know she was a woman at the time.

Time Travel In The Sixties

Compared to the action-packed realism of time travel films like the *Terminator* series, *12 Monkeys (1995)* and *Planet of the Apes (1968)*, the black-and-white video technology of *The Star Wagon*, a 1966 television play, written by Maxwell Anderson and directed by Karl Genus, is archaic. But Genus' direction and the relaxed and intimate acting of a cast that includes Orson Bean, Joan Lorring, Eileen Brennan and Dustin Hoffman make *The Star Wagon* one of the most entertaining attempts to use the idea of time travel to dramatize the tension between free will and destiny I've seen.

The Star Wagon, produced for WNET and NET Playhouse at the time that National Educational Television was evolving into the Public Broadcasting System, is one of the television plays available from distributors like Broadway Theatre Archive who specialize in early television productions.

It's also available as a rental from Netflix.

Taped mainly on location, *The Star Wagon* follows Bean, a dreamy inventor, and his earthy sidekick, Hoffman, as they try to reverse their fortunes by turning back time. If the outcome of their journey through time seems sappy and predictable nowadays, that may say more about the cynicism of the 21st Century than it does about the *naiveté* of television audiences in the Sixties, who were comfortable with Hollywood endings, the triumph of good over evil and the idea that innocence, lost in time, can be restored. And some of Anderson's themes — that there are no great men, that nothing matters more than freedom, and that the business of business is the fleecing of the unwary – seem, in this age of Ponzi schemes and bailouts, downright timeless.

Television is an intimate medium, suited for low-key performances, and Genus' cast, led by Bean and Lorring in the role of Bean's long-suffering wife, deliver the kind of casual intimacy seldom seen in film. Genus uses his performers and the low resolution images of early black-and-white video to create a unique mix of impressionism and naturalism. The high contrast images of Genus' actors, overexposed to the extent that the actors' bodies seem to glow, are painterly and impressionistic, but the performances Genus and his actors create are natural and realistic.

Genus' cast has a remarkable ability to be with one another, to be with Maxwell Anderson's script, and to demonstrate that good acting is, in fact, reacting. The result is a kind of naturalness that even directors like John Cassavetes, who were completely committed to naturalism and improvisation, never achieved. Cassavetes was able to use improvisation to structure his films by creating realistic situations, but the dialogue his actors improvised seldom matches Anderson's ear for small talk, flip comments, and the kind of gentle razzing we see in *The Star Wagon*.

Anderson and Genus deliver poetry as well. Standing on the star wagon, Hoffman looks like an angel with one good wing. There is a dreamlike, druggy quality to Bean and Hoffman's laughter as they launch themselves back through time. Bean moves effortlessly from innocence, as he rehearses a hymn, The Holy City, with Lorring, to funny sexuality as Eileen Brennan digs in his front pocket for candy at a picnic; and Bean's dark and violent rebirth leaves the impression of opera, of voices singing together to reveal the dark underside of Anderson's comedy before Hoffman yanks Bean from the river to begin life over, half-drowned and miserable, lying in the mud with his head in Brennan's wet lap.

Technically, these scenes of Bean's death and rebirth by the river are as advanced as any experimental cinema of the Sixties. Bean's passage begins with the sound of Hoffman pushing Brennan out to the way and jumping into the river, but we aren't allowed to see Hoffman pull Bean out of the water until we enter the drowning Bean's thoughts and contemplate nothing less than the meaning of life.

It is possible to think of life as a long series of paths not taken, doors opened or not opened, decisions made one way instead of another. It is a convention of most time travel films that the journey back through time will either change nothing, or it will change everything. The art of those films is to show why this should be so, to explain in a satisfying way why history had to happen exactly as it did. In *The Star Wagon*, Anderson breaks with that convention. He raises the possibility of changing history by going back in time, and then rejects that possibility as an act of will. Orson Bean's Stephen returns to the present tense of his life as we found him, not because he has to, but because he wants to. But he is better for having made the journey, even if the world is not, and, watching the film, I felt the sweetness of life in a way I had not felt it since those summer evenings long ago, when I was a boy and I waited nervously at shortstop for our pitcher to deliver his first pitch.

At the end of the play, Stephen tells us his time machine is just a way of remembering the past. Karl Genus' *The Star Wagon* is as good a way as any of remembering some of broadcast television's best years. And that's something, in my view, upon which it is worth spending some time.

Escape To Reality

When the world gets to be too much for me, I pull out one of my video collections and escape for a couple of days. I have *Angels In America*, all of *The Sopranos*, *Rome*, *Lonesome Dove*, and a ton of Bergman. Most of the time they'll do, but when things get really rough, I turn to my John Cassavetes Criterion Collection.

More than any other director, John Cassavetes portrays people at their limits, bound up, penned in by their marriages, their friends, their sex, their race, their age, the limits of their talent, and any other cage or corner Cassavetes can cram them into. And they usually don't get out. They find salvation, if they find it, inside their cages.

The Criterion Collection's five Cassavetes films provide an easy, though expensive, way to acquire a taste for Cassavetes. The collection has *Shadows (1959)*, *Faces (1968)*, *A*

Woman Under the Influence (1974), *The Killing of a Chinese Bookie (1976)*, *Opening Night (1977)* and the 2000 documentary, *A Constant Forge: The Life and Art of John Cassavetes*. Or you can watch Cassavetes' films and the documentary individually on Netflix or Amazon Prime.

Cassavetes was, arguably, the father of American independent film. His first film, *Shadows*, was made at about the time French directors were creating the New Wave and Cassavetes, like the French, subordinated plot to the *mise-en-scène*. The story is often beside the point; just something to hang the film on. To Cassavetes and the French *auteurs*, film was synthesized experience, the story was an occasion for that synthesis, and the quality of the film depended on the quality of the experience the *auteur* was able to create. The French bought the rights to dime store novels for their plots. Cassavetes invented situations. His films have beginnings and ends, but they are, like direct cinema and *cinéma vérité* documentaries, essentially situational and episodic. The end of each episode and the way it's resolved are determined, not by the requirements of a plot, but by the inner workings of the episode itself. Affairs end. Men go home to their wives. Women who have nervous breakdowns come home to their families when they get out of the hospital. They put their kids to bed, clean up the dishes and go to bed with their husbands. Strip joint owners who get mixed up with the mob get killed. And the play must go on.

To the *cinéma vérité* style and structure, Cassavetes added improvisation. He worked out scenes in collaboration with his actors instead of forcing his view of the scenes on them. Cassavetes' approach to directing let his actors bring their own life experiences to situations and allowed him to add their sense of what is authentic and what is not to his own. The tension between rigid direction and improvisation, between conformity and self-expression, is a recurring subtext in Cassavetes' films, from *Shadows* to his Pirandellian masterpiece, *Opening Night*.

Shadows is frenetic. Hip. Beat. A film portrait of Lelia, a young, black artist, cornered by race, gender and family who ends up on a dance floor in the arms of a middle-class black man she meets at a party, the kind of man Lelia and her brothers know is square but others might call solid.

In *Shadows*, Cassavetes crammed the action and the feeling of the beat Fifties into one black-and-white box. It was ten years later before he was able to make his next independent film, *Faces*, a portrait of a marriage on the rocks. It was the beginning of a body of work that eventually exhausted the themes Cassavetes took up in *Shadows*: women on the edge, the way families and friends tie us up but make us strong, the life and death struggle to be authentic and spontaneous instead of phony. *Faces* is Cassavetes' least successful film, although it's his most accessible and appreciated effort. It's his least filmic and most photographic film. In addition to Rowlands, Carlin and Cassel, the cast of *Faces* included Fred Draper, Val Avery and Elizabeth Deering, actors Cassavetes worked with for the next ten years. *Faces* was Rowland's first shot at portraying a woman on the verge of a breakdown. By the time Cassavetes made *A Woman Under the Influence*, she had the role down pat.

There is something almost unbearably tense about the young Rowlands in *A Woman Under the Influence*. It's as if somebody has jammed a 220v wire into her brain. It takes her about two minutes to convince me she's the most troubled woman I'll ever see on the screen.

There is an acceptance of violence against women in the film I find deeply disturbing. And yet, *A Woman Under the Influence* is about the kind of people I know well. Working class people who never have enough living space, not much education and culture, and sometimes not enough money.

They fight at the dinner table. But there is redemption in the physicality of these Cassavetes' characters, in their muscle. It's a roundhouse right that brings Rowlands down to earth and restores her to her family. To her kids. To the dirty dishes that, when all is said and done, have to be taken from the table to the sink. In *A Woman Under the Influence*, Cassavetes shows us a family coming together, closing the doors on the outside world and making what they can of their lives. *A Woman Under the Influence* added Lady Rowlands and Katherine Cassavetes to Cassavetes' troop of actors.

The Killing of a Chinese Bookie is Cassavetes' *film noir* classic. It's the darkest of Cassavetes' films, not just visually — most of it was filmed at night with available light — but emotionally as well. It's Cassavetes' bitterest film. When the mob decides to kill him for his club, escape is never an option for Cosmo Vitelli. He has no family or real friends. The only important thing in his life is a third-rate floor show he created for his tawdry strip joint. Vitelli, played by Ben Gazzara, gets shot in the gut while he's trying to murder a Chinese bookie to pay off a debt to the mob. He ends up bleeding to death, slowly, while he paces the sidewalk outside his club.

Opening Night wraps up the collection. Gena Rowlands stars as an aging actress, struggling with her age, her relationship with her co-star, played by Cassavetes, the demands of her director, the limits of the script, and the death of a young fan. Rowlands is haunted by the girl's ghost. On the verge of breaking down, Rowlands brutally murders the girl's ghost and her own youth. Playing a scene with Cassavetes, she saves the show and her career with an improvised performance on opening night. The film is a triumph for Cassavetes. As the writer and director of *Opening Night*, he can do what he was never able to do in the real world. He can direct the play's audience and its reaction to him and his wife. The audience loves them, of course. I guess I do, too. Cassavetes knew that it's not what you see, but what you remember that counts. It's the way films live in our memories that matters. And he gave us a lot to remember. He gave us close-ups, and he gave us enough time with his characters to get to know them well.

I remember Ben Carruthers in *Shadows*, walking down the street in a coat that's too light for New York City in the wintertime; Seymour Cassel fleeing down a hill in *Faces*; Gena Rowlands dancing, Peter Falk with his crew, Katherine Cassavetes guarding the stairs to keep Rowlands away from the kids in *A Woman Under the Influence*; Ben Gazzara in the dark, getting his orders from the mob, and Gazzara in the light, standing in the spotlight with Mr. Sophistication and his strippers in *The Killing of a Chinese Bookie*. I remember Rowlands, beating her youth to death, crawling toward her dressing room, putting up her dukes in *Opening Night*. And I remember John Cassavetes, laughing and bounding around the stage in *Opening Night*, while the audience laughs out loud and applauds.

When I watch Cassavetes' films I feel I'm in the presence of myths. Can I name the myths? Can I say who Cassavetes' characters remind me of, who the major and minor deities are in Cassavetes' pantheon? Who is that with the wound that will not heal? Who driven mad by humdrum? Who is that, chasing the suitor from his house? Who is that, leading his men out to work? Who leading the women out to dance? Can I name them? Not a chance. It was Cassavetes' achievement to create a pantheon of characters who suggest mythic figures without names. I could no more name them than the Greeks, gathered around the hearth to listen to the poet spin his yarns, could say who Achilles and Odysseus reminded them of.

Bergman

Turner Classic Movies has Bergman on all night, beginning at 9:00 PM Eastern with *The Seventh Seal (1957)*, followed by *Wild Strawberries (1957)* and *Persona (1966)*. And the Criterion Collection is releasing *The Seventh Seal* on DVD in a couple of weeks.

The *Seventh Seal* is the first Bergman film I saw. I saw it at a foreign film theater just off-campus when I was a college freshman in Lubbock. They ran *And God Created Woman (1956)* a week later, and I was hooked on foreign films until the '80s when, for reasons I can't explain, except for the films of Tarkovsky and a couple of other directors, I lost interest in them. Maybe it was because "my" directors had died off or petered out.

I think of *Persona* and *Cries and Whispers (1972)* as Bergman's masterpieces, but *The Seventh Seal* was my first encounter with the collision of idealism and naturalism in film. To my romantic 18-year-old mind, the knight, Antonius Block, and Death were fascinating allegorical figures. They were in the natural world, but not of it. As I grew older, I was drawn more and more to the rich natural world of Bergman's films, but, in the beginning, like Block, I imagined a life of the intellect was superior far to a life of the flesh.

4 COMMENTS:

Tom Manoff said...

I saw the last half of *The Seventh Seal* yesterday also. Powerful myth these 50 years later. Classical style. Powerful when I saw it as a kid, and deeper now. You can't beat black-and-white, I think, unless you're David Lean. Black-and-white seems less vulnerable to dating the style.

JUNE 5, 2009 AT 3:12 PM

Billy Glad said...

I hadn't thought of that. Hard to imagine anyone choosing to do a film in black-and-white nowadays, but I suppose there are exceptions.

JUNE 5, 2009 AT 3:38 PM

Tom Manoff said...

I watched Lean's *A Passage to India* the other day. It's a pain that it wasn't in full letterbox. Even so, the long shots of the Ganges, a train crossing a bridge in the distance, the moon above a temple were the best moments of the picture for me. The acting seemed dated. But the acting in *Doctor Zhivago* doesn't. Have to think on that. The acting in *The Seventh Seal* is stylized and retains immediacy through that classicism. I wonder if realism in acting is more vulnerable to outdating than the stylization of *The Seventh Seal*?

JUNE 5, 2009 AT 4:14 PM

Billy Glad said...

Funny, but the British films are my least favorite foreign films now, except for *Tunes of Glory*. I did like them during the Seventies.

JUNE 8, 2009 AT 12:50 PM

Equus

A child is born into a world of phenomena, all equal in their power to enslave. It sniffs, it sucks, it strokes its eyes over the whole, uncountable range. Suddenly, one strikes. Then another. Then another. Why? Moments snap together, like magnets forging a chain of shackles. Why?" — Equus (1977) United Artists

Equus is art that manages to be about violence without adding to the culture of violence. Neither the Peter Shaffer play nor the 1977 film adaptation by Sidney Lumet are likely to provoke copycats to act out the violence that is the subject of their art. Alan Strang, the boy who blinds six horses with a metal spike, doesn't inspire admiration or contempt, only pity. His cruel attack on demigods of his own creation is a desperate act, performed in the midst of despair and

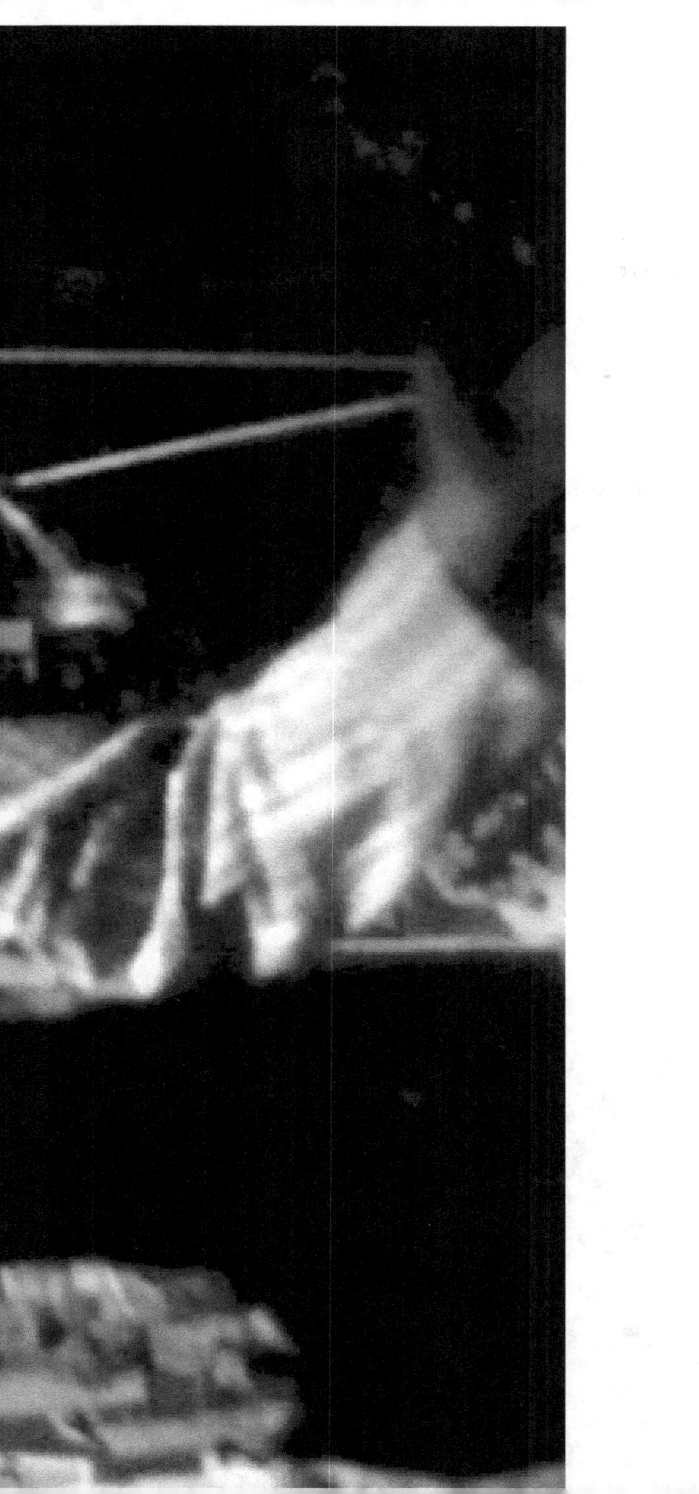

excruciating mental pain.

Alan Strang's parents are unable to understand their son's madness and they're not willing to shoulder responsibility for Strang. While Shaffer hints at the roles Strang's mother's religiosity and repressed sexuality and his father's hypocrisy may have played in Alan's descent into a secret world, ruled by improbable gods, ultimately, Shaffer lets the parents and society off the hook. The connections are just too complex.

One of the reasons *Equus* works is that it grounds itself in antiquity and refers to fundamentally important things like the struggle between reason and emotion, the Apollonian versus the Dionysian in culture. The role of psychiatry in Shaffer's *Equus* is to civilize the child, to bend the individual's will, even his grasp of reality, to the demands of society, even if the unique and creative individual is destroyed in the process.

Equus distances us from the violence it portrays by beginning and ending with: "Why?"

As a play, *Equus* naturally involves the viewer as spectator more than participant. And, being a British play by a British playwright, it lacks the cultural references to the Westward Expansion that are so readily available to American artists. But even the film version by American director Sidney Lumet, though it occasionally adopts a subjective point of view and graphically depicts the blinding of horses, manages balance. It doesn't just dramatize the struggle between nature and civilization — between what Levi-Strauss called the raw and the cooked — it honestly wrestles with the dilemma and achieves, if not a solution, at least a resolution to the conflict between freedom and conformity. It wraps the action of the film up in literate and reasonable discourse about a difficult subject. For better or for worse, it is a cerebral film. And it's an honest one, because the author doesn't pretend to answer the unanswerable. He — and we — must settle for stasis — as painful as that may be.

Ultimately, of course, it is not Alan Strang but Martin Dysart, the child psychiatrist appointed by a British court to ease Alan's pain — and the one person in the film who has a moral dilemma — who ends up in chains.

Account for me, the horse god Equus demands.

Dysart can no more account for Equus than I can rule out the possibility that some word of mine, some thought, floating loose in the blogosphere where everything is connected to everything else, will forge the last link in a lethal chain some sad day.

1 COMMENT

Antepilani said...

I watched the documentary *Exit Through the Gift Shop* last night while streaming Netflix through my Xbox360, reclining in my Herman Miller chair and sipping a nice glass of Drencrom.

It was early yet.

January 21, 2011 at 2:15 PM

Lady Macbeth In Iraq

Bring forth men-children only, for thy undaunted mettle should compose nothing but males. — Macbeth

Why do women tear other women down? I ran across a hatchet job on Kathryn Bigelow by film critic Martha Nochimson at Salon this morning. Nochimson's attack is personal, and, in a nutshell, boils down to the charge that Bigelow ditched her femininity to succeed in a man's world. A lesser included offense is the rather strange charge that Bigelow's Sgt. James in *The Hurt Locker (2008)* is less manly than — of all people — John Wayne, who consistently glorified war, but whom Nochimson characterizes as a "meaningful mentor" to young men.

There has always been tension between creative people like Bigelow and the critics who crash their parties, but this "criticism" — which reminds me of the gender issues raised around exceptional female athletes — is less an example of second-rate criticism than an example of the way women tear each other down. While Bigelow is trying to crash through Hollywood's glass ceiling, Nochimson is hanging onto her legs. When will women stop acting like crabs in a basket, crawling over one another to get out?

Make no mistake about it, Nochimson's article is not about *The Hurt Locker*. It's about Bigelow and the kind of woman she is.

Bigelow deserves and will get the Best Director Oscar for her work on *The Hurt Locker*. Her film conveys both the incredible pressure American troops in Iraq have been under to make instant life-and-death decisions and the limits of high-tech to take the pressure off of them. As she develops the film's premise, that something about war is addictive, we realize it's not just Sgt. James who's addicted. All of us are. In Sgt. James' case, it's the unmediated experience of danger that's addictive. He disarms bombs with his own hands. For the rest of us, it's war as the central reality of our time.

That Sgt. James is unable to find his way home, that by the end of the film all he wants is another moonwalk down a deserted Baghdad street in search of another bomb, says something important, though disturbing, about what it means to be a human being — or a nation — at war.

Ms. Nochimson should watch *The Hurt Locker* standing up next time. Clearly, most of it went over her head. And she should give up criticizing films until she learns what irony and metaphor are for.

Hollywood's Real Glass Ceiling

Kathyrn Bigelow is about to become the first woman to win an Academy Award for Best Director.

Whether she deserves the Best Director prize — and I happen to think she does — is beside the point. Ms. Bigelow will come away with the Oscar for Best Director as a consolation prize, because the Academy can't afford to admit that *The Hurt Locker (2008)* was the best picture of the year.

The Hurt Locker is up against Hollywood's real glass ceiling: the industry's profit margin.

Can Hollywood acknowledge that a low-budget movie that has grossed less than $20 million is a better film than the box office event *Avatar (2009)*, a blockbuster that has grossed over $1 billion and is on its way to becoming one of the most profitable films of all time? Can the industry tell moviegoers: Thanks for the bucks, but the 3D spectacle

you blew your money on last Christmas wasn't a great movie after all?

The face-off between *The Hurt Locker* and *Avatar* has been billed as a battle of the sexes, ex-wife against ex-husband, and as blockbuster against art house breakout. But, in the most basic sense, the confrontation looming at the Academy Awards is about whether movies can come to grips with the human condition instead of trying to escape from it.

Can we afford to make movies that synthesize real experience, to support producers and directors who engage the world as artists, or can we only support escapist spectaculars that distract us from the real world?

Rejecting *The Hurt Locker* will be a clear statement that Hollywood doesn't have the heart to take on the real world. In the head-to-head matchup between *The Hurt Locker* and *Avatar*, there is no question that *The Hurt Locker* is the better film.

Avatar is a significant motion picture event, designed to revive a floundering industry by providing a 3D experience that can't be matched by television or DVDs. Its release has been accompanied by the kind of marketing campaign you'd expect for a film that took over 10 years and a few hundred million dollars to produce. It's probably the first of many 3D blockbusters Hollywood will crank out over the next couple of years, and, in that sense at least, it represents the future of the industry.

Unfortunately, *Avatar* is a very bad film. The story, dialogue, art, characters, sound and music are all trite. It's even weak in the one area you'd expect a 3D film to deliver: retinal pressure and the sensation of movement. There's not enough subjective viewpoint to suck the viewer into the action and provide real thrills. Worst of all, the film consciously tries to rise to the level of myth, but can't quite make it. That's what happens when a filmmaker succumbs to the idea that he can create myths rather than channel them. In a medium that lends itself to metaphor, *Avatar* is remarkably without characters, scenes or images that point to anything beyond themselves. Cameron's images, like his film, are, essentially, meaningless.

There is more real meaning in any single scene of *The Hurt Locker* than there is in all of *Avatar*.

Ms. Bigelow's film conveys both the incredible pressure American troops in Iraq have been under to make instant life-and-death decisions and the limits of high-tech to take the pressure off of them. As she develops the film's premise that war is addictive, it doesn't take us long to discover it's not just Sgt. James who's addicted to war, it's America itself that's addicted as well. In James' case, it's an addiction that craves the unmediated experience of danger. He disarms bombs with his own hands. But it's an addiction that's tempered by James' and his team's regard for human life.

Ms. Bigelow's GIs are reluctant killers who risk their own lives to save the lives of others. Somehow, as we watch James' teammate, Specialist Eldridge, struggle to engage the enemy, Ms. Bigelow leads us to the realization that we are all Specialists now.

Critics of the Iraq occupation will find no cheap shots at America or the American military in *The Hurt Locker*. Ms. Bigelow invites us to see the war from the point of view of our best kind of soldier — one whose job is to save lives, not take them.

That one of them is unable to find his way home, that by the end of the film all he wants is another moonwalk down a deserted Baghdad street in search of another bomb, says something important, though disturbing, about what it means to be a human being — or a nation — at war.

Nevertheless, Hollywood will split the Oscars between Ms. Bigelow and Mr. Cameron. Ms. Bigelow will win the Best Director Oscar, but the Best Picture award will go to *Avatar*. That's the bottom line.

Avatar: Cameron's Epic Failure

Be sure you see the 3D version of James Cameron's *Avatar (2009)*. The 3D visuals are the only thing *Avatar* has going for it. Without them, it's a second-rate effort with a hackneyed plot and dialogue from a director who seems to have entered his long fingernails phase. Cameron spent so much time making *Avatar* that the world moved on, leaving him to obsess over yesterday's themes alone.

While *Avatar*, like American banks, is probably too big to fail, it will be interesting to see if America embraces *Avatar* the way it did Cameron's most important film, *Terminator 2: Judgment Day (1991)*, or Michael Bay's excellent summer blockbuster, *Transformers: Revenge of the Fallen (2009)*.

In his *Transformers* films, Bay goes beyond the man vs. machine myth to pursue a vision of machines transcendent. Bay's machines embody the best and the worst of human nature, while in *Avatar* Cameron rejects humanity to pursue a comic book vision of nature in revolt against man and his efforts to subdue it. Bay celebrates the kickass technology of the U.S. military and its projection of power anywhere at any time, Cameron comes down on the side of the men and women who oppose the cynical exploitation of people and nature by corporations — a theme he developed far more successfully years ago in *Aliens (1986)* and in *The Abyss (1989)* — although Cameron's efforts along those lines never approached Roland Joffe's moving and historically accurate film, *The Mission (1986)* . They still don't.

Avatar has too many film-historical references to be considered original art. The warmed-over plot and characters will appeal to viewers who think of the Battle Of The Little Big Horn as the high point of the westward expansion or of *Dances With Wolves (1990)* as a good film. The rest of us will have to wait for a new director with fresh ideas to exploit the 3D technology Cameron has pursued so faithfully and so completely frittered away.

The 3D Bubble

After single-handedly creating a 3D bubble with *Avatar*, James Cameron is trying to fill it. Since *Avatar* was released last year, the universe of available 3D screens has doubled internationally. That's a lot of seats to fill. So Cameron's A*vatar*, already the highest grossing movie of all time, is being re-released today.

The marketing angle for the re-release, aimed at filling some of those seats in the over-built world of 3D theaters, is nine — yes, nine — previously unseen minutes of film, picked up from the cutting room floor.

Avatar fans will see their beloved Na'vis mourn the death of a fallen warrior in a "big, emotional scene" that Cameron claims is the best CG he's done. (Like Jesus, Cameron has saved his best wine for last.) We're also promised a "rousing action-adventure, pulse-pounding" hunting sequence.

Following the re-release today, an extended *Avatar* DVD will be released in November that includes the new footage,

plus an "alternate reality version" of the film that is 16 minutes longer than the original.

Cameron says it will be a long time before there is an *Avatar* sequel — if we're lucky, it will be a very long time — but, apparently, Cameron will be able to find plenty of scraps to keep *Avatar* fans on the hook during the long wait.

The success of *Avatar* is a sign of the times. It tells us more about ourselves and the world we live in now than about whether *Avatar* is a particularly good film, or even a particularly entertaining one.

Escapist movies do well in hard times. And the times these days are hard enough to require exceptionally escapist movies. *Avatar* fills the bill. More than anything else, it's a movie about escaping from the reality of the human condition.

Sadly, it's not a good movie to boot. In fact, *Avatar* is a very bad film. The story, dialogue, art, characters, sound and music are all trite. It's even weak in the one area you'd expect a 3D film to deliver: retinal pressure and the sensation of movement. There's not enough subjective viewpoint to suck the viewer into the action and provide real thrills.

Worst of all, *Avatar* consciously tries to rise to the level of myth, but can't quite make it. That's what happens when a filmmaker succumbs to the idea he can create myths rather than channel them. In a medium that lends itself to metaphor, *Avatar* is remarkably without characters, scenes or images that point to anything beyond themselves. Cameron's images, like his film, are, essentially, meaningless. Maybe the times are too hard for films that synthesize real experience. Maybe Hollywood can't afford to support producers and directors who engage the world as artists.

Avatar is a significant motion picture event. It was designed to revive a floundering industry by providing a 3D experience that can't be matched by television or DVDs. Its release was accompanied by the kind of marketing campaign you'd expect for a film that took over 10 years and a few hundred million dollars to produce. The industry is betting it will be the first of many 3D blockbusters that will be cranked out over the next couple of years. The theaters and seats are waiting. And Cameron has set the bar low enough that *Avatar* might represent the future of the industry. That's a pity, because Cameron has done much better in the past. In *Avatar*, the 3D technology Cameron pursued so faithfully and so completely was just frittered away.

In his best film, *T2*, Cameron reconciled human beings and machines by uniting the best of humans and the best of machines in Schwarzenegger's cyborg. But in *Avatar* Cameron rejects humanity to pursue a comic book vision of nature in revolt against man and his efforts to subdue it.

To his credit, Cameron has always sided with men and women who oppose the cynical exploitation of people and nature by corporations. But that's a theme he developed far more successfully years ago in *Aliens (1986)* and in *The Abyss (1989)*, although Cameron's efforts along those lines never approached the movie *Avatar* reduces most blatantly, Roland Joffe's moving and historically accurate film, *The Mission (1986)*. Cameron's reprise of *The Mission* is pure escapism that offers his audience the temporary and vicarious thrill of watching alien natives defeat well-armed corporate mercenaries.

Ultimately, films exist as memories. I saw *Avatar* twice when it was first released, once in digital 3D and once in IMAX 3D. I don't vividly remember a single image from the film. Maybe that's the key to a successful re-release. If you don't remember a film at all, it makes sense to see it again. In the inside out, upside down world of pop culture, the most forgettable films will have the longest lives. Viewers will watch them again and again, as though they're seeing them for the very first time.

The Hurt Locker May Have a Chance

Just when I thought Kathryn Bigelow's *The Hurt Locker* didn't have a chance to win the Academy Award for Best Picture, the AP reports that some pesky Palestinians have decided to get into the act. Palestinian protesters at *Bil'in* have painted themselves blue and posed as characters from *Avatar*. Apparently, the demonstrators equate their fight at *Bil'in* to the Na'vi's fight against intergalactic corporatism in Cameron's film.

With the Best Director Oscar already in the bag for Bigelow, Cameron now finds his Best Picture Oscar in jeopardy. Hollywood needs 3D, but do they need it enough to associate themselves with a film that's been picked up on by those controversial Palestinians?

Could be a sweep for Bigelow.

The Cyborg

Conflicts between opposites like good and evil can never be fully resolved, but sometimes they can be reconciled by myths. For me, the struggle of human against the not so human, which has been the subject of myth since Homer, is reconciled best by the myth of The Cyborg, a creation that is part human and part machine. The Cyborg re-unites humans with characteristics we projected onto the world of machines and set ourselves in opposition to around the time of the Industrial Revolution. Machines are cold, dead and hard, but living human beings are warm and, compared to machines, very soft. The fragility of human beings is revealed in war, murders, car wrecks and plane crashes, the art of Schwarzkogler, Chris Burden and Mark Pauline, the reproductions of Andy Warhol, and the films of motion picture directors whose forte is the action sequence, and piling action sequence upon action sequence and genre upon genre, the Action Adventure Science Fiction Fantasy film.

The struggle of humans against machines, as it has played out in our best films, has two main variations. In the first variation, machines are evil. In the second variation, machines are just dangerous and it's the "mad scientists" who create or use them who are evil or insane. Machines have a potential for evil, but they usually include a built-in safety mechanism to protect people — the first law of robotics is not to harm a human being or, through inaction, allow a human being to come to harm — but, of course, the safety mechanism doesn't always work. *Forbidden Planet (1956)* is an especially bleak rendering of the mad scientist myth. After thousands of years of rationality, with the assistance of a machine to end all machines, the Krell are destroyed by monsters from the id. Morbius, in his pursuit of the knowledge and power of the Krell, is transformed into a monster who, subconsciously, seeks to destroy anyone who opposes him. In masterful renditions of the myth like Stanley Kubrick's 1968 film, *Dr. Strangelove Or How I Learned To Stop Worrying and Love the Bomb*, both the evil machine and the mad scientist versions of the struggle between human and machine resonate at once. Dangerous men are caught up in dangerous machines. We can see the Strategic Air Command as a machine out of control, we can see it as a machine in the hands of a mad general, or we can see SAC as a cog in the menacing machine we used to call the Cold War, a concept that comes close to what the Hindus mean by karma. A clockwork.

Until the Eighties, most Science Fiction films, and in particular the ones in which the machine is a robot, cyborg, or some combination of human and machine, favored the evil machine story and reflected the ambivalence and caution toward machines that had informed the Science Fiction film since Fritz Lang created the evil robot, Maria (the original material girl) in *Metropolis (1926)*. These films include *2001: A Space Odyssey (1968)*, *Colossus: The Forbin Project (1969)*, *Westworld (1973)*, *The Demon Seed (1977)*, *Alien (1979)*, and, finally, James Cameron and Gale Anne Hurd's *The Terminator (1984)*, the genre's last solid rendition of a truly evil machine. The machine in *T1*, like Skynet, the Artificial Intelligence that created it, is bad to its alloy bone.

The space between humans and machines in popular culture began to narrow in the 1980's. In Ridley Scott's *Blade Runner (1982)*, more physical damage is sustained by replicants than by people, the replicants have pitifully short life spans, and, in fact, all of the women in the film are replicants. Scott's film stands Philip K. Dick's 1968 novel, *Do Androids Dream of Electric Sheep?* on its head. Dicks' novel portrays a bounty hunter who is so human he is capable of empathizing with the ruthless machines he hunts down and kills. That capacity almost destroys him. Fourteen years later, in *Blade Runner*, the machines are more human and compassionate than the humans. It's the machines who recite poetry and philosophy and who have "seen things you people wouldn't believe," and it's pain that keeps Roy Baty alive long enough to redeem the bounty hunter, Rick Deckard. In *Robocop (1987)* the human, torn down and reconstructed with machine parts replacing limbs and organs, sustains massive injuries in his first encounter with a killer robot. And, in Cameron and Hurd's *Aliens (1986)*, their sequel to Ridley Scott's *Alien (1979)*, the robot or "artificial person" is ripped in half by WATCH OUT! A XENOMORPH! Cameron and Hurd's word for a non-human life form. The humans and the machines are on the same side, and, at the film's climax, it is the badly damaged "artificial person" — his legless torso resembling a broken, plastic doll — who saves the human child from being sucked into space.

By the time Cameron and Hurd released the sequel to their first Terminator film, *Terminator 2: Judgment Day (1991)*, the chasm separating people and machines was gone. *T2*, like *The Terminator*, is set within the context of an apocalyptic war between humans and machines that follows a 1997 nuclear war between the United States and Russia. The nuclear war begins when Skynet, the U.S.A.'s computer-based defense system, achieves self-awareness and attacks the Russians, hoping the human race will be destroyed in the nuclear holocaust that follows. In this, both films are consistent with each other, and with *Dr. Strangelove*, *Colossus: The Forbin Project* and other films of the Cold War era. And *Terminator 2: Judgment Day* and *The Terminator* have the same basic plot. Skynet sends a terminator back from the future to kill Sarah Connor or her son John before John can be born, grow up, and lead the humans in their war against the machines. In both films, the humans send a warrior back through time to protect John and his mother. It is at this point that *T1* and *T2* diverge. In *The Terminator*, the protector is a human being, and the terminator is a machine. In *T2*, the protector is a machine, and the terminator is neither human nor machine. He is something else.

T2 is a brilliant rendition of the mad scientist myth. Three heroes, John Connor, his mom, and John's cyborg protector, hustle to stop the mad scientist before he can invent the basic technology that leads to Skynet. To stay alive, they have to stay out of the clutches of a new kind of terminator who, though Cameron and Hurd call him a machine, is depicted, especially in his grotesque death throes, as essentially organic or worse. Unlike the terminator in *T1*, who is a machine disguised as a man, the terminator in *T2* is an organic whole, not an assemblage of parts, and, although it's possible to read "machine" into his strength, agility and relentless focus, when he's consigned to a cauldron of molten steel at the climax of the film, he shape shifts, writhes and bellows in agony like a monstrous animal or demon.

T2 is remarkably misanthropic and predictably iconoclastic in its assault on the usual people and institutions, including Ma Bell, bank machines, cops, bikers, foster parents and the city of Los Angeles, which is flattened by a hydrogen bomb. But *T2*'s rendition of the cyborg who is sent back through time to protect John Connor is heroic. And, just in case we can't follow the sub-text, *T2* spells it out for us in a voice-over by Sarah Connor. "Watching John with the machine, it was suddenly so clear. The terminator would never stop. It would never leave him. And it would never hurt him, never shout at him, or get drunk and hit him, or say it was too busy to spend time with him. It would always be there. And it would die to protect him. Of all the would-be fathers who came and went over the years, this thing, this machine, was the only one who measured up. In an insane world, it was the sanest choice."

In the film's Wagnerian finale, the cyborg sacrifices itself to save the human race by following its evil counterpart into the cauldron making sure that the last remnant of the mad scientist's work, the computer chip inside the cyborg's own head, is destroyed. As the cyborg prepares to enter the flames, Cameron and Hurd use a series of close-ups to create a beautiful portrait of The Cyborg. Half of the face is human, the other half, where the skin has been torn away to reveal the gleaming metal armor underneath, is machine.

But there is more. In *Terminator 2: Judgment Day*, James Cameron and Gayle Anne Hurd gave us our first glimpse of a new, still unformed technology that might replace the machine as the not-us adversary upon which we project our worst fears. Having united human and machine through the myth of The Cyborg, having accepted the machine model of human intelligence and anatomy to the extent that we un-

derstand ourselves better as machines than as animals, having realized that we are evolving, not into angels but into machines, we have joined with The Cyborg to face the uncertain and, because our paranoia stays one step ahead of us, always dangerous natural and supernatural worlds. The myth of the evil machine is dead. We are ready to confront, in myth and in art, the potential of bioengineering and of our own overheated subconscious minds.

Grey Gardens Revisited

There is an element of the hunt in documentary films, a delicious kind of trophy hunting at its lightest, but, at its heaviest, a predatory savaging of people and events that exposes the dark side of subjects and the exploitative nature of documentary film.

The Maysles brothers' *Grey Gardens (1975)* is a film portrait of Big Edie and Little Edie Beale. It's a film about eccentrics and eccentricity, about marginal people whose living conditions reflect the condition of their lives.

Film lends itself exceptionally well to the substitution of one thing for another when two things regularly appear together. Over the course of the Maysles brothers' film, the Grey Gardens estate comes to stand for the lives of the Beales in the same way the American flag has come to stand for America and the White House for the President.

If there were nothing more to *Grey Gardens* than that – and there is – it would still be an important work of art, because it's a wonderful example of film as sympathetic magic. It gives us the illusion of power over the world by reducing complicated people and situations, even horrific ones, to a manageable size.

The genre the Maysles brothers chose to work in had rules, and they were accused from time to time of breaking them, of manipulating events, of straying outside the boundaries of direct cinema and cinéma vérité, particularly in the case of *Gimme Shelter (1970)*, a sensational film that features the murder of a black Rolling Stones fan at Altamont.

Direct cinema captures real events as they happen, without interfering with them in any way. There is no direction in direct cinema, no "do this" or "do that again." No questions. No staged scenes. Nature documentaries are perhaps the purest example of the form. The filmmakers witness horrific events, but never interfere. *Cinéma vérité*, another style of modern documentary, has some latitude. It's more about truth than about reality, and, as long as the film conveys the truth, it may wander away from real events.

In the case of films like *Grey Gardens (2009)*, a historical drama that HBO has run off and on since its triumph at the Emmys, neither the rules of direct cinema nor *cinéma vérité* apply. The intention of the producers is simply entertainment, and they're free to pick over the bones of the Maysles' kill any way they can. HBO doesn't broadcast *Grey Gardens (2009)* as part of its regular schedule anymore, but, in a move that harks back to the days when movies were all glitz and glitter to brighten the lives of the little people, they put it up on HBO On Demand over the Christmas holidays. "They were steeped in affluence and privilege," the HBO promo proclaims. "Yet their lives in East Hampton became a riches-to-rags story that made national headlines." There is a metaphor lurking around there somewhere.

A cottage industry has sprung up around Grey Gardens and the Beales since the Maysles first documented the squalor and decay of the Beales' lives. Since *Grey Gardens (1975)* the documentary, we've had *Grey Gardens* the musical, Grey Gardens the book, *Grey Gardens* the web site and, finally, HBO's version of the Beales' story. And I doubt HBO will have the last word.

Over the years, the Beales have attracted a cult following: people who know what it's like to live on the fringe. But the audience for works based on the lives of the Edies is more general than a cult. It includes any of us who have ever slowed down to look at the scene of an accident.

The story of the Edies coincides with the long, downhill slide of American society, the decay of the American dream, and the slow stratification of America into two cultures, one affluent and above ground, the other underground, it's people trapped in poverty. If it could happen to the Edies, it could happen to anyone.

American capitalism has always had two spurs to keep us moving up the steep hill of success. One boot prods us with the promise of fortune and fame, the other with the specter of disaster, with the threat of losing all we have suddenly or, like the Beales, gradually, as we get older. The Beales' story is frightening and fascinating. It's hard to look at it, but it's harder to look away.

The Maysles brothers had an eye for the wounded straggler, for the animal ready to die. Perhaps it's because their subjects knew they were damaged that the Maysles brothers were able to stay above the people and events they filmed, to appear to be superior to their subjects, to have the upper hand. Their contemporary, D. A. Pennebaker, seemed more respectful, more deferential to his subjects – even, as in the case of the *The War Room (1993)* when Pennebaker's cam-

era grovels at the feet of James Carville and Mary Matalin, obsequious.

Pennebaker had a knack for getting in on the beginning of things: Timothy Leary and the Counterculture; Bob Dylan; Joplin and Hendrix at the Monterey Pop Festival; and, finally, the Clintons. The Maysles brothers, Al and David, had a knack for being there at the end of things, the final acts, the death throes of the traveling salesman and the Counterculture, the unraveling of Camelot.

By the time he filmed *Grey Gardens*, Al Maysles was one of the best cinematographers in the world, and the Maysles brothers had mastered the art of manipulating subjects and situations. They had developed a gift for narrative unmatched in documentary film. No one tells a story the way the Maysles brothers do.

"Once you've lost that push, you've had it," Paul Brennan, the "Badger," tells the camera in *Salesman (1968)*. Brennan suffers from too much awareness. He knows he's a dead-ender in a dying profession. Negativity is the unpardonable sin of Brennan's world, and Al Maysles patiently and carefully documents Brennan's descent into negativity during Brennan's last days as a bible salesman.

"We can get it together," Mick Jagger tells the crowd at Altamont, just before a shot of what appears to be the Hell's Angels killing a black fan who pulled a gun on them. Earlier in the concert, when Grace Slick, watching the Hell's Angels beat her fans with pool cues, said: "People get weird, and you need people like the Angels to keep people in line," she was, at that spaced-out, sappy moment, more in touch with the direction of American society than the slightly confused Jagger who believed Altamont was going to set an example for America about how to behave at large gatherings.

The Maysles brothers persuaded Jagger and the Stones to let Al film them watching a rough cut of *Gimme Shelter* on a Steenbeck editing table, ostensibly to provide a gimmick to structure the film. The brothers' real reason was to make the apparent knifing of a fan by the Angels the central point of the film. Without the knifing and the opportunity to make Jagger eat his words, the Maysles brothers would have had a mediocre, though beautifully photographed concert film, whose high points were scenes of Jagger expressing his androgynous sexuality and young Tina Turner fellating her microphone. The violence and the obvious naiveté of the Stones and Grace Slick gave the brothers a chance for something much bigger, a chance to take down the Stones, Slick and the Counterculture at the same time. Eerily, Jagger's helicopter exit from the Altamont speedway foreshadowed America's final exit from Saigon, and, by the end of *Gimme Shelter*, Jagger's stare is as vacant as the barren landscape in the last shot of the film.

For big-game hunters like the Maysles brothers, who already had bagged the "Badger", the Stones, Grace Slick and the beginning of the end of the Counterculture, two eccentric ladies in a rundown mansion were sitting ducks.

The September Issue

The 83rd Academy Award nominations for documentary film were announced last week. Collectively, this year's nominees documented the global financial meltdown, fracking for natural gas, edgy street art, dumpster diving on a massive scale, and war on the ground in Afghanistan.

More than other genres, documentary films tend to be political and, sometimes, combative. Their intent is to document something, and it's hard, if not impossible, to separate the importance of what they document from the skill with which they document it. One suspects that *Restrepo*, an important film that's not particularly well made, is the odds on favorite this year, especially because the first living GI to win the Medal of Honor since the Vietnam War fought in the combat operation *Restrepo* documents. I jotted down some thoughts about *Restrepo* earlier this year. But it's en-

SE/ VOG

A-EXTRA
GE!

r
gest
e Ever
40
es of
RLESS
HION

SIEN
MIL
Fas
Feisties

A MARR
OF EG
Michelle G
Perfect P

tirely possible that the Academy will decide that the global financial crisis or what natural gas producers are doing to the environment outweighs the war in Afghanistan, or even that the artistry of *Waste Land* or *Exit Through The Gift Shop* deserves the Best Documentary award. The Academy often surprises me. Last year, when I commented on "Hollywood's Real Glass Ceiling," I was convinced the Academy would hand Kathryn Bigelow the Best Director Oscar, but wouldn't — couldn't afford to, really — give the Best Picture award to *The Hurt Locker* in the face of *Avatar*'s overwhelming box office and the massive build-out in 3D venues that was going on all over the world. The Academy proved me wrong. They showed me they did "have the heart to take on the real world." Unless, of course, it was those pesky Palestinians who did *Avatar* in by painting themselves blue in *Bil'in* — a case of bad timing for James Cameron.

Documentary films about current events and living people are very much about timing. In the Sixties, Fred W. Friendly and Edward R. Murrow's *Harvest of Shame* ran an hour and was considered gutsy journalism. Fifty years later, a CBS follow-up on migrant farm workers merited only 5 minutes of air time.

The *September Issue (2009)*, directed by R.J. Cutler and filmed by Robert Richman, is a documentary film that illustrates the importance of — and the surreal nature of — timing. The film is a portrait of Anna Wintour, *Vogue*'s U.S. editor-in-chief, and Grace Coddington, her creative director, shot in the context of the roll-out of *Vogue*'s colossal September 2007 Fall fashion issue.

The *September Issue* is an examination of power and manipulation, and, especially, of power in the hands of a competent and confident woman. Most film portraits of women executives show embattled women, under fire and hanging on by their fingernails. In 2007, Anna Wintour was firmly entrenched and riding the wave of a booming economy and fashion industry. The subtext of *The September Issue* is an examination of a successful collaboration, of the way editors and artists work in the real world, and of the way *auteurs* like Wintour and Coddington make signature art out of the work of creative people. And it is, finally, a comment on relevance, satisfaction, and the underlying insecurity that saps joy from even the most successful celebrities.

Formally, *The September Issue* is an example of *cinéma vérité* in its simplest, least challenging form. It mixes more or less coherent shots of live action with interviews. The problem with that approach is that it turns the film into a contest of sorts. The filmmaker tries to get at the truth, the subjects of the film try to hide it — or, at least, to slant the truth. Interviews are like testimony, the characters tell you what they want you to know.

Not surprisingly, the live action scenes tell us more about Anna Wintour than she tells us about herself. Her center stage seat at shows and the nervous fawning of the designers she visits deliver a convincing picture of her position atop the world of design in 2007.

The September Issue was filmed in 2007, just before the beginning of the global financial meltdown and the Great Recession. If the world's business cycle were depicted as a giant roller coaster, the lift sweeping up to dizzying heights, the first drop plunging down at the steepest angle the human body can tolerate without blacking out, Anna Wintour and *Vogue* were, in September of 2007, poised on the brink of the fall. The September issue of *Vogue*, essentially an extravagantly produced catalog of designer clothes and accessories, ran 840 pages. The issue has become a collector's item, selling on eBay for as much as $500 a copy. In 2007, it was a celebration of the fashion industry, a self-congratulatory revel in wealth reminiscent of Versailles with one important difference: the world of fashion and the incomes that sustain it have barely taken a hit from what has been, for the ordinary men and women who used to pick up *Vogue* on their way out of the supermarket, a devastating recession. To be sure, *Vogue*'s advertising revenues are down from 2007, and one of *Vogue*'s advertisers, Burton Tansky of Neiman Marcus implored Anna Wintour to pressure the designers she had under her thumb to deliver their creations faster. He got a pat on his hand. But the drop in ad revenue may be more a reflection of a general feeling of discontent in an industry whose players were personally bilked by money managers than a reflection of specific worries about the global demand for designer clothes or the bang for the buck of advertising dollars. After all, weren't most of those ads in the September issue a display of plumage, a demonstration of the wealth and importance of the advertiser?

Last night, ploughing through a copy of *Vogue*'s September issue I borrowed from my public library, I was struck by the fact that I had to wade through 313 pages of ads before I encountered the first snippet of text pretending not to be advertising.

Then, in a typical pop culture collision, I found a Rebecca Johnson profile of Michelle Obama, complete with gorgeous photographs by Annie Leibovitz, sandwiched between a Grace Coddington fashion spread and a charming essay about life at the top of the New York scene in a Greenwich Village townhouse whose decor, according to the article, was inspired by the Barbra Streisand 1976 remake of *A Star Is Born*.

Was Hillary Clinton just not fashionable enough for her party's elite? Is Michelle Obama as perfect as the *Vogue* interview and Leibovitz photographs make her seem? Or were the images of Michelle Obama manipulated like the images of the models in the Coddington photo shoots with their

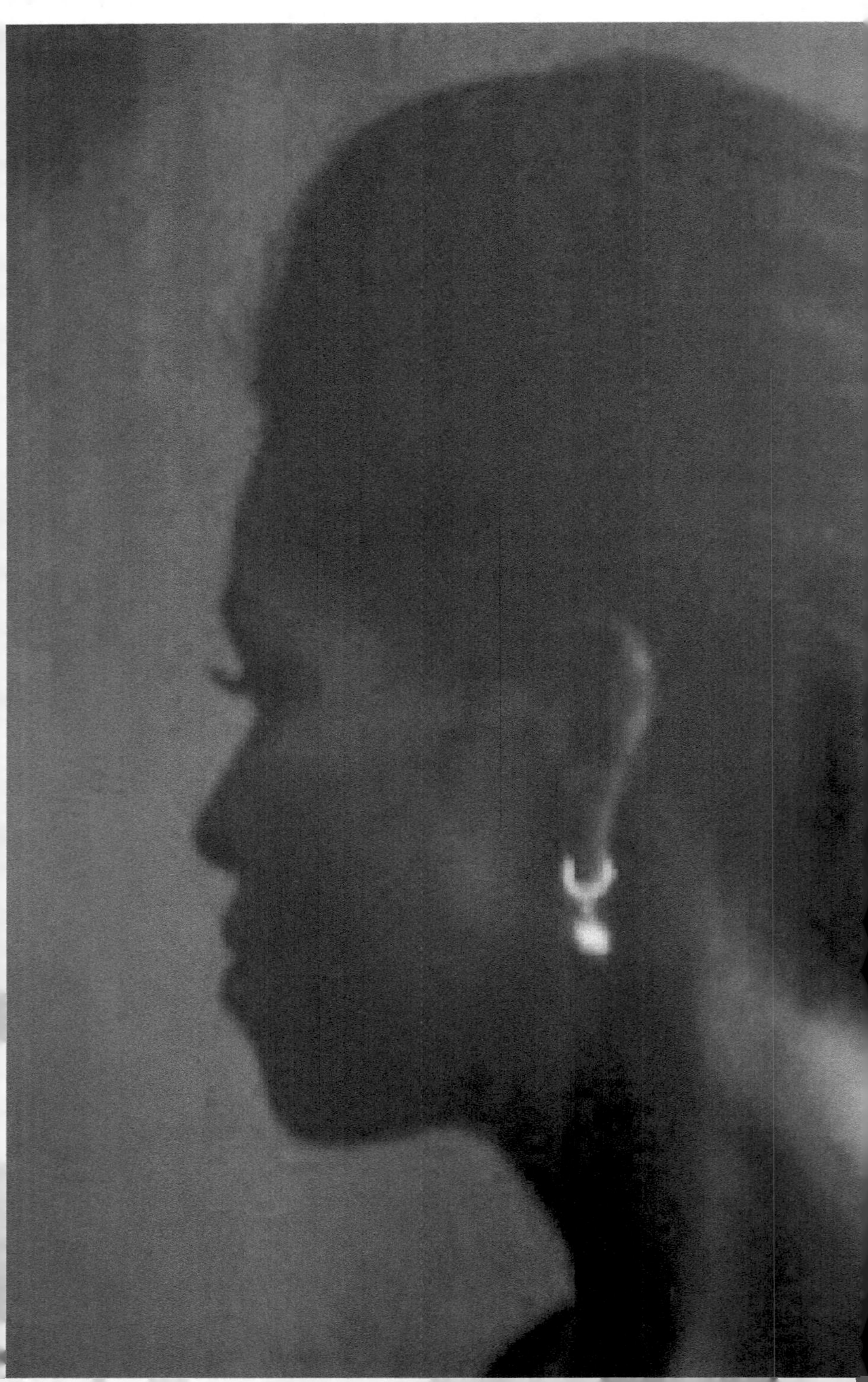

"Why would food taste good?
Why would sex feel good?
Everything [illegible] to certain things.
Life is about being happy."

interchangeable heads, bodies and airbrushed skin, photoshopped to perfection? Did *Vogue* prepare the small town Iowa battleground for an Obama victory? Did a media empire help bring down Hillary Clinton because she was no longer chic, no longer the face of the future toward which fashion — at least in the mind of Anna Wintour — must incline? I suppose that's a stretch, more the stuff of fiction than of some documentary that might have been made. But I think it's self-evident that the Obamas' style is rather neatly tuned to the style of Conde Naste publications like *Vogue*, *The New Yorker* and *Wired*.

Of course, there are no scenes of the Michelle Obama interview in Cutler and Richman's documentary film. Successful politicians learned as far back as the Kennedy era to keep documentary filmmakers at a distance.

The people who get scrutinized in *The September Issue* are Wintour and Coddington, and the element of suspense that holds the film together — even documentaries require some kind of glue — is Grace Coddington's struggle to get her art into the issue intact, even though it is often at odds with Wintour's vision. In the end, Grace gets most of her work in — at one point she observes that she has the entire issue nearly to herself — because she can do what artists do: synthesize experience. Everything is grist for Coddington's mill and her imagination, even the documentary filmmakers themselves. Before the film is over she has Richman jumping — if not through hoops — at least up and down.

Coddington may be the resident genius at *Vogue*, but she doesn't get the cover. For that job, Wintour brings in Italian photographer Mario Testino. And, to my eye, it is Testino, not Coddington, who, in a homage to Fellini, manages to produce the only images that are distinguishable from and rise above the pages and pages of ads.

The real winner in The September Issue is, of course, Anna

Wintour. After living for four years with the rumor — or the fact — that she was the inspiration for *The Devil Wears Prada (2006)*, *The September Issue* gave Wintour an opportunity to create her own image. She comes across as determined and opinionated, without seeming abusive, a far cry from the editor in *The Devil Wears Prada.* If anything, Wintour manages, as improbable as it seems, to portray herself as quite vulnerable. She appears to have gotten what she wanted from the film. Not that I'm completely surprised.

Maybe it was the faint scent of expensive perfume still lingering on the pages of my library copy of *Vogue* or maybe I overdosed on the images of beautiful women, but watching *The September Issue* and Anna Wintour, I suddenly remembered filming an interview with Lady Bird Johnson — a woman I had not thought of as particularly attractive — at her television station in Austin. After the interview, I rode down in an elevator with her, and I was shocked to find myself suddenly overwhelmed by her perfume, her dark red lipstick, perfect make-up and luxuriant fur coat, her obvious wealth and power. Maybe it was pheromones. I could barely breathe, and when we got off of the elevator, my hands were shaking and I was feeling weak in the knees.

The September Issue is available from Amazon and Netflix.

Waste Land

Lucy Walker took some risks when she made *Waste Land (2010)*. There were physical risks — dengue fever and kidnapping — and there were artistic risks, too, hazards in the landscape that could have tripped up an emerging talent, seriously damaging her reputation as a filmmaker. She had to make her way carefully, avoiding sentimentality on the one hand, cynicism and exploitation on the other. She played with scale, filming the landscape from a great distance, so that the *catadores*, working the garbage at Rio's Jardim Gramacho landfill, looked like ants, until, gradually, as she approached them, coming closer and closer, they were revealed as beautiful people. But that could have gone the other way. Had she slipped, she might have filmed interesting patterns, moving across a colorful landscape, that, on closer inspection, turned out to be grotesque. Walker had to trust her cinematographers — Dudu Miranda, Heloisa Passos and Aaron Phillips — and they delivered.

Walker tried, unsuccessfully I think, to contrast the poverty of the catadores with the conspicuous wealth of Rio's south zone. Ironically, in a film that makes a point of the enormous gap, separating rich Brazilians from the poor catadores who dig through their waste for recyclables, the only rich people in the film are the artists and the collectors they serve. *Waste Land* starts out promisingly enough, with shots of *Carnaval* and a short montage that follows the costumes and other garbage from *Carnaval* as it's loaded into garbage trucks and hauled off to the landfill. But after that, to contrast rich and poor, Walker uses the artists, auctioneers and art collectors who move Vik Muniz's images of the *catadores* through *le monde*. That narrows the field considerably. (But don't you worry, Reader. Charles Ferguson's *Inside Job (2010)*, another Oscar contender, has enough rich people to go around.)

In a blog she wrote while she was making the film, Walker distances herself from *le monde*. She says Muniz describes Rio as St. Tropez, surrounded by Mogadishu. The "garbage-clad open sewer" *favela* her *catadores* live in is the worst in town. The landfill is the place where "posh rubbish from the south zone mixes with the cheap trash from the *favelas*."

"Evenings we return to the south zone, she writes. I sulk as I head to a delicious dinner in a bulletproof car, I'd rather be with the catadores than these billionaires moaning about the price of contemporary art. These are the people who are going to buy the artwork that Vik is making in the garbage for our charity auction at Phillips. And these are the people whose garbage will be part of the piece. We're going to trace all these comings-and-goings of things."

Does she? Well, not quite, but if you've been around l*e monde* a little, you can fill in the blanks. I remember wandering around the Museum of Fine Arts in Houston one afternoon and coming across a cocktail party in the sculpture garden. I asked the guard, a tall woman in a dark, blue suit: "What are they celebrating?"

"Being so rich, I guess," she said.

All right. There always has been tension between artists and the patrons they serve. Why go to the dinner parties? Better yet, why not go and take a camera along? Even a little Flip would do. Or, best of all, why not broaden the scope of the film and give us a look at the life-style of the fat cats who live in the south zone? All of them, not just the collectors of art.

Walker does step in a hole now and then.

Nevertheless, when all is said and done, she comes through the Jardim Gramacho landfill and the making of *Waste Land* with her artistic limbs, her integrity, and her reputation intact. Lucy Walker is an increasingly important talent, and *Waste Land* is a timely and engrossing film.

Early in *Waste Land*, while Walker's crew is filming the *catadores* who separate recyclables from the garbage at Jardim Gramacho, a *catador*, noticing the cameras, calls out: "They're filming Animal Planet!" Walker includes the remark in the film to confront the issue of exploitation head on, but the *catador* could not have been more wrong. Nature films are pure direct cinema. Lions maul a baby elephant. The filmmakers don't interfere. They record the kill and move on. Walker is up to something else.

In a statement about *Waste Land*, Walker tells us documentary filmmakers can't help interfering with their subjects. "Your presence is changing everything," she says, "there's no mistaking it. And you have a responsibility." Walker tells us that *Waste Land*, like all of her work, is about getting to know people who you do not normally meet in your life. She aims, she says, to create an opportunity for the audience to emotionally connect with the people on the screen. That's actually a pretty limited goal. In fact, she has done much more. Walker and her collaborator, photographer Vik Muniz, have made a genuinely anti-Fascist film.

It is the intention of Fascist art, architecture and film to reduce individual human beings to insignificance, to make them feel small. (Visit the National Gallery in Washington, D.C., or watch Leni Riefenstahl's Fascist documentary *Triumph Of The Will (1935)* and you'll see what I mean.) Walker and Muniz have the opposite in mind. The footage of Vik Muniz flying into Rio to make portraits of the *catadores* out of the recyclables they collect at Jardim Gramacho is strikingly similar to Riefenstahl's footage of Adolf Hitler flying into Nuremberg for the 1934 Nazi Party Congress. The similarity could be a coincidence, but Walker is a student of film as well as a maker of films, and my guess is that she — on some level — made that connection. The intention of the Riefenstahl film is the glorification of Hitler and the Fascist Third Reich, while the intention of *Waste Land* is homage to the little "guy," to the working poor. If anything is glorified in *Waste Land*, it is humanity.

Vik Muniz wanted to find out if he could change the lives of a group of people, using the same materials they dealt with every day. Muniz showed the *catadores* at Jardim Gramacho how to get big bucks for their recyclables by repackaging them as art. He put together a social experiment, and *Waste Land* documents that experiment. Unfortunately, the *Pictures of Garbage (2008)* series doesn't come through in the film. The process Muniz uses to create the work is complex and abstract. He photographs catadores, posing as figures in well-known works of art, *La Mort de Marat*, for example, then projects a giant image of the photographs on the floor. The *catadores* use recyclables to realize paintings — collages really — from the projected images, and Muniz photographs the *catadores*' "paintings" to make the final work of art. There are seven of them in the *Pictures of Garbage* series.

Oddly enough, "*Pictures of Garbage*" — as a title — is most interesting in English, where it picks up some real complexity from the play on the word "garbage." The pictures are of people, not garbage. And the materials used to paint them aren't garbage either. They're recyclables. The recyclables are used to outline and shade — you might say they are where the people are not — so the people seem to emerge from the materials, from what Muniz calls: the "garbage." All of that nuance appears to be lost in Portuguese. I checked around, and I hear Brazilians never use the word *lixo* to refer to people. Muniz is lucky to be working in the U.S.A., a mean country that has the idioms it needs to adequately express it's meanness.

It doesn't matter. The *Pictures of Garbage* series isn't about art anyway. It's about action.

And, if Muniz's images don't come through, Walker's do. And, for me, they deliver what Walker promised, an opportunity to emotionally connect with the people on the screen. Walker makes that connection in an exceptionally filmic way.

When Walker started filming *Waste Land*, she met a *catador*, Valter dos Santos, riding his bicycle, and, Walker says, right then she knew she had a film. She describes Valter as the landfill's elder statesman, recycling guru and resident bard. He's been working at Jardim Gramacho for 26 years. "It's not bad to be poor," Valter teaches. "It's bad to be rich at the height of fame with your morals a dirty shame."

Vik Muniz doesn't make a portrait of Valter, and, while Vik and young Tiao dos Santos, the charismatic president of the pickers co-op, are out on the art circuit, Valter is back at the landfill. Walker dedicated *Waste Land* to Valter dos

Santos.

Look. We need more artists like Lucy Walker and Vik Muniz, artists who have the power to remind us of who we were, back when we had a sense of community.

And — at the risk of sounding too nationalistic — we need American filmmakers to give us a James Agee, Walker Evans look at America — and, yes, a Lucy Walker look at America — and at the sore — to borrow an image from Agee — the hard, flat, incurable sore of poverty that is spreading across America.

We need American filmmakers to point the steady, unafraid lenses of their cameras at the real face of America, and we need to have faith that something magnificent can come from the simple act of seeing one another as we really are.

After watching *Waste Land*, I realize that I have chosen not to see, too often I have chosen not to even look. I have chosen not to look, because, if I looked, I might have seen, and, seeing, I might have had to do something. I have chosen not to look. But my eyes are wide open now. Are yours?

Next week, *Inside Job (2010)*.

This has been a good year for documentary film. The five documentaries the Academy's mysterious nominating system picked are so good that I honestly can't say which one I'd vote for. Fortunately, I don't have to vote. The Academy, in its infinite wisdom, has not given me a vote, just as the universe has not given the poor ostrich the power of flight.

Inside Job

Inside Job (2010), Charles Ferguson's *exposé* of the takeover of American government by greedy financiers, is full of information. It adds important details to the history of the worldwide financial disaster that triggered the Great Recession, and, even when Ferguson is being redundant, recounting facts that are generally well-known, he's entertaining. Sunday night, Ferguson won an Academy Award.

The question is: How relevant is the history of a ponzi scheme that caused a global financial disaster back in 2008 now that the folks *Inside Job* calls our "Wall Street government" have moved on to undermining civil liberties, torpedoing single-payer health insurance, busting unions and generally shredding the safety net we cobbled together during the Great Depression?

Will Charles Ferguson's documentary film bring down

the Wall Street government? Will it even break its stride?

I have no doubt that *Inside Job* will do what film and art are uniquely suited to do. It will change the way we look at the world. I don't think anyone who sees *Inside Job* will ever look at bankers and the finance industry, academia, our government, or the history of America over the last 30 years in the same way again. But will we be able to do anything to break the oligarchy's stranglehold on America?

Inside Job unfolds like a criminal trial as Ferguson carefully builds a case against the most prominent financial figures in America, many of whom are now in the Obama administration. By the end of the trial, the verdict of history — or at least of the historian, Ferguson — is clear. The finance industry and the government of the United States, on purpose, wrecked the world economy and destroyed millions of lives.

Ferguson's explanation of how subprime mortgages were bundled as derivatives, called Collateralized Debt Obligations — CDOs for short — and sold in unregulated markets along with Credit Default Swaps — insurance policies that paid off when borrowers defaulted on the subprime loans in a CDO — is easy to follow. Because anyone could buy a Credit Default Swap against a CDO, whether they owned the CDO or not, firms like Goldman Sachs could sell CDOs and bet against them at the same time. AIG, the main writer of Credit Default Swaps, collapsed — and got bailed out — when it couldn't pay off on the Credit Default Swaps it had written. The financiers held on to the commissions and bonuses they made selling the CDOs and Credit Default Swaps, even after the bubble burst. The taxpayers held on to the dirty end of the stick.

Ferguson is a skillful interviewer who balances skepticism with naiveté and knows how to follow up when he gets an opening. The big names in finance and government were smart to dodge his interviews. He is especially savage when he unmasks the academics — the professors of economics and finance — who sold out to the finance industry, covered up for crooks, and even invented economic theories to justify and defend Credit Default Swaps.

Inside Job is a film in the tradition of documentaries like Edward R. Murrow and Fred Friendly's *Harvest of Shame (1960)*. It combines interviews and narration with archival video and photographs to make a point. It's not particularly filmic, but the cinematography of Svetlana Cvetko and Kalyanee Mam is crisp and sophisticated. It fits the subject. The settings for the interviews are well chosen. A fast-moving montage of mansions, yachts, jets, drugs and whores — but where were the male prostitutes? — adds a dimension to the history of the meltdown that was missing from the Congressional hearings on C-SPAN. To his credit, Ferguson sees Wall Street's obsession with wealth and its use of drugs and prostitutes more as character issues than as moral ones. And he's not without humor. The irony of Eliot Spitzer being reluctant to use the personal vices of Wall Street underlings to force them to flip on their overlords is not lost on him, or on us. Equally ironic is the Bush administration's sacrifice of Lehman Brothers to "calm the markets," like Greeks, sacrificing to Poseidon to calm the seas. If *Inside Job* has a weakness, it's in the way Ferguson brings the pain of the financial crisis down to the individual level. Why interview workers in China when so many workers in the Midwest had lost their jobs?

Inside Job won the Academy Award for Best Documentary this year, but, in spite of Matt Damon's sappy reminder — delivered as we gaze at the Statue of Liberty — that "some things are worth fighting for," *Inside Job* may not accomplish as much as Ferguson hopes.

What we — the survivors — need now, instead of warnings and history, are tools. We need to know how to get on down this Cormac McCarthy kind of road, past the charred, asphalt-covered bodies of the refugees who died when the death ray caught them pushing shopping carts, burdened with their last belongings, along the interstate. We need stuff we can use.

And we need to know what the overlords — the financiers who are, as Ferguson reminds us, still in power — are going to do next. What will they package and sell to create the next bubble? Maybe we can get in on the ground floor.

Exit Through The Gift Shop

Whether or not *Exit Through The Gift Shop (2010)* wins the Academy Award for Best Documentary, British artist Banksy's light-hearted romp through the world of underground street art is shaping up as a win for Banksy, for his fellow street artists, and even for the collectors who, according to Banksy, bought $1 million worth of kitsch, conceived and produced with Banksy's help by the documentary filmmaker turned street artist: Thierry Guetta, a.k.a. "Mr. Brainwash." If the eBay value of the work the L.A. art geeks bought at Mr. Brainwash's massive 2008 *Life Is Beautiful* show is rising and falling with his fame, the geeks should be in better shape now than they were before Banksy released his chronicle of MBW's rise to stardom.

MBW himself has made out quite well. In addition to the cash from his 2008 show, he landed a Madonna CD cover — thereby meeting the minimum requirement for consideration as a serious graphic artist — and he treated himself to a NYC show last year. But the biggest winner of all is the Academy of Motion Picture Arts and Sciences' mysterious "demopol", the nominating system that filled the Academy's hand in the category of Best Documentary by including Banksy's comedy among the five contenders.

As the voting draws to a close, Academy members can choose from a list of documentaries that includes *exposés* of the global financial system and the natural gas industry, a film portrait of a rifle platoon on the ground in Afghanistan, and, remarkably, two documentaries about artists and the impact art has on people's lives. One of them is *Waste Land (2010)*, Lucy Walker's sensitive study of Brazilian-born artist Vik Munoz and the catadores who separate recyclables from garbage at Rio's Jardim Gramacho, the biggest landfill in the world. *Exit Through The Gift Shop (2010)* is the other one. It is, at the same time, an entertaining recollection and an "exposé" of the art scene. Lucy Walker had to walk a thin line between portraying her subjects and exploiting them. Banksy never had that problem. He just had to have fun.

Exploitation and expropriation is the main — if not the only — point to street art, formerly known as graffiti. The streets are the canvas, and, in Banksyland at night, they belong to art and to artists in search of a perfect wall. *Exit Through The Gift Shop* puts Banksy's permanent mark on street art and the L.A. art scene. It's a clever expropriation of underground street art and the artists who make it, especially Mr. Brainwash, who set out to document Banksy and got documented himself. The streets and street art belong to whomever can control them, and, in *Exit Through the Gift Shop* at least, Banksy is in full control.

Artists synthesize experience. The successful ones also manage to create self-sustaining systems in which the sale of their work fuels the creation of more work until the balance tips in their favor and they are making enough money to expand the scope of their work. They become a brand. Banksy, of course, is there. He's able to sustain his own work, run an art factory, finance the work of other artists, and move out into new forms. And, in spite of his protestations to the contrary, Banksy has a flair for film.

Exit Through The Gift Shop is the most personal of the documentaries up for an Academy Award this year. It's *cinéma vérité* that is exceptionally well done, and it neatly demonstrates the power of narrative to structure time and to entertain.

Banksy has the conventions of the exposé film down pat: the hooded sweatshirt, the pixelated faces, the voice-over that ties fragments of film together. He understands the use of foreshadowing as well as he understands what Tom Wolfe called "*le monde*", the insular little world of art makers, art dealers and art collectors. The first time we meet Mr. Brainwash, he's pawning off cheap clothes with unusual stitching as expensive designer clothes. The last time we see him, he's just sold a million bucks worth of art that's as questionable, from Banksy's point of view, as the money Banksy forged — with Princess Di's face in place of the Queen's — but was afraid to distribute. There is no law against the sale of bad art. As Wolfe famously noticed, *le monde* is very small, and collectors have always been driven to get in on the ground floor, running the risk of buying bargain basement clothes at designer prices, or near art — the equivalent of the peripheral junk you pick up when you exit a museum through the gift shop.

But it is the brilliance of his editing, the way he alters reality by juxtaposing events, sequencing and resequencing time and space to sculpt a reality that never was or could be in the so-called real world, that finally sets Banksy apart. Somehow, from fragments of experience, recorded on hundreds of tapes, Banksy pulls together a complete narrative that, really, could not be any other narrative and still fit together so well. What's real and what isn't? Does it matter? I doubt there are two viewers anywhere who would agree on how much of Banksy's documentary is "made up" to provide continuity and context, or just to make a point. Personally, I doubt Mr. Brainwash's grilling at the hands of Disneyland security after Banksy — in one of the film's funniest scenes — inserts a life-size, blow-up doll, wearing a black hood and orange Gitmo jumpsuit, into the Disney landscape. But I enjoy the Disneyland footage anyway.

If *Exit Through The Gift Shop* — and Banksy's work in general — has a weakness, it's that his work is political. Banksy has a message. It's a cool message, but a message nevertheless, and Banksy has to lock it down. He can't leave room for the viewer to miss the point. He can't chance the kind of complexity that would make his art polyreferential, the kind of work that points to a multitude of things at once. Maybe that kind of work — work that empowers the viewer to participate more in making the art — would require Banksy to give up more control of his turf than he's willing to do right now.

And, finally, there is this. *The Life Is Beautiful* show's success is all the more remarkable, because it occurs in 2008 when the American economy was already in free fall and the fault line, separating rich America and poor America — a fissure conservatives had been hammering on since Reagan — finally split, sending the two Americas drifting apart, though not so far apart that the poor Americans can't still see rich America and the American dream sailing away, forever out of reach. Will the Academy of Motion Picture Arts and Sciences be able to ignore that coincidence and judge Banksy's work on its artistic merits alone?

Exit Through The Gift Shop (2010) is available from Netflix and Amazon.

GasLand

Every race has a dark horse, running at long odds. In this year's race for the Academy Award for Best Documentary Film, the dark horse may be *GasLand (2010),* a film by Josh Fox that takes on almost everyone in the Oil and Gas Industry, including George W. Bush, Dick Cheney and Halliburton over the use of "fracking" — hydraulic fracturing — to extract natural gas from vast deposits all over the United States.

While he was Vice President, Dick Cheney forced a bill through Congress that exempts fracking from the reporting requirements of the Clean Air and Water Act. The drillers don't have to tell the public what's in the fracking liquid they mix with water and shoot into gas deposits where it can seep into the water supply or return to the surface, either to evaporate or to be carried off and dumped.

Fox makes the case that fracking injects dangerous chemicals deep underground to break up rock and shale, releasing vast quantities of natural gas, while polluting the water supplies of homes and towns near the wells, which, if natural gas drilling proceeds as planned, will be just about every home and town in America. The industry denies the charge that fracking poisons the environment and the people and animals who depend on the environment for clean water.

Formally, *GasLand* is about as simple as documentary film gets. Maybe a Ken Burns special, cobbled together from old photos, with voice over and dramatic music, requires less of the filmmaker, but not much less. The subject of *GasLand* is Fox and his quest for information about what fracking is and what it is doing to people and the environment. We tag along, learning as we go. The form will be familiar to anyone who has seen *Supersize Me (2004)*, *Religulous (2008)*, or any of Michael Moore's films. *GasLand* adheres closely to the form. We take a road trip, talk to people who have had their water poisoned by the frackers, see some drinking water catching fire right out of the tap, animals losing their fur, sick people describing their symptoms, big names in the oil and gas industry, including Boone Pickens, refusing to be interviewed, politicians ducking and obfuscating.

Fox has a personal stake in the issue. He owns 14 acres of unspoiled land in Pennsylvania — his boyhood home — that the gas industry is trying to lease for $100,000. Fox doesn't try to make the industry's offer into a will he lease or won't he lease cliff hanger. We find out he won't early in the film. The element of suspense in *GasLand* is situational. The issue of fracking is far from settled. Legislation to undo Cheney's exemption of natural gas drilling from the reporting requirements of the Clean Air and Water Act is still working its way through Congress, and Pennsylvania and New York are struggling with the problem of how to protect their water supplies from the frackers. All of that counts in *GasLand*'s favor. Timeliness is a plus for documentaries.

Fox is immensely likable. His rap is pleasant, his voice easy on the ears. Strangely enough — and maybe it's the landscape he's traveling through — he reminds me of Don Johnson in *A Boy And His Dog (1975)*. That Fox is able to conjure up an apocalyptic premonition of the future, using video of natural gas drillers at work in people's backyards and tap water catching fire, is a sign of his considerable talent.

Nevertheless, *GasLand* is a dark horse in the Oscar sweepstakes, because it's ahead of its time. To work as exposé, it has to make fracking relevant and build some outrage against the natural gas industry. Two of its competitors, *Inside Job (2010)* and *Restrepo (2010)* just have to tap into the outrage over the global financial meltdown and the war in Afghanistan that already exists.

Restrepo

Afghanistan's Korengal Valley is on the Pech River, northwest of Asadabad, near the Pakistan border. The Korengal valley is the location of what has been, arguably, the most documented engagement between U.S. forces and the local Taliban and their allied foreign fighters in Afghanistan. The fight for control of the Korengal Valley has been recorded in award-winning photographs, a long article in the New York Times Magazine, and, of particular interest, in *Restrepo (2010)*, a direct cinema film by Tim Hetherington and Sebastian Junger that's available for sale or rental as a DVD and as streaming video from Netflix and Amazon. The film won an award at Sundance last year, and it's been nominated for an Academy Award. There is not a lot of direct cinema around anymore, and this one deals with a serious subject, with life and death decisions. On top of that, it must have been an exceptionally hard film to make.

The Hetherington-Junger documentary illustrates the difference between documentary film on the one hand and photographs and print on the other for practitioners of the art and for viewers of documentary films as well. The challenges the filmmakers face in *Restrepo* are the same challenges direct cinema and *cinéma vérité* filmmakers always face: telling a story without narration, tying episodes together seamlessly, slapping on enough detail to make the film come to life and give viewers a sense of being there. In addition, they had to stay alive.

(Update: Tim Hetherington was killed by mortar fire in Misrata, Libya, 4/20/2011.)

The efforts of the filmmakers and the film's subjects, the professional soldiers of the Second Platoon of Battle Company, are exceptional, but, as film, Restrepo is not exceptional. As document, it fills some gaps that photography and print can't fill, and, for a few minutes, it achieves brilliance, but it relies too much on photography, print and a viewer's personal memories to fill the gaps in its incarnation as a 90-minute feature film. I suspect there is an exceptional 30-minute film buried in Restrepo, but, if it's there, Junger and Hetherington didn't find it.

The experience of art is a collaboration between the artist and the audience, and fragmented videos like Restrepo require viewers to participate to an unusual extent. The more we know about combat, the more gaps we can fill and the more complete and convincing Restrepo seems, especially as we recall the film a couple of days later, after the images have sunk in.

Restrepo was brought to my attention by a Marine who thought it captured the essence of combat better than any film he'd seen. He and I are both aware of the movie's many shortcomings, its lack of a central theme beyond the notion that war is hell, its episodic and elliptical nature, the absence of a point-of-view that reveals what the GIs are shooting at — we see bombs, rockets and mortars going off in the valley, but most of the time the soldiers could be firing their weapons into thin air for all we know — but, for him, the personalities of the soldiers make the film worthwhile. For me, it's the greasy grill in the snack bar, the cramped bunks, the mysterious spotting device that looks like it was covered up to keep us from seeing what it is. More cerebral than my Marine friend, I admire the idea of OP Restrepo, the gesture, while he admires the spirit of the men who manned the post.

For others, the appeal of *Restrepo* may lie in the irony of viewing a film about combat in the Korengal Valley, knowing that American troops withdrew from that valley in April of 2010, after entering it 5 years earlier specifically to pick a fight with the Taliban and the foreign fighters there. America did not stay the course in the Korengal Valley. Some might say the soldiers and Marines who died there died in vain. And some might say that the valley is a metaphor for America's war in Afghanistan, a war that is sure to end in some kind of stalemate, with neither the United Nations nor the Taliban winning a clear-cut victory.

Tim Hetherington and Sebastian Junger were embedded with U.S. troops in the Korengal Valley off and on during 2007 and 2008. Other reporters were there at the same time, notably Elizabeth Rubin. Her story for the New York Times Magazine, "Battle Company Is Out There," with photos by Lynsey Addario, fills most of *Restrepo*'s gaps. Indeed, *Restrepo* works best for me when I think of it as video that illustrates Rubin's article.

Restrepo The Movie, a web site devoted to promoting the film and Junger's book version of the fight for the Korengal Valley, *War*, has photos of the 2nd Platoon, video interviews, some outtakes from the film and some Hetherington pictures. A little blog at the site has an entry that reminds us that Juan Restrepo was a real person who died in combat and is remembered and mourned by his family.

Reading the Rubin article and spending some time at the *Restrepo* web site before you watch the film — or reading Rubin and visiting the film's web site, then viewing the film again if you've already seen it — may add to the depth of your viewing experience. It's something I'd recommend you do.

The web site tells us that *Restrepo* is "an entirely experiential film: the cameras never leave the valley; there are no interviews with generals or diplomats. The only goal is to make viewers feel as if they have just been through a 90-minute deployment. This is war, full stop. The conclusions are up to you." And, describing their film — in all modesty I suppose, —- the directors themselves assure us that: "This is reality."

But the reality is that Junger and Hetherington do leave the valley. They go to Italy with Battle Company when the company redeploys, and the filmmakers take the soldiers of Battle Company into a studio and interview them there. Ironically, those interviews, those remembrances of combat, provide the glue that holds the video fragments Junger and Hetherington recorded on the ground in Afghanistan together. And it is the interviews that come just before some fragments of video shot in the middle of Operation Rock Avalanche, a six-day fight around the village of Yaka China, that — for a few minutes — lift *Restrepo* to the level of brilliant documentary.

Like Junger's documentary book, *A Perfect Storm*, Junger and Hetherington's *Restrepo* is about death, even to the extent that, if nobody had been killed during the year they spent making the film, it's doubtful *Restrepo* would have been distributed. But American soldiers did die in the Korengal Valley that year, and, as he did in *A Perfect Storm*, although he does not attend their deaths, Junger recreates their dying. To be sure, Junger does not presume to tell us how it feels to die in combat the way he told us how it feels to drown in *A Perfect Storm*. We learn from the soldiers that "Doc" Restrepo, the medic for whom outpost Restrepo and the film are named, was wounded soon after he arrived in the valley and bled to death in a medevac helicopter on the way to a field hospital. We're not there when Restrepo dies. But when another soldier, Staff Sergeant Larry Rougle, is killed, we're as close to the action and to the emotions of his comrades as it's possible to get without being there.

There is something uncomfortable — disrespectful maybe —about deconstructing a film that shows an American soldier dying in a war that is, for some of us, morally, strategically and even tactically ambiguous. After five years of fighting for the valley, the battleground turned out to be of no strategic value. The tactic of seizing the high ground and setting up an outpost — OP Restrepo — to draw the enemy in did not work. The attack on the outpost never came, and Battle Company's CO, Dan Kearney, was forced to take his soldiers down the valley to engage the Taliban in Operation Rock Avalanche, a long battle that is the climax of the film and the low point of Battle Company's deployment in the Korengal Valley.

Veteran combat photographers used to advise rookies to use fast film, a fast shutter, stop down, focus at 10 meters and shoot anything that moves. That works to illustrate a story, but to tell a story with pictures, especially one that unfolds over months of fighting, much of it at night, needs a better plan.

Elizabeth Rubin says she went to Afghanistan with a question: Why, with all our technology, were we killing so many civilians in air strikes? After a few days, that question sparked others. Was there a deeper problem in the counterinsurgency campaign? Why were more American troops being killed every year?

Those questions led Rubin to focus her article on the life and death decisions being made every day in the Korengal Valley and on the man making most of them: Dan Kearney, the lord of the Korengal Valley. She follows Kearney through a fire fight that ends with him killing a woman and a child when he destroys a house with armor-piercing missiles, and on into Operation Rock Avalanche, a mission Rubin says many thought insane. It's during Rock Avalanche that Rubin's rendition of the battle for the Korengal Valley syncs up with Junger's and Hetherington's in her account of the action that cost Staff Sergeant Rougle his life.

> I followed Piosa through the brush toward the ridge. We came upon Rice and Specialist Carl Vandenberge behind some trees. Vandenberge was drenched in blood. The shot to his arm had hit an artery. Rice was shot in the stomach. A soldier was using the heating chemicals from a Meal Ready to Eat to warm Vandenberge and keep him from going into shock.
>
> Piosa moved on to the hill where the men had been overrun. I saw big blue-eyed John Clinard, a sergeant from North Carolina, falling to pieces. He worshiped Rougle. "Sergeant Rougle is dying. It's my fault. . . . I'm sorry. . . . I tried to get up the hill. . . ." Sergeant Rougle was lying behind him. Someone had already covered him with a blanket. Only the soles of his boots were visible.
>
> "There's nothing you could do," Piosa said, grabbing Clinard's shoulder. "You got to be the man now. You can do it. I need you to get down to Rice and Vandenberge and get them to the medevac." Clinard wiped

his face, seemed to snap to and headed off through the trees.

It may be that someday someone like Sebastian Junger or Elizabeth Rubin will write a book, and the electronic version of that book will include hyperlinks to video clips that illustrate the author's prose. The words and images and sounds will all come together in the same work, a new kind of art that combines the best of narrative, video, photography and sound.

Or maybe we'll have to keep pulling that kind of work together ourselves, creating cathedrals of our own imagining like my recollection of *Restrepo*, with chapels by Rubin and Junger, stained glass windows by Hetherington and Addario, statues of Restrepo, Rougle, Kearney and Sal Giunta, the first living Medal of Honor recipient since the Vietnam War, clips from YouTube put up there by GIs — and, high up on a back roof, a little gargoyle fashioned from these thoughts.

1 COMMENT

Anonymous said...

I've been reading Junger's *War*, watching *Restrepo* on YouTube, searching through videos and articles on Korengal, and just came across Rubin's article. How odd is it that she's not mentioned by Junger? A pregnant woman in Korengal? Or she not mentioning Junger? And yes, I like the idea of multimedia reading. I worked way too hard on filling the gaps on this.

April 11, 2013 at 2:30 AM

LASTING FINISH BY KATE LIPSTICK/ROSSETTO/ROUGE À LÈVRES
107

Combat Obscura

When she finished reading *Into The Wild*, my daughter wrote "one in which he would be free to wallow in unfiltered experience" on her full-length mirror in greasy, red lipstick from Lasting Finish's Kate Moss collection.

In the age of streamers and unlimited bandwidth, the World Wide Web offers more than its share of unfiltered viewing experiences to eat up the bandwidth of the Web and of people the center of whose lives the Web has become.

Of the two best known streamers, Netflix seems to be streaming better video than Amazon Prime these days. Both *The Keepers (2017)* and *Roma (2018)*, a film that probably should have been a series, were worth watching. But Amazon has streamed *Combat Obscura (2019)*, distributed and promoted by Oscilloscope Labs, a viewing experience that may turn out to be more iconic and important than anything

Netflix has come up with yet.

Combat Obscura is episodic, elliptical and, yes, unfiltered by anything except the time and bandwidth allotted to it by Amazon. Taped by Miles Lagoze, a Marine Corps videographer assigned to Helmand Province in Afghanistan from 2011 to 2012, shortly after Tim Hetherington and Sebastian Junger were nominated for an Academy Award for *Restrepo (2010)*, *Combat Obscura* is a fragmented and blurred view of combat, obscured not so much by the fog of war as by the videographer's tunnel vision, his shaky camera and his inability to decide what if anything is important. It's a restless, no point, no center, no grasp, searching but not finding kind of video. We never know where we are or when we are. Restlessness and indecision worry and finally defeat the entire video. Even video of a firefight and a Marine with a head wound, the best combat footage in the video, fails to satisfy. The camera moves away from the wounded Marine just as the realization that he has been shot begins to sink in. Institutions like the Marine Corps imprint themselves on people like bulldog tattoos. Lagoze has a chance to mine that vein. He lets the moment pass him by.

I don't doubt there are viewers who will find Lagoze's tapes hard hitting and revealing. But for others they will be a collection of tropes. We've seen Marines and soldiers smoking dope so many times it would be surprising if they didn't smoke in front of Lagoze. And we've seen things far worse on YouTube than the body of Lagoze's dead shopkeeper, an Afghan apparently shot by mistake. Even the Marine Corps finally decided the stolen tapes weren't worth worrying about.

It's amazing how little we see that is new in the 68 minutes *Combat Obscura* takes up in our lives. Except for a few scenes and images whose promises are unfulfilled, most of the content is uninspired. The form of the video may be worth talking about, however, if we can find a way to do that.

Since the footage is only structured by the videographer's tour of duty and what he could steal of his own and other videographers' work when his tour ended, deconstructing it ("unpacking" is the current buzzword) would do more harm than good. Although you might think that deconstruction would lighten the load a film or video carries, the opposite is true. Deconstruction lays on a heavy burden of significance that a little video like *Combat Obscura* would never bear up under. We should settle for describing it if we can. What we need is something to compare it to.

Except it's not that easy to say what *Combat Obscura* is like. Is it a Marine videographer's journey from youth to manhood? A coming of age story, a personal odyssey as Lagoze claims? We would have to take his word for that. There is no evidence of growth in the video itself. Even the fact that the videography seems to improve over time might be explained by the fact that Lagoze didn't shoot those segments. Is it a "home movie" then? It seems too intentional for that. And the aim is negative. Most of us don't shoot video of our friends and family to embarrass them. There is an urban myth that demonstrators spat on soldiers and Marines returning from Vietnam. That never happened. But Lagoze appears to have something like that in mind. "Stop looking at these kids as heroes," he told *Stars and Stripes* during a phone interview before the video's release.

As a "war film" *Combat Obscura* begs to be compared to *Restrepo*. Lagoze actually told The Daily Beast that he thought he was up to something "*Restrepoesque*" when he was on assignment in Afghanistan. If he was, he failed to pull it off. Unlike *Combat Obscura*, *Restrepo* has a focal point. We know where we are, when we are and why we are there. Operation Rock Avalanche, a long battle at the climax of *Restrepo*, fixes the action of that film in time and space.

Nothing in *Combat Obscura* even comes close. The creators of *Combat Obscura* ask us to buy the idea that narrative and structure are unnecessary to film and video, even undesirable, but Lagoze and Oscilloscope Labs haven't closed that sale with me.

What *Combat Obscura* is most like is the information leaks that WikiLeaks dumps into the blogosphere now and then for the media to amplify. And in a world where journalism professors call leaks the lifeblood of journalism, that may be the future of streaming video. If that's the case, distributors like Oscilloscope Labs should give up the idea that the leaks have to be feature length and bundle short videos like tranches of sub-prime mortgages or collections of lipsticks. And beyond that, maybe the way of the future is to cut out middle men like WikiLeaks and Oscilloscope Labs and stream video from drones, satellites, surveillance cameras and videographers like Miles Lagoze in real time to pump a constant intravenous fix of unfiltered experience directly into our bruised and swollen brains.

The Legacy Of Edward R. Murrow

In 1960, Fred W. Friendly and Edward R. Murrow teamed up to make *Harvest of Shame*. The film was Murrow's last television documentary before he left CBS to head up John F. Kennedy's United States Information Agency and the Voice of America. Ironically, so the story goes, as a U.S.I.A bureaucrat, Murrow tried, unsuccessfully, to suppress a B.B.C. broadcast of *Harvest of Shame*.

Harvest of Shame documented the living conditions of American migrant farm workers and recorded the prevailing attitude of big business, lobbyists and government officials toward the farm workers and their living conditions.

Edward R. Murrow has had many imitators, but none of them has managed to channel Murrow's combination of serious journalism and real concern for people who were unable to manage in any way the oppressive political and economic culture that impinged on their lives.

Harvest of Shame is one of television's most respected documentaries, not because it was especially effective, but because of its intention and style.

Harvest of Shame originally aired just after Thanksgiving Day in November 1960. A follow-up report by CBS last year — a 5 minute segment, compared to the 50 minutes of the original — found that the migrants' pauper wages were a little better and the workers were mostly poor Hispanics now instead of poor blacks and whites, but the working conditions and daily lives of migrant farm workers have not much changed.

Harvest of Shame gave a face to the faceless, advocated for the powerless, and created a lasting example of how television documentaries — and journalism in general — can engage important issues without bias or polemics, with compassion instead of passion, and with respect for its subjects.

The shots of workers, voicing their frustration about trying to make a living at the bottom of the American economy, and the shots of a corporate lobbyist, reducing and explaining away the tragedy of people permanently abandoned to poverty, could, in these times of massive, permanent unemployment and underemployment — especially of the undereducated and people over 50 — be filmed today. We only lack the film makers, journalists, and the subjects who — like the migrant farm workers of the 60's — convincingly demonstrate the flaws in American society, the disjunction between our basic values and the way we allow some of our fellow

Americans to live.

Harvest of Shame, for the most part, let's the workers and bureaucrats speak for themselves, admittedly in the context of Murrow's narration. But the film manages to balance Murrow's narration with the true faces and voices of the workers, captured by David Lowe, in a way that never overpowers the workers and their story. Typically, Murrow closed the show with a comment that conveys his belief that words — and reason — matter, that it is possible to talk about occasions for anger, without histrionics and without acting anger out.

Are there real barriers to producing documentaries like *Harvest of Shame* these days? In many ways, they should be easier to do. The cost of video equipment is more affordable than it's ever been, and venues like YouTube let documentary filmmakers "self publish." The problem for filmmakers, if there is one, lies in finding subjects. The problem for the rest of us lies in finding the serious work once it gets produced.

Harvest of Shame can be purchased on DVD at Amazon, or, with a leading commercial, be viewed for free at YouTube or CBS News.

The West Virginia Mine Wars

The Republicans in Congress are trying to cut the Corporation for Public Broadcasting, the National Endowment for the Arts and the National Endowment for the Humanities out of the federal budget, essentially eliminating all federal support for the arts, including support for documentary films. That's just one more way to stifle independent voices.

At a time when protests — both non-violent and violent — are sweeping the Middle East and Africa, and American unions — supported by college students — are struggling to fight off Republican attacks on the remnants of the labor movement, let's recall the kind of documentaries public money has helped produce.

Even the Heavens Weep: The West Virginia Mine Wars (1985), directed and edited by Danny L. McGuire, was produced by WPBY-TV and the West Virginia Educational

Broadcasting Authority with money from The Humanities Foundation of West Virginia and the National Endowment for the Humanities. It's a simple documentary — narration, still photos and interviews — that recreates the beginning of the labor movement in America, and the battle of Blair Mountain in West Virginia. It packs a surprising wallop.

In 1921, 10,000 armed coal miners — many of them WWI vets — marched up Blair Mountain to get at the coal mines and company towns on the other side of the mountain, triggering the bloodiest fight between labor and capital in America's history. The mine owners defended their mines and shanty towns with 3,000 hired thugs — armed with rifles, machine guns and a small cannon — dug in at the top of Blair Mountain, and hired private planes to bomb the miners with explosives and tear gas. Finally, Warren G. Harding sent federal troops to Blair Mountain to disarm both sides. Until the documentary was made in 1985, Blair Mountain had dropped out of American history.

Even the Heavens Weep is an important historical document, pulled together from archival photos and news clippings, framed by a good script. The photographs of the working conditions in coal mines before the unions and of the living conditions in the "company towns" at the West Virginia mines are, at the same time, a grim reminder of the past and a terrifying glimpse into what the future of workers might look like in America, Inc.

It's hard not to see similarities between the mine owners' determination to smother the nascent union movement early in the 20th Century and corporate government's determination to finish off the vestiges of the union movement now. But it's even harder not to see the differences. The early unions had the energy of youth and the excitement of their discovery of solidarity and brotherhood on their side, and the course of history was in their favor, even if it took ten more years, the Great Depression and the New Deal to establish the unions. By the time Roosevelt threw the weight of the federal government behind the unions, every working man and woman in American would be hurting from the economic collapse that followed the drastic consolidation of wealth into the hands of a few privileged Americans that touched off the Great Depression.

Nowadays, the union movement is on the wane. Fighting to protect public employee unions feels almost like fighting to protect an endangered species. Many Americans are hurting, and, in fact, will never work again. But there are too many Americans who are not hurting this time. The country and the economy is too big for 10,000 marchers to make a difference, even if they were armed — is that even conceivable anymore — and could find somebody to march against. It feels like the only thing left to document is the end of the labor movement in America. And maybe we won't even bother to do that.

Films like *Even the Heavens Weep* don't cost a lot of money to make, but they do take time and dedication. And it takes backing to get the kind of interviews with historians McGuire uses to pull the archival footage and photos together. Without the mantle of the CPB, the NEA or the NEH, particularly for young filmmakers, getting access to credible sources can be extremely difficult —almost impossible — to do.

1 COMMENT:

Rachel said...

I wonder how many of the 7,000 or so families of the original group are even aware of this documentary.

MARCH 17, 2011 AT 11:34 PM

The Most Dangerous Man In America

I finally got around to watching *The Most Dangerous Man in America: Daniel Ellsberg and the Pentagon Papers (2009)* last weekend, and I think this POV segment directed by Judith Ehrlich and Rick Goldsmith is full of bad news for Pfc. Manning, the young soldier accused of stealing secret files from the Department of Defense and the State Department.

Since he copied the Pentagon Papers and distributed them to the press in 1971, Ellsberg has continued to be a prominent figure in the chronic anti-war movement that periodically obsesses American Progressives. No question he's sincere. But I can't help thinking Ellsberg should wear a t-shirt that says something like: "Don't try this at home, kids." Compared to Ellsberg, Manning is a clerk.

Unlike Pfc. Manning, Ellsberg wasn't in the military

when he stole the Pentagon Papers from the Rand Corporation. He was a prominent defense analyst on a first name basis with people like Henry Kissinger and editors and reporters at the New York Times and the Washington Post. He had been a Captain in the Marine Corps and was friends with John Paul Vann. Ellsberg is in a class by himself.

Ellsberg was charged with and tried for espionage. He faced life in prison, but he beat the rap. What was his pretrial confinement like? There wasn't any. After his arrest, Ellsberg was released on his own recognizance.

The very bad news for Pfc. Manning and is supporters is that, while the Supreme Court upheld the right of the New York Times and other newspapers to publish The Pentagon Papers, Ellsberg's acquittal had nothing to do with either the facts of his case or with Constitutional rights beyond his right to a fair trial. Ellsberg was acquitted when his judge declared a mistrial after Nixon blatantly tried to interfere with the trial and the judge concluded Nixon had made it impossible for Ellsberg to get a fair trial anywhere in America. Nixon ticked the judge off, and the judge let Ellsberg go.

The Obama administration is not likely to make that mistake.

Pfc. Manning's conviction by a military court is a foregone conclusion. The only question now is whether or not the military will be able to get Manning to flip on Julian Assange. My guess is that when his trial date approaches and he figures out he's not Ellsberg after all, Manning will cooperate.

The film itself is a strange mishmash of historical and contemporary interviews, news footage and excerpts from the Nixon tapes. My favorite moment is an audio clip of Richard Nixon, urging Kissinger to think outside the box and support a plan to nuke Hanoi.

The Most Dangerous Man in America: Daniel Ellsberg and the Pentagon Papers (2009) is available from Netflix.

It's A New World

I woke up this morning in a new world. Last night, I learned Michigan used to be on the equator. It was completely covered by warm, salt water just 350 million years ago. My attitude toward the Great Lakes and the little town I live in changed overnight. I live where a great ocean used to be.

8 COMMENTS:

quinn the eskimo said...

I'd just like to point out the last two Word Verification offerings:

- Extrudodog
- Cottony Underpants

JUNE 3, 2009 AT 11:05 AM

Billy Glad said...

Looking out my window, I can imagine waves, lapping at the trunk of the big maple tree I'll have to cut down if I add a bedroom and bath to the house. It seems to me the auto bailout has ended up about where I expected. A colossal pass-through to Obama's union base that, unfortunately, is far from over. The sad thing about American culture is that people who were getting $65,000 per year and a ton of benefits to assemble cars weren't able to save any money or get out while the getting was good. Did you know Michigan has a plan to turn the Detroit area into Hollywood in the Midwest? Remember *Robocop*? T5 and T6 can be set in Detroit!

JUNE 3, 2009 AT 11:33 AM

Tom Manoff said...

I should have kept my 55 Chevy. Bought it in 1963 from my girlfriend's parents for $75 which is what a dealer offered them. Three on the column. Gave me 60,000 miles. Then I had to have a Thunderbird. And the nonsense began. Of all those cars, I'd take the Chevy.

This post deals with cars right? Michigan. Passing of American culture. Bye bye Mrs. American Pie. Look for the Union Label. Duck and Cover. Right ? Not reptiles.

JUNE 3, 2009 AT 5:46 PM

Billy Glad said...

That's the best part! As far as I can tell, there were no early Devonian reptiles! There may have been sharks, though. I hate them, too. Don't even get me started on sharks. I'd club a baby shark as quick as I'd club a baby Komo.

JUNE 3, 2009 AT 8:21 PM

Billy Glad said...

I wonder if there is any place in the United States where the two Americas are more evident than in Michigan.

JUNE 3, 2009 AT 8:48 PM

Tom Manoff said...

So. No one talking to me again. So long boys. I'm done.

JUNE 4, 2009 AT 10:39 AM

quinn the eskimo said...

I can't talk old cars. Never owned a car. Which, more than anything else in our culture, marks me as a freak. Where I relate to this Michigan is knowing what it's like to be from a place where the economy is gone. Just gone. And it's part of what makes me want to beat the bejesus out of liberal-Dem writers who wax nostalgic about it. Suuuch pretty words, sooo caring, and not God's own first clue what it means.

Nova Scotia used to be a Titan in transportation. You guys may not give a damn, I donno, but you wanna understand Michigan? Go see how life shifted in other places that fell. NS made ships. The greatest sailing ships the world's ever seen. We built the fastest ships that ever went under sail. Wiki: Bluenose.

And not just at one or two big yards. Every little cove

imaginable had shipyards. My village is 480 people. My beach has little pieces of soft brown wood sticking up 4" from the sand. We never knew what they were from. But my Dad dove and swam off the end of the dock they were once part of. And his Dad was Harbormaster. 5 miles down the road there were these incredible shipyards, and 12 miles down the road, and so on. They cut every single tall tree in the whole province, to build the British Navy. I remember how shocked I was at how tall trees could grow when I went to the States. There were none left in NS. And after that, the great emptying began. Because we never had the political power to force reinvestment in new shipbuilding.

Which means our culture, for 100 years, was poverty, the dole, fading nostalgia for those beautiful ships. Just like your beautiful big cars. And then... we all "went down the road." I donno if that phrase means anything to you guys, but every Canadian understands it. There's a movie, *Goin' Down The Road*. Wiki it. Every single family, every single one, lost kids who had to move thousands of miles away. And these people were Scots, Irish, who'd already come through this before.

You think it's hard to say goodbye to ice cream stands and assembly plants? How about saying goodbye to the Sea. Ship-building. Land you frigging owned. Your family. And all of it on land your family considered Holy Salvation itself after starving in Europe.

JUNE 4, 2009 AT 5:00 PM

quinn the eskimo said...

Just looked it up to check memory. *Goin' Down The Road*. Shot for $26,000. Always makes the Top 10 Canadian Films list. Pauline Kael loved it. Said it showed up the forced honesty of Cassavetes. And it still makes me want to kill somebody. Down home the Dust Bowl lasted 100 years. Which is why saving GM in some form and making stuff like the Chevy Volt work is so important.

JUNE 4, 2009 AT 5:29 PM

Shamananana Nanananana

Winter lasts longer on this side of the lake. At least it seems to. And we've been traveling in the ice and snow more this year than we usually do. If I had a ceremony or an incantation that would end the winter now, I'd use it. If I were a shaman, I'd construct a complicated mechanism, a string of batteries maybe, to jump start the sun.

My father died in the winter. He was in a hospice in Mississippi, where he had a warm room with big windows and four beautiful women to change his pajamas and his sheets every night, laughing and singing while they put the old man to bed.

When he lapsed into a coma, we drove over from Houston, and he was still alive, but breathing in a labored way that lifted his shoulders off the bed with every wheezing breath. We sat with him for nine or ten hours, talking to him and wetting his lips with a piece of gauze, soaked in cold water.

I was holding his hand when he suddenly opened his eyes and squeezed my hand, and I said hey, he's awake, then no, he's gone as he died. And I felt that something had just left that body. Took one last look and moved on, leaving me next in line.

For an entire year after that, I had a recurring dream. I dreamed I was being roasted slowly, like a pig in a pit. The strange thing about the dream was it really hurt. I could feel the intense heat from the coals, charring my skin. It took a year for the fire to burn my skin away and prepare me to carry on in my father's place. And he was a very ordinary man.

Unit D

This morning I took the kid to Big Boy for breakfast. On the way, she told me if she had been born in the old days we would still be in New York where her name was written in the book. People couldn't move around back then she said, couldn't leave New York the way we did right after 9/11, a move we'd planned to make to the Midwest, made easier by the dust in the air and the smell like a burned out motor or lamp and the scorched pieces of paper that floated into the courtyard of our co-op the day after the towers fell down. That was the day I got back to Brooklyn, drove all night in a rented car, came in across Staten Island with the heavy trucks, ambulances, and military vehicles of all kinds, everything but tanks. The tanks were just in my mind. But I heard the helicopters when the rental threw a rod a couple of blocks from my apartment and I parked it in front of a corner grocery and walked the rest of the way home.

If it had been the old days, we'd have stayed in New York instead of laying in a supply of Cipro and Amoxicillin and flying out to the Midwest, and I never would have put that guy's eye out at the dump. It was about the time Saddam's sons, Uday and the other one, were killed, gunned down or blown up, and right after I took the wood from the kitchen cabinets we tore out to make room for the new refrigerator down to the dump. Right before that, the night before or maybe the night before that I dreamed I was trapped in the basement and the house was on fire, and I was yelling at my wife to throw the .357 magnum through the narrow basement window so I could blow my brains out to keep from burning alive, the kind of dream that stays with you all day. And right after that dream I took the wood to the dump. Long pieces of wood with nails sticking out that I tried to hammer down, but they kept bending and sliding under the hammer and I couldn't get them all out or bent down flat, and I had to be careful not to jam one into my hand when I was loading the wood into the back of my truck. When I got to the dump, the attendant helped me pull the wood out of the back of the truck and throw it over the side of the walk-in dumpster. And when we were almost finished a guy came out of the dumpster, holding his head and saying what the hell were we doing, and the attendant told him he wasn't supposed to be going inside the dumpster like that. You're lucky you didn't get killed the attendant told him. I could see the guy had a cut next to his eye, and he was sticking his finger through a hole in his baseball cap and saying you ruined my cap. Then he went over and got in his car and his wife was looking at his eye, and I backed out and drove off, thinking they were probably writing down my license plate number, or maybe they would come back to the dump every Saturday and try to find me. But I was thinking maybe he wouldn't have much of a case, even if he lost that eye, because he probably shouldn't have been in the dumpster. But just to make sure, I called a lawyer so he could set my mind at ease. They say when you leave a place you get a unique perspective on it, see things the people who stay behind don't see. All I get is homesick now and then.

At Big Boy, we ended up in a booth next to some kind of old timers' breakfast club, four guys from the local VFW, talking about draft dodgers in the Seventies and a local doctor who did a tour on a medevac plane, flying critically hurt GIs from Iraq to Germany, the kind of old men and the kind of conversation makes you want to say if I get that way please put a bullet in my brain pan. But just to show you how confusing free association can get, I sat there thinking all at once about four or five things, all jumbled up, that I have to put down in some linear way here, because the narrative won't let me tell it all at once. The VFW has to let you use their big, portable barbeque pits if you're a veteran. You just reserve the pit. Tow it home with your truck. Leon told me that at Leon's World Famous Barbeque in Galveston while I waited for my take-out ribs, reading the menu on the wall, reading cold yard bird, a phrase my wife picked off the menu and put in a poem, you cold yardbirds, I know the names of poets in high places, while Carmen, whose craziness landed me in the Army, waited for her order, standing alongside me at the counter, wondering who I was. I made the mistake of going to see her at Unit D, you don't even have to explain to anybody what a place called Unit D is about, after she slashed her wrists, and the cops, doing me a favor, figuring me, an officer of a local bank, for a respectable guy who happened, unwittingly, to be mixed up with the criminally insane, took me down to the station and showed me her rap sheet. How were they to know that inside that thick file was where I longed to be?

The Time Machine

In 1926, the Russian filmmaker, Vsevolod Pudovkin, created one of film's most famous metaphors by cutting back and forth between images of the ice in a frozen river breaking up and workers storming a prison. The montage starts with the ice-clogged river, cuts to marching workers, back to the river beginning to flow and marching workers reflected in the water, the water and broken ice cascading down river.

I wonder what a modern day Pudovkin would juxtapose with the river thawing and slowly turning into a torrent of water to create a metaphor for the financial system thawing out. Start with the Spring thaw maybe. Water dripping from the trees. I got a phone call from the bank that holds the mortgage on my house the other day, offering me a line of credit. Cut to a rivulet of water flowing downhill into a stream. Today, the bank offered to refinance my mortgage for free and give me a half-point discount if I open an account and let them deduct my monthly payments automatically. Cut to mail going into mail boxes, people calling the bank, kids trying on new shoes.

I can't wait for the part where the ACDs at the banks start to light up and we get to film those flashing lights on the computer consoles and data flying across the CRTs, images that took the place of tapes spinning back and forth to show those big computers working. Money piling up in corporate accounts.

The hyenas have started buying "distressed" properties in Detroit, Florida and New Jersey. Cut to those jagged black cracks streaking across the ice. Millions of people drowning in the cold water. Bodies swept out to sea.

1 COMMENT:

Billy Glad said...

It's easy to imagine creating a metaphor that compares the revolution to a spring thaw and a torrential river by alternating shots of marchers and the river, but the vocabulary of film has evolved for almost 100 years. It's not clear to me that someone watching *Mother* in 1926 would have immediately realized that two things, happening at the same time, were related figuratively as well as temporally.

MARCH 10, 2009 AT 3:16 AM

Power Failure

The power went out in our neighborhood late this afternoon. Still light enough with the shades up to search for candles and the kerosene lamp that was our main source of light during hurricanes when I was growing up. I don't know how I ended up with the lamp. I think I dug it out of my mother's attic when I got back from Germany and moved into the upstairs of an old house in Galveston's historical district with a friend from Seattle. We had some statues and some big scheffleras that looked good in the lamplight. A gray kitten that attacked our feet when we were sleeping. Bach on a reel to reel tape deck I blew my first paycheck from ANICO on. And a big staircase down to the front porch that had a way of ending halfway down, like something had pushed it in against the wall, so I couldn't get out of the house. I slept in a room off that staircase, and later, after I was married and my son was born and we had spent some time in Arkansas making films, when we moved back to Galveston, we rented that same upstairs apartment and my son slept in that room. The ceiling of his closet fell in one night.

This afternoon, I found the lamp oil right off, but it was almost dark by the time I found the lamp and the glass chimney, and some of the time I was looking with a flashlight, its narrow beam highlighting the TV, some books, the top shelf of a closet, and, finally, the kerosene lamp. I showed my daughter how to fill it, trim the wick, light it and adjust the flame, then how to put the chimney on. The lamp oil burns with a whiter flame than the kerosene did, and it has a different smell, but the light is still soft.

When my wife got home, we went out to dinner. For some reason, during dinner and on the way home tonight, the three of us were exceptionally gay.

2 COMMENTS:

Cypher Blueman said...

I had to look up ANICO which for some reason I'd read as ANCIO. Not to be maudlin, but these writings will have special meaning for your kid down the years. I can't quite get at it, but I wonder why I liked the big storms in New York. No school. But more. I liked that three day black out in the city in '65. I read *The Lord of the Ring*s by candle light. I'm not sure I would like a blackout today though. I'd miss the chance of seeing *Doctor Zhivago* on TCM. I like to see him snowed into the Urals, writing poetry.

FEBRUARY 28, 2009 AT 8:25 AM

Hilarym99 said...

I loved when the power would go out when I was a kid. Just loved it. Something magical about it. The silence maybe, or the different kind of light when there's no flashing screens, only flickering candles. I have a friend whose family had a generator. They'd plug in their video game system to the plug that got the power. I think they missed something doing that.

A few years back, in college, I was hanging out with an ex, watching TV. We were in that awkward, trying to be friends, but something was still there stage, I think. The power went out. We just sat. It seemed uncomfortable, at least to me, without the TV to focus on. I couldn't stop thinking about what we would have done three months earlier to pass the time.

FEBRUARY 28, 2009 AT 10:06 AM

Unity

Sitting in my wife's car in the garage tonight, lights on, windshield wipers going, it's easy to see how people get depressed. I'm just back from the store, and had to maneuver past my old 4Runner to get into the one-car garage. I left the truck's lights on when we came back from the PTO pancake breakfast this morning. Thai soup for lunch. I made the soup last night because I went down to the faculty practice at Northwestern by myself Wednesday, and my wife and daughter missed out on lunch at a good Thai restaurant. I had a glass of champagne at lunch today. An ounce of cognac in the champagne. And I fell asleep reading Niall Ferguson's *The Ascent Of Money*. When I woke up, I knew I'd left the lights on and I knew the battery would be dead when I went outside and tried to start the truck.

This is the first winter we've had a one-car garage. We

park my wife's VW in the garage and leave the Toyota in the driveway, close to the furnace exhaust where it's a little warmer. The battery is probably finished. I'll jump it in the morning and drive the truck tomorrow, but I'm not hopeful the battery will hold its charge. Getting my daughter to school Monday may be a hassle, I'm thinking, sitting in the warm car, staring at the odds and ends stacked on the shelf at the end of the garage, above the bicycles and the snow-blower. A yellow sprayer I used to spray nematodes on the grubs infesting my yard back in Wisconsin in a futile attempt to avoid chemicals. The "for sale" sign from the lot we bought down by the beach here in Michigan last summer with the address and the outline of the lot on it. When we bought the lot, down near the water where a Jack Nicklaus golf course is under construction, I distinctly remember saying "how can we lose?"

I grew old reading John Updike's books. I read *Rabbit, Run* the first time in a reading room at the Student Union of the University of Texas in 1961. I think I puzzled over the punctuation of the title for an hour before I started reading the book. Updike is a little older than I am, but close enough in age for us to have seen and done some of the same things at the same time. It was Updike's genius to take his time with Harry Angstrom, to let him live, taking him up every ten years or so when the world had changed enough for new things to be important. Updike saw the end of Detroit coming. And he knew it would not be the foreign cars that undid us, but the easy money, the fast deals and cooked books. If I never quite believed Rabbit was real, I always understood him. I could relate to him as he got older and richer, then poorer and, finally, died.

The jump start worked. The battery held its charge. Fat Boy, my 1993 Toyota 4Runner, is parked in my driveway, charged up and ready to go, icicles hanging from his shiny grill like frozen snot.

The Wolf of Winter

A long time ago, I told my son, I think he was in the first grade then, that Kenneth Patchen's "The Wolf Of Winter" was about the winter cold killing poor people. I doubt we got into nice distinctions between body and spirit or into the idea that there is a pessimism born of winter that afflicts boys who grow up in the South. A winter depression that settles into your bones and makes it hard to move.

Economic hard times are bound to hit people in the North, in the big frozen cities, harder than they hit people in the South. Finding a way to stay warm, a place to sleep, has to be tough. In Seattle, they open up the public buildings at night and the homeless sleep in the halls. For the poor, winter is hard. During a depression, it's going to be deadly.

The first panhandler of the winter turned up on our street yesterday. It was recycling day, and, in retrospect, I imagine she was working the snow-covered sidewalk for bottles and saw me dragging my little green tub of bottles and cans to the curb.

Her story was one I'd heard before. Just moved into the neighborhood. Family in trouble somewhere. Gas money to get to them. Pay me back in a couple of days. God bless me. Can she give me a hug? We settle for shaking hands.

I've never turned a panhandler down. It's a deep superstition of some kind. The way I buy off the bad luck that stalks me, just out of sight. Like a wolf.

I Was Born Too Soon

A new female condom is coming on the market.

The FC2 Female Condom is made with a soft material for quieter use. Its original version failed to gain a foothold in the U.S. marketplace because it was noisy to use, as well as too expensive.

Too noisy? Hell, why not make them even noisier, but with better sounds?

How about the "Flight Of The Valkyries?" Or something wet and squishy, like rubber boots slogging through the mud of a rice paddy?

7 COMMENTS:

GirlFromTheBronx said...

I had to give a listening exam after reading this post. While playing Wagner's *Wesendonck Lieder* for my students, what comes strolling into my brain? Yep, you got it. Squishy, wet, slogging, rubber boots.

MARCH 11, 2009 AT 9:22 PM

Antepilani said...

I totally missed out on Rock and Roll. I got in just in time to hear the death rattle. Where is the Misty Mountain Hop? Where is the Smoke on the Water? Kiss in the Kingdome? Everything now is beer and lifestyle music. I got the left-overs of the Stones and the other ancients just grinding it out to make a living.

MARCH 12, 2009 AT 9:25 PM

Billy Glad said...

Sounds like you were born too late. My son, who is about your age, got to climb a tree and sit right over the stage at an outdoor Talking Heads concert when he was a kid. On the way out, we saw people slam dancing.

MARCH 12, 2009 AT 9:28 PM

Antepilani said...

Once in a lifetime.

MARCH 12, 2009 AT 9:32 PM

Tom Manoff said...

Keep on Orpheus. Set loose those Maenads on fearful flesh. Make those crazy girls sing backup to your own mad song.

MARCH 12, 2009 AT 9:45 PM

Billy Glad said...

I think I can use that, Mansky.

OCTOBER 10, 2017 AT 9:55 PM

Billy Glad said...

You be poet, man.

OCTOBER 10, 2017 AT 9:57 PM

Lang Lang's Fingers

I got an email from the Lyric Opera of Chicago today, promoting an upcoming performance by pianist Lang Lang. Struck me as strange. The overhead camera and screen on the stage seem designed to dehumanize the event. Like if opera singers had cameras pointing down their throats so you could see their vocal cords moving. All that's missing is a whispered commentary, slo-mo of Lang Lang's crazy fingers and instant replays. Yet another example of the power of technology to dehumanize human experience.

"An overhead camera and onstage screen will allow every audience member to witness Lang Lang's energy and grace at the piano."

6 COMMENTS:

quinn the eskimo said...

I want a Bum-Cam. Seat placement is critical. I need to see all of the energy and grace. Also, Smell-O-Vision.

MAY 9, 2012 AT 10:11 AM

Billy Glad said...

I swear, man, sometimes I think I'm going crazy. The world around me is turning into a completely virtual flux. The web and the blogosphere are bad enough, but when you go to a game or concert and end up watching the screens more than the live performance — and now this — I mean, doesn't it turn the performer into some kind of wind-up piano player? Deconstructed. Depersonalized. A bad montage where the sum of the parts is less than the whole. I just don't know.

MAY 9, 2012 AT 10:37 AM

Tom Manoff said...

In about 1962 I went to a movie in Times Square about China. It had what quinn calls "smell-0-vision." Actual smells were injected into the theater. I thought it was wonderful. I wondered why it never came back. Who knows what the "smells" were? But I'm with quinn on smell. Billy, I think also that the virtual world works as long as you balance it with the real world. I garden and practice. I've been working on my garden for 10 years. I'm back to practicing the piano for significant hours as I did as a youth. All of this balances out the web stuff. And also, Billy, what is film if not virtual life? Is it more "real" or "organic" than video? I think it is more real and organic. The dividing line is analog/video. Analog is a continuum. Video is digital. Digital means cutting reality into small bits. That has an impact on the harmony of the body and soul. Who wouldn't want real film over digital? Big screens help. Why? The images have to move through the air. Air by its nature acts as a disperser of sound and light. Thus the digital source is blurred into more of a reality.

MAY 9, 2012 AT 1:52 PM

Billy Glad said...

I suppose you're right. I don't want to be mean about it. I hope the people who go to the recital enjoy watching Lang's hands while they listen to him play. I guess I come down on the analog or continuous side. I know you're talking about something more basic, but at a cruder level I prefer deep focus and continuous shots in movies to montage. Funny that I should be complaining about seeing more. To me that's as bad — or worse — than seeing less. What about opera? Do they throw close-ups of the singers up on big screens now? Do they run a montage of the best moments during intermission? They might. They might be doing that while I'm out in the lobby drinking cheap Rioja.

MAY 9, 2012 AT 2:16 PM

GirlfromtheBronx said...

As with most things, I think the priorities behind the deed, the action, the development, is what matters. This just reeks of a PR stunt. But I don't doubt it will catch on. There have been times when I have had a knee jerk response to technology getting in the way of the pure event.

I reacted with great negativity to the introduction of subtitles at the Opera. That was in 1983! I finally got over it. But my original objections remain intact. I even got my panties in a twist when NY Times switched over to using color. I'm not sure why that annoyed me so much, but there you have it.

Anyway, this kind of thing just seems vulgar and unnecessary. It brings attention to one aspect of the playing— the finger dexterity. I doubt the average person watching a close-up of fingers will be able to integrate the entire musical experience when they have been guided to focus on one part of it. That annoys me. I also wonder if all artists will have to sign a release to allow this or if they will have an option to reject.

MAY 11, 2012 AT 11:40 AM

Billy Glad said...

It's like putting a performer in a jar. But what the hell can you expect from a world where fans of Pavarotti can turn up for the Met opening of Turandot wearing sports coats and green-and-white checkered pants? And the worst part is everyone of those tacky dweebs knows more about Turandot and Pavarotti than I ever will.

MAY 11, 2012 AT 1:23 PM

FLIR

Forward Looking Infrared has been around a long time. I first saw it in use over 30 years ago, cruising along the Rio Grande in an INS helicopter. FLIR has given U.S. troops the ability to see at night without being seen. It has completely altered the nature of modern warfare. It's incredible stuff. It reduces the human beings at the receiving end of a weapon to mere targets on a screen. If it's true, as I was told growing up in Texas, that distant is polite, FLIR makes killing about as polite as it gets.

I read recently that some researchers believe playing kill-or-be-killed war games improves cognition. According to Daphne Bavelier, an assistant professor in the department of brain and cognitive science at the University of Rochester, people who play fast-paced games "have better vision, better attention and better cognition." The AP says Bavelier was a presenter at a symposium on the educational uses of video and computer games.

I'm constantly running into reports that suggest video game players make the best surgeons, pilots and CAD monkeys.

I guess that depends on the individual. My first video game was Doom, and after playing it for a month or so, I developed tunnel vision that lasted for weeks after I stopped playing the game. It was like walking around, looking at the world through a tube about the size of a coffee can. Last year, Jane Mayer reported in *The New Yorke*r that some of the CIA agents who fly the lethal drones over Afghanistan wear flight suits at work. Mayer's October 2009 article, "The Predator War", explores the risks of using predator drones as our weapon of choice in the war on terror.

I don't doubt that video games are educational and have real potential for making work more fun. One of the best games I've heard about was used by currency traders. The traders sat in the cockpit of a virtual fighter jet and gunned down stacks of foreign currency with bullets denominated in dollars to exchange dollars for Euros, Francs or Marks. To buy dollars, they loaded up with a foreign currency and gunned down piles of dollars.

You could develop a Madoff version of that game that helped investment advisors gun down their clients fortunes, and, in the advanced version, gun down their clients themselves, saving them the trouble of jumping out of windows.

According to the AP, Professor Bavelier had some good ideas about ways to "harness the positive effects" of first-person shooter games without violence.

"As you know," she said, "most of us females just hate those action video games. You don't have to use shooting. You can use, for example, a princess who has a magic wand and whenever she touches something, it turns into a butterfly and sparkles."

Put that into the targeting system of an Apache helicopter and you might have something.

Personally, I'm looking forward to smart weapons that know when to shoot and when not to.

7 COMMENTS:

quinn the eskimo said...

Viddy games were my life in '79-80. Space Invaders. I played for hours every day. Absolutely addictive. I got good. Won prizes on campus, toured around playing. Does it change you? Hell, yeah. The side effects included words turning into little marching men when I read. And my mind and motor controls got "re-wired" to become faster at certain tasks, perceive patterns of certain types.

What's not right is to say it creates "better vision, better attention and better cognition." Your vision can become fabulous at picking up certain objects on a 2-D screen but worse at even seeing other kinds of objects and at working with real-world 3-D. Any activity you do repeatedly is going to make your brain respond and change. Becoming a baseball player? Huge brain changes. Learning to drive a car while talking? Ditto. Learning to read. Learning to relax and enjoy sex with animals. Same.

But these games don't change you more than reading does. Jesus. Reading drags you away from colour, from 3-D, from the external world, damages your eyesight and produces solitary beings. It's the readers I worry about when it comes to "distancing" people from killing. 'Cause it's since we started reading that we really got into mass killing. When you have to strangle a guy up close, even if he's a different colour, he still looks an awful lot the same, eh? But hype you up on book-learned differences and you'll kill him in a second. Books. Satan's tools.

DECEMBER 17, 2010 AT 11:35 AM

Billy Glad said...

I've become convinced that this is the future of the "war against terrorism" in Afghanistan and other places. I haven't completely thought it through, but I think what we're doing in Afghanistan now is "preparing the battlefield" for special ops and the remotes. It's really too bad for the Iraqis that the Predators weren't developed enough for us to invade, prepare the battlefield and withdraw — even as late as the point in time when we had completely determined there were no WMDs and Saddam was caught and hanged. Almost no US casualties at that point and nothing like the Iraqi casualties we eventually saw. I remember Bush authorizing some "smart bomb" strikes right before the invasion, hoping to kill Saddam. Nowadays, a "pilot" in Virginia could fly a little Predator through a window at Saddam's palace and land it on his bed. But I still have to figure out exactly what "preparing the battlefield" entails. Then I might have a good article.

DECEMBER 17, 2010 AT 11:50 AM

Miguel de las Animas Perdidas said...

Not so sure that "a pilot in Virginia could fly a little Predator through a window at Saddam's palace and land it on his bed" now either. It is a fact that of the over 50 launches of the so-called "smart bombs" at the beginning of the Iraq War II none hit their intended targets.

DECEMBER 28, 2010 AT 5:04 PM

Tom Manoff said...

Do I dare say that I own an Xbox? That I've flown many a mission over Iraq and shot down mysterious looking jets vaguely Soviet-meets-Darth-Vader in design.

DECEMBER 31, 2010 AT 7:03 PM

Miguel de las Animas Perdidas said...

You lucky sod!

DECEMBER 31, 2010 AT 8:17 PM

Billy Glad said...

Probably why you enjoyed *Restrepo*, Mansky. Did you notice the secret spotting device, covered with a blanket so we couldn't tell what it was? When I was a kid, I got my shoes at Clark's shoe store, and they had this fluoroscope device you put your feet in and you could see how the shoes fit — even see the bones in your feet. Nothing has impressed me since.

DECEMBER 31, 2010 AT 8:45 PM

Tom Manoff said...

X-rayed feet up. Christ. That's scary. Saw the bones of your feet, you say? Duck and cover.

JANUARY 1, 2011 AT 2:32 PM

YouTube

Web 2.0 has witnessed the rise of citizen journalism and a brand of publishing that reminds me of the wild, wild West, compared to the staid publications of the East Coast with their European sensibilities and, as Norman Mailer put it, their "bloodless, gutless restraint. "

Cyberspace tends to be combative and ideological. And Julian Assange, publisher of WikiLeaks, is one of the most combative and ideological publishers on the web. Assange and the leaked documents and videos he has published are now at the red hot center of the battle to control the flow of information over the world wide web. Although Assange is not the first publisher to make government documents available to the public, his publication of gun camera videos and U.S. Department of State cables is massive, both in terms of its sheer volume and in terms of its buzz. And it is the only leak around right now. In my view, there is nothing on WikiLeaks as sensational as the Abu Ghraib photos, and, in fact, nothing as shocking as some of the videos that have been up on YouTube since the start of the Iraq occupation, but Assange has made the leaks personal and part of a private war with the U.S. government. He has given the publication of leaks a human face. He has become the center of attention. That's too bad. Because it may be too hot at the center for Assange.

When I first saw the gun camera video Assange published, I was struck by the fact that the gunship was adhering to General Petraeus' regrettable rules of engagement for Baghdad. The rules should have been stricter, but at least they prevented the gunships from finishing off the wounded the way this gunship did.

This kind of video, depicting the actual murder of a wounded insurgent, has been available on YouTube for years, along with countless home videos put up there — self-published, if you will — by American soldiers and Marines, and also by insurgents. Most of the insurgent videos seem to have been removed quietly over the years on the grounds that they violate YouTube's terms of service. I say "quietly" because YouTube, a publisher whose significance dwarfs the personal soap opera of Assange and WikiLeaks, has never identified itself as a publisher with an ax to grind. In fact, YouTube doesn't pretend to be a publisher at all. Putatively, they are simply providing a forum for the free exchange of information. Therein, it seems to me, lies YouTube's safety, if not legally — and I don't pretend to understand the legal issues around the free flow of information — at least morally. For YouTube does not notice us, unless we draw attention to one another. They have adopted at least the appearance of ignorance and neutrality. Assange has not.

Assange has, in fact, made quite a big deal out of knowing exactly what he's publishing. He has probably been led down that path by the establishment press who are very high on "responsibility" and insist on things like verifying sources, redacting classified information, and making a determination about whether the public's right to know outweighs the danger of exposing operators and operations. Having consented to work with the establishment in making those judgments, Assange has exposed himself to the moral, if not the legal responsibility to get it right. I suspect that is something Julian Assange is poorly equipped to do.

(Update. 3/24/2019. YouTube removed the video of an American gunship murdering a wounded insurgent.)

2 COMMENTS:

Billy Glad said...

I actually thought WikiLeaks was going to be a place where people put things up as opposed to Assange and company "publishing" them, but it turns out Assange needed to be at the center of attention. He got there, and now his mama is worried he'll end up in the general population where some 300 lb. psycho whose little brother got killed in Afghanistan can get at him. It appears that some of WikiLeaks' co-founders think Assange has been too engaged with the content, too. They are promising a site that just forwards leaked info to a publication of your choice. I'm torn between sending the Hives secrets to the National Enquirer or to NPR. By the way, I have discovered a good little news blog run by a couple of old guys at the NPR site, Frank James and Mark Memmott, called *The Two-Way*. I have figured out what they do — if anything — except cut and paste, but their selection of news items is interesting. Yesterday, they had a short clipping up about Pfc Bradley Manning, the kid who is actually going to have to deal with those 300 lb gorillas in the general population some day. Glenn Greenwald has latched on to his cause. His best hope is Greenwald will file an *amicus* brief and it will take the court 100 years to read it. Christ. You'd think Greenwald was being paid by the word.

DECEMBER 16, 2010 AT 7:22 AM

Billy Glad said...

Reviewing this old post this morning I note that YouTube finally got around to deleting the most violent video from the occupation, the government did get Assange, Chelsea Manning made it through and revealed the fact that she is a trans woman, *The Two-Way* has evolved into something else, and Greenwald has moved to Brazil. Life does go on all around us.

OCTOBER 1, 2018 AT 9:54 AM

Julian Assange

Both sides of the WikiLeaks debate seem determined to misrepresent the issues in the Assange drama by hotly arguing over whether Assange is a journalist or not. Of course he isn't. Assange is a publisher, and he's entitled to the same protections — no more and no less – as any other publisher.

File this under topics for further research.

Do journalists have better or worse protections under the U.S. Constitution than publishers have? Are they held to different standards? Do people respect journalists more than they respect publishers? Who raised the issue of whether Assange is a journalist in the first place? Does being perceived as a journalist help or hurt Assange?

And what, if anything, do the charges a Swedish prosecutor wants to question Assange about have to do with

WikiLeaks? For the record, I don't think the charges have much to do with the WikiLeaks drama at all. Sex shouldn't be a death-defying act. If Assange did what the two women have accused him of doing — if he exposed them to the risk of AIDS by forcing them to have unprotected sex — he committed a crime under Swedish law. That doesn't mean he's not entitled to protection as a publisher when he publishes government tapes and documents.

The Manning Debate

After years of war in Afghanistan and Iraq, examining the conditions of Pfc. Bradley Manning's confinement at Quantico, Va., could be the first step in a process of national reconciliation. President Obama could begin that process now, with a simple act of compassion. He could direct the Department of Defense to find a better way to safeguard Pfc. Manning while he awaits trial. The President will not be able to risk lifting the Prevention of Injury (POI) watch Pfc. Manning is being subjected to, but he can and should make the POI watch more humane.

Sooner or later, Americans do find ways to reconcile their differences. For me, reconciliation after the Vietnam War came with the dedication of Maya Ying Lin's Vietnam Veterans Memorial, a sad, retiring monument to the fallen of a sad war. I've always felt the Vietnam Veterans

Memorial was a more fitting conclusion to the Vietnam War experience than America's victory in the Gulf War, a victory that, according to George H. W. Bush, "kicked the Vietnam syndrome" and, it turns out, restored the confidence America needed to undertake further adventures — adventures Pfc. Manning is accused of trying to thwart by stealing classified documents.

In the case of Pfc. Manning, as the wars in Iraq and Afghanistan grind to a close, Americans have a chance to start reconciling our differences over at least one aspect of the conduct of those wars: our treatment of prisoners of war and captive "enemies" of all kinds.

The Department of Defense's treatment of Pfc. Manning has been opposed by the left for a long time — especially by Glenn Greenwald and by bloggers at Jane Hamsher's Firedoglake — but now Pfc. Manning's physical and mental health, and the conditions under which he is being held at Quantico, have begun to concern more Americans. It has become clear that, whatever the reasons, those conditions include sleep deprivation, solitary confinement and intentional humiliation. They are conditions that have been denounced as "stupid" by the Department of State's top spokesman, P.J. Crowley, at the cost of his job.

There is something disturbing about seeing the force of the United States government directed against a single individual, in this case a 23-year-old soldier.

Understandably, the Obama administration is angry at Pfc. Manning. They believe he leaked embarrassing details about the wars in Afghanistan and Iraq and about State Department operations around the globe. Just as understandably, they would like him to implicate WikiLeaks — the site that first published the documents they claim Pfc. Manning stole — in the theft of the documents. But does that anger and that desire to get at the publishers of the documents justify treating

Pfc. Manning in a way that many are beginning to describe as torture?

Facts about Pfc. Manning's life at the brig are hard to come by. It's not clear if Pfc. Manning is still being interrogated, or if he's just waiting for his trial. The military insists that Pfc. Manning is being treated the same as any prisoner in his circumstances would be — whatever that means — and President Obama is content to take their word for it. But Pfc. Manning and his lawyer dispute that claim. They say Pfc. Manning is being abused and punished under the guise of protecting him.

Most of the information we have about Pfc. Manning's confinement comes from him and his lawyer, David Coombs, and, to be fair, there are contradictions in their story. On the one hand, Mr. Coombs says Pfc. Manning sleeps naked in a cold cell; on the other hand he says the brig has given Pfc. Manning a blanket he can't tear. And Pfc. Manning admits that, out of frustration with his living conditions, he has become upset, yelled and pulled his hair.

To be even more fair, the military has responded — in a way — to criticism from Pfc. Manning's supporters. When Pfc. Manning complained about having to sleep naked and stand inspection every morning in the nude, the brig gave him a rough garment to wear. (But then the Marine guards proceeded to mock and humiliate him by calling the garment a "smock.")

This much is clear. Pfc. Manning has been held in solitary confinement since he arrived at the Quantico brig on July 29, 2010.

For 23 hours a day, Pfc. Manning sits in his cell. The guards check on him every five minutes by asking him if he is "okay." He is required to respond. At night, if the guards can't see him clearly, because he has a blanket over his head or he is curled up, facing the wall, they wake him to make sure he is unharmed, forcing him to choose between sleeping without covers or not sleeping at all. He eats all of his meals in his cell. He is not allowed to exercise in his cell, and he only gets one hour of exercise in a closed room outside of his cell each day.

Considering the torture and abuse of prisoners by the U.S military at Abu Ghraib — where the guards assisted interrogators by softening the prisoners up — it's not unreasonable for people concerned with civil liberties to demand an objective review of the way Pfc. Manning is being treated. And it makes sense to wonder why the military is stonewalling attempts by members of Congress to get access to the brig.

On the other hand, it was the U.S. Military itself that uncovered and publicized the crimes at Abu Ghraib. And no one would dispute that it's reasonable for the military and the Obama administration to make Pfc. Manning's safety during his pretrial confinement a top priority.

Pfc. Manning, his lawyer, and his supporters all want the military to lift the POI watch Pfc. Bradley is living under. His lawyer cites brig psychiatrists who say there is no mental health reason for keeping Pfc. Bradley under POI. But is such a demand realistic?

Preventing injury to Pfc. Manning is a political issue. Simply put, the President can't afford to take the chance — no matter how remote — that Pfc. Manning might come to harm.

There is plenty of reason to believe that someone might try to hurt Pfc. Manning if they got the chance. And, while there may be no good reason to believe he would harm himself, his suicide, if it did happen, would deal a devastating blow to the reputation of the military and the Obama administration. It would undoubtedly lead to investigations, conspiracy theories, and attacks on the administration from all sides.

Political suicides are rare, but there have been enough of

them to give President Obama pause. The suicides of the monk Thích Quảng Đức in Saigon and the Quaker Norman Morrison outside the Pentagon in Washington, D.C., for example, had a profound impact on the Vietnam War.

The risk of an individual throwing his body into a war machine to gum up its works may be something psychiatrists are less qualified to assess than politicians are. The Obama administration has no desire to see the young soldier who embarrassed them by showing that they couldn't protect their secrets embarrass them further by killing himself while in their custody. Forget about lifting that POI watch.

But let's make sure the watch is as humane as it can be.

There is no reason why the conditions of Pfc. Manning's POI watch can't be modified to eliminate sleep deprivation and humiliation. And certainly his jailers can find a safe way to relieve the isolation of Pfc. Manning's solitary confinement, including letting him exercise in his cell and get some sunlight and fresh air.

The brig needs to deliver Pfc. Manning for trial unharmed physically — and unharmed mentally as well. There is no justification for destroying Pfc. Manning in the course of protecting him. If the idea is to prevent Pfc. Manning from harming himself, shouldn't the military consider the fact that loss, hopelessness and isolation are all on the CDC's list of risk factors for suicide?

If he is convicted, Pfc. Manning, whose motive for taking on the United States government may have been to stop killing and torture, will probably end up in Leavenworth, where, in further irony, he will join William Calley, Hasan Akbar and Charles Graner, a guard convicted of prisoner abuse at Abu Ghraib.

Maximum security prisons like Leavenworth subject some dangerous prisoners — those who have attacked other prisoners or guards, for example — to solitary confinement with the goal of conditioning them so that they can be returned to the general population. Pfc. Manning, who no one has suggested is a danger to anyone else, will have done that much time in solitary before he ever comes to trial.

All of us, from the left and from the right as well, should demand that President Obama act now. He should direct the military to immediately cooperate with the Congress. He should direct the Department of Defense to devise humane ways to prevent injury to Pfc. Manning while he awaits trial. If the Department of Defense can't do that, he should get them the advice of experts who can.

Wouldn't America be better off if the debate about Pfc. Manning's pretrial confinement could be shifted from whether he is being tortured to whether the treatment he is getting is a little too kind? Is there a society on earth that doesn't admire empathy, compassion and mercy?

No matter what we believe about America's role in the world, no matter what we believe about America's wars in Iraq and Afghanistan, and no matter how much or how little damage we believe Pfc. Manning may have done, if we cannot reconcile our differences over something as simple as the pretrial treatment of Pfc. Manning, a young man whose life is effectively over, we may not be able to reconcile our differences at all.

3 COMMENTS:

CraneStation said...

Billy, thank you for posting this. There is a book called *The Sutras of Abu Ghraib*, written by Aidan Delgado. He is a Buddhist. Upon seeing the abuses there, he decided to leave the military on conscientious objector status. At this point, they took away all of his protective gear. Kicked off the island, I guess. It is important for those of us who still have our humanity intact to keep writing about the inhumanity that is happening all around us.

MARCH 18, 2011 AT 9:29 PM

Cypher Blueman said...

I was once deprived of sleep and worse by police. I've decided that it wasn't a fluke but human nature for many people who become police. When given a political/social reason, whatever inhibitions these enforcers have loosen. They like to torture. Everywhere and for all time.

MARCH 28, 2011 AT 7:24 AM

Billy Glad said...

The Manning issue is difficult on a number of levels. The determination of the human rights activists to get his prevention of injury watch lifted instead of modified to make it more humane is troubling, because you don't have to be very sophisticated to see who would profit most from Manning coming to harm. I shudder to think of the outrage and clicks on the popular muckraking sites in the liberal blogosphere that would follow any kind of injury — self-inflicted or otherwise — to Pfc. Manning. I wonder how the pretrial treatment of Daniel Ellsberg compares. Ellsberg was older, successful, not in the military, and on a first name basis with people like Kissinger. He should have been walking around with a t-shirt that said: Don't try this at home, kids. Maybe that's why he's so active in the Manning case.

MARCH 28, 2011 AT 8:43 AM

Nattering Nabobs

The Associated Press is reporting that the Army will move Pfc. Manning from Quantico to Leavenworth soon. According to the Army, Pfc. Manning will be jailed in the medium security facility at Leavenworth while he awaits trial, because the interview to determine his competency to stand trial has been completed. (Does that mean Army interrogators have what they need from Manning, or that they've given up on getting him to implicate Julian Assange in the theft of Pentagon and State Department secrets?)

Manning's new cell opens on to a common area where he can mingle with other "pretrial confines."

If Manning is convicted, it will be a short walk to his permanent home. The military's maximum security prison is located at Fort Leavenworth, too. If he graduates to the maximum security block at Leavenworth, Manning will join William Calley, Hasan Akbar and Charles Graner, a guard convicted of prisoner abuse at Abu Ghraib. That prospect may have influenced the information he provided Army investigators.

Or maybe Manning's interrogation is still going on, and the Army wants him to get a good look at where he could end up if he doesn't cooperate.

Either way, Manning's move might mean big trouble for Assange. It is definitely a thumb in the eye for the blogosphere personalities who have been milking Manning's pretrial confinement. They are already complaining about the improvement in Manning's confinement conditions they so desperately sought. Kansas is a long way from Washington, D.C., where most of the "nattering nabobs" hang out. (Hat tip to John Milius and Francis Ford Coppola.)

Ennui

I've lost interest in the news. The World Wide Web in general has become a colossal bore. I was already starting to lose interest in the websites I had developed the habit of visiting every day, when, suddenly, The New York Times fell apart. Following current events seems so meaningless now, even as a spectator sport. I feel like I'm bringing the plants and lawn furniture in for the winter, just when I should be putting them outside. Sigh.

Spring has been a long time coming to the shores of Lake Michigan this year.

Following the YouTube links from It Might As Well Be Spring," I noticed that Dana Andrews was in *State Fair (1945)*. Andrews made some good films, including *Laura (1944)* and *The Best Years of Our Lives (1946)*. Sometimes I think my obsession with the auteur theory has caused me to underestimate the contribution actors make to films. Maybe they contribute more to the *mise en scène* than I've given them credit for. I've always thought Andrews would have made a great Phillip Marlowe.

As of this morning, there are 1,223 documentary films available to view instantly on Netflix and many, many more available by mail. I can't imagine being able to make a list of 1,223 things worth documenting, but I suppose it only took 1,223 people who were able to raise some cash to make a documentary to produce that body of work. Everybody does a little, nobody does a lot. The last documentary I watched was *The Most Dangerous Man In America: Daniel Ellsberg and the Pentagon Papers (2009)*, a strange little film I played out of curiosity about the similarities and differences between Ellsberg, who was on a first name basis with Henry Kissinger, and Pfc. Bradley Manning.

The government is going to risk holding Pfc. Manning in "medium security" at Fort Leavenworth, Kansas, while he awaits trial. The military has concluded that Manning is no longer a danger to himself or anyone else, and that he's not likely to be harmed by guards or other prisoners before he's tried. If the Obama administration is wrong about that, they will have a mess to clean up in the middle of a political campaign. Personally, I hope Manning is no longer in danger because he's cut a deal and given the government Assange.

The first page of the Netflix documentary list includes *Modify (2005)*, an 84 minute film about "branding, piercing, tattooing, tongue splitting and every body modification imaginable." The blurb says *Modify* has "an original soundtrack featuring more than 20 new musical artists." Might be worth a look for somebody, though probably not for me. I couldn't even sit through *Ilsa: She Wolf Of The SS (1975)* the last time I tried to watch it, and they don't even cut anyone for real.

Rise Of The Planet Of The Apes

The tide of popular culture turns amazingly fast. The rise of one myth flows in over the ebb of another, wiping out all traces of the receding myth, until that myth returns to lap even farther up the beach than before. So it goes with pop culture versions of the fall of man. They keep coming back.

In the Fifties, the French writer Romain Gary raised the issue of mankind's survival in *The Roots of Heaven*. Gary's protagonist is Morel, an ordinary French dentist who goes over to the elephants in French Equatorial Africa. Morel is a misanthrope, but Gary, it turns out, is not. The ending of the novel is a tribute to the human spirit. The Fifties were the time of the beat generation, of cool, of jazz, grass, the Korean War, the rise and fall of McCarthy, the presidency of Eisenhower, the post-war boom, the poetry of Patchen and Ginsberg, the death of Robert Capa, the fall of Dien

Bien Phu and Brown v. Board of Education.

Just seven years later, Pierre Boulle's 1963 novel, *Planet of the Apes*, contemplated the extinction of mankind and the rise of the ape as the torchbearer of civilization throughout the universe. The Sixties were the time of the hippies, the Cold War ascendant, the Kennedy and Johnson presidencies, the Civil Rights movement, acid and acid rock, the Vietnam War, the fall of Lyndon Johnson and the rise of Nixon. Alan Ginsberg lived to see Chicago cops riot against the sons and daughters of America's middle class who had tuned in, turned on, dropped out and come back swinging against the war and the draft. I was just back from Germany where I had put in my two years as a medic at an Army hospital, getting high and shooting up Thorazine to improve my tan, so I passed on Chicago myself, but I did show my younger brother how to curl up into a ball to protect his nuts when the cops started beating him. I sent him off to Chicago with a bright red bandanna to cover his nose and mouth when the tear gas began to fly. Or maybe I hallucinated that.

Boulle's *Planet of the Apes* didn't speculate about the causes of the rise of the apes as the dominant species in the far reaches of the galaxy, or about the extinction of man and the rise of the apes on our own planet. Boulle simply presented the success of ape culture and the failure of mankind as a fact. For some unknown reason, man was just not good enough.

When Twentieth Century Fox produced the film version of Boulle's book, they apparently thought they owed the viewer an explanation. The plot of *Planet of the Apes (1968)* hangs on a malfunctioning starship that plunges back to Earth instead of landing on a planet at the far end of the galaxy, and on a nuclear war that wipes out the human race, letting apes take over the planet while the starship and its astronauts are gone.

In Fox's *Rise of the Planet of the Apes (2011)*, the human race is wiped out — probably — by a virus. Since the collapse of the Soviet Union, nobody takes seriously the idea that man will be wiped out in a nuclear holocaust. And we're not worried about rogue computers turning on the human race anymore. The peril now is biological. In *Rise of the Planet of the Apes*, a virus that makes apes smart enough to talk and to break out of an ape jail in San Francisco is deadly to humans and highly contagious to boot. Good thing for the apes, of course, since without the intervention of the virus they would have had one good day of beating up on the cops before the bombs started to fall.

The idea that apes can beat up cops is as silly as the notion that hippies can beat up cops. It's just more Hollywood eyewash in the style of the Na'vi beating down the guns and machines of corporate America to liberate Pandora in Fox's *Avatar (2009)*. But there is a strong odor of misanthropy and self-hatred about the idea that resonates with establishment critics like David Denby of *The New Yorker*.

Here's Denby, waxing poetic over scenes of apes, invading a research facility. "When the apes, like water bursting through a dam, pour through the building's glass walls at different levels," Denby exults, "the image is a pop epiphany of freedom."

Something like ice breaking up and cascading down a raging river as a metaphor for revolution I suppose.

The high water mark is definitely creeping up the sand.

2 COMMENTS:

Miguelitoh2o said...

Got to see the film yesterday. My thought which I expressed aloud to my theater companion, as the apes headed out to the Muir Woods after sacking the research facility and the battle on the Golden Gate Bridge was: "Well it's open season on apes in the Muir Woods, now". I think they'd have been lucky to have a breeding pair survive until the virus had reduced humanity to the point where humans wouldn't be blasting the Muir Woods into oblivion. I thought it was an interesting twist on the story nonetheless. One of my friends is the chimp vet at the Save the Chimps sanctuary, and I'm curious to hear her take on the film. I know their organization is founded on the principle that their chimps are never loaned out to research facilities like the Sanctuary in the film did, so I think that part of the film was kinda a caricature of evil villains/Snidely Whiplash.

OCTOBER 6, 2011 AT 9:15 PM

Billy Glad said...

Have to wonder how Occupy Wall Street and October 2011 look from your vantage point. I wish them luck, but I'm not that hopeful. Boulle's apes sailed around space using solar sails. Poignant.

OCTOBER 6, 2011 AT 9:31 PM

The Hunger Games

Apparently, somebody convinced Suzanne Collins that the narrative of *The Hunger Games*, her teeny-bopper dystopian novel, needed some "fixing" for the film version of the book. So Collins, whose millions of avid readers turned out for the opening of *The Hunger Games (2012)* last weekend, tinkered with the story to explain why the "game maker" — the fellow charged with making the gladiatorial Hunger Games of a future Fascist America entertaining and instructive for the survivors of a failed rebellion — would change the games' rules of engagement on the fly. And she destroyed the focus that was crucial to the success of her novel.

Why Collins would agree to fix something that wasn't broken is a mystery to me. I'm guessing some of the money men and women behind the film were too dull to under-

stand the overarching importance of young love, star-crossed lovers and love triangles to Collins' readers. That a cynical game maker would play up the love angle for a sappy and spoiled audience and then sadistically pull the rug out from under the lovers didn't require any explanation at all. Neither did the fact that the idea of the lovers committing suicide — the ultimate symbol of rebellion against a dystopia — would panic the game maker.

Certainly, there is no reason why a film should conform slavishly to the novel it's based on. The novel is one thing and the film quite another. But these are not trivial changes. They go beyond "tweaks." They are irritating shifts in the narrative that complicate rather than clarify the story. They distort the story's point of view and diminish the story's heroine, young Katniss Everdeen, played by Jennifer Lawrence.

And Jennifer Lawrence is exactly what *The Hunger Games* has going for it. She is immensely likable; someone an audience can care about. She moves well, and her face is large enough and smooth enough for the camera to linger on, to turn into the kind of landscape that's missing from most of the film. Simply put, *The Hunger Games* doesn't need a single scene that doesn't have Jennifer Lawrence in it.

If anybody deserves a poison berry for the *The Hunger Games*, it's Gary Ross. His direction was even worse than the script. He never found the right mix of action and contemplation to make his film work. Ross never catches the power of nature, violence and unreason that drives the book.

Whence had they come,
The hand and lash that beat down frigid Rome?

Gary Ross doesn't have a clue.

It's hard to get from a first-person novel to a third-person film. That may explain why the producers of *The Hunger*

Games ended up with a second-rate director. Maybe the good directors shied away from the script. What Katniss is thinking dominates the book, and, when you take that away, an enormous weight is placed on Lawrence's delivery and body language to communicate what's going on in her mind. In the novel, Katniss Everdeen makes a dangerous passage from a young girl to a woman, from a huntress to a warrior, and, at the end, back to a teenage girl. If *The Hunger Games* team had pulled that off, they would have had a great movie. All of that teenage energy, confusion and drama, dropped into the middle of gladiatorial training and combat. My god!

It turns out, of course, that a PG-13 rating was more important. The bad news is the team planning the sequel may be just as inept. The producers couldn't get Tony Scott, whose *Man On Fire (2004)* had exactly what *The Hunger Games* films so badly need. The buzz is they'll soon sign music video director Francis Lawrence who made *I Am Legend (2007)*, a boring remake of *The Omega Man (1971)*. The one ray of hope is that someone on the project has signaled by dumping Ross that they think there is more at stake here than a massive box office that's already a dead hog cinch. There are moments in popular culture when great myths finally crystallize. Maybe somebody understands that *The Hunger Games* novels and films could be that kind of moment. It's a damn shame if they're not holding out for a director and writers who are equal to the task.

2 COMMENTS:

Billy Glad said...

I'm going to go back into this piece now and then over the next week or so. The books embody some interesting themes. Raw v. Cooked, Nature v. Civilization, Altruism v. Selfishness, and are clearly intended to invoke the decline and fall of the Roman Empire. *The Hunger Games* trilogy is, apparently, a step up for Collins from the 4th to 6th grade audience she previously wrote for. Gregor this and Gregor that. I understand Rowling is doing an adult book, hoping to cash in on an aging Harry Potter audience. So maybe the strategy is to follow your readership into adulthood, becoming a more mature writer on the way. If I didn't have a younger reader in the family, I doubt I would have read Collins' trilogy. Collins has worked hard I think to reference the decadence of Rome, and the Katniss character is complex enough to satisfy me. Collins has obviously read a lot and let her reading shade her own work in ways I like. Satisfying to watch a pawn in the game fight her way to the top, a symbol of the revolution become a real revolutionary.

APRIL 2, 2012 AT 6:48 PM

Miguelitoh2o said...

Well I am a fan of the book. The description of Panem as a government totally at odds with the welfare of 12/13ths of the population does seem to be a fairly apt metaphor for what our current political reality is, so I can understand why you place the weight on the film and it's direction that you do. I'm going to try to catch the movie this week, as it's in town now.

APRIL 29, 2012 AT 2:39 PM

The Green Hornet

He had it all. Biomimicry, a gas gun that made a weird sound, a big, fast car, called the Black Beauty, an Asian sidekick and The Flight Of The Bumblebee. I listened to The Hornet on the radio; read the comic books; watched the movie serial on Saturdays. Van Williams played the Hornet and Bruce Lee played Kato on TV. There's a great scene of Lee taking a Green Hornet set apart in the Bruce Lee biopic: *Dragon: The Bruce Lee Story (1993)*. So, I had high expectations for *The Green Hornet (2011)*, the Seth Rogen and Jay Chou movie directed by Michel Gondry that opened this weekend.

But, once you get past the twist that the movie is a comedy based on a premise that would have made a good Saturday Night Live skit, there's not much there, unless you think it's fun to play Name That Team and come up with

GREEN HORNET FIGHTS CRIME
33 MAR-APR
GREEN HORNET
COMICS
10¢

interesting duos that Rogen and Chou remind you of. I figure Aykroyd and Belushi or Aykroyd and Murray or Aykroyd and just about anyone.

Rogen was one of the Hornet's writers, and he's probably a better writer than a comedian. Some of the gags and one-liners in *The Green Hornet* are laugh-out-loud funny. But be sure to see the 3D version. I imagine the film would be incredibly boring in 2D, mainly because *The Green Hornet* lacks an interesting villain. Making a fun, comic rendition of a comic book is at least as good an idea as making an exceptionally dark one, but comedy or no, comic book heroes and comic book movies need interesting villains, and *The Green Hornet*'s Chudnofsky falls flat on his face.

Cameron Diaz is adequate in the Girl Friday role. Her face is the only image from *The Green Hornet* that sticks in my memory. It's as if she's the first real person I've seen in 3D. Tom Wilkinson does a brilliant turn as the Hornet's dad.

Hollywood badly needs to come up with a new superhero worthy of sequels and prequels, and some blockbuster films to fill the 3D bubble created by *Avatar*. *The Green Hornet* doesn't seem likely to fill either bill.

6 COMMENTS:

quinn the eskimo said...

The obvious one is *Swamp Thing*. Alan Moore did some of his best stuff with the Swampy Elemental, maybe even as good as *V for Vendetta* and *Watchmen*. Plus, my fave from childhood, *Captain America*, is out this year. Sigh. Dude only had a shield, really. Not much in the way of special weaponry. I donno though. Might be good to have *the* "American" superhero come out and show us how to operate without a lab full of special weapons.

JANUARY 15, 2011 AT 11:10 AM

Billy Glad said...

Have you noticed that except for you, running across the river in your blue suit, there are no Canadian superheros? Or are there and you've been keeping them to yourselves all these years. Is there a Captain Canada? The Iceman maybe? Cheesehead? I'm looking forward to *Captain America*. Hard to believe they won't update his weapons, though. I saw the previews of *Thor* last night. I'll probably go just for the moment when he wakes up after being hurled down to Earth and realizes where he is!

JANUARY 15, 2011 AT 12:20 PM

quinn the eskimo said...

How could you forget Captain Canuck? Okay. *Wolverine* is an awesome Canadian superhero. Created by an American. But that's okay, 'cause Superman was 1/2 designed by a Canadian. Shuster.

JANUARY 15, 2011 AT 3:27 PM

Antepilani said...

I thought *Hancock* could have really been good but it fell apart quickly. They had the right actor and casting him as an anti-hero should have made for a good story. *Watchmen* clearly demonstrates the lack of need for heroes of the day types. We outgrow them. Our heroes are based on our society's current fears and obstacles. What would our modern heroes be named?

Morgan Chaser. Fights injustice in brokerage houses! He has a really cool pen.

Put Captain America to work over in the Korengal Valley. That would be an awesome movie.

Nothing will ever compare to sitting on the floor listening to the *Hornet*. That was an event. Or I picture it as such. Like a really good narrator reading aloud in class.

I'm going to see it today after school so I'll let you know. Honestly I've been looking forward to it...for a laugh at least!

JANUARY 21, 2011 AT 12:27 PM

Billy Glad said...

Morgan Chaser. Very good. Be sure you see the 3D. Maybe we have enough heroes and it's better villains me need now. What was *Watchmen* if not villain against villain? *Thor* is going to have a good cast. They used him in the *Parallax View* montage. *Shane* or *Thor*?

JANUARY 21, 2011 AT 12:47 PM

Antepilani said...

Great call on *Swamp Thing*, quinn. That would be excellent. One problem. Adrienne Barbeau is irreplaceable.

Saw Green Bee last night. They picked the wrong genre. It just wasn't that good as a comedy. A quick redo as action/adventure and it would have been solid. Kato is very good. Villain was a limp noodle, but a good actor. Wife and son loved it so it was not a wasted trip.

JANUARY 22, 2011 AT 5:11 PM

Passion Play

Here is the main thing I want to say.
I'm working 24 hours a day.
I fix broken films.
You know I really can.

A long time ago, I figured out the only reason to create anything is that no one else has. The books I want to write are the books I want to read, but nobody has written them yet. The films I want to make are the films I want to see, but nobody has made them yet.

My wife used to drive me crazy by starting to fix films the minute we left the theater. I don't think we've seen more than one or two films over the years she didn't have ideas about ways to make them better. I wrote it off to her politics. Well, hell, I'd say. Go make your own film if you don't like that one. Go make a film that fits your politics or your aesthetics or whatever.

Lately, I've come around to her way of thinking. Why not fix broken films? Why not start with the idea that what's missing in the world is a better version of a film somebody made or a book somebody wrote? Where does it say you have to start from scratch?

Now you take *Passion Play (2010)*, a first film by screenwriter Mitch Glazer. That's a gorgeous little film that never comes together. It has two pretty people: Mickey Rourke all broken down and Megan Fox just coming into womanhood. It has Bill Murray, reprising the gangster he created for *Mad Dog and Glory (1993)*, jazz, the desert, a freak show, LA, a woman with wings. What's not to like? The realization of the script for one thing. And, ironically, the script itself for another.

Rent the movie and come back. We're going to fix it by making it clear that for most of the movie Mickey is dying or dead and that the entire film from the moment that Mickey is improbably rescued by Native American sharpshooters takes place on a plane between life and death.

As a comedy writer, Glazer has never had to trouble himself with thoughts about what is real and what is not. In fact, the unexpected is an essential element of comedy. But, in a movie that mixes comedy with surrealism, allegory and film noir, keeping things orderly — keeping images, characters and events on their proper plane — is what distinguishes the work of filmmakers like Fellini and Bergman from gutsy but unfinished efforts like *Passion Play*. The problem with *Passion Play* is that everything exists on the same plane. The viewer is forced to process everything in the movie — winged women who learn to fly, broken down musicians, miraculous rescues by Native American warriors, ironic dialogue, cool humor, incongruous locations — all on a plane that represents a gritty, slightly droll reality — in spite of the fact that the beat up, beat down, booze and drug-whacked brain of the Mickey Rourke anti-hero who rescues the winged girl and, in turn, is rescued himself, though not redeemed, seems perfect for processing alternate realities.

The quick fix for *Passion Play* is simple. It comes down to one shot. At the end of the film, Rourke is being transported in the arms of an angel. He looks down and, in a wide shot, sees his dead body, lying in a ravine and his murderer driving away. Glazer intends for us to realize at that moment that the film has been Rourke's experience of his transition from life to death — a dying hallucination that calls to mind the last scenes of Terry Gilliam's brilliant *Brazil (1985)*. What I need is a close shot of the body as Rourke leaves it behind to nail that moment of realization down in memory.

Glazer doesn't get close enough to Rourke's dead body to make that scene work. I need to see Rourke's dead face.

It would help to fade out on the Native Americans and fade in on Rourke, walking in the desert, to mark the transition to the dying hallucination earlier in the movie, too. And I'd cut the rest of the film in half. The arbitrary length of "feature" films has done in more than one first film.

I'd get Fox past the idea that she won't be taken seriously as an actress if she does nude scenes. I'm dying and I imagine Fox with her clothes on? Please.

That's the quick fix. A complete makeover of Glazer's beautiful but personal film would require too much work. The problem is that Rourke dies so early in the film that the revelation at the end of the film that the action has taken place on some spiritual plane feels like a clever gimmick. Frankly, I'm not sure I care enough about the Rourke character for it to make a difference to me whether he's dead or not. And does it really matter if the film is taken literally or not? Would anyone care if Glazer left out the shot of Rourke's dead body altogether? Is *Passion Play* some kind of filmic

Book Of The Dead, full of hidden images and code words scholars could spend years discovering?

It could be that the best news about *Passion Play* is that a film as personal and esoteric as *Passion Play* can even get produced. Or maybe it's that Megan Fox can act.

20 COMMENTS:

Tom Manoff said...

" Why not fix broken films? Why not start with the idea that what's missing in the world is a better version of a film somebody made or a book somebody wrote? Where does it say you have to start from scratch?"

I'm down with this big time. Make some version though discussion that makes the movie have another version or variant. That's the structuralist view — any myth can only exist in all its versions which include all variants by the tellers, critics, etc. All one Story. Like that *True Grit*, The "real" version includes both films and their reviews.

JUNE 21, 2011 AT 11:47 AM

Billy Glad said...

I like *Passion Play* better without the gimmick. I think of *Juliet of the Spirits* as the best example of the intersection of the spiritual and deadening reality planes. In *Brazil*, the moment of realization that Sam Lowry hasn't really escaped but just withdrawn from reality under torture is poignant and bitter, because you want him to escape. And, what I think of as one of the most clever exploitations of the thinks he's alive but is really dead gimmick, *The Sixth Sense*, involves a sense of redemption that is missing from *Passion Play*. The elements are there, but they never come together in a meaningful way. It needs to be more simply about freeing the angel who will carry him to the afterlife. That part of the myth is just too messy.

JUNE 21, 2011 AT 5:15 PM

quinn the eskimo said...

Great idea. Fix 'em up. Like *Tree of Life*. Just saw it. Wanted it to be great. Don't think it is, though I found it moving in places, even with all that "Texas" business. Perfect for fixing.

JUNE 24, 2011 AT 1:06 AM

Billy Glad said...

Funny you should mention Malick. For some reason I got the urge to watch *Days of Heaven* a couple of weeks ago. May have been because Manoff and I were talking about *mise-en-scène* — or maybe something in the air. Every now and then I look at the sitemeter details of visitors to the Hive. This morning, somebody got here by googling "is Mickey Rourke dead in Passion Play?" What kind of world lets caped crusaders and Nordic gods, wielding hammers, run free, but insists on gimmicks like dying fantasies to make films about angels "real?" What if it turns out that when we die we have to find the angels we abandoned as kids or lose our souls? The immortal soul. What an invention!

JUNE 24, 2011 AT 7:22 AM

GirlfromtheBronx said...

This is too funny. We play "Film Doctor" too! Mostly we recast the entire film when we think the actors chosen were inadequate. We also come up with much better endings too. It's amazing how many okay movies peter out at the end and make you feel like you just wasted two hours. And what about the sound in movies? Sometimes I think that 102-year-old deaf people are doing the sound. It goes from inaudible whispers to ear drum shattering levels within seconds. And what's with the music being so loud that you can't hear the dialogue?

JUNE 24, 2011 AT 3:22 PM

quinn the eskimo said...

I think the angels needed a bit more colour. Some primaries—yellow is nice—and I think they shoulda been written better roles. Same with souls. They're going to have to become something more playful, like the daemons in *The Golden Compass*, or just fa-fa-fade away.

JUNE 24, 2011 AT 4:34 PM

Billy Glad said...

I was thinking about sound when I was watching the new *True Grit*. Carter Burwell is such an enormous asset for the Coen brothers. And the daemons in the Golden Compass struck me a incredibly inventive, quinn. Big improvement on souls. Don't the Jews get out of all that immortality and soul garbage? How did they do that?

JUNE 24, 2011 AT 5:57 PM

quinn the eskimo said...

I think the daemon shows our culture struggling with new ways to "see" all this, but not sure of itself. Having an animal daemon is interesting, but does it signify more our "self," or is it closer to being an "other," like a totem? Reading Pullman, it felt more like my self. Seeing it in a film, two visual images, made it more totem, separate. Plus, we've all been taught that our truest natures, the ones God would take to heaven, are the bloodless ones—our non-physical, un-animal, ghostlike natures. However, our truest selves may actually be closer to how we are when we're pushed to be more animal, feral.

Then there's the world of online avatars and all that, so maybe we'll all just see our spirits as electrical sparks, or code.

JUNE 25, 2011 AT 11:18 AM

Billy Glad said...

Apparently, the planned sequel to *The Golden Compass* was killed by protests from the Catholic Church and other religious organizations, because Pullman's work is viewed as anti-religious. I didn't get that impression from the film itself, but, to tell the truth, I don't have a very clear idea of what the different sects will tolerate or not tolerate anymore.

If we are ever forced to live as our avatars, some of us are going to come out better than others. Just noticing.

JUNE 25, 2011 AT 12:54 PM

Tom Manoff said...

I'll add that avatars can show our demons....which is why I like a good one...

JUNE 27, 2011 AT 11:32 AM

Billy Glad said...

Uh huh. Right. At least you won't be stuck throwing up for all eternity like the chimp that used to hang out here.

JUNE 27, 2011 AT 1:12 PM

Tom Manoff said...

" We need to see Rourke's dead face."
Been seeing it for a long time, bless him.

JUNE 27, 2011 AT 9:10 PM

Billy Glad said...

The best thing about the end of the film is that if you look at the clip, look at Rourke's face as he touches his hat, just before he dives off the building, and, at that angle, for just a second, the young Mickey Rourke is there.

JUNE 27, 2011 AT 10:02 PM

GirlfromtheBronx said...

Has anyone seen *The Adjustment Bureau*? Does anyone think it needs the Doc? I enjoyed it as a summer, desperately looking for something to watch, entertainment kind of flick.

Maybe we need a Top 10 most in need of a fix list.

But I think the idea is not a film makeover, right Billy? Isn't the fix for basically good films that could have used a better eye to things? Cause I don't think the Film Doc wants to waste his time with hopeless cases.

Funny, when I want to come up with something for the category, I go blank. Maybe it's just summer malaise. Lots of that going around.

JULY 6, 2011 AT 5:58 PM

Billy Glad said...

You got that right, girl. Malaise. *Enuii*. The no dos. What difference does it make if those films get fixed or not? quinn wants a film fixed, he can fix it himself. Did you see Winter's Bones? I'm going to fix that one. Push Teardrop over the top instead of dialing him back. Soon as I get around to it. Or spend my time thinking about films that don't need fixing? Change them one iota and you diminish them. That's easier to do. *Valmont*. *The Sacrifice*. *Solaris*. And what about *Michael Clayton*? A first film!

JULY 6, 2011 AT 6:20 PM

GirlfromtheBronx said...

I'll be back. I gotta go whip up some Summer Malaise Spaghetti. Später Gator

JULY 6, 2011 AT 6:53 PM

Billy Glad said...

I've got arugula, cherry tomatoes and basil growing out back right now. I bring them all together in a good olive oil-based sauce with pasta and Parmesan cheese. I'll trade you for the recipe, girl.

JULY 6, 2011 AT 8:06 PM

GirlfromtheBronx said...

I'm bad. I do everything alla fast and furious. I'm a mix 'n match kind of cooker. A little bit of fresh, a little bit of canned or frozen and mix it all together for something that tastes okay. I doubt you'd really want to trade. I'd get the better part of the deal. Your fresh basil, arugula and tomatoes sounded great. But I did make a fabulous potato salad the other day all from scratch. My father's recipe.

Okay, back to film doctoring. I can remember *Dangerous Liasons* vividly but not *Valmont*. I guess that proves *Valmont* could use a visit from the Doc. And speaking of John Malkovich, have you ever seen *Color me Kubrick*? Just saw it a few weeks ago and was really taken with JM's performance. I haven't seen *The Sacrifice*.

JULY 6, 2011 AT 11:08 PM

Billy Glad said...

Valmont, *The Sacrifice*, *Solaris* and *Michael Clayton* are examples of films I wouldn't change. Interesting that you remember *Dangerous Liasons* while I remember *Valmont*.

JULY 7, 2011 AT 4:47 AM

GirlfromtheBronx said...

It could be that my ability to remember things in the last 10 years has become increasing difficult. Sometimes, I can't remember the name of a movie I saw a week ago. So, I'm sure that has a lot to do with it. And it seems that in present time I also have trouble with reading comprehension, too!

Here's what I do remember. The performances of each of the main characters in *Dangerous Liasons* and how the plot unfolded. I can still see specific scenes.

For *Valmont*, I remember Annette Benning best, then comes Meg Tilly. But for some reason, I don't recall how the plot unfolds. How whacked is that? I know I enjoyed it.

And I couldn't remember if I had seen *Solaris*. I had to go look it up. I did see it, but I couldn't come up with a reason to fix it. Since *you* are the Film Doc, I'm happy to see that we're on the same wave length!

JULY 7, 2011 AT 11:24 AM

Jonah Hex

It's easy to be dismissive of *Jonah Hex (2010)*, Jimmy Hayward's box office flop. The film grossed a meager 5 million bucks the weekend it opened, far behind *Toy Story 3 (2010)*, and was universally panned by reviewers. And not without good reason.

The plot is trite and hard to follow, the acting average, and most of the time Hayward's visualization of the comic book material is boring. Ironically, Hayward got his start in the *Toy Story* franchise. He was an animator on *Toy Story (1995)* and *Toy Story 2 (1999)*. But, watching Hayward's *Jonah Hex*, I was reminded of an old friend's put down of Midland, Texas. I spent a week there one night, he told me.

Josh Brolin, a talented and intelligent actor who has been on a roll lately, plods along in the title role. John Malkovitch seems to have dropped in for a couple of disconnected

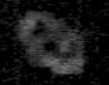

JOSH BROLIN
MEGAN FOX
JONAH HEX
2010

scenes. Malkovich can play villains like Quentin Turnbull, Hex's archenemy, in his sleep, but there is so little connection between him and Brolin that you have to wonder if they were ever on the same set at the same time.

Megan Fox is billed as a star, but comes across as a bit player, making a cameo appearance. Fox badly needs to make the transition from teenager to woman to put the *Transformer* franchise behind her, but in Hex she comes across as a kid, dressing up in her grandma's clothes. There is something about her voice that works against Fox. She hasn't learned to make the slight disconnect between her body and her voice work for her the way Monroe did. She came close in *Jennifer's Body (2009)* but lost it, or maybe a dialogue coach took it away.

Hex won't appeal to fans of the *Jonah Hex* comic books, either. The writers left too much good stuff out. Fox's Tallulah Black is a far cry from the disfigured female bounty hunter of the *Hex* books, and El Diablo and Lazarus Lane, two — or one, depending on how you look at it — of the books' most imaginative creations, are missing completely.

Unlike *Watchmen*, the seminal graphic novel that established the form, the *Hex* books spanned so many years and versions that the writers had to boil the comics down in an attempt to distill the essential Jonah Hex from the books. In deciding what to leave in and what to leave out, they invariably chose to use the most hackneyed elements of the comics.

The next blockbuster franchise and comic book superhero turned movie icon won't be *Jonah Hex*. And yet, for anyone who is interested in pop culture and genre films, *Jonah Hex* is an important movie. Jimmy Hayward has made a very bad film. But, in making it, he has — inadvertently, perhaps — tested the limits of turning graphic novels into films.

Jonah Hex looks exactly like what it is, a first film by a

director who knows absolutely nothing about the way real people move through real space. It ends up being a jumble of disconnected portraits, shots — panels, if you will — and, in memory, exists as an exact replica of a comic book. Watching *Jonah Hex* is like spending 90 minutes reading a graphic novel. No one will come closer to literally translating a graphic novel into film than Jimmy Hayward has.

But will anyone want to? Is thumbing through a graphic novel what most of us go to the movies to do?

Genre films, especially action-adventure films, require a compelling narrative and fast action. Action that is suggested by the static panels of a comic book must be realized in film. If you want to see what happens when a director ignores that basic truth, go see *Jonah Hex*. If not, save your money and catch *Watchmen (2009)* on cable TV.

Fantastic Mr. Fox

Fantastic Mr. Fox (2009) was released on DVD this week, and cable television is showing *Mr. Fox* as video on demand, another format that lets viewers pause the film or re-play scenes.

Wes Anderson has crammed so much visual information into every scene of *Fantastic Mr. Fox* that it's easy to make the case that the DVD or video on demand experience of *Mr. Fox* is even better than the experience of watching it on the big screen. Watching *Mr. Fox* in real time, you get the Richard Scarry feel of it, but until you freeze a frame, it's impossible to see all of the detail that's working to make *Mr. Fox* easily the most original visual experience among last year's films.

There are cave drawings from Altamira on the walls of the foxes' cave; strange books in Bean's kitchen. The long, traveling shot through Badger's Flint-Mine is too rich to take in all at once. The drawings of tunnels and sewers are like treasure maps, and Mrs. Fox's landscapes are wonderfully complex.

Anderson added characters and scenes to Roald Dahl's book to get the story of *Mr. Fox* up to feature film length. And that, unfortunately, is where Anderson stumbles. For Anderson's story, when all is said and done, disappoints.

In spite of a too familiar scene in which Mr. Fox protests that he loves his son just the way he is, when the young fox finally succeeds it's on his father's terms, not his own. And the other scene required for a PG audience — Mr. Fox's realization that he's not the center of the universe — seems contrived and lacking in irony.

But though he stumbles, Anderson does not fall. He finds redemption in the ending of his film, where up is down, in is out, and the happy ending turns out to be more dismal than it seems. Dahl's animals only end up stuck underground; Anderson's end up stuck in a supermarket.

Anderson's Mr. Fox imagines he's wild. But in the most poignant moment of the film, Anderson lets us see how domesticated Mr. Fox really is by showing us powerful images of a wild wolf — the only truly free animal in the film.

Stasis

What's fascinating about an academic like Stanley Fish deigning to share his views on the best American films with us is not so much his arrogance as it is his ignorance. But there are clues here about Fish and about the Obama world to come, so it's worth taking a minute to explore how far out of touch with reality selective perception can put us.

Here's Fish on *The Best Years Of Our Lives (1946)*, a William Wyler film that Fish considers the best American film ever made.

"The three intertwined stories are resolved with a measure of optimism, but with more than a residue of disappointment and bitterness. Al Stephenson is still a drunk. Fred Derry is still poor and without skills. Homer Parrish still has no hands."

Still. As in stasis. As in nothing has changed.

I think not.

Al may be a drunk, but he's a drunk making loans to GIs, based on their character and his own judgment. Fred may be poor and without skills, but he's not a soda jerk anymore. He's just landed a job beating swords into plowshares and building post-war America. And Homer Parrish may still have no hands, but, by the end of the film, it's Homer's girlfriend helping him into his PJs instead of his dad.

That's narrative. That's character development. And if it's not great film, it is solid literature.

Flip it on its head. If a guy like Fish can't see that the characters in a film he thinks is the best American movie ever made are changing in front of his eyes, can we expect him to see that Bill Ayers and Bernadine Dohrn, people he thinks are a couple of the solidist citizens around, haven't changed at all? They're still the over-privileged white kids who couldn't make it in the Civil Rights and anti-war movements and set out on their own, starting a two-bit, terrorist organization that ended up making zero difference, except to the people who got hurt and killed by the Weathermen. Just a couple of saps with a dumb idea who've never owned up to their sappiness or the dumbness of their idea.

Cut to Europe, where Government officials and Jewish leaders are concerned that the conflict in Gaza may spill over into violence in Europe as attacks are reported against Jews and synagogues in France, Sweden and Britain.

But, what the hell? Those people, according to Mr. Ayers' and Ms. Dohrn's code, are honor bound to attack those Jews, aren't they?

Years from now, they might even wish they had done more.

But don't get me wrong. I could care less about the Weathermen. I thought they were entertaining. I wasn't political in the '60s. By 1967, I had tuned in, turned on and dropped out. I wasn't looking for a street fight, I was looking for sex, drugs and rock and roll. I was looking for long hair, long legs and conical breasts that year. It was much later that I realized, stoned and watching Nixon on TV, that even the President Of The United States could go insane. Then panic set in until Tim Leary told me a few years later not to worry about the government, the people who were stealing hubcaps at the Atlanta film festival a couple of years ago were now running it. I decided to join them.

So you tell me. Should I worry about the Obama administration or not?

3 COMMENTS:

Cypher Blueman said...

At first it was hard to figure why this Fish guy and his list of movies annoyed me. It started with the *New York Times*. How does something like this Fish thing make it? I looked at the date. Christmas vacation. The grownup editors must have been on vacation.

The Fish likes the films of Billy Wilder. Who doesn't? But can Wilder survive the Fish? Fish writes about *The Best Years of our Lives*: "the movie is filled with thrilling and affecting scenes." Thrilling? When the wife realizes her husband is home from the war it's "thrilling?" Come on Fish. "Affecting" does it. "Thrilling" is a word you might save for a chariot race. Edit please.

Then he writes: "the movie ends with a residue of disappointment." Dude. Ya kinda missed the point. And this sentence about *Sunset Boulevard* actually made it into print at the Times? "But even before the final incredible scene of Desmond descending a staircase while the camera, empty of film, rolls, she has earned the sympathy we extend to the terribly needy, and he has revealed himself to be the true monster, a betrayer of Desmond, of the young girl who sees more in him than there is, and of himself." Yikes. Fish, I know that you know that Wilder, himself, of whom you speak in tones that are at once thrilling and affecting, was, at first, from Austria. So are you translating your own writing from the German?

Thrilling words keep a'coming. The father in *Shane* is characterized as "a tree-like Van Heflin." About *Red River* he writes: "brooding over all these characters is the cattle drive itself, a force both of nature and history." About *Vertigo*: "There's no getting to the bottom of this movie; its vertiginous." Christ. Is he putting us on?

Wait a minute, Blueman. Pull up. Where have you read crap like this before? There's something familiar in these words about *Red River*. "There are two triangles and one dyad." Now that's an odd line to read about a movie. And "dyad" isn't your everyday word even for the *New York Times*. Hey. It's dime store structural anthropology. Fish! You wouldn't be an academic by any chance?

He is. And ungifted. But I'm still annoyed. Something about the list. Something about how all these characters move thrillingly yet vaguely through binary oppositions as dyads.

Ah. Here it is at the end of his piece: "So there they are, 10 movies marked by sentiment and cynicism in equal doses, but with sentiment winning out more often than not." A rather cynical way to assess the best American movies of all time. They're great because sentiment wins out at the end.

Fish-dude! What about a moral? What about a narrative

that leads to a place of certainty, a point when the movie makes a case for right or wrong? There are more than a few movies on your list that do.

But the Fish ain't having none of it. The Fish ain't happy in Heaven nor Hell, but floating between, a dyad of "this-or-that" because neither matters. He's an elitist, our Fish. No accident that most of these films are half a century gone. Academic elitists are uncomfortable with the present, with what is close and populist. No accident that he prefers *Shane* to the *Unforgiven*. Our dyad-drinking professor wouldn't be caught dead nor alive with Clint.

By claiming sentimentality as the defining element in the best American movies of all time, Fish has missed what makes these films American.

I couldn't resist a Google on Fish. I found another of his articles. It seems he has a regular blog for the *New York Times*. I hear he was taken in by the Sokal Hoax. It all makes sense now. Darn dyads, dagnabit.

JANUARY 8, 2009 AT 7:25 PM

Billy Glad said...

Does he translate his own writing from the German? Pretty damn funny, Blueman. And the Sokal hoax is priceless. Working over these elite, ungifted but tenured academics with their two homes and their hidden agendas could keep us amused for years. Can we spare the time, or do we have bigger fish to fry? I say we let this fish off the hook. Put him in a footnote.

For me, your question about how a guy like Fish becomes a regular around the *Times* is fascinating. Obviously, if Murdoch gets his hands on the *Times*, that will come to a screeching halt. So I imagine the restructuring of the *New*

York Times will become a fight to the death between the Left and the Right to see who comes away with the Grey Lady.

JANUARY 9, 2009 AT 7:38 AM

Cypher Blueman said...

I feel guilty that I terminated my daily *New York Times*. I've read that thing since I was in 10th grade. Speaking of change, what high school today would assign editorials from the *Times* to 15 year olds?

We'll miss it if it goes down. And ideas will never have the possible gravitas that print imparts compared with the web. The Fish souffle is a sign of the downfall, with the underpaid and depressed editors drinking heavy Christmas grog while the 20-somethings run the shop.

JANUARY 9, 2009 AT 7:38 AM

You've Come A Long Way, Baby

Yesterday afternoon, I spent 15 minutes watching Fred Zinneman's 1977 film *Julia*. The film is based on a book by Lillian Hellman, author of *The Children's Hour*. Ms Hellman's relationship with Dashiell Hammet, the detective story writer, is pretty well known, as is the fact that she was a prominent and controversial, maybe a fascinating figure in the McCarthy saga. There are people around who know a lot more about that than I do.

I'm interested in the relationship between Hellman and

Hammet, Lilly and Dash, as portrayed by Fonda and Robards, that I caught a glimpse of yesterday.

I started watching at about the time Hellman is finishing her first play. Hammet sends her back to rewrite it. The second try meets his approval. It's a success on Broadway. She gets royalty checks, he gives her the benefit of his wisdom on the subject of money, fame and writing.

"Free me glazies!" Little Alex cried.

I can't explain why, but that piece of film literally made me sick to my stomach.

I won't inflict the needy, cloying Fonda and the smug, condescending Robards on you here. Be grateful for small favors.

7 COMMENTS:

Tom Manoff said...

When I saw the name Fred Zinnemann and I realized that I didn't know all of his movies. It's quite a list. Among them: *The Day of the Jackal*, *A Man for All Seasons*, *Oklahoma*, *From Here to Eternity* and *High Noon*. *Julia* is not one of my favorites, though, as you say, it does open the door on the relationship between Hellman and Hammett. There's a book of Hammett's letters which I ordered thinking about this. Two bucks plus shipping. What I remember most about the movie is the performance by Vanessa Redgrave, an actress I like quite a bit.

Lots of issues on the blacklist here. Hellman's famous book about it is *Scoundrel Time*, which has been criticized as self-serving and loose with the facts.

Hammett seems the most interesting person here, at least

to me, his writing so influential in what would become *film noir*.

MARCH 12, 2009 AT 6:40 AM

Billy Glad said...

I'm sure a director and actors of that caliber knew exactly what they were doing. The question is: Did Hellman?

MARCH 12, 2009 AT 6:56 AM

Tom Manoff said...

Do you mean Hellman as the author of the screenplay or her work in general?

MARCH 12, 2009 AT 7:35 AM

Billy Glad said...

As a viewer of the film. When you put your life story in someone else's hands, I wonder if you can ever be completely satisfied with the results.

MARCH 12, 2009 AT 7:39 AM

Tom Manoff said...

Looking up *Julia* on IMDB, I see that she wrote the novel not the screenplay. Following the links, I find that Alvin Sargent wrote the screenplay for *Julia*. Now he's a writer I like more than a bit. He wrote episodes of *Route 65* and *Naked City*. Films like *Ordinary People*, *Stalking Moon*.

Bobby Deerfield and more recently, two films I really like, *Spider-Man* 2 and *Spider-Man 3*. *Naked City* to *Spider-Man* with *Ordinary People* in the middle shows a real talent. Putting your life in the hands of a writer and director. Scary I would imagine. Wouldn't casting be the first issue?

MARCH 12, 2009 AT 8:26 AM

Billy Glad said...

I wonder if there is any public personality I like more than Jane Fonda. Probably the result of watching *Barbarella* in an altered state. I was pleased to discover that she has a web site.

MARCH 12, 2009 AT 6:40 AM

Billy Glad said...

I write, post, then edit constantly, confounding my critics.

MARCH 12, 2009 AT 6:40 AM

Madison Avenue

Madison Avenue hacks have been ripping off talented artists since the early days of advertising, but the ripoffs seem to get worse every year.

The people producing ads these days don't have the art historical references to understand the work they're ripping off. Their knockoffs aren't just unoriginal. They're bad.

The latest example is an AT&T ripoff of Christo and Jeanne-Claude. The producer probably saw an article about Christo and Jeanne-Claude somewhere — though I doubt he or she ever actually saw a Christo/Jeanne-Claude project — and figured it would be a good idea to make a visual pun on the word "cover" by showing buildings and other landmarks being draped in colored cloth.

This pretentious commercial, the latest in AT&T's ongoing "coverage" war with Verizon, is a good example of how man-

AT&T Blanket Commerci

Rethink Possi...

gled art turns up in advertising, and it could have some unintended consequences for AT&T. That's what they get. As every school child knows, you're not supposed to "touch the art." If AT&T rethinks anything, they should rethink this ad, before Verizon jumps on it with an ad that takes the wraps off.

I see people working in an office with big windows and a fantastic view. Some of them are talking on their cell phones. Suddenly, their windows are covered by falling drapes, the room gets dark and the cell phones stop working. We see AT&T covering buildings, cities, a beach. Everything stops until Verizon starts tearing down the drapes, uncovering buildings, rolling up the fabric covering the beach. The cell phones start working again.

If the ad person who produced the AT&T ad had actually experienced a Christo/Jeanne-Claude project, he or she might have realized that wrapping an object confines it, hides it, interferes with it, shuts it up and closes it in. Something wrapped is limited by the wrapping. It's the unwrapping that's the significant event.

Christo's *Valley Curtain* at Rifle Gap, Colorado. The size and shape of the "waves" are based on Coast Guard research and designed to evoke feelings of dread.

AT&T has had to remake their commercial and add a disclaimer, saying that Christo and Jeanne-Claude have nothing to do with AT&T. One more obnoxious commercial like this one and I'll join them.

Weaver Ants. From *The Superorganism* by B
Wilson, W.W. Norton, N.Y. with permission.

What are those ants doing? I never get tired of looking at them.

When I was making art, I was fascinated by metonymy, a figure of speech that substitutes one word for another word that it's closely associated with. Over time, the crown comes to stand for the king.

It is metonymy that gives documentary film and other forms of sympathetic magic their power over us. And it is metonymy that connects the unseen and unseeable theoretical concepts of science to their manifestations in the realm of the senses.

In the physical world, films and photographs are instantly metonymic. The weaver ants in the header stand for actual ants in a completely realistic and convincing way. The ants in the header may be suspended in time and space, immutable, undying, but, to our minds, they are real. And they are doing a real ant thing, a thing they were caught in the act of doing by the biologist who snapped their picture and generously gave us permission to use it here. They will continue to do that one ant thing and nothing else as long as the photograph lasts. They will not sting us to move us off their trail, they will not turn around and head in the opposite direction, and the major worker will not put the minor worker down. They will move forward together, always tending toward some place outside the frame of the photograph, but never getting there.

Now the scientist who took the picture of these weaver ants, Bert Hölldobler, knows as much about ants as anyone alive, and he tells us that what is literally going on in that picture is an example of the division of labor. What Professor Hölldobler's photograph shows is a major worker carrying a minor worker "to a place where the minor worker is needed for special work, such as attending honeydew-secreting homopterans or nursing small larvae."

That's the observable fact of the picture. The denotative meaning of it. But we do not live by metonymy alone.

Beyond metonymy, there is metaphor, a figure of speech in which a word that literally denotes one thing or idea is used in place of another to suggest a likeness. As metaphor, the picture of our ants points to something beyond itself. It refers to other things that it is like. And, as a picture that is a metaphor for something else, the more things it refers to, the more delightful it is. As metaphor, Professor Hölldobler's weaver ants are amazingly polyreferential.

Trust

I just got home from the experience of 5 hours of small-town American healthcare, watching my wife work her way through nurse practitioners, X-ray techs, X-rays and cat scans after her car was hit from the rear by an uninsured driver.

When we first moved to this little town, a neighbor recommended the clinic we go to. It's run by a religious organization. All of the doctors are missionaries who base here but travel to the underdeveloped world to heal the sick and spread the word of the Lord.

In the waiting rooms I sat in yesterday, I saw loops of Doctor Gupta explaining lung cancer, Wolf Blitzer reporting on the Iranian riots, and a painting of Jesus, guiding the hand of a surgeon. I thought the painting was the most interesting. I couldn't help imagining different versions of it and variations on its theme.

Maybe we could add Moses and Mohammed to the painting. Show Jesus and the other prophets — peace be unto them — jostling one another and arguing about how to guide the doctor's hand.

Or, we could show them guiding other hands. The bombadier's hand as he drops bombs on Pearl Harbor, Hiroshima or Dresden. Or the executioner's hand as he tightens a noose, lights a fire or slits a throat. How about a guiding hand at the gas chambers and ovens?

It must be comforting to believe that every slip of the knife is God's will.

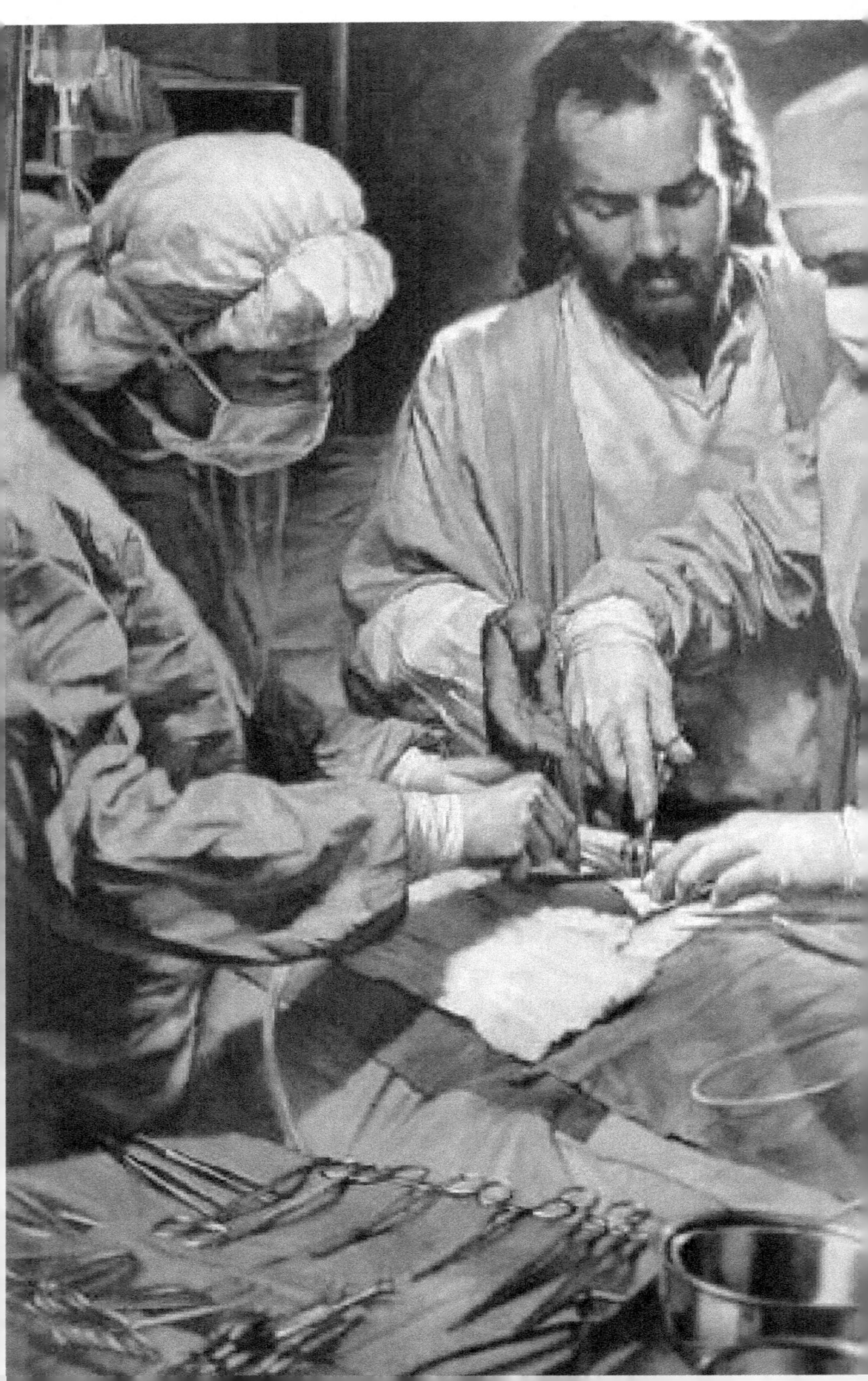

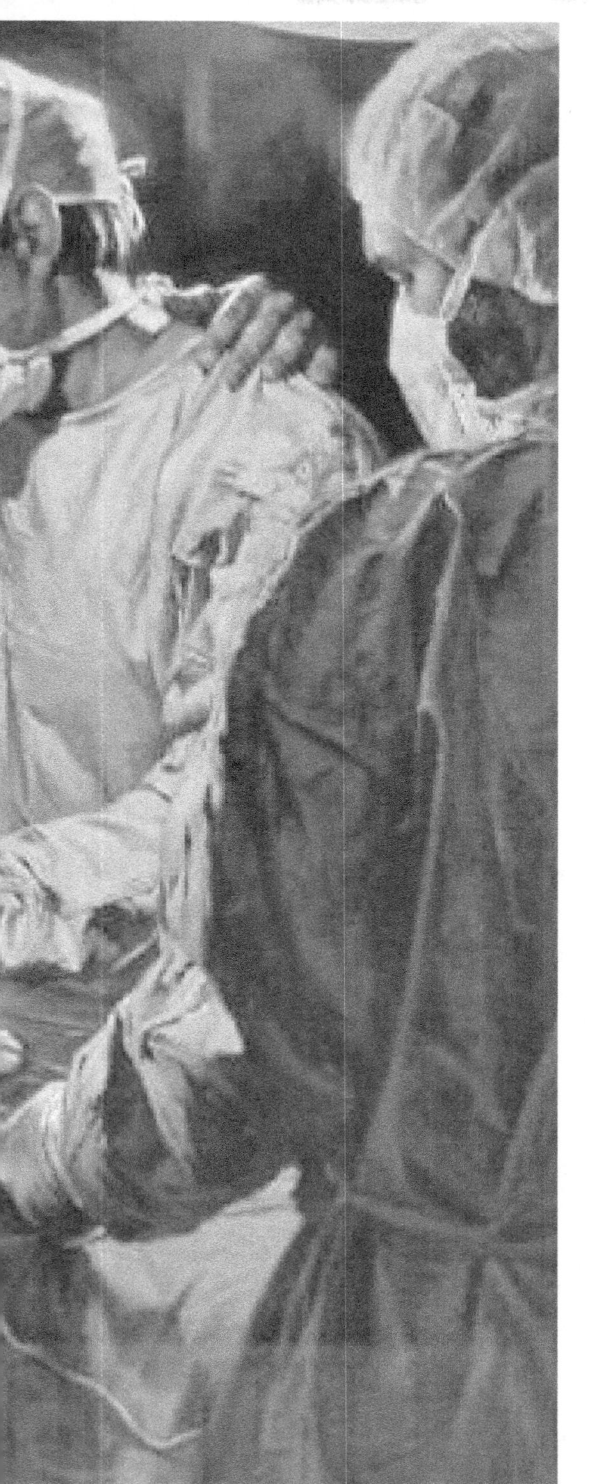

Outside The Echo Chamber

Thanksgiving is a good time to reflect on who we are, where we came from and where we're going.

Adam Goodheart has a Homer Winslow cartoon up on the *New York Times* opinion pages today, courtesy of the Smithsonian American Art Museum. The cartoon was published in *Harper's Weekly* in 1860.

I was struck by Goodheart's observation that "there is precious little celebration in Homer's tribute to the national holiday, let alone flattery of well-heeled Harper's readers."

Contrast that with Ted Koppel's "Olbermann, O'Reilly and the death of real news" at the *Washington Post*. Koppel, commenting on the echo chamber phenomenon so familiar to anyone who spends time in the blogosphere, notices that "we live now in a cable news universe that celebrates the opinions of Olbermann, Rachel Maddow, Chris Matthews,

THANKSGIVING DAY, 1860.—T

[GR]EAT CLASSES OF SOCIETY.

Glenn Beck, Sean Hannity and Bill O'Reilly—individuals who hold up the twin pillars of political partisanship and who are encouraged to do so by their parent organizations because their brand of analysis and commentary is highly profitable."

This analysis and commentary drowns television viewers in a flood of opinions designed to confirm their own biases. Commentators like Olbermann and O'Reilly "show us the world not as it is, but as partisans (and loyal viewers) at either end of the political spectrum would like it to be. This is to journalism what Bernie Madoff was to investment: He told his customers what they wanted to hear, and by the time they learned the truth, their money was gone."

Ironically, the Koppel piece at the *Post* is so cluttered with on-line ads and scripts, including an ad aimed at investors with at least a $500,000 portfolio, that it's practically unreadable. If it didn't confirm my own biases, I wouldn't mention it.

Receding Out Of Sight

Funny how the background/foreground thing works. I know that things that suddenly grab my attention are there in the background all the time and I don't notice them until something snaps them into focus, but I swear it seems like somebody sneaks them into the world when I'm not looking.

I've been rereading Sherwood's *Roosevelt and Hopkins: An Intimate History*, and the other day my wife was in the office, listening to Terry Gross interview Tim Weiner, author of *Enemies: A History of the FBI*. As I listened to the interview in the background, what struck me right off was that Ms. Gross, who may be the best interviewer who ever lived and is at the top of my list of people I'd like to interview, seemed to be having a hard time getting her head around the fact that J. Edgar Hoover may have done some things that needed to be done, and may have done them in the only way they could have been done. The way she closes the interview with a conversation between Hoover and L.B.J. makes me think she may have been giving me time to get my own head around that possibility.

I flipped to the index of Sherwood's book and found that Hoover was only mentioned twice: once in relation to a report the FBI sent Roosevelt about a dinner Hopkins attended in England, and again in relation to the fact that Hoover was decorated by the British after WWII "for exploits which could hardly be advertised at the time."

I've become convinced lately that I was born and grew up during America's very best years, between 1939, when America was finally coming out of the Great Depression and about to enter WWII, and the Seventies, when America began to fall apart. I'm sure other generations have felt and will feel the same way about their time in the sun; even my daughter, as she commutes in an armored SUV between her fortified apartment complex and her office in the secure zone — whatever color it is that year — may have the feeling that her America is the best America that ever was. But I think of the war years, the post-war boom of the Fifties and Sixties, and the rise and fall of the Counterculture as a rush to the top of the world, followed by a slow decline, a breaking up and drifting apart that has literally torn holes in the fabric of our society.

And I'm glad the generation that came before mine and included flawed men like J. Edgar Hoover held America together as long as they did, and sad that my own generation let go of her hand.

3 COMMENTS:

quinn the eskimo said...

I'm loathe to engage on this one. But I'm feelin' lucky. Hoover, for starters, is and should be burning in Hell. So there's that. And I don't buy that the disaster we see around us was created or developed by the Boomer generation. I think a lot of the crap we see was seeded by the very generation you praise. Whether it was a big military or multinational corporate money movements or an addiction to cheap imports or ads everywhere or putting off paying for things until tomorrow this stuff was created long before the Boomers. What's missing in this is that the Greatest Generation—the ones who actually fought WW2 and lived as adults through the joblessness and the Depression—were actually born pretty much in 1920 or prior, right? Which leaves us 20 years worth of people before the Boomers arrived. A generation. Those born roughly between 1925 and 1945. A group that never fought in WW2. A group that never fought unemployment during the Depression. And that group wanted stuff. They wanted stuff. Now. And they forged tools required to get it.

But now we Boomers gotta take the blame for the fall of America, Canada and the rest? Not sure I'm buying that. If anything, I think our generation has helped create what the future will see as the tools, the attitudes, the necessary ways forward. Thing is, it'll take another generation or two for those new tools and attitudes to finish their work.

FEBRUARY 22, 2012 AT 2:55 PM

Billy Glad said...

The generation before the Boomers was The Silent Generation. We lived in and enjoyed the world the Greatest Generation gave us, and along with the Boomers we mucked it up.

FEBRUARY 22, 2012 AT 2:59 PM

Tom Manoff said...

I have to think about this bastard. Easy for you to say. You weren't on the receiving side of the persecution. What counts is could that guy have done it within the Constitution, and even if not, to what degree will you allow him to terrorize citizens? Just because we weren't shot in the Gulag doesn't mean we weren't terrorized.

"J. Edgar Hoover may have done some things that needed to be done, and may have done them in the only way they could have been done."

Yeah. Needed to be done. It was great fun.

FEBRUARY 22, 2012 AT 4:01 PM

The Trouble With *Noir*

I've been thinking about Hollywood *film noir*: dark, edgy films from the Forties and Fifties. Moody. Quirky characters.

It occurs to me that *film noir* was connected in a special way to the *auteur* theory that French critics like Bazin pushed and that Andrew Sarris popularized writing for *The Village Voice*, if "popularized" is a term that makes sense in relation to esoteric subjects like film criticism and film history. But, for those of us who do find the cinema worth thinking about, it might be interesting to talk about how film noir fits the *auteur* theory, a way of talking about film history that insists that directors are the real authors of films — even Hollywood films — and that good directors have a style of filmmaking that is consistent throughout their body of work, and, in some cases, work over the same motifs again and again. On one hand, there is a Wells style, a Ford style, a Lang style, a Losey style and an Huston style, even a Bud Boetticher style that is unique and recognizable. On the other hand, some directors also deal with the same themes over and over. Arguably, preoccupation with the same themes throughout a body of work is a higher level of authorship than simply imposing elements of style on themes that change from film to film, depending on what the producers and the script writers come up with.

What I want to suggest is that the directors shine in *film noir*, precisely because the *film noir* screenplays are, generally, lousy.

Although any film that emphasizes cynicism, sex and crime can resemble *film noir*, the classic *noir* period spans the 40's and 50's and is closely linked to the detective fiction of the Depression and the following twenty years. The films are typically black-and-white and shot on location, often at night. Films like Huston's *The Maltese Falcon (1941)*, based on a novel by Dashiell Hammett, and Howard Hawks' *The Big Sleep (1946)*, based on Raymond Chandler's novel, exemplify the style. Neither Hammett nor Chandler worked on the screenplays for the films that were made from their books. John Huston, the director of *The Maltese Falcon*, wrote the screenplay for his film, but William Faulkner, Leigh Brackett and Jules Furthman, three writers who often worked with Hawks, collaborated on the script for *The Big Sleep*. It turns out that comparing the way *The Maltese Falcon* and *The Big Sleep* were made into films reveals some interesting things about the relationship between screenplays and novels, and about the *auteur* theory as well. Huston's authorship of *The Maltese Falcon* is not in doubt. He wrote and realized the screenplay that reduced the Hammett novel to film. Hawks' authorship of *The Big Sleep* doesn't seem to be quite as complete. I have to give some thought to that.

2 COMMENTS:

Anonymous said...

Dan Zukovic's *Dark Arc*, a bizarre modern *noir* dark comedy called "Absolutely brilliant...truly and completely different..." in Film Threat, was recently released on DVD through Vanguard Cinema and is currently debuting on Cable Video On Demand. The film had its World Premiere at the Montreal Festival, and it's US Premiere at the Cinequest Film Festival. Featuring Sarah Strange (*White Noise*), Kurt Max Runte (*X-Men*, *Battlestar Galactica*) and Dan Zukovic (director and star of the cult comedy *The Last Big Thing*). Featuring the glam/punk tunes "Dark Fruition", "Ire and Angst" and "F. ByronFitz Baudelaire", and a dark orchestral score by Neil Burnett. "Equal parts *film noir* intrigue, pop culture send-up, brain teaser and visual feast." — American Cinematheque.

APRIL 20, 2012 AT 12:21 PM

Billy Glad said...

In the Sixties, researchers fed spiders LSD, and the spiders wove crazy, misshapen webs. That was nothing compared to these drive-by, context sensitive ads thrown up by bots. This is what has become of the World Wide Web.

APRIL 20, 2012 AT 3:25 PM

From Novel To Film

There are several ways an *auteur* can turn a novel into a film. The easiest way, probably, is to ignore the book's characters and plot and recreate the "essence" of the book in film. Warhol's *Vinyl (1965)*, for example, captures the essence of the Anthony Burgess novel *A Clockwork Orange*, without burdening the film with Burgess's characters and plot. But that's probably not the most commercially successful way to turn a book into a film.

The commercially successful way, the Hollywood way, is to respect the narrative and characters of the novel and to recreate those elements with acting, cinematography, sound and editing in a way that "brings the novel to life." The quality of the novel, of its characters and plot, matter. If necessary, the film may deviate from the novel, but changes to the original are made in the spirit of improvement. Stanley Kubrick was faithful to Anthony Burgess's plot in his film version of *A Clockwork Orange*. Ridley Scott, on the other hand, probably intended *Blade Runner (1982)* to be an improved version of *Do Androids Dream Of Electric Sheep?* by Philip K. Dick. Scott's departures from Dick's narrative and characters were intended to produce a better, more successful story. In either case, the director creates the *mise en scène*, everything that you can't get by just reading the script.

The third way is to use the novel's characters and plot simply as a place to start, as something to wrap the film around. French New Wave directors bought the rights to dime store novels for their plots. Almost any plot would do, because the films they made weren't about the narrative. The story was beside the point. Art is synthesized experience. For filmmakers like Jean-Luc Godard, the story was just an occasion for that synthesis.

I think my preoccupation with the *auteur* theory and the director as auteur caused me to underestimate the role of the screenwriter in authoring films. Looking recently at the way Frank Nugent reshaped Alan Le May's *The Searchers* for John Ford raises the possibility that Nugent had as much to do with the recurring themes and the feel of Ford's work as Ford did. Ford's preoccupation with women as the carriers of civilization, for example, is completely absent in Le May. The way that Nugent introduced that and other Ford themes into *The Searchers (1956)* is an example of craftsmanship that's worth studying.

The fastest, most practical way into the motion picture industry for aspiring filmmakers is to begin by writing screenplays. In the Sixties and Seventies many of us gravitated to documentary films. They were easy to make with the equipment and people we had access to. A direct cinema documentary was something we could make by ourselves. A handheld 16mm camera and a compelling subject put us in the *avant-garde* of a long line of filmmakers, descended directly from the great Robert Flaherty. The problem back then was finding outlets and audiences for our work. And, for many of us, an even greater problem was finding a way to get from documentaries to feature films and the big screen. Direct cinema and *cinéma vérité* have evolved over the years. The dominant form nowadays is a kind of film essay that puts the filmmaker at the center of the documentary as witness, pundit and entertainer. YouTube has already made it possible for some film and video essayists to attain celebrity status. As video streamers struggle to fill almost limitless bandwidth, film and video essays may be a good way forward for beginning filmmakers with winning personalities and a flair for entertainment. The problem of finding outlets and audiences for documentaries may no longer exist. But the leap from essays to feature films will be as difficult to make as it ever was. The path from screenwriter to director is obvious and direct. But the path from novel to screenplay on the other hand is not as direct as I once imagined it was. The connection between novels and screenplays is complex. It goes beyond the simplistic idea that screenplays turn books into films. I wish I had spent more time thinking about how good screenplays are created and how they are turned into films. Any screenplay, it seems to me, whether it is based on a novel or written instead of a novel, is literary. It exists in the context of novels, other screenplays and even the writing we think of as history itself. The work of realizing a screenplay, the work of making it into a film, proceeds in that context. Good films are made by filmmakers who are able to bring more to a screenplay than is already there and by critics and viewers who are able to do the same. That's the boat we are in.

It Was Hemingway, I Think

I've always been fascinated by what writers have to say about writing, actors about acting, directors about directing. But I can think of only one good piece of advice I ever gleaned from all those interviews. It was Hemingway, I think, who said something like: The trick is to stop writing while you still know what's going to happen next.

2 COMMENTS:

Tom Manoff said...

Of course he killed himself.

MARCH 25, 2009 AT 8:50 AM

Billy Glad said...

Yes. Apparently, he knew what was going to happen next and decided on a different ending. I've often wondered how somebody gets to that place.

MARCH 25, 2009 AT 8:56 AM

Noir

I woke up early and went down to the Corner Bakery for a cup of coffee. I sat at the window, next to a table of Russians. I couldn't understand a word they were saying.

I was watching the raindrops race each other down the window, the big ones gobbling up the little ones that got in their way, and thinking about Raymond Chandler and *The Long Goodbye*, a Chandler book I'd been reading the night before, when it hit me that *The Long Goodbye* is Chandler's most personal and autobiographical novel.

They say Chandler's agent was disappointed by *The Long Goodbye*. He thought the Philip Marlowe character had gone soft. Personally, I think Marlowe comes across as more bitter and cynical than he is in Chandler's earlier work, and more political, more angry at the rich people who shaped the West Coast.

Noir

I woke up early and went down to the Corner Bakery for a cup of coffee. I sat at the window, next to a table of Russians. I couldn't understand a word they were saying.

I was watching the raindrops race each other down the window, the big ones gobbling up the little ones that got in their way, and thinking about Raymond Chandler and *The Long Goodbye*, a Chandler book I'd been reading the night before, when it hit me that *The Long Goodbye* is Chandler's most personal and autobiographical novel.

They say Chandler's agent was disappointed by *The Long Goodbye*. He thought the Philip Marlowe character had gone soft. Personally, I think Marlowe comes across as more bitter and cynical than he is in Chandler's earlier work, and more political, more angry at the rich people who shaped the West Coast.

CVS

Some people say: When you dream, everything in the dream is you. I've never looked at novels and films that way, but maybe I should.

Chandler died in 1959. He developed pneumonia after a binge.

The chronology that accompanies The Library of America's *Chandler (Stories and Early Novels)*, ends with: "1959 ... Returns alone to La Jolla where he intended to live. Drinks heavily, develops pneumonia, and is hospitalized on March 23. Dies in Scripps Clinic at 3:50 P.M. on March 26. Buried on March 30 at Mount Hope Cemetery in San Diego."

Robert Altman made a film version of *The Long Goodbye* in 1973. In a send-up of the detective genre, Altman cast Elliot Gould as a mumbling, bumbling Marlowe who talks to his cat.

The thing about *noir* in books and films is there is never enough rain for me.

8 COMMENTS:

Tom Manoff said...

Well, I feel the same. So is there such a thing as a "*Noir* Soul?"

APRIL 12, 2011 AT 12:20 PM

Billy Glad said...

There must be. Here is the passage made me think the book is autobiographical. Why I can't say.

"What sort of guy is he sober?"

She smiled. "Well, I'm rather prejudiced. I think he is a very nice guy indeed."

"And how is he drunk?"

"Horrible. Bright and hard and cruel. He thinks he is being witty when he is only being nasty."

"You left out violent."

APRIL 12, 2011 AT 9:50 PM

Tom Manoff said...

I always thought I'd interview Lumet. Thought of you when he died last week. I wonder who's left that I'd better get to before the end. I thought about asking Sean Penn for an interview on the blacklist and acting. The worst he could do is say no. Are all the directors of that generation gone now?

APRIL 13, 2011 AT 4:33 PM

GirlfromtheBronx said...

That's a great picture, Billy, and when you write I can smell the sidewalk.

APRIL 13, 2011 AT 11:05 PM

Billy Glad said...

It's a funny thing, girl. I grew up reading Chandler, Mickey Spillane and Rex Stout. I still have all of Chandler's and Spillane's books, and I reread them every five or six years, for comfort maybe. I think Spillane has influenced the graphic novel and comic book writers who create dark, violent superheroes. He and Chandler certainly influenced me.

APRIL 14, 2011 AT 9:10 AM

Billy Glad said...

Jesus, Tom. I think they may all be dead now. Sean Penn would be a good interview all right. He's in a class by himself. Clint Eastwood, too.

APRIL 14, 2011 AT 9:17 AM

Tom Manoff said...

Name a movie from the last several years that stands up to something like a *Doctor Zhivago*, an epic that occasionally dips into *noir* shadows for contrast. But skip the *noir* aspect. Just name something you really can put on the same level.

APRIL 16, 2011 AT 2:13 PM

Billy Glad said...

I like *Zhivago*, but I don't watch it as often as I watch some other films. I suppose the others hold up better for me. I'm not a big fan of Lean's. And I actually prefer *Lawrence of Arabia* to *Zhivago*. Recently? I'd say Oliver Stone's *Alexander* and Ridley Scott's *Body of Lies* hold up for me. Also *Kingdom of Heaven*, another Ridley Scott film. I like places where the desert goes down to the sea. I'm afraid I won't be visiting any now.

APRIL 16, 2011 AT 4:59 PM

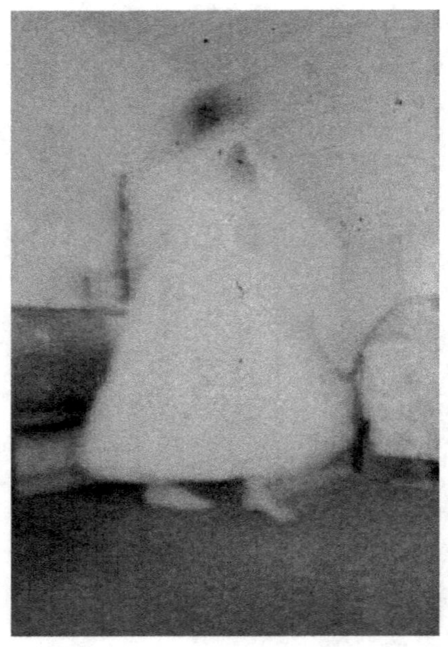

Foreclosed Spaces

Spaces retain the imprints of the people who once occupied them long after the people have moved on. This is true of rooms and ruins above and under the ground, of large and small spaces alike.

5 COMMENTS:

GirlfromtheBronx said...

I have this weird thing that happens to me whenever I sleep in a hotel. The first night or two in a strange place or hotel, I dream about people, places and things that have absolutely nothing to do with my life. I call it "dreaming other people's dreams."

MARCH 24, 2009 AT 10:23 AM

Billy Glad said...

I'll watch out for that next time I'm sleeping in a strange place.

MARCH 24, 2009 AT 10:56 AM

GirlfromtheBronx said...

Okay, here's the part I left out. I wrote this last night and shut down my computer. I thought I'd think about whether I should post it or not. My husband was already asleep when I wrote it. As I was watching David Letterman, he wakes up for a second and leans over and mumbles "hey dream girl" and in this half asleep state, starts singing that 50's song with the refrain, Dream, dream, dream, dream.

MARCH 24, 2009 AT 1:52 PM

Billy Glad said...

You probably need to take a chicken and some holy water to that house. The bedroom anyway.

MARCH 24, 2009 AT 2:07 PM

GirlfromtheBronx said...

Okay, Billy, this is really getting weird. I just received an email from an old friend who says to me: "You popped into my dream the other night. You had strangely become the mother of my friend's 2-year-old I was babysitting. That's all I remember." One more and I'm walking myself over to the psych ward!

MARCH 24, 2009 AT 4:28 PM

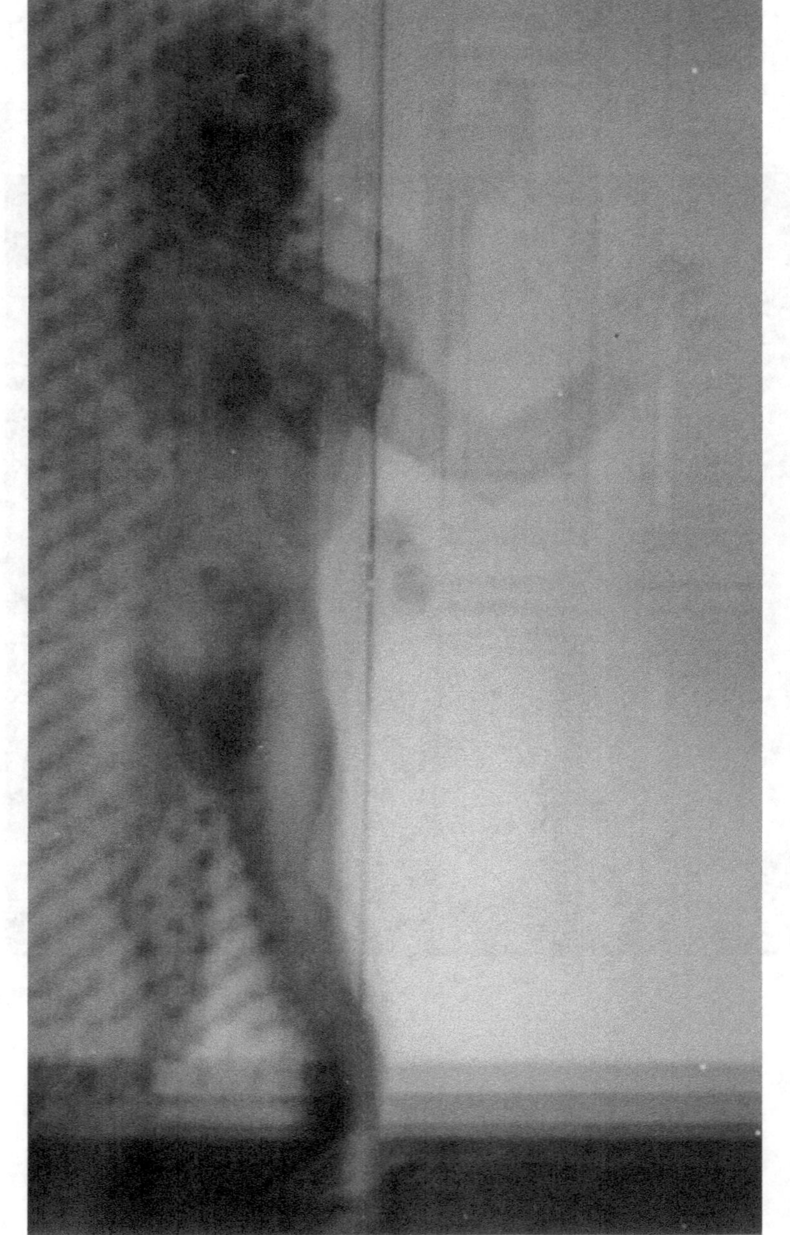

Public Broadcasting

Yesterday, I was listening to some kind of NPR afternoon concert on the car radio while I waited for my daughter to get out of school, and I had the satisfying experience of realizing I knew the opera I had tuned in on was by Wagner. The long, melodic baritone solo in German, joined by a chorus at the end, had to be Wagner. Did he ever compose voices singing in harmony? Maybe he did, but all I remember are conversations. When the piece ended, I found out I had been listening to *Die Meistersinger von Nürnberg*, and it struck me that there are people who would have immediately recognized the opera, the baritone and the conductor as well, maybe even remembered the exact date of the performance. But I don't need to know that much to enjoy, at some level anyway, a few minutes of Wagner on a bright Thursday afternoon while I wait for my daughter to come out of school. I just have to have a radio of some kind and tune it to my public radio station, or some other station that broadcasts classical music. As long as those stations exist. As long as nobody comes along and decides classical music is a waste of time. A waste of money. The same goes for Public Television, doesn't it? Anyway, I think it does.

I've been trying to remember the programs I saw in Austin the night PBS programming came on the air in 1969. No luck so far. There was something about Joplin and Hendrix about that time, but I don't know if I saw it that first night.

I saw some good things on PBS. Sometimes, I wonder why they don't pull out all that tape and put together a week-long best of PBS. I remember Orson Bean in *The Star Wagon*, singing Jerusalem, telling his sidekick Hoffman as long as I've got a dollar, you've got fifty cents. Krishnamurti. Alan Watts in the afternoon. Documentaries like *High School (1968)*.

I was at Arden House in New York at a Corporation For Public Broadcasting bash for documentary filmmakers the night Richard Nixon cracked down on PBS and the CPB. Rumor had it the disaster had something to do with Frederick Wiseman's *Basic Training (1971)*. I never found out. But after that week it seems to me the story of PBS has been the saga of a long, slow climb back into the light. It still has a long way to go.

6 COMMENTS:

GirlFromTheBronx said...

I still have a tremendous amount of regret for having squandered many opportunities to hear *The Ring* for free while living in Germany. Politics won out here. It was only at the very end of my time there that I allowed my political responses to recede to open up some space to appreciate the music. I never turned back. It may take a week for me to get to the other topics in this post.

MARCH 13, 2009 AT 10:58 AM

Billy Glad said...

We used to see *The Ring* in Seattle when a few people still dressed for it. Sat front row center in the seats they roped off and put fire and smoke warnings up for the night of *Gotterdammerung*. I really love Wagner. I could watch the conversation between the Wanderer and Alberich in *Siegfried* a thousand times. Ominous fate. When I think of that word, I think of the Wanderer. Foreboding. Cruel. Connecting that to the Nazis is like opening the door of a white hot furnace. Not even your bones can survive.

MARCH 13, 2009 AT 11:13 AM

GirlFromTheBronx said...

Amazing how many great artists have been tainted for many of us because of their ties to the Nazis. Wagner is still such a hard pill to swallow for so many Jews. His anti-semitism is indisputable. I have friends, Holocaust survivors, who when flying to Europe, refuse to do any connecting flights in Germany that would force them to step foot into that country. Too much pain.

So I did my part in boycotting all Wagner while in Germany. But then one day, a Jewish colleague and I were assigned to sing two of the nine *Walküries*. We both thought long and hard about it.

We ended up doing it and had the time of our lives. Neither one of us had big Wagnerian voices. But screaming our heads off, making love to our steeds, and running around with our spears, singing that incredible music. Man, it was amazing!

MARCH 13, 2009 AT 3:01 PM

Billy Glad said...

You should have sung Brunhilde, refusing to obey Wotan. It's clear Wagner thought of the Jews as Nibelungen. Coppola used the music brilliantly to convey the US Army's attitude toward the Viet Cong. Or I guess I should say he made it available to me so I could make that connection if I wanted to.

MARCH 13, 2009 AT 3:21 PM

GirlFromTheBronx said...

Great scene in the movie. I remember the first time I saw it. Getting back to metaphor and metonymy for a minute here. I assume we can consider this an example of metaphor. But it's still hard for me to grasp completely. I imagine metaphor and metonymy can be in the eyes of the beholder? No? I mean isn't it possible that person A, unfamiliar with Wagner's politics might hear the music as simply beautiful and as a result inelegantly applied to a horrific moment? Then person B, who is relatively familiar with Wagner's politics might likely transfer only the Nazi connection to indicate power over the victims and nothing of the symbolism inherent in the Ring. And the next person C, more familiar with Wagner and the Ring, would go as far as you did and supply the connection of the Nibelungen to the American attitude.

So, is person C on his/her way to metonymy when the images and connections they bring from what they know about Wagner and the existing metaphoric links from *The Ring* are applied to that scene? Is that more like the river and the workers in Pudovkin's film, but done in the mind of the viewer?

MARCH 14, 2009 AT 8:37 AM

Billy Glad said...

If you don't have any other associations, it's just thrilling music playing while things get blown up. Could be it's based on fact of some kind, too, though I doubt it. All that Wagner/Nibelungen/Jews/VC stuff is going on in my noodle. Whether it was in Coppola's, too, is anybody's guess. In Pudovkin's case, you don't have to guess. He puts the river and workers together in the same shot in a way that tells you what he means.

MARCH 14, 2009 AT 1:07 PM

Jasmine

My Night Blooming Jasmine has started to bloom already. I have two big plants in pots in my sun room. I bring them inside in the Fall and put them back out on the porch in the Summer. They've never bloomed this early before. It's amazing to sit in my sun room in the evening, look out at the moonlit snow and smell Jasmine. I just have one little cluster of about 10 flowers on one plant, which is lucky, since my wife hates the smell. But I grew up with it. One whiff transports me back to hot summer nights in Galveston, Texas, reminds me of the warm waters of the Gulf Of Mexico, brings back the heavy scent of the perfume on the necks of the girls I held in the back seat of my old man's Pontiac. I worry about what kinds of smells my young daughter is going to remember from her childhood, growing up in Wisconsin. Wood fires maybe. Other Winter smells. But Jasmine, too, come to think of it. She loves it. She tears off one flower every night and takes it to her room.

The End of Time

As I near the end of my own time, Updike's *Toward The End Of Time* provides a kind of reference point for me. I've outlived Harry Angstrom. Ben Turnbull, Updike's 66-year-old ex-financier, failing in body and mind, is my benchmark now.

Ben lives in an alternate future that features Al Gore as a former President, nuclear war with China, the collapse of the federal government and security services from FedEx. The latter makes sense. They have the trucks and people, and they know the neighborhoods. I've often thought FedEx or UPS should deliver our bombs for us. Problem is, I suppose, that, as international corporations, they might take contracts from other countries, too, maybe even contracts to turn around in mid-flight and drop our bombs on us.

One of the permissions Updike gives us is to treat fiction

as fiction. After all, centaurs and witches are no less believable than FedEx providing security in the absence of police or rich old Ben Turnbull consorting with teenage whores as he works through a dying marriage and approaches his inevitable confrontation with impotence and incontinence, unless death intervenes first.

1 COMMENT:

artappraiser said...

Every time I see Updike's name and whatever new thing he is up to, I think of how when he is gone people will wonder why we did not better recognize a giant of American culture walking among us. I suppose Twain was taken for granted in his time, too, as was Dickens in another culture. He's the real thing. Tom Wolfe, for example, is a pitiful charlatan in comparison, and that's coming from someone who enjoys much of Wolfe's work. Unlike many of his generational colleagues like Pynchon or Doctorow or Connell, there is nothing precious about his work. It's not "literature." It is all American. I don't know if he holds secrets as much as he is continually seeking them out. I think his interest in writing on American visual art is part of that.

DECEMBER 15, 2008 AT 10:33 PM

I'm On My Own

John Updike is dead. Who'll keep me company over the next 20 years or so?

1 COMMENT:

Cypher Blueman said...

I liked the end of the New York Times Updike obit.

His standing within the literary community may never have been greater than in 2006 when he delivered a passionate defense of bookstores and words, words on paper, at publishing's annual national convention. Responding to a recent New York Times essay predicting a digital future, he scorned this "pretty grisly" scenario and praised the paper book as the site of an encounter, in silence, of two minds.

"So, booksellers," he concluded, "defend your lonely forts."

JANUARY 27, 2009 AT 9:03 PM

In Conclusion

I'm thinking about turning my attention to the Hollywood studio system. I'm even thinking of defending the studio system against promiscuous "*auteurism*." I suspect the studio system may be our best chance to maintain some semblance of quality in film by acting as a gatekeeper, a bestower of some kind of "Good Housekeeping Seal of Approval," an imprimatur that narrows our viewing options to an almost manageable way too many when streaming kicks into high gear.

That's a role critics have played in the past and the *auteur* theory was the perfect instrument for separating the wheat from the chaff, the quality art from the kitsch. But in a streaming world of dozens of streamers and tens of thousands of directors, concentrating on the work of a handful of *auteurs* seems, well, limited. And the number of true *au-*

teurs may be much smaller than some critics believe. Many so-called *auteurs* only made the list in the first place, because we stretched the definition of authorship.

I still believe there have been, are and will be *auteurs*, but my take now is that only makers like Ingmar Bergman, Pier Paolo Pasolini, John Cassavetes and others who write their own screenplays as well as realize them should be considered authors of films. That reduces the candidates for the exalted status of *auteur* considerably. "Pantheon" directors like John Ford who primarily realized scripts written by other makers, would be immediately demoted, directors like Tarantino, Wes Anderson, Paul Thomas Anderson, Terence Malick, young Greta Gerwig, Francis Ford and Sofia Coppola, Kubrick, and Oliver Stone would be promoted and directors like Scorcese, Cameron, Bigelow and Scott would become questionable *auteurs*. Certainly someone like Antoine Fuqua would never make the cut. But wait.

About fifteen years ago I missed *King Arthur (2004)* when it was first released. There are probably a number of reasons I wasn't interested in seeing it, primarily, I think, because I had no great interest in Fuqua the director. I had seen *Training Day (2001)* but wasn't particularly impressed, and I probably counted Fuqua's music videos against him. But why I dismissed Fuqua's film doesn't matter really, because if I had seen *King Arthur* in 2004 I would have seen an entirely different film from the one I saw one evening last month when I was bored, clicking through the movies on Cinemax, and decided to give *King Arthur* a look.

Back in 2004, I hadn't read Kazuo Ishiguro's *The Buried Giant* and tried to imagine ways Ishiguro's foggy Arthurian England could be rendered on film. And, although it was first published in 1956, I hadn't read Winston Churchill's *A History of the English-Speaking Peoples* yet either. When I read the first volume, I realized the history of the Saxon conquest of England was as vague as the memories of Ishiguro's characters in *The Buried Giant*. The Fifth Century generally is a murky, empty space, lost in time and waiting to be filled.

This was in my mind when I had my first look at Fuqua's *King Arthur*. I've watched it three times now and I still can't explain why I am so intrigued and, yes, moved by the film. I understand some of it. I was struck by how much *King Arthur* resembles a John Ford Western set in the darkness, grime and poverty of Fuqua's 5th Century England, not just because of the similarities between King Arthur's knights and Ford's cavalry officers and cowboys, but also because Fuqua uses portrait shots of his characters to freeze them in time and in our memories the way Ford did, and even goes John Ford one better by using portrait-like close-ups of King Arthur's knights to transform them from Romans to Sarmatians and to restore them to the Middle East at the end of his film.

King Arthur is a striking example of the way the confluence, the synthesis, of film and literature creates a rich experience for viewers who can bring something of their own to a film. Fuqua's portrayal of the Romans, Britons and Saxons fits my picture of the Britons, Arthur, his knights and the Saxons in *The Buried Giant* and in Churchill's history better than the Medieval rendition of those characters in typical Arthurian films. Fuqua's *mise-en-scène* is, for me, poignant. Like all great myths, the legend of Arthur never fails to entertain. And Fuqua's *King Arthur* is a dark and fascinating retelling of that myth. But was it Fuqua the director who did all that, and if it was, how did he get to that place?

King Arthur is a Jerry Bruckheimer production, based on a screenplay by David Franzoni. Without interviewing them it's impossible to know if the *King Arthur* project originated with Bruckheimer or Franzoni, but almost certainly it did not originate with Fuqua. And that's the point. In the case of *King Arthur*, the track records of the producer and the screenwriter are better guides to the quality of the film than the *oeuvre* of the director. And that's very neat, because it is going to be easier to keep track of and predict the quality of the work of production studios than it is to get a handle on the talent of individual makers of streaming film and video, especially if the studios and streaming services step up to the job of making sure that "the quality goes in before their names go on."

For the would-be makers of screenplays and films, information about how the studio system works, how projects are conceived and realized in the real world, will become an increasingly essential part of their education. Surprisingly, just when an explosion of bandwidth makes it easier than ever to make and distribute independent films, studios may become more important to filmmakers and audiences than they were in the heyday of Hollywood.

Everything old is new again. (Hat tip to Peter Allen.)

Lists

Films

Bambi (1942), Storm Warning (1951), The Story of Bob and Sally (1948), Peter Pan (1953), Peter Pan on NBC (1955), Scorpio Rising (1963), Blow-Up (1966), Juliet of the Spirits (1965), Persona (1966), The Loved One (1965), Vinyl (1965), Godzilla (1954), Kiss Me Deadly (1955), Rome (2005 - 2007), Game of Thrones (2011 - 2019), The Searchers (1956), The Sopranos (1999 - 2007), Lonesome Dove (1989), Angels in America (2003), In Harm's Way (1965), Sleep (1963), Blow Job (1963), The Keepers (2017), Rise Of The Planet Of The Apes (2011), The Best Years of Our Lives (1946), The Terminator (1984), Terminator 2: Judgment Day (1991), 12 Monkeys (1995), Planet of the Apes (1968), The

Star Wagon (1966), Shadows (1959), Faces (1968), A Woman Under the Influence (1974), The Killing of a Chinese Bookie (1976), Opening Night (1977), A Constant Forge: The Life and Art of John Cassavetes (2000), The Seventh Seal (1957), Wild Strawberries (1957), And God Created Woman (1956), Cries and Whispers (1972), A Passage to India (1984), Doctor Zhivago (1965), Tunes of Glory (1960), Equus (1977), The Hurt Locker (2008), Avatar (2009), Transformers: Revenge of the Fallen (2009), Aliens (1986), The Abyss (1989), The Mission (1986), Dances With Wolves (1990), Forbidden Planet (1956), Dr. Strangelove Or How I Learned To Stop Worrying and Love the Bomb (1968), Metropolis (1926), 2001: A Space Odyssey (1968), Colossus: The Forbin Project (1969), Westworld (1973), Demon Seed (1977), Alien (1979), Blade Runner (1982), Robocop (1987), Aliens (1986), Alien (1979), Grey Gardens (1975), Gimme Shelter (1970), Grey Gardens (2009), The War Room (1993), Salesman (1968), Inside Job (2010), Triumph of the Will (1935), Harvest of Shame (1960), Exit Through The Gift Shop (2010), GasLand (2010), Supersize Me (2004), Religulous (2008), A Boy And His Dog (1975), Restrepo (2010), Combat Obscura (2019), Roma (2018), The September Issue (2009), The Devil Wears Prada (2006), A Star is Born (1976), Harvest of Shame (1960), Even the Heavens Weep: The West Virginia Mine Wars (1985), The Most Dangerous Man in America: Daniel Ellsberg and the Pentagon Papers (2009), Goin' Down the Road (1970), Mother (1926), State Fair (1945), Laura (1944), Modify (2005), Ilsa: She Wolf Of The SS (1975), Planet of the Apes (1968), Rise of the Planet of the Apes (2011), Man On Fire (2004), I Am Legend (2007), The Omega Man (1971), The Green Hornet (2011), Dragon: The Bruce Lee Story (1993), Armageddon (1998), Passion Play (2010), Mad Dog and Glory (1993), Brazil (1985),

True Grit (1969), *True Grit (2010)*, *The Sixth Sense (1999)*, *Tree of Life (2011)*, *Days of Heaven (1978)*, *The Golden Compass (2007)*, *The Adjustment Bureau (2011)*, *Winter's Bone (2010)*, *Valmont (1989)*, *The Sacrifice (1986)*, *Solaris (1972)*, *Michael Clayton (2007)*, *Dangerous Liaisons (1988)*, *Color Me Kubrick (2005)*, *Jonah Hex (2010)*, *Toy Story (1995)*, *Toy Story 2 (1999)*, *Toy Story 3 (2010)*, *Watchmen (2009)*, *Fantastic Mr. Fox (2009)*, *Julia (1977)*, *The Day of the Jackal (1973)*, *A Man for All Seasons (1966)*, *Oklahoma! (1955)*, *From Here to Eternity (1953)*, *High Noon (1952)*, *Route 66 (1960 - 1964) and Naked City (1958 - 1963)*, *Ordinary People (1980)*, *The Stalking Moon (1968)*. *Bobby Deerfield (1977)*, *Spider-Man 2 (2004)*, *Spider-Man 3 (2007)*, *Barbarella (1968)*, *The Maltese Falcon (1941)*, *The Big Sleep (1946)*, *A Clockwork Orange (1971)*, *The Long Goodbye (1973)*, *Lawrence of Arabia (1962)*, *Alexander (2004)*, *Body of Lies (2008)*, *Kingdom of Heaven (2005)*, *High School (1968)*, *Basic Training (1971)*, *Training Day (2001)* and *King Arthur (2004)*.

Influencers

The Yellow Dwarf, *Phaethon*, mothers of friends, other older women, L. Rust Hills, a museum director's Greek wife, Larry McMurtry's creative writing teacher, Wyatt Earp, Mike Hammer and Rick Deckard, one Texas Tech English professor who knew his stuff, Crazy Horse, Michael Tracy, Clarence Ayres, the Castillo family, a first reader at the Scott Meredith literary agency, an editor at Avon Books, Walter Lee Younger, Kimani Wa Karanja and Eddie Cook, Harry Bridges, Malcolm, Robert Capa, Elizabeth I, the Catholic Church, the United States Army, Galveston, Texas, the Gulf of Mexico and the Southwest, my draft board, Sandoz Pharmaceuticals and Panama Red.

Places and Things

The water holes in the desert around Fort Davis, Texas, on the San Antonio-El Paso Road, Galveston, Lubbock, Ciudad Acuna, Austin, Houston, Baumholder, Frankfurt, Denton, Conway, Arkansas, Washington, D.C., New York City, Seattle, Vietnam on television, in books, films and in the press, the Vietnam War memorial, Texas Tech, UT Austin, *The Overseas Weekly*, North Texas State, KUHT-TV, my '65 Plymouth Barracuda, my 1982 Ford Mustang and my 1993 Toyota 4Runner, my Canon F-1 35mm black top SLR, Eclair 16mm cameras, Nagra recorders, Steenbeck editing tables, Sheboygan, Wisconsin and Saint Joseph, Michigan, King Kong on top of the Empire State Building, my Buck knife, a .30-06 Springfield rifle I sold but can't remember why, Levis, Timberland shoes and Izod Lacoste shirts, La Rumba, the Omar Khayyam, Jeffrey's, Leon's World Famous BBQ, Gaido's on the beach, Gulf shrimp, speckled trout, Chablis, Le Chambertin, the Buffalo River, the winter wind in NYC, the hawk in Baumholder, my school of Yukimitsu tanto, poppies, Mack Trucks, hurricanes, kerosene lamps, baseballs, bats and gloves, neatsfoot oil, folded caps, shortstop and second base, night blooming jasmine and grounded freighters looming in the dark.

Credits

22	Ginger Rogers, *Storm Warning*
28	Norman Mailer, *Advertisements for Myself*
29	Pauline Kael, *I Lost It At The Movies*
29	Alfred North Whitehead, *An Introduction To Mathematics*
29	Tom Wolfe, *The Painted Word*
31	B.H. Friedman, *Jackson Pollock: Energy Made Visible*
32	Marshall McLuhan, *Understanding Media: The Extensions of Man*
36	*The Star Wagon*, WNET and NET Playhouse
54-56	*Equus*, United Artists
61	Martha P. Nochimson, "Kathryn Bigelow: Feminist pioneer or tough guy in drag?", *Slate*, February 25, 2010
66-67	*The Hurt Locker*, Voltage Pictures
75	Sandy Cohen, "Avatar returns to 3D theaters with 9 min. additional footage", The Associated Press, August 26, 2010
76	*Avatar*, Twentieth Century Fox
81	Associated Press, February 12, 2010 2:23 PM
88	The Cyborg, *Terminator 2: Judgment Day*, Carolco Pictures
92-93	Maysles Films, Inc.
96	HBO Films
102	*Vogue*, September 2007
106-107	Annie Leibovitz for *Vogue*, September 2007
108-109	Mario Testino for *Vogue*, September 2007
112-113	*The September Issue*, A&E IndieFilms and Actual Reality Pictures
144-145	Elizabeth Rubin, "Battle Company Is Out There", *New York Times Magazine*

147 Jon Krakauer, *Into The Wild*

164 Billy Glad 2019, Photograph by Kate Glad, Drawing by Suzanne Berberet

200-201 Condom

204-205 Lang Lang

211 The Associated Press, May 28, 2010 10:02 AM

212 Jane Mayer, “The Predator War”, *The New Yorker*, October 26, 2009

235 The Associated Press, April 20, 2011 10:15 AM

244-245 *Rise of the Planet of the Apes*, 20th Century Fox

247 David Denby, “Noble Creatures”, *The New Yorker*, August 29, 2011

252-253 Jennifer Lawrence, *The Hunger Games*, Lionsgate and Color Force

254 William Butler Yeats, “Whence Had They Come”

260 *Green Hornet Comics*, Harvey Publishing, 1947

278 Josh Brolin and Megan Fox, *Jonah Hex*, Warner Bros.

280-282 Black, El Diablo, and Jonah Hex, *Jonah Hex*, DC Comics

289 Stanley Fish, “The 10 Best American Movies”, *The New York Times*, January 4, 2009

304-305. AT&T Blanket Commercial: Rethink Possible

306 Christo and Jeanne-Claude, Australian Beach

308-309 Christo’s Valley Curtain at Rifle Gap, Colorado. The size and shape of the “waves” are based on Coast Guard research and designed to evoke feelings of dread.

316-317	Nathan Green, "The Healer"
319	Ted Koppel, "Olbermann, O'Reilly and the death of real news", *Washington Post*, November 14, 2010
319	Adam Goodheart, "An American Thanksgiving, Skewered and Roasted," *The New York Times*, November 23, 2010
320-321	Winslow Homer, "Thanksgiving Day, 1860, The Two Great Classes of Society", *Harper's Weekly*, December 1, 1860
325	Robert Sherwood, *Roosevelt and Hopkins: An Intimate History*
346	The Library of America, *Chandler (Stories and Early Novels)*
350-351	Billy Glad, George Shaw, Ron Weiss

www.ingramcontent.com/pod-product-compliance
Lightning Source LLC
LaVergne TN
LVHW010223110826
845148LV00022B/1334

* 9 7 8 1 7 3 3 4 9 1 4 0 2 *